EJITURU'S DREAM

EJITURU'S DREAM

NWANGANGA G. SHIELDS

Primix Publishing
11620 Wilshire Blvd
Suite 900, West Wilshire Center, Los Angeles, CA, 90025
www.primixpublishing.com
Phone: 1 (888) 585-7476

Published by Primix Publishing   03/23/2021

ISBN: 978-1-954886-02-5(sc)
ISBN: 978-1-954886-03-2(e)

Library of Congress Control Number: 2021902551

This edition of the Book is dedicated to my mother,
Esther Mboro Oti, to whom I owe my success in life.

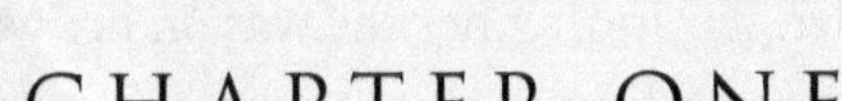

CHAPTER ONE

Ejituru stood in the courtyard of her late grandfather's spacious home, contemplating what lay ahead. It had rained the previous night, and water still dripped from the roof. A beautiful, tall, brown-skinned girl, Ejituru had led a sheltered life from the time she was born. She had attended the primary school where her mother was headmistress, and now went to a prestigious girls' boarding school where she was under the protection of the principal, a friend of her mother's.

A good student throughout her six years as a boarder, Ejituru was ready to put her secondary education behind her. It was a foregone conclusion she would breeze through her final exams with distinction. She looked forward to the next step in her life—going to university to become a doctor. She wouldn't let anything stand in the way of achieving her mostcherished ambition.

Frowning, she fleetingly thought of her father. Since her return, he'd been dropping hints she needed to find a suitor. She put her hand to her face, trying to wipe sleep from her eyes, as she surveyed her surroundings. The concrete floor of the courtyard—the space between the main house and the kitchen, servants' rooms, and storage rooms— was still wet. Beside the main house stood tanks for collecting rainwater. Beside them, rusty drums stored water from the stream.

She picked up a bucket of cold water and turned to look at the main house she just left. It had two stories, with four bedrooms and a sitting room on each level. Each floor had a space that functioned as a dining area beside the staircase. The top dining area was reserved for her father, with a small table with a basin of water for the diner to wash his hands before and after eating. The top floor could also be entered from the front of the house, facing the street, through a staircase that led up to the entrance balcony. As she stood there, she felt raindrops on her bare shoulder, reminding her she was on her way to have a bath.

When she was young, Ejituru went to the stream every morning and evening to fetch water. She returned balancing the earthen water pot, sometimes a pail, on her head. During the morning visit, she normally bathed in the stream, returning home only to put on her uniform and go to school. In those days, she used to enjoy splashing with the other children in the stream a mile from her parents' house.

Those days were behind her, and no one expected a grown woman who had completed secondary school to visit the stream to bathe. She could have taken a bath in the courtyard bathroom her father used, but she hated the windowless room with its slimy concrete floor, mildewed walls, and dirty towels hanging on a rope tied to hooks hammered into the walls. That, and deference to her elders, persuaded her to carry the bucket of cold water to the back of the house, where she used the small enclosed area in the backyard reserved for servants. There, at least she could see what was on the ground.

The fenced backyard had an area designated for bathing. In the corner, a thatched hut contained the latrine. The rest of the backyard belonged to the vegetable garden, where gourds, water leaves, bitter leaf, and okra flourished, along with fruits like plantains, pawpaws, and bananas. Since it was the rainy season, the gourd, melon, and water leaf plants had plenty of healthy green leaves. Ejituru's mother wouldn't have to buy vegetables any time soon.

When she entered the backyard, she saw some of the pawpaws were at the stage where they could be plucked and eaten. She made a mental note to ask her mother if she could have one for a midday snack. The pawpaw trees weren't tall, and she could harvest what she wanted herself, but her mother, Nkechi, would protest, arguing that Ejituru shouldn't strain herself, since a servant could do that for her. After all, what other use did her mother have for all the people she fed?

After her bath, with her wrapper tied under her armpits and her cornrowed hair still wet, Ejituru entered the courtyard through the narrow passage separating the kitchen area from the servant and storage rooms. She noticed her mother had started converting one of the unenclosed spaces on the opposite side of her father's bathroom to Western toilets and bathrooms. With the project just starting, a big hole was dug and a cement base for the two rooms was finished, but the rooms weren't enclosed. A new porcelain toilet and cover sat nearby, waiting to be affixed to the hole.

It'll be nice to have a modern toilet, Ejituru thought.

She always hated the toilet in the backyard, where she had to sit on a stool with a hole in it, and users often forget to replace the lid. A new bathroom with a window would be an improvement. Her mother told her that the new toilet required water instead of the ash customarily dumped into the old one.

The sound of voices in the kitchen alerted her to her mother's presence. She saw Nkechi, a light-skinned woman with freckles on her face, sitting in the anteroom with its raised mud benches, instructing the kitchen servants. Her mother must have awakened early and had her bath, because she wore a long batik skirt and matching blouse, with a scarf tied loosely on her head, indicating she wasn't dressed for outside and that her hair wasn't yet combed.

Ejituru frowned. Though she loved coming home, especially to see Nkechi, with whom she had a close relationship, she hated sharing a room with so many different relatives without knowing who would be in the room each night. She had no privacy. Coming home in that respect was no different from being in boarding school, except that at home she was surrounded by relatives who loved her. In school, she had to depend on so-called school friends who might or might not love her.

Before she left for boarding school, Ejituru had hated sleeping alone and was happy to share a room with someone. In those days, there were always two or three girls sleeping on mats on the floor in the room with her. At her current age, she felt she deserved a room of her own whenever she stayed with her parents. She didn't want to feel like she lived in a dormitory.

A frown passed over her face as she retied her wrapper. The smell of fried plantains and fried balls of black-eyed pea flour, known as *akara*, drew her irresistibly, so she walked into the kitchen, even though she would be teased for wearing nothing but a wrap.

"Ejituru, is that you?"

The slap of flip-flops on the floor must have alerted her mother to her presence. As Ejituru approached the kitchen area, she saw the raffia mats covering the mud beds were unraveling at the ends and needed replacing. Particularly fond of that space, Nkechi often received her female friends there. It was usually the first place visitors saw when using the back door beside the bathroom when they wanted to avoid traversing the main house to reach the kitchen.

As soon as her mother saw her, she sat up and said in a firm but affectionate voice, "Ejituru, go put something on, please. You're no longer a child."

"But, Mama, I just wanted to relax a little. There's no one here but family. Besides, the *akara* balls smell so delicious, and my stomach's growling." She grabbed a small slice of fried plantain from a bowl.

"I don't know what they taught you in that school for the past six years," Nkechi teased. "Come, then. Sit down and have breakfast. You're very skinny. You need fattening."

"Mama, we no longer need fattening. That's an ancient tradition. Men of my generation prefer slim women."

Laughter erupted from the many busy helpers in the kitchen. While Nkechi issued instructions for the morning tasks, a young nephew sat on the opposite bench, washing and drying containers and pots. Two young nieces, straddling low stools inside the kitchen area, tackled various morning chores. They coaxed flames from the embers of the charcoal with a fan, pounded black-eyed peas for *akara* balls, fried plantains, and prepared corn porridge, called *ogi*, for breakfast.

All young relatives who lived with Ejituru's parents had their school expenses paid for in exchange for housework. The gentle teasing and show of love was what Ejituru looked forward to, because that was her family, where she belonged.

"Okay, *Nwamu,* my child, I know. You still need to add some flesh, even if we won't put you in a fattening room like the old days. Who wants to marry a skinny woman anyway? There's nothing to hold."

As her mother's only surviving child, Ejituru knew Nkechi wanted to spoil her, especially since she had just returned from boarding school. Nkechi gave her the name Ejituru, because she felt Ejituru was a gift that could be taken away from the family any time God wished.

On the morning Ejituru left for boarding school for the first time, the rain had fallen as if the heavens opened to release all the water they contained. She liked to imagine it was sharing her sorrow over leaving the bosom of her family. With no direct route from her village of Ndi Otusi to Ibiaku, Nkechi accompanied her to the motor park, where she would catch a bus to Aba, then change buses for Ikot Ekpene.

At the motor park, Nkechi's tears, indistinguishable from the rainwater, left Ejituru with a heavy heart as she boarded the small bus. She huddled in a window seat, straining to see her mother and letting the chatter of the other passengers wash over her. She felt lost by the time the bus reached Aba. The din of vendors carrying prepared food bombarded the disembarking passengers, adding to Ejituru's confusion. Little kids shoved food at her—*akara* balls, *moinmoin, suya,* or peanuts wrapped in small cellophane packages—extolling their taste and competing for a sale. She pushed and shoved past the vendors to look for her connecting bus. It was quite a struggle. She nearly missed her bus, but for the help of the driver to whom her mother entrusted her.

Ejituru was her mother's seventh child, the only one to survive past the age of five. Because of that, Nkechi lived in constant fear of losing her. It was a tiresome burden for a child, but she had learned to respect her mother's love and fears by trying to be careful to avoid danger. In school, she was ridiculed mercilessly for not participating in basketball, soccer, or any athletic activity that might result in injury. She earned the nickname of "Snail" for always picking her way carefully and avoiding obstacles in her path. She walked around a fallen tree rather than climb over it. During school holidays, she stayed close to home, giving in readily to Nkechi's whims.

Ignoring the reproving look Nkechi sent her that morning, Ejituru gobbled four *akara* balls and washed them down with a bowl of watery, sugared corn pap, or *akamu,* to which she added evaporated milk. It was so much better than her typical school breakfast of *akamu* with milk and sugar, or sometimes boiled yams with tomato and onion stew.

As she ate, she considered how to spend the day and listened to the desultory conversation in the kitchen. It was mainly about tasks needing to be done and upcoming community events. Ejituru, disassociated from what happened around her, longed for the time when she would graduate from secondary school, but once she finished, she looked forward to new experiences. She tried to enjoy the time with her parents until the examination results came, and she already knew which university she would attend.

For the moment, she wondered how to spend her day. Turning to her mother, she said, "Mama? I was thinking of visiting Auntie Erimma today."

Scowling, Nkechi said, "You know she's been very ill." "Yes. That's why I want to go."

"Since it rained last night, and the road to the village isn't paved and will be full of puddles this time of year, you must be careful. Take six bottles of Coca-Cola as your gift to her."

"That's a good idea, Mama. I'll get dressed and set out. It'll be too hot later. The morning's always the best time to visit the sick. I promise to be careful."

"By the way," Nkechi added, retying her headdress, which had come slightly unraveled, "did you hear that one of the women in the compound lost her life savings and her special-occasion wrappers to termite infestation?"

Ejituru covered her mouth in dismay.

Twisting and untwisting her hands, Nkechi said, "She had everything hidden in a bundle in a dark corner of her room, where she hoped her children wouldn't look. She only checked when she had unexpected expenses. She's in tears, the poor woman. You know such a loss was quite common in my grandfather's time. You'll probably get an earful in the compound."

Before Ejituru could respond, the window on the top floor facing the courtyard flew open. Nwakama, Ejituru's father, a slightly built dark man with hair parted on the left, poked out his closely cropped head. The top floor was his preserve. He occupied two rooms, his bedroom and a room used as an office, which held a table, chair, and two bookshelves, though the books had been looted during the civil war, and none were left. When visitors filled the house, that room became a temporary bedroom. Ejituru shared a room on that level with her cousins. Ordinarily, Nwakama didn't enter the kitchen area, unless he couldn't avoid it.

"Mama Ejituru," he shouted excitedly, "you remember what we discussed the other day? Chief Iro and Chief Okoro Ukwu are on their way to visit. They sent a young man to ensure we had nothing planned. Since it's only a courtesy call, I told the boy it would be all right to come this morning. I should have my breakfast before they arrive."

Frowning, Nkechi said, "I have nothing to discuss, so I don't feel like going upstairs to talk about what I already said I won't accept."

"The chiefs will be here in about an hour. We should at least discuss how to handle the visit."

Nkechi's tone became harsh. "Papa Ejituru, I told you I don't think this meeting should happen. I don't agree!"

"Let us allow them to present their case," he replied, trying to sound authoritative.

"No. I'm against it. I don't want to be involved with that family. You can have your meeting, but I won't show my face."

"It's just an introductory visit." He tried to be conciliatory. "That's all. It's not as if the event would take place tomorrow. It might never happen, but we should keep an open mind."

Ejituru had no idea what they were talking about. *I hope this fight is nothing to do with me,* she thought. Shrugging, she wished they would resolve their differences in private. She knew she had to leave as soon as possible, because her mother never gave in and would continue to voice her objections until her husband gave up.

Nwakama and Nkechi had been married for over twenty years, but the relationship had always been somewhat antagonistic. Both felt they married beneath them. Nwakama regarded Nkechi as his social inferior, and couldn't understand why she didn't give him the respect he was due as a member of a prominent family. Nkechi felt that Nwakama should accord her all due respect as the family's breadwinner.

Before she went to boarding school, Ejituru believed her mother was on the verge of throwing her father out. The house belonged to Nkechi, as it had been her father's. Somehow, Ejituru's parents always made up after their fights. She loved them and wanted them to stay together, but she realized they coexisted largely because her father accepted his inability to support himself. Sometimes she felt sorry for him, even though many men of his generation in surrounding villages found themselves in the same situation.

Ejituru sighed in relief when her father decided to abandon the argument, but she knew the quarrel was only postponed and would resume later. She left the kitchen, walking quickly across the courtyard into the main room. As she climbed the stairs to the second floor, she greeted her father, who sat in the dining area eating breakfast and shaking his head over the exchange with Nkechi. He wore an old wrapper and washed-out singlet. His cropped hair was almost white.

"I'll be going to Ndi Otusi to visit Aunt Erimma," Ejituru said, glaring at him.

"I saw her only yesterday, and her health seems to be improving," he replied. "She'll be glad to see you." He waved her off lightheartedly.

Ejituru left for the spacious room she shared with her young cousin. It had two windows overlooking the street, two beds, a standing mirror in the corner, and several suitcases piled to one side. Only one bed had a mosquito net, and Ejituru chose that one to use. The other bed had only a raffia mat on a mattress and a thin wrapper used as a blanket by whichever cousin shared the room with her. While she had her bath and breakfast, the room was swept, and her nightdress, which she dropped lazily to the floor in her haste to get to the bathroom, was folded and placed on the bed.

She opened the windows and looked out at the road. For a short time, she watched the parade of villagers go by. Several unfurled umbrellas sheltered passersby, and she wondered if the rain had started again. If so, she had to take an umbrella with her. Rain or no, she had to leave the house as soon as possible.

Ejituru rummaged in her suitcase for body cream and gently applied it, then carefully oiled her hair, making sure she covered her entire scalp. She quickly pulled out her favorite tie-dyed caftan from the suitcase, hunted in her bag for a matching head tie, and changed out of flip-flops into sandals, determined to visit her aunt. As she dressed, she wondered what the chiefs wanted with her parents and why her mother was so opposed to whatever they had to say. She decided not to worry about it. Her parents disagreed on many things. Though they still lived together, they led independent lives. With her mother wrapped up in her activities, and her father busy with local politics, they appeared to have little in common. Nkechi always focused on her work and the affairs of her own family. She had scant interest in her husband's activities, except when they intruded into her life.

Ejituru wondered what her future held in store. She had promised herself not to marry until she made something of her life. Village girls of her acquaintance usually married when they reached puberty and never completed their education. She was relieved that she was her mother's child. Nkechi always placed education above all else and made many sacrifices to ensure that her only daughter received the best education the country offered. Ejituru vowed she wouldn't disappoint her.

The rain stopped by the time she left her parents' house. The umbrellas she saw from her room provided protection from raindrops falling from trees on both sides of the road. She walked the hundred yards to the road on the path her grandfather created.

She always admired their front yard. On both sides of the path, grassy areas with coconuts, dwarf oil palms, and orange trees separated her grandfather's plot from his neighbors. A hedge of croton plants grew on the side near the road. Ejituru loved their beautiful yellow, green, and orange leaves, interspersed with bougainvillea and other flowering plants. Lemongrass bushes lined the path, serving not only as ornamentals but as plants for medicinal purposes. Within the grassy area were beds of frangipani and hibiscus plants, their flowers less abundant during the rainy season than at other times. Ejituru couldn't resist the urge to pluck a few frangipani flowers and savor their beautiful scent. Her grandfather was meticulous about having the grass cut and hedges trimmed regularly, and her mother followed suit. As a little girl, Ejituru and her friends played silly games catching crickets and praying mantises, tying strings on them and trying to race them. It was a cruel game, something she stopped indulging in after she grew up.

Okoro, her maternal grandfather, a primary school teacher, had started building the house as soon as he married. Before then, he had lived in a mission-provided house during the school year and returned to his mother's house during vacations. As a married man, he had to move away from his mother's house. There was a saying among his people that having two women share a kitchen was courting disaster.

Okoro negotiated for a piece of land two miles from his ancestral compound. A close friend had built a magnificent house nearby and urged him to move out of the cramped compound to start his own home. He built a replica of his friend's house, a handsome building with four bedrooms on each floor and two sitting rooms, on the main road leading from the villages to the farming areas. Nkechi always said it was worth waiting for.

Proud of his new domain, Okoro left mission housing as soon as he could. Most villagers passed it as they went to the farm, the market, or the stream, and it became second nature for them to stop by, even if just to say "Hello" and move on. As was the custom, people dropped in at any time, leaving no privacy for those who lived in the house. People came at all hours of the day and entered whichever occupied room they found to make their presence felt. To stop them or claim privacy would seem like self-aggrandizement, cutting the family off from their poorer relatives.

A long time in the past, the road leading to the villages had been paved. Patches of tarmac clung to the soil in places, but overall the road reverted to its original dirt. When it rained as it had the previous night, people tried to circumnavigate the many puddles. Occasionally, a car, truck, or motorcycle swooped by and splashed water on the trekkers, and the drivers traded insults with them.

"Hey!" people on the road called. "Watch where you're driving! Go slow, you madman!"

"Get out of the road," the driver shouted back. "Watch out, you fool!" Groups of early risers were on the roads, returning with basins of cassavas, yams, coco yams, and assorted vegetables balanced on their heads, with babies on their backs. Others were just setting out for the market or the farm. Several cyclists carrying passengers rushed past.

People called out to Ejituru from both sides of the road. *"Ada Anyi!* When did you come back?"

Ejituru crossed the road to speak with the woman who had trouble with termites and to pay her respect. The woman wore an ill-fitting, baggy, Western dress, presumably a gift to replace some of the clothes she lost the previous month.

"Your mother has been very kind to me," she said. "God bless her. She paid my church dues."

Several passersby spoke to Ejituru.

"We hear Nkechi has malaria. Is she better? This is the season for it. The Sunday medicine is very costly. Tell her she isn't alone. Many people in the village are down with malaria right now."

Ejituru marveled at how the term "Sunday medicine" had taken over as the name for Daraprim, a popular malaria drug. Billboards across the country proclaimed its efficacy if taken every Sunday.

"Are you coming to the age group meeting tonight?" a young woman asked her.

"Perhaps." She thought she should, because a lot of things had happened during her absence. She could learn about recent events during the get-together. Moonlight gatherings with made-up songs about perceived transgressions of some members could be fun, except if one were the object of such songs.

Ejituru answered all questions politely, knowing whatever she said would be repeated and embellished so many times that people would think they knew her innermost thoughts. She shied away from an elderly woman who would undoubtedly inquire about the health of Ejituru's entire family, listing each member by name and expecting Ejituru to reciprocate by listing and inquiring about the health of every member of the woman's family in return. That would take at least five to ten minutes. Besides, she would have to kneel to be blessed in front of the old woman throughout the whole thing. Reflecting on the traditional mode of greeting, she wondered how long the custom would survive, given the pace of modern life.

Ejituru walked past the government primary school, where small groups of children played soccer, taking advantage of the break in the weather. Although the school was near her grandfather's house, her mother had sent her to an all-girl mission primary school near Grandfather's original village. She'd been in the mission school for only three years before Nkechi was transferred to a school outside the area, and Ejituru had to move to her mother's school. Before the civil war, various indigenous fruit trees—oranges, several species of palms, *udara*, and native pear—grew along that strip of road, but they were cut down for development. As a child, she had enjoyed picking *udara* fruit and eating them on her way to the village.

On the opposite side of the school, several thatched huts served as shops. Some were bars where one could buy roasted meat, mainly chicken and goat, along with palm wine, fresh or fermented. Some offered prepared food, ground nuts, roasted fresh corn, and more. Others offered assorted manufactured goods and yard goods. Competing music blared from each shed.

Someone called out a greeting as she passed a carpenter's shed. Since the village seamstress was just opening her shop, Ejituru poked her head in to greet her and inquire about her health. She had known the woman a long time. Before the civil war, she had been the best seamstress in the area, but with so many new tailoring businesses springing up, she faced stiff competition. Ejituru noticed the old foot-operated sewing machine in the corner. Several finished dresses hung on the line waiting to be claimed, and piles of lace for sale occupied a table beside the door. A young woman Ejituru's age sat inside the shop, her nails bitten down to the cuticles.

"Hi, Ifeoma. Is that you?" Ejituru asked. "I haven't seen you since we left the mission primary school. *Ewoh!* What have you been doing?"

"I enrolled in a primary teacher training college and should finish soon. I plan to teach kindergarten. And you? I heard you were in Ibiaku. Have you graduated? What are your plans? Will you teach, like your mother?"

"Oh, no. Not teaching. Too many annoyances. I hope to go to medical school."

"Ejituru, my sister, I'm so glad for you. I hope you gain admission to Nsukka. Are you going to Ndi Otusi?"

It took Ejituru longer than anticipated to reach the outskirts of Umu Ukwu, her father's village, and even longer to reach Ndi Otusi, one of the nine compounds making up the village. The twenty villages in the Cross River area had been settled by three kinsmen bound together by their religious belief in one God and grouped according to which ancestor founded the village. Nwakama's village was one of four with a common ancestor. The compounds were contiguous, with a public space where traditional events were held, along with a village hall built with contributions from sons living overseas.

Since it had rained during the night and early morning, mud covered the entrance to the compound. Ejituru had to watch her step to avoid messing up her new sandals. To enter, she had to pass the hall used for village meetings. No meeting was in progress, though groups of elderly men huddled in front of the building to talk. Ejituru greeted them as she passed.

Before the civil war, a cocoa grove had separated Ndi Otusi from the next adjacent compound, and an area was set aside for human waste disposal. That grove was gone. In its place stood a jumble of houses built with cement blocks and roofed with corrugated iron sheets. Within the compound stood a cluster of mud houses with thatched roofs.

Originally, the arrangement of the houses formed the shape of a horseshoe, with only a few houses in the center. After the civil war, many people built houses with no consideration for order. As a result, the compound lost its common area where villagers could gather in the evenings to trade stories and gossip. The houses clustered in the middle of the horseshoe lacked space for gardens, unlike the older houses, which had space behind them for small plots where women could grow vegetables and have one or two banana, plantain, or pawpaw trees. Despite that, one or two bitter leaf and water leaf plants grew in front of each house.

As Ejituru approached the compound, she thought of her parents and the conflict they had that day. Her face clouded. She could think of only one reason for her mother's anger. Her parents always disagreed about her education. Her father wanted her to become a primary school teacher, a career suitable for a married woman, while her mother encouraged Ejituru to aspire higher. Ejituru vowed to make sure she availed herself of all educational opportunities. Education would give her the means to escape the fate of many girls she knew, who, because of early marriage, ended up as petty traders.

As she entered the compound, a variety of odors assailed her. She caught the smell of rotting maize leaves, the scent of banana, orange, and cassava peels strewn everywhere, the sweet smell of ripe, rotting pawpaws falling from the tree, maize roasting on the hearth, and, more strongly, the powerful odor of fermented, boiled cassava and its fried variety, *gari,* being readied for market. Goats and chickens scampered about, competing for food among the rotting garbage. Clusters of children in various stages of undress latched onto Ejituru, shouting and asking for presents. Knowing the village schools were on a short break, she had expected that. "Sister Ejituru!" they shouted. *"Ilo ne?* Are you back home? Did you bring us anything? When did you get back?"

"I have nothing to give," she replied, glaring at them. "I just came back from school a few days ago, and I'm here to visit Aunt Erimma. Where would I get the money to buy you something? Get out of my way."

Then she remembered that in her haste to leave the house she had forgotten to pick up the sodas Nkechi told her to offer her aunt. *Oh well,* she thought, *I can tell Aunt Erimma about it and send someone to bring the Coca-Cola later.*

"Stop!" she told a small girl relieving herself in the middle of the narrow path. She shooed away a dog attracted by the stench. "Where is your big sister or your mother? She should clean this immediately before someone steps in it. This spot isn't a toilet. You should know better."

She stepped over the mess, remembering how her mother had told her the same thing when she was growing up. Each compound always set aside a space in the back for such waste. The civil war had swelled the village population so much that land had become scarce. Any available space already had a structure on it, so owners had to provide their own toilet facilities. Nkechi often bemoaned the way the village women seemed unconcerned about their surroundings. She rarely entered the compound anymore because of the poor conditions.

When Nkechi was growing up, wives competed to see who could keep the neatest house. They spent hours one day a week to polish the mud floor with mixtures of charcoal and coco yam leaves. Wives who kept untidy houses were ridiculed. Unfortunately, the world had changed, and one had to watch one's step. Most of the houses in the compound looked like they needed to be replastered with mud. Many had heaps of rubbish and wood piled outside the walls.

"I want to get away from all this," Ejituru muttered.

CHAPTER TWO

Da Erimma lived in a house at the bend of the horseshoe, so Ejituru had to walk past several houses to reach it. Halfway there, she met Nwada, the wife of her father's half-brother. A small, thin woman with unkempt, uncovered hair, she wore a wrap tied under her armpits, and flip-flops. She must have heard the commotion caused by the children following Ejituru and come out to see what was happening.

"Leave her alone!" Nwada shouted at the kids. "Don't you have anything better to do?"

The children ran off.

"Ada Anyi!" she exclaimed. "Are you on holiday? How long will you be with us?"

"Yes, Auntie. I'm on a short break from school."

"How is your mother? We heard she had malaria. This rainy season is the time for it."

"She's feeling better, Auntie. Thank you for your concern. *Nda aga imere?* How have you been?"

Nwada took five minutes to tell Ejituru of her various ailments and the termite infestation, while Ejituru impatiently made sympathetic noises.

"Were you told of the arrival of Ignatius from America?" Nwada asked. "We thought he was in the north. Your mother must have told you."

"Who is he? I've heard nothing. I got back only three days ago, Auntie."

"You must've heard. It's all we talk about here."

Puzzled, Ejituru asked, "Auntie, who is he? A distant relative, perhaps?" "*Mbaa!* Of course not." She blew her nose loudly. "He's not a relative. Perhaps you don't know him. He's much older than you. You weren't of school age when he graduated from Ndukka Secondary School near Amangwu. You must know his mother. We all bought fish from her, and I'm sure Da Nkechi must have sent you to her stall many times."

"Yes, I remember the woman. Didn't she die in a car accident? I remember hearing only that her son lived in the north and didn't return for the funeral. That was the news during one of my Easter vacations."

"Exactly! That was him. He arrived suddenly last week. As we know now, he was in America all that time. You should see the car he drives. He refused to stay at his father's house and moved into his mother's old house. His father has that big house in the village extension, the one with armed men outside the gate. His father stays there only during festivals, preferring his house in Aba. Apparently, Ignatius alerted his maternal uncle of his impending visit and sent money to rehabilitate his mother's house. He eats at his mother's brother's house and sleeps in his mother's house." Words poured from Nwada while she gestured wildly.

"Is this true? I didn't know he and his father weren't on good terms." "It's rumored that his father refused to pay for him to go to college, and he had to go to the north to stay with his mother's brother before he found his way abroad. He hates his father and refuses to have anything to do with him. I understand his father's trying to find a wife for him."

"Is that what he wants?" Ejituru asked, confused.

"*Imara aga ndi anyi di*. You know how it is. The chiefs have been trying to reconcile him with his father. I hear that since Ignatius came back, Chief Iro has been talking to him, telling him that his father performed all the traditional burial rites for his mother, and he should be happy to have a father who did that and should forgive his past actions."

"How sad for him to come back home and not see his mother." In a firm voice, Ejituru said, "Auntie, I'll visit you sometime soon, but I must visit Aunt Erimma. Then I have to get back home. My parents expect me in an hour. We're expecting guests."

At that rate, Ejituru felt she'd never get back in time. From past experience, she knew her mother would prefer she spent as little time as possible in the compound. She sensed Nkechi somehow blamed her father's relatives for all her miscarriages and other losses, and she tried to prevent Ejituru from having any prolonged contact with them. As Ejituru grew older, she had ignored those fears and made an effort to get to know them.

Nwada accompanied her to the front of Erimma's house. "I understand she's been ill," Ejituru said.

"Yes, our daughter. She's been very ill, but God has been gracious and she's recovering. I just fetched water for her and helped her with breakfast."

"Oh, Auntie, I'm so glad. That's why family is important. Thank you for helping Da Erimma."

Da Erimma was the third child of Ejituru's paternal grandmother. She had been born at a time when the locusts swarmed, defoliating every tree in the area. All food crops withered and died, leaving nothing to eat except the locusts. People gathered them in baskets and roasted them. Soon, the locusts outlived their lifespan, and only their shells remained. Ejituru's paternal grandmother had given birth to her third child alone.

She got out of her mud bed, cleaned herself, looked for a knife to cut the umbilical cord, and was cradling her baby by the time her co-wives realized what had happened. When the loud cry of her seven-year-old daughter, who had just returned from the stream, alerted her co-wives of the birth, all the women rushed in and carried the baby out to be bathed. They buried the umbilical cord in a specially prepared bed where a shrub could be planted, then sent for the father to tell him of the new arrival.

From the time she was born, Da Erimma—so named because she wasn't a beautiful baby but was very scrawny—exhibited a spirit of independence, unconstrained by tradition. She preferred to live her life as dictated by her aspirations. Conscious of her limits, she knew when to give in to the norms of society.

Following the death of her husband, Da Erimma moved back to her father's compound and occupied her mother's house, where she raised her two daughters. She refused to have anything to do with her husband's compound, saying she had never belonged there. Shortly after her return, her mother died, so Erimma assumed the premier position in the senior wife's household, and looked after her unmarried brother, Ejituru's father, until his marriage. She still lived in that house.

Da Erimma was Ejituru's favorite aunt, and she knew she would be happy to see her, especially since Ejituru had been away at boarding school during the worst of Erimma's illness. She'd been ill for some time, and the doctors seemed unable to diagnose the problem.

Da Erimma's house resembled most of the original wives' houses in the village. It had a small outer room in front, with dwarf walls and mud benches where visitors sat. Once, that room doubled as a kitchen, but the spot where the hearth had been was now cleaned out and replastered. The original thatched roof was replaced with corrugated iron sheets, though the mud walls remained. A door connected the outer room to the bedroom. An open hearth at the rear of the house overlooking the vegetable garden served as the present kitchen.

Ejituru stepped into the outer room and called, *"Kpam. Kpam.* Is anybody in?"

"Who is it?" her aunt asked. "Come into the room." Her reedy voice lacked its usual strong tone.

As Ejituru entered, she asked, "Where are you, Auntie?" The room had no window, and she had difficulty seeing the silhouette of her aunt on the bed. "Let me open the doors to let in some light."

With the doors open, the room came into focus. Apart from the mud bed, she saw several tin boxes piled in one corner, presumably containing Erimma's most-cherished wrappers and blouses, several pots and pans, and several tin plates and bowls stacked together. Beside the bed, a small table held a jug of water with a cup over it, assorted containers for ointments, and small packages held together with different-colored ribbons. Ejituru surmised those contained the drugs Erimma took.

Several wrappers and matching blouses hung on a rope strung across the room.

Da Erimma looked up from her mud bed. When she saw Ejituru, she exclaimed, "*Ewoh!* Ada Anyi is back and has come to visit. Come here, my child, and give me a big hug. Let this old woman feel a young breast." Ejituru went to the bed to hug her aunt, then sat near her on a low stool that one of the little girls who lived in the house brought to her. She was struck by how thin and gaunt her aunt was. Da Erimma was once plump, with a round, fleshy face and beautiful dark-brown eyes, someone who always took pride in her appearance and house. The woman in the bed didn't resemble the person Ejituru knew and loved.

Ejituru turned away to hide her tears. "How are you, Auntie? I hear you've been quite ill. I hope the worst is over."

"Yes. It was very bad for some time, but thanks to God, who looks after us and decides when it's our turn to be united with him, I'm still here. Look at you! You're a grown woman and very soon will have suitors." She placed a pinch of snuff in her nose.

"No, no, Auntie. I still have a long way to go. I want to go to college and become a doctor so I can care for you."

"Praise be to God. I know you'll do it. I pray I live to witness such a blessing."

"Auntie, let me help you get up so we can sit together in the outer room for a little while. You need fresh air."

Her aunt sat up, and, with Ejituru's help, she walked to the mud bed in the outer room. She blew her nose into the rag she clutched and said, "Ejituru, my child, your mother used to get me out of bed, even when I was very ill, and bring me out here for the same reason. She brooked no nonsense."

Da Erimma lay on the bed, and Ejituru sat beside her. As they conversed, passersby called out greetings.

"We're glad to see you up, thank God!"

"I give thanks I saw you today!" Erimma replied.

A young girl who lived with Erimma rushed in with a bowl of fried fish for Ejituru, which was sent by Nwada. She couldn't refuse.

Though not hungry, Ejituru had to eat everything on the plate to spare people's feelings.

"You know, Ejituru, seeing you has cured me of my illness." Covering herself with a wrapper the child gave her, Da Erimma continued, "How is your mother? I heard she had malaria. It's been seven days since she visited."

"She's better, thank you."

"Your mother has been very kind to us. She arranged for me to go to the hospital to see the doctor, and she bought all the medicines. I told her many times that God will bless her for her kindness to me. Have you seen Onyeka?"

Ejituru swallowed, her mouth suddenly dry, as she considered how to reply. "Auntie, I returned only three days ago. As I understand it, Onyeka now lives permanently in a farm village and visits on market days. I just missed her. She left green corn and some corn pears to be given to me on my arrival. I'm sorry I didn't get to see her, but I hope to on the next market day."

"Well, she's the burden your mother has to bear. That girl doesn't know what's good for her. She let those foolish women in the village fill her head with all sorts of nonsense."

Ejituru, not knowing what to say, stared at her hands. She wouldn't want to say anything that might be construed as criticism of her mother or Onyeka, her mother's gift to her husband. Ejituru loved them both. Onyeka was, to her, the older sister she never had, someone who looked after her as a child and comforted her when she needed it. Any negative comment would seem like a betrayal of both women, so she ignored the subject and asked about people in the compound.

Looking brighter, Da Erimma sat up. She and Ejituru remained silent for a time, lost in thought.

She startled Ejituru when she said, "I have to tell you about my last week's visitor. It was a big surprise. Ignatius came to thank me for being a good friend to his mother. She was my friend, and we hid nothing from each other. She knew I could keep her secrets, and she told only me and her brother that Ignatius went to America to study. She wanted to keep it quiet to avoid difficulties with her husband's family.

"After the war, Ignatius sent her small sums of money through his uncle, her brother. He also helped his uncle after he lost everything in the north. His uncle said he didn't know what would have become of him if it hadn't been for Ignatius. Everyone thought it was the uncle who maintained Ignatius' mother, but it wasn't. That was what they wanted people to think."

Ejituru stared at her aunt, listening intently and trying to make sense of it. She felt uneasy at all the talk about a young man she never met. *What does his return have to do with me?* she wondered.

"Her death was so sudden," Erimma said. "His uncle told me that Ignatius had no legal papers in America. If he had come for the funeral, he wouldn't have been allowed to go back. His uncle wrote to tell him the circumstances of his mother's death and all the events that happened. Ignatius wrote that he would visit as soon as he was able.

"What was the point of coming for the funeral when he couldn't come home while she was alive? He's here now though. Even those who cursed him during the funeral fawn over him, because they think he has bags of money."

Da Erimma sank back, feeling tired, and Ejituru helped her settle more comfortably.

"How sad for him to be so badly thought of," Ejituru murmured. "All that time he was thousands of miles away, feeling sad and alone."

"Since he arrived, he's been making the rounds of the villages to thank people who cared for his mother. All isn't well between him and his father. I don't blame Ignatius. The man never really supported either him or his mother. Look at most of the men in our villages. How many support their families? On the other hand, his father had the money to help his son go to university, but he refused, because the silly man didn't know the value of education." She was breathing hard.

"Oh, Auntie, rest a little now," Ejituru said. "For a person who never left her village, you're very wise."

"Well, my princess, it's true I never left the village, but I have eyes and ears. I watch and listen. In any case, Ignatius was here a few days ago. We wept together for his mother, may her soul rest in peace. She was a good woman who lived an exemplary life. Despite the way she was treated by her husband, she never said a bad word against him. Whenever he visited, she always acted like a good wife, preparing food for him even when he never gave her money to buy it."

"What a selfish man!" Ejituru said indignantly. "I suppose they're all selfish when you think about it, Auntie."

Da Erimma nodded. "Yes, most of them certainly are. Ignatius told me the chiefs are trying to make peace between the two of them. I told him to let bygones be bygones and not to hold a grudge forever. We have only one father in this world, and I'm sure he has regrets too. Look at his actions during his wife's burial! He gave her one of the most lavish funerals we've seen in years. Everyone talked about it, saying he was trying to make up for neglecting the woman during her lifetime. I told Ignatius to forgive his father, and he said he'd try."

As Erimma closed her eyes, Ejituru held her hand and stroked it, thinking she'd drop off to sleep, but the old woman's eyes snapped open. "He also confided that his uncle is pushing him to marry. He said he promised his mother he'd marry someone from the area, but, with her gone, he wasn't sure how to proceed. It would have been nice if the mother chose a girl for him, but she died suddenly. His uncle wants him to decide during this visit, but it's short. He spent most of the time trying to settle his mother's affairs. He said the chiefs have gotten involved in the marriage business too. They're trying to arrange a wife for him."

Da Erimma looked hard at Ejituru, her almost-black eyes clear and young in her gaunt, lined face. Ejituru saw how thin she was. The rag covering her head didn't mask her bald patches.

Though not the first person in the village to study abroad or have a rich father, Ignatius had attracted a lot of attention.

Ejituru, feeling uneasy, shrugged it off, saying defiantly, "Auntie, Mama knows I'll go to university in September and become a doctor. No one thinks I'm getting married now, do they? Because I don't want to. I won't." "Tread carefully, *Ada Anyi*. What you want and what the world wants of you are two different things."

"I must leave now, Auntie. My parents are expecting a visit from Chief Iro and others. I must be there to greet them."

Her aunt laughed. "If the visit is about what I think, you shouldn't rush home. Take your time. On the other hand, I wouldn't want you upsetting your parents. Come to visit again, and we'll talk some more."

Ejituru felt agitated. What was going on? Why hadn't her mother mentioned Ignatius? That was probably the reason for the quarrel that morning. What was her father thinking of even entertaining such an idea?

Her mind in turmoil, she tried to control herself. Turning to her aunt, she said, "Auntie, I'm very sorry. My mother wanted me to bring you some drinks. In my rush to come here, I left them in my room. I'll ask one of the girls at home to bring them to you later today."

Ejituru hugged her and left quickly, barely acknowledging those who called to her as she passed. How could she avoid seeing the elders without angering her father?

CHAPTER THREE

Ignatius, the object of the villagers' intense scrutiny, arrived one week earlier from the US, where he had lived for the past ten years. Tall with an athletic build, he had light-brown skin and a pleasant face. He surveyed the room in his mother's house, where he sat waiting to hear from the chiefs that the visit to his prospective bride was still on.

The room was as he remembered it, except it had a fresh coat of paint, as did the rest of the house. Okoro, his uncle, wisely retained the original ochre-colored paint, presumably to keep the memory of Ignatius's mother alive. Ignatius noticed other changes. There was a toilet at the back of the house, with an enclosed space for a bath. The small porch at the rear where his mother prepared many meals for him was just as he remembered. The parlor where he sat contained mismatched wooden chairs grouped near the walls and a small, round table in the middle.

He regretted having agreed to the visit. Was he ready to assume the responsibility of marriage?

I feel sad that since I returned I've been listening to these people advise me on whom to marry, without my mother being present, he thought. *Ever since I came back, nobody has asked about my life in America. My mind is in turmoil. This visit was to become reacquainted with my uncle, to whom I owe so much, and to take care of my mother's house. Now I'm being pushed in another direction.*

He interlaced his fingers, muttering, "I'm only going along with this because I know in my heart it was my mother's wish."

Looking at the opposite wall, he saw his mother's photograph among those of other family members. It showed her as a beautiful, tall woman with a light-brown complexion and a head full of hair. She often plaited her hair, tying it in a bunch behind her back, and that was how he chose to remember her.

She peered at him from the photograph, making him think she was remonstrating with him for missing her funeral and asking him to do this for her. He felt that marriage to a girl from his village was what his mother wanted, but he would have been more accepting of the visit if his mother were alive to help select his wife.

Ada Ngwu refused to follow her husband, Ugo Chuku, to Aba when he moved, claiming she wouldn't feel at home in the town. She would never become accustomed to the traffic and noise. She loved her little house, and was glad that, unlike the houses in her compound, it had a corrugated iron roof, cement-plastered walls, and a backyard where she could bathe in private. In those days, Ugo returned on weekends to visit his wife and son.

Ignatius looked out at the yard and chuckled as he saw children kicking around a tin of evaporated milk. *I was once like them,* he thought.

Ignatius's mother paid for his primary and secondary education from the proceeds of her dried-fish trade. His father by then had another wife who lived in town with him, and he had other children by her. As was customary in a polygamous household, each wife assumed total responsibility for her family unit, so Ada thought nothing of it, as long as she received her share of gifts from her husband on major feast days.

Ignatius never really knew his father. By going away to secondary boarding school, he rarely met him. He saw his father only on those days when Ugo came to the village for a short time, usually at Christmas and New Yam Festival periods, when those abroad were traditionally expected to come back for village meetings.

Ugo's achievement amazed Ignatius, given the man's limited education. Broad-shouldered, slim, and athletic in his youth, Ugo changed with wealth and an inactive lifestyle and developed a paunch. In an age where success depended so much on one's education qualifications, he went unrecognized, but the civil war gave him the opportunity for success. The war disrupted the social structure, and each person fought for his or her survival while living through it. Ugo wasn't afraid of manual labor, which saved him and enabled him to make a fortune. He contracted to deliver food to the troops. Rumor had it he worked for both sides, trading in Nigerian and Biafran currencies, and at the end of the war, unlike many others, he had no Biafran currency, because he had secretly opened an account in the liberated areas.

His contacts during the war served him well in the postwar period, because he became a major supplier of food and material to the Nigerian Army. After the war, he added the production and distribution of cocaine and marijuana to his list of products. By the time Ignatius saw him again, he was the largest drug dealer in the country. Though many people in town despised him for the way he made his money, they tolerated him and his excesses because of his wealth and the ability to pay off many of his enemies. He was also lavish with money on occasion.

That was very different from when Ignatius grew up in the area. Ugo had always said he rose from nothing. True, he built a house in the village where Ada Ngwu and Ignatius lived, and he was generous when he visited, but it was Ada to whom Ignatius felt he owed everything.

He crossed himself as he sat in the living room watching the comings and goings of villagers outside and thinking about the rift with his father. When the University of Nigeria at Nsukka had accepted Ignatius after his secondary education, his mother persuaded him to go to Aba to seek financial assistance, because she couldn't afford the fees with her meager earnings. Ignatius turned toward the room where his mother was buried, remembering the meeting as if it just happened.

He left home early in the morning and took the first bus for Aba, where he arrived at 9:00 a.m. He didn't know where his father lived, and had never met his stepmother or half-siblings. His mother forbade him to have anything to do with the second wife, and his father believed in keeping the two families apart.

From the motor park, Ignatius went to the wholesale market, where he was told he could find his father. He arrived and saw Ugo, dressed in a dirty white singlet over tattered, short khaki pants, in the middle of a ferocious argument with a customer. It went on and on, with the parties posturing and pointing fingers at each other, trying to emphasize their views, while onlookers shouted encouragement to the side they supported.

The argument almost degenerated into a fight, when an elderly man stepped in and told both parties to cool off. The raucous crowd thinned out once the main attraction ended. Shoppers remembered they still had to shop, and the unemployed left to seek other diversions.

Ignatius waited patiently until the shouting subsided. Still visibly upset, Ugo dragged his son aside and didn't look pleased to see him. "Look who's here," he announced. "This is my son, here on holidays."

He turned to Ignatius. "I didn't know you were coming. Where's your bag? Since school is out, I presume you're looking for something to do."

Those around them sniggered.

Confused, Ignatius said, "I just came to tell you that my results are out.

I did well and gained admission into the university."

Everyone congratulated him on his achievement, but Ugo looked bemused and let the news wash over him. "As you can see," he said, "I'm very busy and don't have time to talk. You should make yourself useful by helping load carts with merchandise. *Mgwa buru otu ihe!* Get to work!"

Ignatius looked around the deafening noise. Carts, cart pushers, and merchandise filled the place. People shouted at the distributors, trying to catch their attention. Each person was assigned several cartons. Glad to help, Ignatius loaded his father's share of the assignment—cartons of evaporated milk, cabin and digestive biscuits, and other goods to be ferried to customers in the retail part of the market. Despite the acrid smell of the unwashed, the noise, and being jostled by the crowd, Ignatius enjoyed working alongside his father, and hoped his mood improved by the time they talked.

In late afternoon, Ugo said, "Let's start for home, so we can talk. I don't want everyone here to know my business."

Thinking he would finally meet the other branch of the family made Ignatius happy.

As the two walked down the dusty, overcrowded Aba road, stepping over gutters full of putrid rubbish, Ignatius said, "Papa, I've gained admission to Nsukka University. If I go, I'll study engineering."

His father seemed distracted and wasn't paying much attention to the conversation. Occasionally, he stopped and held lengthy conversations with passing acquaintances.

"What happened to you? Why didn't you come as we agreed?" He turned to Ignatius. "Bush man! He can't even keep an appointment."

Ignatius continued where he left off, fighting to control his tears. "Even though I gained admission, I didn't merit a scholarship. My going depends on having someone pay my tuition. Papa, as you know, my mother paid for all my education to this point. She would have difficulty meeting my university tuition and board. I wouldn't ask you to do this if she could pay for it. I've never asked for anything. This is important to me."

Ugo turned angrily toward him. "How can you even think of such a thing? Where would I get the money? You have a secondary school certificate, which is more than I have. You should be satisfied with that."

He became extremely agitated and shouted, *"N'ga ezuru ya na banki, eh?* Steal from the bank? What you should be thinking of is getting a job and working to support yourself and your mother. *M'muru akwukwo?* Do I have any education? You've had more education than I ever had. That should be enough. I don't have the money for university, and that's that. If you want work, I can help you find a job as a salesman with one of the traders I know in Aba, and you can earn a few pennies. *Ikwesiri icho oru eema aru enweta ego igeji nyere nnegi aka.* You ought to work to support your mother.

"It must be your mother who put the idea of attending college in your head. If she wants you to go, she should pay for it. I never wanted you to go to secondary school. That was her idea. I'll never consider it. I've always tried to do my best for her and you and the kids I have in Aba. For some reason, she thinks I have money to waste for education.

I've seen so-called educated people, and they earn only a pittance. *Oke akwukwo abagi uru.* Too much education is no use."

Ignatius couldn't believe what his father said.

"Here's some money for the bus," his father continued. "You should go home to your mother and tell her I have no money for education," he shouted, the veins on his neck bulging.

Passersby gathered around, eager to see a fight.

"I'm trying to build my business," Ugo said. "That's my only concern."

Sitting in his mother's house, waiting, Ignatius remembered the image of his angry father before him, as if it were taking place right then. He remembered how he feared his father would fall down or die from his own anger. He hadn't known what to do. He had cried as he stood there listening to his father rant, wondering if the madman in front of him was his father or some stranger. When a crowd had gathered, he wanted the earth to part and swallow him. He didn't want to be the object of pity or derision.

Caught up in his anger, Ugo seemed unaware of what was happening around him, impervious to the crowd and Ignatius's feelings. To Ignatius, it looked as if he were no longer aware of his presence. To hide his anger and tears, he had turned his back on his father.

Ugo Chuku never looked at Ignatius or offered to take him to his house to meet his wife and other children. On reflection, Ignatius felt he shouldn't have expected any other reaction. In their culture, men never had responsibility for their children. That was the duty of wives. Husbands provided land for cultivation of crops, while women produced food and took responsibility for the offspring of any union.

In hindsight, Ignatius felt he could have understood his father's point of view if he had sat down with him and explained his financial situation. Perhaps he really didn't have the money to pay for Ignatius's education at the time. How was Ignatius to know? His father spent lavishly whenever he visited the village.

Crushed, Ignatius had run all the way to the motor park and cried all the way home. His future plans were in ruins.

When Ignatius had told his mother of the meeting with his father, she knelt near her bed, crestfallen, and prayed, asking God to show her the way out of her predicament. Her small-scale fish business would scarcely be enough to maintain Ignatius at the university. Since he hadn't been a good student in secondary school, he didn't have high enough scores on the General Certificate of Education to merit a government scholarship. For days, Ignatius had stayed inside on the bed beside his mother's, unable to face the world. He wished he were dead. Beside herself, Ada Ngwu ran from one relative to another like a madwoman, soliciting help. They, too, struggled to come up with enough for Ignatius's school fees. John, Ignatius's uncle, had one child at secondary school and had in recent months been to Ada Ngwu for help with school fees. She wasn't able to accommodate him. She could barely help with occasional gifts of fish or vegetables, as she, too, struggled to maintain her family.

Another uncle, a day laborer at the government station, had very little money. He came to Ada Ngwu for food every day. The third uncle lived in the north, and she had no way to contact him. Besides, she reasoned, he must be in financial difficulty, because he hadn't come home during the New Yam Festival.

For weeks, Ignatius walked around in a fog. He stopped attending Christian union meetings at the church and tried to avoid fellow members. By September, his friends who were university bound had departed, and others left the village to go to relatives in town. He vowed he wouldn't return to Aba to grovel at his father's feet and ask for help getting a job. If need be, he would stay in the village and help his mother with her fish marketing or farming.

However, she decided to send him north to stay with her brother.

Ignatius didn't see his father again for a long time.

After his mother died, Ignatius became overwrought with anger and sorrow. *I owe everything to her and her family.* He sighed and wrapped his arms around his torso, swaying gently from side-to-side. *My heart is full of bitterness that my mother was taken from me just when I'm in a position to help her. She's not here to help me make this important decision.*

True, my father carried out his responsibility for the funeral, but, apart from that, has he ever done anything for me? Nothing!

He saw the chiefs approaching to accompany him to Nwakama's house. Wiping away his tears, he went out to join them.

CHAPTER FOUR

It took Ejituru thirty minutes to walk from the village to her parents' house. Rather than entering through the front, she came in through the courtyard and entered the outer room of the kitchen to tell her mother about the visit.

Visibly irritated, Nkechi said, "There you are. It's about time you returned. Your father's visitors are here, and he's been looking for you. You need to go to the sitting room upstairs and pay your respects to Chief Iro immediately."

"Mama, I came as quickly as I could," Ejituru replied angrily. "You know how it is when you've been away for a long time. One must pay respects to many people."

She sat on a stool opposite her mother. "We always have visitors. This isn't the first time Chief Iro has been to our house. Why am I required to go pay my respects for this visit in particular? Since you retired, hardly a minute passes in this house without visitors."

"Ejituru, you know I said this morning that I wouldn't see these people. However, sending a maid with welcoming gifts would give offense." Her tone softened. "I'm sorry if I sounded angry, my dear. Now would you please take this up and pay your respects?" She handed Ejituru a bowl of kola nuts and a bottle of schnapps. "Your cousin will carry the glasses. You don't need to stay with them long."

Ejituru set her teeth and took the offerings. Her mother still hadn't mentioned Ignatius, so perhaps Da Erimma read more into the situation than was warranted. Village life was like that. People often misconstrued situations. There were other eligible secondary school girls in the village after all. Perhaps her name was mentioned to her aunt as one of several. Since she'd been away at boarding school for six years and hadn't been home for three months, Nkechi probably wanted to show off her only child.

Relieved she didn't have to send a maid with the welcoming gifts, Nkechi said, "Ask your father whether he requires any other types of refreshment for his guests."

Grateful her daughter heeded her instructions to return as soon as possible, Nkechi felt sorry for her harsh words. Even though she was against the visit, Nkechi felt it wasn't in her best interests to stop her daughter from meeting the visitors. If Nkechi were to meet them, the elders would feel she was giving tacit agreement for further discussion.

Thinking it over, Nkechi decided she would snub the visitors by not showing her face. Let her husband make whatever excuses he felt comfortable with. Nkechi would stay in the kitchen the whole time and brood.

Her only regret was that she refrained from telling Ejituru what was going to happen. She feared that if Ejituru knew she was the object of the visit, she would linger longer in the village, hoping to avoid the visitors altogether. Nkechi needed Ejituru to meet the visitors, because she would remain in the kitchen. She wanted her daughter to report what happened during the meeting.

Ejituru peeked around the corner of the room entrance, where four guests gathered with her father. The visitors sat around a table, with Nwakama occupying the chair nearest the door. She saw Okoro Ukwu, an elderly man from the village and a member of Eze Ukwu's advisory council. As an important member of Nwakama's family, he was consulted on all significant matters. He and Nwakama grew up together. A tall, dark man with sunken cheeks, having lost quite a few teeth, he nevertheless had an imposing presence. Life hadn't always treated him kindly. He had lost two sons during the civil war. He was the only one in town to have joined the Nigerian Brigade during World War Two, and fought with the British in North Africa. The villagers had all heard the stories of his exploits so often that the children could finish the stories for him. He still received a small pension, going proudly to the district office to get it.

She recognized the second man, Ugo Chuku, a rich man who lived primarily in Aba and visited his house in the village extension only during important festivals. He made a fortune during the civil war, providing supplies for the troops on both sides, some said. She didn't know his current position, but some thought he produced and distributed drugs, especially to soldiers. He had a large walled compound comprised of several houses. To enter, one had to pass through an imposing gate with two watchmen on either side, in addition to an armed guard, and one had to be announced. As befitted a rich man in the post-civil-war era, he liked to go out accompanied by several men who announced his presence.

She was surprised to see him. Nkechi, in particular, disliked such ostentatious behavior. Old-fashioned villagers ridiculed him behind his back, while young men saw him as a role model, someone who achieved what they wanted in life. Modestly dressed in a white shirt and traditional Igbo wrap and cap, he wore strings of cowry shells. On his left fingers were rings of various stones and sizes. Ejituru couldn't identify the stones, but the gold ring was quite large. In his right hand he clasped an intricately carved staff with a gold handle.

He exuded power—the kind that came from wealth that could also disappear like a puff of air. She could tell by his posture that he wasn't at ease in the company and was there only out of necessity. Nkechi always claimed she had a knack for summing up a man in a moment, and Ejituru knew her initial observation was usually correct. She tagged him as a villain of the worst order. In contrast, the village elders, whose power and stature derived from their positions in the village and the trust in which they were held, appeared relaxed and calm.

Something was brewing. She had never seen Ugo Chuku in her parents' house before. Why was he there, and who was the young man beside him?

It suddenly dawned on her that the third man was Ugo Chuku's son, Ignatius, about whom everyone was talking. What was her father up to? She judged Ignatius to be in his late thirties. He had a pleasant face, a somewhat fair complexion, and short, cropped hair. Muscular and tall, he looked very different from his father, who developed the inevitable paunch of the well-to-do. He must have inherited his complexion and height from his mother, she thought, because his father was short and quite dark.

Ejituru tried to recall an image of Ignatius's mother, but all she could vaguely remember was a slim, light-skinned woman crouched over a basin of fish in the market. There were many fish traders, so she wasn't sure. She met some of his father's daughters, who were about her age, and their mothers. Ignatius wore a long, light-blue eyelet shirt over khaki trousers, whereas the other men wore the traditional Igbo costume of a longsleeved shirt, loincloth, and woven cap.

Ignatius looked very sad. Was he thinking of his mother? Was he forced there by his father, just as she was being forced to serve them kola nuts?

The fourth visitor was Eze Iro, the titular head of Ugo Chuku's village, a small, brown-skinned man whose bald head was covered by the woolen cap commonly worn by men in the area. Highly respected in the Council of Elders, he was the family friend of several highly placed people in the clan. Ejituru's mother spoke highly of his integrity and sound judgment. He had come to the house several times, and if her father could be said to have a friend, it was, perhaps, Chief Iro. He had a trusting, open face, the kind of man whose word was his bond. He had not had the privilege of education, but he was wise.

Ejituru wondered why he'd let himself be persuaded to accompany Ugo Chuku, a man of such unsavory character that no self-respecting person would be seen in his company. Some said money bought everything, including respectability, so perhaps Ugo Chuku paid to ensure the chiefs accompanied him.

Ejituru entered. "Welcome," she told the room at large as she presented the bowl of kola nuts to her father. She went on her knees in front of Chief Okoro Ukwu, her relative, and greeted him, as was the custom. She repeated the same gesture in front of Chief Iro, then asked her father if anything else was needed.

"No, my child," Nwakama replied. "This will do for now. *Soro anyi n'oro.* You should stay and keep us company."

He uttered the traditional greetings as he handed around the bowl of kola nuts. He presented the knife and bottle of schnapps and small glasses to the oldest chief, who accepted the gift and said the blessing to the ancestors before opening the bottle and pouring a libation to the ancestors into one glass.

"I'm afraid you can't pour the traditional libation," Nwakama said, "since we aren't at ground level." He gave each person a thimble of schnapps to drink.

After the ritual of the breaking of the kola nuts, Ejituru sidled to the door but was stopped by Okoro Ukwu. Escape became impossible.

"Ada Anyi Ejituru, welcome back from school." Chief Iro blew his snuff-filled nose into a rag he pulled from a shirt pocket. "I haven't seen you around. When did you return? How did you do in your exams? Where do you want to attend college?"

"*Mazi*, I came back only a few days ago. I've just been resting, making up for lost sleep before the examination. I've only been to our compound today to pay my respects to Da Erimma. I'm not sure where I will be next year, as that depends on my exam results."

The others made sympathetic noises.

"What do you want to study?" Chief Iro asked. "Medicine, preferably at Nsukka."

"Oh!" they exclaimed.

Nwakama said, "I'm very proud of her. I wish her stepbrother would be as good a student as she has been, but it has yet to happen."

"This one knows what she wants to do in life," Ugo Chuku said out of the blue.

Ejituru kept her gaze down to avoid looking at him.

After a pause, Chief Iro motioned toward where Ugo Chuku sat and turned to Ignatius. "This young man is Ignatius. He said he can't remember you at all, because you were very young when he left the area, though he's heard many good things about you from his relatives. He lives in America now. He arrived a week ago and will return in another week, a regrettably short visit."

The others agreed it was too short.

On hearing his name, Ignatius eyed his father beside him. Ugo Chuku looked uncomfortable, shifting his weight from side to side, as if he wished he were elsewhere. He fiddled with his rings and used his handkerchief to wipe sweat from his face, despite the fresh morning breeze coming in through the open windows on both sides of the room.

Ugo Chuku was a bit distant and uncomfortable when the party entered Nwakama's. Ignatius sensed it was an unfamiliar place to his father, who he believed had never set foot in the house or spoke to the owner before. He felt his father would have preferred to be surrounded by his sycophants in his walled compound rather than be there. However, his father *had* to be there. He couldn't afford to miss the opportunity to enter into the arrangement, which would help him rehabilitate socially in town, where one's social standing was more important than one's financial status.

In contrast, the two men with him, Chief Iro and Chief Ukwu, seemed at home in the house. They joked with Nwakama and discussed current news relating to the villages. Though they discussed nothing substantial at the get-acquainted meeting, Ignatius felt the chiefs had already indicated the purpose of their visit to the host.

During his second week back home, his Uncle Okoro and his father had suggested he should consider marrying someone the family would feel comfortable with. Many eligible girls in the village would fit. It would be a shame on his mother's memory if he were to marry a foreign woman. His uncle wanted to make sure Ignatius was fully anchored in the village. With a wife from a good family, he would be constantly obliged to return and put down roots. His uncle and father had suggested several girls. In the end, they decided the family would consult one of the village elders for his advice.

That was how Ignatius found himself at the home of Ejituru's parents. Prior to the meeting, Ugo Chuku sought a private meeting with him, in which he stressed the importance of the visit. He indicated it would be a great achievement if his son married into that family, which was wellknown and respected throughout the area. Tired of fighting his relatives during the short visit home, Ignatius agreed to meet the family. He already refused to consider negotiating for a piece of land, and fought of requests to put more money into his uncle's business. He would meet the girl, but taking the step of actually marrying her was his decision. No one would force him into a marriage he didn't want.

During his visit, he had to entertain the entire village and meet many minor requests for financial support. Every day, someone asked for help with school fees, food, or payment for drugs or doctors. Everyone assumed he had bags of money to satisfy their needs. When he said he didn't, he was branded selfish. It seemed no one cared about him as a person, only as a source of money. Even the chiefs who sat with his father in the house seemed concerned only about the financial benefit of any deals they could conclude.

When the visit was first proposed, he demurred, arguing that finding a wife wasn't his first priority. He needed to become established in the US. He hoped his relatives or chiefs would ask about his life and how he had managed to enter the States when everyone thought he was in Kaduna. They assumed that, since he could afford to visit, he was wealthy. After all, everyone in America was rich. What would they say if they knew about his life there?

He snapped his thoughts back to the present when Chief Iro continued the introduction.

"Ignatius doesn't know any of the young ones in the village," he said. "He's here to be introduced to you, so he'll have some young educated person to talk with while visiting. At this time of year, there aren't many of them around. Ejituru?"

Surprised at being addressed, Ejituru, who kept her eyes fixed on the photographs of her maternal grandparents on the opposite wall, snapped back to the present. "I'm not the best of company, since I've only just come back from boarding school. I hardly know anything about happenings in the village." She didn't want to keep the eligible young man company, or any other bachelor for that matter.

Chief Iro laughed, wiping his nose with a rag pulled from a pocket. "You'd be surprised how much there is to talk about."

"This one is very clever," Nwakama said grandly. "I expect her to pass all her examinations with distinction. The results are due in a few weeks. Many students try to get into the university, but only a few succeed. To be accepted into medicine depends on how well someone does on the science exams. Ejituru has been a good student. I have no doubt she'll be selected, given her past results."

Feeling awkward about her father's words, Ejituru looked outside the window to the road across the way.

"Ignatius," her father asked, "where are you in your studies?"

Not prepared to answer the question, he knew he had to say something. "I'm finished. I'm an engineer. I graduated a little while ago with a degree in electrical engineering and am working now." Wanting badly to roll his eyes, he raised his eyebrows to stop himself. "You know, in America, we take longer to graduate. Many of us have to work to earn money to pay for college fees."

The fact that he didn't have an American accent surprised her.

Chief Okoro Ukwu, who'd been silent most of the time, coughed loudly. "Working while in college is impossible in Nigeria. Where are the jobs for students, when so many with degrees aren't working? Even if the jobs exist, the children of big shots get them." He sipped a little of the schnapps and turned to Ignatius. "What's your job? Was it hard for you to work and go to college?"

"Yes. That's why it took so long," Ignatius replied. "I've completed college and am working now. I wasn't able to return for my mother's funeral because, at the time, I had no legal status in America."

The old man persisted. "But you were still able to go to school and work?"

Ignatius replied tiredly. "You do what you must to survive. When my mother died, I had just applied for permanent resident status, and I didn't want to jeopardize my chance. I have it now, and that's why I was able to visit home for the first time in ten years."

"So, you're an engineer!" Nwakama exclaimed, as if just hearing the news. "You must be very clever. They say people in America make a lot of money, and life isn't as hard as it is here. You're lucky to live in such a rich country."

"It's hard to get well-paying jobs in America," Ignatius said. "If one isn't choosy, there are jobs available."

His father spoke with pride, startling Ejituru. "Yes, it's my son we're talking about, even people who regard me as dirt."

Chief Iro, glowering at him, ignored the outburst.

The discussion shifted to general questions about life in America, the climate, the treatment of foreigners, the living conditions, how difficult it was for Nigerians to get visas to study abroad, and the difficult economic situation in Nigeria, especially the lack of employment opportunities for university graduates.

"Those studying abroad should stay there," Chief Iro intoned. "What are they coming home for?'

"Amen," the others chorused.

"Coming home to join the ranks of the unemployed? *Mba!*"

Chief Ukwu addressed a young man who sat quietly in the corner. "Bring that bag of yours. Let's see what's inside."

Opening it, he produced a bottle of schnapps, the dried front and back legs of a goat, and twelve kola nuts. He turned to Nwakama. "My brother, as you know, this visit is just a peeping through the door. As relatives within the clan, we're obligated to present a small gift to the family. This visit was for Ignatius and his father to better know the family. I'm sorry Nkechi isn't well enough to be present, but we hope to see her when we come again."

Accepting the gifts, Nwakama said, "I apologize for Nkechi. As you know, this is malaria season. She joins me in thanking you for the gifts. They aren't necessary, but custom requires that I accept them. For what you had in mind, I'm not presently in a position to say yes."

"We understand," the chiefs replied.

They stood and began the lengthy leave-taking process.

Ejituru followed them down the steps to the front of the house. *Agreement to what? Marriage?* Her father wouldn't force her to marry instead of following her dream of going to university, would he?

As the visitors finished leave-taking, Chief Iro went into the courtyard to say hello to Nkechi and inquire about her health.

"*Mazi,*" she said, "I stayed away not out of disrespect, but because I don't want to pass on my cold to you."

He looked at her sidelong. Everyone knew she didn't have a cold, just a mild form of malaria. He made cursory remarks about the new additions and asked, "Who's doing the construction?"

"Kanu Ukwu."

"He's well known for his fine workmanship, but he takes too long to finish a project. I hope your work is an exception." He left to rejoin the group.

As the chief approached, Ignatius hesitated at the entrance and turned to Ejituru. "May I visit tomorrow? Perhaps you can show me around. I've been away for more than ten years, so I haven't seen the improvement in our town."

Everyone stopped to listen as Ejituru gave an affirmative reply. What choice did she have?

Ignatius felt that asking her out was a mark of respect for the elders, no more. Besides, he needed to know more about her views. He knew full well that most modern Nigerian girls would jump at the chance to marry someone who lived in the States, which was regarded as the utmost achievement. He heard from friends that the girls' main concern was to get to Europe or America, and love wasn't part of the decision. They all wanted to leave Nigeria.

Ejituru seemed to treat him as a stranger she just met and would probably not meet again. Her mind wasn't needed for the meeting, and she acted as if she wanted it to end it as quickly as possible, so she could get back to her other activities. He realized no one bothered to explain the real reason for the visit.

On one level, he was relieved, because that lessened his burden of having to pretend that asking her out was anything more than it seemed: the chance to become reacquainted with his village and the new developments. She wouldn't expect anything from him the next day.

On another level, he was disappointed that she showed no interest in him as a "been to." He expected her to be dazzled by the attention he gave her, but she wasn't. The chiefs raved about her beauty, intelligence, and family background, but he had reservations. Would she fit into his life in the US? She would want to complete her education. Was he willing to pay for it if her parents demanded that? Her father was very coy about his demands, and her mother's intense dislike of Ugo Chuku clouded her judgment. Hence, she stayed away from the meeting.

After Ignatius and the others took their leave, Nwakama went back to the sitting room, calling for helpers to clear the table and take the gifts to Nkechi.

Ejituru joined her family in the kitchen.

"Tell us, sister, what happened upstairs?" they asked. "Is he handsome?"

"Nothing happened!" she replied, visibly upset.

"Tell us what they said." Her young cousins bubbled with excitement. Nkechi quickly shooed away her young helpers, telling them off for not accomplishing their various tasks. When Ejituru realized they all knew that she was the object of the visit, her anger mounted. She thought of all the ways families tried to hide special events from the affected, such as odd glances they gave each other, a jaunty walk, or the accidental touching in a knowing way—all hinting at private secrets shared but hidden from those specifically involved. Ejituru recalled many such situations. Some were associated with good events, while others forebode tragedies. Fuming, she had difficulty controlling herself. Suddenly, she was a victim of the process. Her young cousins, and especially her mother, hid important information from her.

It was unlike her mother not to pay respects to visitors, especially since Chief Iro was among them. Ejituru wanted to find out why her mother hid the truth from her. She must have known the purpose of the visit. Was that why her mother was vehemently opposed to the visit in the first place? Was that why she feigned illness to avoid greeting the visitors?

Those questions whirled through Ejituru's mind as she answered her mother's questions about what transpired in the parlor.

"How did your father handle the visit? Tell me what the chiefs said."

Ejituru tried to hide her irritation. If her mother was interested in the visit, why hadn't she met the guests instead of gathering knowledge secondhand? She answered truthfully, hoping her mother would reciprocate. "As far as I could tell from what was said, the visit was to introduce Ignatius to all of you, then everyone talked in a strange way. At no point was the purpose of the visit, other than what it seemed, mentioned. In the end, Chief Okoro Ukwu remarked that the visit should be regarded as 'peeping through the door,' but that my father should think about it before the next visit. Why would anyone be peeping at our door? Only Ugo Chuku and his son were strangers."

Nkechi looked angry, then gave a hollow laugh. "The next visit will be over my dead body."

"Oh, Mama, don't say that," she replied angrily. "Visits don't kill. You're being melodramatic."

"My child, what did you think of Ignatius?" She tried to hide the tears in her eyes.

"He's a bit full of himself. Then again, he's an engineer with an American degree, so I presume he has a right to feel a bit pompous." She didn't want to show her anger at her mother for hiding important events from her. "His father seemed out of place and uncomfortable. The only time he said something, it was really out of context. The chiefs did all the talking. I was surprised when Ignatius asked me if I'd like to take him to the new extension. I thought he should be familiar with it, since his father lives there."

"When will this outing take place?"

"Apparently, he'll come midday tomorrow to pick me up in his big car."

"What did your father say?"

"He apologized for your absence, saying it was malaria season. He didn't object to the proposed outing tomorrow."

"I won't stop you, but be careful, okay? There are things you don't understand." She scrutinized her daughter's face, trying to read her thoughts.

"Mama, I've been in a girls' school, and you'd be surprised to know what we talk about!"

"Just be careful of those people."

"Mama, what do you mean, 'those people'?"

"I'm just telling you that the apple doesn't fall far from the tree. Heed my warning."

Ejituru, seeing her mother scowling, didn't reply. She would have said more, but her father shouted from the balcony.

"Mama Ejituru, did you see the gifts? You won't have to buy any meat for some time."

"I hope they didn't inject poison in it," Nkechi muttered.

"Nkechi, look on the bright side. Nothing has been decided. You may have to change your mind fairly soon."

"Change my mind? Never." Chuckling, he closed the window.

Nkechi got up and went after him. Ejituru shook her head. The argument would continue for several days, because Nkechi never forgot a slight and knew how to nurture it, bringing it up repeatedly. She knew Nkechi went to argue with him in an attempt to make him see her side of the issue. Ejituru expected there would be several days when, as a way of showing her displeasure, Nkechi would refuse to address him directly. 'What do you think of the man from America?' her cousins asked, slipping back into the room. "Are you looking forward to being with him tomorrow?"

Ejituru became angry again. *What's going on?* she wondered. Her father implied that it was a done deal and Nkechi had better acquiesce. What did he mean?

"Sister Ejituru, is he not the one for you?" one cousin joked.

Ejituru lost control. "I'm annoyed with all of you! I never want to hear that question again! Do you hear me?'

She rushed to her room, hearing her parents shouting at each other as she closed the door and fell onto her bed, weeping.

CHAPTER FIVE

One week earlier, Nkechi was filled with anticipation for her daughter's arrival. Getting bed sheets from the trunk in her room for Ejituru's bed, she happily hummed a song.

Nwakama breezed in, smelling of palm wine and stockfish. "Nkechi, come here a minute. I have something very important to discuss with you."

Nkechi surmised immediately that it meant nothing good. Usually, their private discussions entailed his need for cash to pay off debts or enter into a venture that would result in more debts. That time, however, it was different.

"Sit down. As you know, I'm very close to Chief Iro and Chief Okoro Ukwu. They're like brothers. They look out for me, and they watch my back."

"What have you done?" she demanded.

"I've done nothing," he retorted. "You always think the worst of me. It's not what you think. I'm not involved in anything that requires money. They just want to discuss an important issue—the joining of two families in the village. It concerns us."

"Which two families are they thinking of joining? How does it concern us?" She was bewildered. "Your brothers' sons are all married, and their daughters are too young. Onyeka's daughters aren't old enough for marriage."

"Nkechi! Mama Ejituru!" he said angrily. "Why are you jumping to conclusions? Why don't you, for once, let me tell you what I have to say?" She restrained herself. She knew in her heart whatever he had to say would kill her. Even though he said he loved her, he always hurt her when she least expected it. She stood by him because she married him in church, and she wouldn't go against her vows. She would try to make the best of the situation, and she never let anyone know that her marriage wasn't anything but happy.

"I apologize. Tell me what you have in mind."

"Please bear with me and listen to what I have to say without interrupting the way you usually do. You remember Ada Ngwu, the fish seller who died last year? Her son, Ignatius, has been in American for several years, studying to be an engineer. This young man has approached Chief Iro to find him a wife from one of the families in our village. He doesn't want to marry a stranger."

Nkechi, taking a deep breath, covered her face with her hands.

Nwakama paused to put a pinch of tobacco into his nose and wipe the remnants away with a rag. "Chief Iro wants to know if we would consider this young man as a possible suitor for our daughter, since they can't think of any other young girl fit for him in the village. He's working as an engineer in America. You know how we like to keep our wealth among us."

"Papa Ejituru!" she shouted in rage. "Over my dead body! She's just completing her secondary education, and she wants to go to university. She's too young to marry. She has a bright future. If they want to marry him off to a village girl, they should look elsewhere. There are many girls whose parents would jump at the privilege of having their daughters married to a man from America."

"But look at it this way," he said, bemused, "she can still continue her education, but it'll be in America, not at Nsukka. I hear that many married women there go to university. We can insist that he pay for her education. You should be happy that we don't have to pay."

"Nonsense! You may not want to pay for it, but I'm prepared to do it rather than subject my only child to a way of life I don't approve of. Why should we expect another family to pay for my only child's education?" Her voice grew louder. "Besides, I don't want to be associated with that family. Look at how his father treated his mother. He doesn't have a good example of marriage."

"Think of it, Mama Ejituru. His maternal uncles are good people, and he has their example."

"I don't want it. Please tell your friends, the chiefs, to look elsewhere."

"Mama Ejituru, why don't you think about it?" he asked in a conciliatory tone. "Besides, nowadays, the decision is entirely up to the young ones. If she decides she isn't interested in the young man, we'll drop the subject. She's under no obligation to marry him. Furthermore, he's never met her and might not like her. Why are we quarreling over something that may never happen?"

Nkechi stormed from the room with a heavy heart. Since then, she had been ill and in bed with a mild form of malaria. Only the thought of Ejituru's return got her out of bed the day before Ejituru was to arrive. She arranged for the airing and cleaning of Ejituru's room and sent to the market for ingredients for her favorite foods. She missed her daughter, whom she regarded as her only true friend in the world. They would spend the day together, discussing Ejituru's plans for the future, since she had completed her secondary education.

Though the rain stopped and the day promised to be sunny, a huge cloud descended on Nkechi. The future, which seemed bright one week earlier, had dimmed since then. Her heart heavy, she went over everything in her mind since Nwakama had broached the subject, and her anger was directed at him. She never had any strong feelings for him, though she'd grown fond of him. To the outside world, theirs was a successful marriage. Deep in her heart, she knew she stayed not out of love or affection but because an unmarried woman lacked respect in her social circle. Nkechi needed the respect her husband's social standing gave her.

She thought of her daughter, home from boarding school, with her future in front of her. Why would Nwakama contemplate marrying her off?

I want her life to be different from mine, she thought. *I want her to have all the opportunities I didn't. Our country is changing, and our women have many opportunities available if they work hard at their studies and go to university.*

Nkechi worked hard and denied herself many things to ensure her only daughter would attend a good boarding school and lack nothing. She sacrificed so that Ejituru would get a good job and look after her in her old age. It wasn't easy. She refrained from wearing fashionable clothes and expensive jewelry, unlike the other women in her social class.

Instead of being satisfied with her small government pension, which often arrived late, she dabbled in many income-generating activities to ensure that school fees wouldn't be a problem. Recently, she bought a cassava-grating machine she could rent to local women to bring in more income. She was in the process of acquiring a grinder that would reduce food preparation time for village women and would bring in a little more revenue. Her sewing shop was also doing well.

She had embarked on all those activities to pay for Ejituru's education, and now her husband had a harebrained idea of marrying her daughter to a young man from a family Nkechi considered her social inferiors.

To have her daughter achieve what she'd been denied herself would be Nkechi's crowning glory. Nkechi had never attended secondary school, because her father, though he was a teacher himself, felt that a primary teacher-training college would take fewer years than a secondary school. Besides, Nkechi had already been betrothed. He felt it was easier for a woman to combine marriage with teaching. Her father did what he thought was wise, but nowadays, with so many opportunities opening up to women, his views could be regarded as old-fashioned.

Nkechi hoped Ejituru would be admitted to the University of Nigeria at Nsukka. If she didn't get a scholarship, Nkechi would pay for her education. She told her daughter, "I won't let the fees stand in the way, no matter what it costs."

Wiping her eyes in desperation, Nkechi cried silently. *Why is my husband trying to sabotage my plans? He hasn't contributed one naira to Ejituru's education. When has he ever contributed to anything except to ensure that Onyeka continues to have babies every two years? I don't want my daughter to think of marriage until she has a profession.*

Her thoughts flew randomly, jumping from one subject to another like dry corn kernels in a hot pan.

Nkechi had married Nwakama just as she completed her primary education. It was touch-and-go whether she could have teacher training, but her father prevailed, making it a condition for the marriage. It took place during the colonial period just before home rule, prior to independence. She thought she was marrying a man with prospects, but her husband wasn't able to support a family, and Nkechi had to become the breadwinner. *He's a big man in name, but social status doesn't feed the family or pay for education,* she thought.

His family, socially prominent but poor, resembled many families in the community. Such families were traditionally prominent, but in the modern age, with its emphasis on education and professional qualifications, they barely survived. They depended on handouts and gifts at special occasions from family members. Their status depended on the past, their position in the village council, and decisions related to allocation of land.

Nkechi had reigned as queen of the household, controlling all the people and making sure each knew his or her station. It was a large household when adding in the uncles, aunts, and offspring. Even then, Nkechi wondered how she was able to feed them all, given her meager income. They never lacked food, and Ejituru never ran around naked or in secondhand clothes like other children.

When Ejituru arrived, brimming with confidence, one look convinced Nkechi that her daughter's dreams would come true. She was going to university, graduate, and get an important job in the government. That would be her and Nkechi's biggest achievement. Ejituru would put to shame those in Nkechi's family who thought educating girls was a waste of money, since they would get married, and the benefit of their education would only accrue to the husband's family.

Nkechi enjoyed being with Ejituru, and they kept no secrets from each other. Ejituru knew her mother's wishes for her, and often assured her that she wouldn't let anything stand in the way of her education. She always dreamed of being a doctor, and Nkechi was happy that Ejituru went to a secondary school with a strong emphasis on science.

Ejituru excelled there, and Nkechi saw no reason why she wouldn't be accepted into Nsukka.

Since Ejituru's return, Nkechi had refrained from mentioning the dark cloud hanging over them. She concentrated on the wonderful things waiting in the future. Since Ejituru's results weren't available yet, they discussed the possibility of her getting a clerical job in the district headquarters as a way to fight boredom. They also discussed the possibility of traveling to Calabar to visit relatives. Nkechi didn't want her daughter hanging around with the other village girls on holiday, listening to their gossip.

Aware that Ejituru had turned eighteen and was on the cusp of a new life with new experiences beyond Nkechi's control, she feared for her daughter. *She'll soon move away from me,* she thought. *I won't be able to control where she goes like I did when she was young.* Nkechi felt she needed to enjoy the short time with Ejituru before she began the next stage of her life.

I intended to spend the day with Ejituru, perhaps go to the market to show her off to my friends. Little did I know my day would be rudely shattered. I'm here preparing breakfast for my daughter, and what do I hear? The chiefs are visiting today with the father and son to meet my daughter! I'm once more plunged into despair.

As she sat in the kitchen surrounded by young girls helping her, all the pent-up anger against her husband and his family surfaced. She again thought of her marriage, which hadn't worked out as she hoped. When she thought of all her wasted pregnancies, stillborn and dead children, tears came to her eyes. She wiped them quickly with the loose end of her wrap.

The lack of a male child had driven her to offer Onyeka, whom she thought would be easy to control, to Nwakama. Nkechi found another woman to give him the precious male child. That wasn't unusual. It was common for a married woman, either because she was barren or because she birthed too many girls, to give in to her husband's wishes and agree to share him with another woman.

Brought up as a family member from the age of fourteen, Onyeka had been carefully chosen. She was a pretty girl with a light-skinned, almostreddish complexion, rich tight hair, and soulful eyes. There was no doubt she would grow into a striking woman. She walked like a gazelle, quick and sure-footed. Onyeka was ten years older than Ejituru, who was in her first year of primary education when Onyeka entered the household and became the older sister Ejituru never had.

Nkechi went through the marriage ceremonies. She gave the parents the traditional dowry of meat and assorted types of traditional wine, paid the required twenty-one guineas, and made sure everyone understand she was marrying an uneducated girl to her husband to produce children for her. Onyeka became part of the family, the nursemaid and general help around the house. She cooked and cleaned, always deferring to Nkechi, and was always anxious to please.

One of Onyeka's brothers, a primary school student, also came to live in the house and was part of the group of servants who made the household function. They fetched water from the stream, bought food on market days, washed and pressed clothes, swept rooms, and cared for the yard. When Nkechi enrolled in a two-year teacher training course at Nsukka after the civil war, Onyeka used Nkechi's money to trade in crayfish and keep the family afloat. Nwakama, lacking a strong educational background, didn't cope as well. To survive during that period, he became a sales agent for a soap-producing entity. Unable to keep that job, he took on odd jobs with the military. He also started cohabiting with Onyeka, instead of waiting for the traditional handing of the gift from Nkechi, and the family finally realized the dream of male children.

Where Onyeka had been subservient, deferring to Nkechi in every respect, the relationship changed after Onyeka had her first son. She became Nkechi's rival for their husband's affection. She befriended members of Nwakama's family who she knew disliked Nkechi, and she began carrying tales of what happened in the home to them. She became neglectful of the children, unwilling to do rudimentary housework. Soon, she demanded her own kitchen and house, arguing that as the mother of the male children, she deserved to be treated with respect, not as a servant. In the end, she moved back to the plantation with her family and only visited occasionally. However, living apart didn't stop her from producing children. She gave birth to five, and any attempt to restrain her fertility failed. Nkechi several times asked her husband to refrain from bringing more children into the world, but to no avail.

Nkechi felt she had no one to blame but herself. She wished she hadn't married Onyeka to her husband but had allowed him to choose a concubine. That way, she wouldn't have been considered responsible for any offspring from that union. Since the children were her husband's children by a marriage she created, Nkechi always felt they were her responsibility and blamed herself for everything. She would have to tackle the problem of Onyeka sometime in the future.

Nwakama sat on a chair in his room, folding his loincloth, preparing to lie down to rest after the visitors left. It had been a rough morning. He had to lie to his trusted friends regarding his wife's failure to welcome them to his house. He wouldn't talk to Nkechi now, because he knew the discussion would deteriorate into a confrontation, which he wanted to avoid. Nkechi had all the power. The house in which they lived belonged to her father, although, over the years, the villagers ceased to think of it as Nkechi's father's house and gradually came to accept Nwakama as the rightful owner, since Nkechi's father had no male heir. Nkechi had a good job as a teacher and was able to build on whatever income she had from it by engaging in many other profitable activities.

He hadn't done anything that was truly worthwhile. He hadn't been a good student in school, and barely managed to get his primary school certificate. Like most men of his generation, he depended on his standing in the community and the belief it was his right to be looked after by his wife. He'd inherited farmland, which he hoped to develop someday. As a member of the council of chiefs, he was often called up to adjudicate minor cases. He was also an elder in the Presbyterian Church in the village and was sometimes asked to preach. He was pleased by his achievement as a member of his generation, but he had no regular income except what Nkechi occasionally gave him.

The proposed marriage, he felt, would be good for him. His prospective son-in-law's father was a very wealthy man, and his most-trusted friend indicated that the marriage would bring him a fortune. He didn't think highly of Ugo Chuku, but money was money. It didn't matter where it came from.

Ejituru would go to America, and, if he played his cards well, Ignatius would come to rely on Nwakama, given that Ignatius had very little contact with his own father. With the union, Nwakama would be in a position to help steer Ignatius into investing in his hometown, buying a piece of land, and building a big house there. Nwakama could even convince Ignatius to help him develop his own land. He heard that at Owerri and Aba, many Nigerians returning from the US were able to start new businesses.

Lost in thought, Nwakama jumped when Nkechi burst into his room. "What were you thinking by encouraging my daughter to go out with a young man she knows nothing about?" she shouted. "You shouldn't have agreed to this meeting or encouraged them to think we would allow Ejituru to go to America with him." She slapped the table with her hand for emphasis.

Nwakama, taking a deep breath, remained quiet. He didn't want to enter into an acrimonious discussion. It would only deteriorate into her recounting all the ways he had hurt her in the past and the grievances his family gave her over the years. He wasn't prepared to rehash old wounds. If he handled the marriage discussion well, Ejituru would see things his way, no matter what Nkechi felt. Ejituru would be able to persuade her mother to accept the inevitable.

Sighing deeply, he turned to her and said confidently, *"O gini ne megi?* What's wrong with you? If she decides not to marry him, I won't force her, but I'm convinced he would be good for her. She would go to America and enjoy a better standard of living than she would have in Nigeria. She would attend the best university in the world, have the best education, and enjoy a different lifestyle than what she would have here."

His attitude incensed Nkechi even more. "Are you sure you're really thinking of Ejituru when you agreed to a discussion of marriage?" She stamped her foot. "I'd bet everything I have that you were just thinking of the benefits to yourself. That's typical of your useless family.

"I've had it with you people. Ejituru is only eighteen, and you're selling her to a man we don't know. We don't know what he does. He says he's an engineer, but how do we know it's true? I've heard some of the Nigerian been-tos lie about their jobs in America. They exaggerate their position to impress people at home. How do you know he's not just telling us what he thinks would impress us? Nwakama, you're gullible! You've allowed your friends, the chiefs, to influence you, and you aren't thinking clearly. I beg you, remove yourself from this situation." He remained silent.

She began to cry. "If they come back to you for the wine ceremony, please say you want Ejituru to finish her education in Nigeria and be able to choose her own husband. The chiefs won't have to live with Ignatius. We can't commit our daughter to a man we don't know." She paused for breath.

He still didn't speak.

"You're right when you say times have changed, but we should allow our daughter to finish her education and make something of her life." She wiped her cheeks. "If you really believe that times have changed, why do you have to bring someone to see your daughter and give him the impression that you favor a union with her?"

She paused to pick up her top wrapper, which had fallen to the floor. In a conciliatory tone, she said, "If Ignatius was staying in Kaduna and came home looking for a suitable bride, and we knew exactly about his situation, it wouldn't be too bad, because if the marriage turned out badly, Ejituru could easily call us to come and bring her home. I'd close my eyes to everything and tell her to try it, promising we'd be there to pick up the pieces if her marriage became intolerable. But America, with a stranger? You must be mad! I don't understand you anymore, Nwakama. This is the last straw."

Without waiting for a response, she stormed from the room. As Nkechi descended the stairs to her own room, she heard Ejituru crying next door, but she was in the wrong mood to be able to comfort her. She went to her room, lay on the bed, and cried.

Speechless, Nwakama scratched his head and sighed. After thinking it over, he decided to ignore Nkechi's anguish. He wouldn't give in on that matter. His friends and acquaintances already saw him as a weak man whose wife wore the pants in the family. True, he owed her a lot. Even his legitimate sons were gifts from her.

Would she feel differently about the marriage proposal if she had a male child? he wondered.

To Nkechi, Ejituru was both a male and a female child. She placed all her hopes and aspirations on their daughter. Nwakama would do everything in his power to prevail and win the battle. He would make Ejituru see things his way. Nkechi would be forced to acquiesce.

Having reached a decision, he stood, dressed, and left the house to seek the company of his friends.

CHAPTER SIX

Unaware of the drama playing out between Nkechi and Nwakama, his prospective parents-in-law, Ignatius trailed behind the chiefs as they walked down the path to the village. Lost in thought, he hardly heard what they said.

What wouldn't he have given when he graduated from high school to be as sure of his future as that girl was? At that stage in his life, he had dreamed of going to university. When he sent his application to Nsukka, he half expected it to be rejected, given the competition. Unlike Ejituru's mother, his mother couldn't afford the fees, but Ignatius reasoned that his father would acknowledge his achievement and agree to pay for his further education if he were accepted. In retrospect, that was never an option, since his father had never contributed a penny toward his schooling before that. Going to Aba only confirmed the inevitable—Ugo Chuku had no interest in his son's education. Ignatius vowed that, as far as he was concerned, his father no longer existed.

Aware of his mother's financial situation, he had decided to give up the idea of further education and concentrate on other means of subsisting to ease her burden. He didn't fault her. She did her best, and the time had come to help her.

He had resisted her plea that he seek help from his uncle in Kaduna, but an incident in the village during that period led to his acquiescence. The village council convicted the father of his best friend of causing the death of several children in the compound who stole oranges from his tree. Villagers alleged that he had buried poison in the roots of the tree and told it to kill any nonfamily members who removed any fruit. Several children in the compound contracted diarrhea and died, and the village council met to ascertain the cause of the deaths. All the children ate oranges from the tree, which was the only common denominator.

Ignatius had trouble accepting the man's guilt, arguing that the entire incident was preposterous. The illness could easily have been caused by a parasite in the water. Even though the culprit contracted with a wellknown native doctor to remove the "poison," the elders unanimously decided he and his family should be expelled from the compound. The village youth carried out their meager household items, and the family had to leave the only home they knew. No village would accept them, so they ended up in Umuahia, where they started new lives.

"Mama, this is wrong," Ignatius told his mother in dismay.

"My son, you're too trusting," she replied. "There are many wicked people in this world. You should know that appearances can be deceiving. That man is wicked. He found a way to protect himself and his family from the poison. The way the case was handled will be a warning to others who have similar intentions."

The case strengthened Ignatius's resolve to leave the village.

When he was growing up, northern Nigeria seemed like Mecca to any hardworking Igbo man who wanted to strike out on his own. Because of population growth, land in Ignatius's area became scarce, and farm plots became smaller and smaller, while the vast north remained underpopulated. With so many in the southeast having difficulty making ends meet through their earnings from subsistence farming, many men from Ignatius's village went north to try their luck.

Okoro, Ada Ngwu's closest brother, went north four years earlier after the New Yam Festival and did relatively well trading. He bought produce in the midwest of the country and sold it in the north. His wife, like Ada Ngwu, traded fried fish, specializing in stockfish. Judging from their appearance during the few times they returned to the village with their young children, they made a comfortable income together. Ada Ngwu had no doubt Okoro would accept Ignatius as his son.

"I want to go," Ignatius said, "but what if I can't get a job immediately? I don't want to be a burden to anyone. Besides, Uncle Okoro already has two children."

"*Mechie onu gi?* Who has ever heard of this?" she countered. "He's my brother, and you're a strong young man. I have no doubt you'll be able to support yourself, as long as you keep an open mind and are willing to take any available job. Remember that a beggar has no choice. He accepts whatever handout is given to him."

The advice became his salvation during his stay in the States, where he didn't hesitate to take any form of menial employment, as long as he was paid.

Ada Ngwu brought out the rusty tin where she kept her money and handed him four pounds for his journey north.

Ignatius caught the night train from Enugu to Kaduna, a big step for a young man who'd only been beyond his village twice in his life. Finding a seat in the packed third-class coach was difficult. He finally found a place squeezed between two heavyset men returning to their station from a funeral in the east. His traveling companions tried to engage him in conversation and invited him to share their food, but he was in no mood to participate.

When the sun rose in the morning, he observed the surrounding countryside. As the train went north past the middle belt, he saw fewer and fewer trees and forests, then scrubland with tall grasses and short, stumpy trees with plenty of open spaces. That was the savannah he had read about in geography class. The train stopped at many of the villages and towns scattered throughout the area, and at each stop passengers could buy food from vendors.

Fascinated by everything he saw during the few times he was awake, he wished he could tell his mother about the new places he was seeing. When he reached Kaduna, he felt lost and didn't know where to go. He had no address, though his mother gave him the name of the market where Okoro Ngwu had a spot. She said he should be easy to find, since he was apparently well-known among the Igbos in Kaduna.

Ignatius emerged from the train tired and hungry. He found Kaduna dusty and hot at that time of year, different from the Cross River villages where he grew up. Flies covered everything, including the containers carried by the food hawkers. Everyone waved fans, but the cool air from the fans lacked the strength to drive away the flies from the food. His stomach growled, and he felt faint.

He got some *akara* balls from a vendor who covered his wares with gauze, stuffing himself quickly while trying to avoid chewing and swallowing flies. He reached for his little portmanteau and wiped flies off with his hands. Why were there so many of them? As he looked around, he saw many people carrying fly swatters, constantly smacking themselves with them.

Ignatius recalled the day he arrived in Kaduna, amazed at how he was able to find his relatives. It must have been the hand of God. He couldn't think of another explanation. He wandered outside the station, feeling drowsy after eating the akara and drinking water he had scrounged from a Hausa man who stood near a small frangipani bush. He'd been about to throw away the water after washing his face and hands in preparation for midday prayers. Ignatius stopped him, begging him in pidgin English for a sip to quench his thirst. He asked someone standing nearby for directions to the market, only to learn the man was a passenger on the train and was waiting for his brother, who seemed to have been held up. The man promised to get directions for him once his brother arrived.

By the time Ignatius reached the market carrying his small portmanteau, it was midafternoon. He tried asking for directions again, but was unable to make himself understood in the jumble of languages being spoken all around. He had almost given up hope, when he thought he heard Igbo being spoken by two men in a stall on his left. Apologizing for the interruption, he asked for directions to the fish market, hoping to at least be able to see his uncle's wife. The strangers gave him good directions.

The Kaduna Sabo market occupied a large space. To reach the fish market beside the produce market five hundred yards from where he stood, he had to navigate many obstacles—hawkers, carts, carriers with large bundles on their heads, and women with babies on their backs and big loads on their heads.

It reminded him of the first time he went to Aba with a message for his father. He had met him at the market. While Ugo Chuku went about his business, Ignatius trotted behind him. Ignatius remembered encountering hawkers selling everything from foodstuffs to writing pens, the carriers, and push carts of every description. Pushed and shoved by the crowd as he followed his father, ten-year-old Ignatius hated the smell and incredible noise. He was determined not to visit Aba again if it meant accompanying his father to the market.

The fish market had twenty stalls, with more people selling off mats on the bare floor or on tables in front of stalls. They mostly sold dried fish and crayfish, but two or three, like his aunt, sold stockfish. He saw Regina, his aunt, in one of the last stalls, busy haggling with a difficult customer. That lasted fifteen minutes and ended with a sale, putting her in a good mood by the time she finally noticed him waiting patiently for her.

A stout woman, Aunt Regina wore a long-sleeved blouse, a wrapper tied loosely around her waist, and a scarf. She held a flyswatter in her right hand, which she moved constantly. She wore a long coral necklace and pair of dangling earrings that moved as she swiveled her head from side to side talking to the people around her. She wore snakeskin slippers. The top portion of her wrap lay on the bench beside her, where she sat when not showing wares to customers, the only other furniture apart from the table on which she displayed her wares. Several bags of stockfish were on the bench, as well as a bag in which Aunt Regina stored her food, drinks, and other things she needed, including her purse. Each time she made a sale, she rummaged in her bag for change and stuffed the paper money into a pocket sewn under her blouse.

"What are you doing here?" she shouted.

"I came for a visit. My mother sends greetings and hopes it will be possible for you and Uncle to take me in for some time. *Na ututua ka nru turu.* I arrived this morning by train."

"*Ewoh!* Why didn't you send a message to say you were coming?"
"Auntie, you know how it is. Letters take too long, and no one from the north has been back for years. Besides, it was a spur-of-the-moment decision by my mother."

"You poor thing. You must be tired. Come and sit down. Let me get you some Fanta, or would you prefer lemonade? If so, I have to wait until the hawkers come by. *Ewoh!*" she said again, pinching herself before turning to her fellow women. "We didn't know he was coming. Have you ever heard of a thing like this? A young man traveling such a distance alone? He miraculously found me."

"Auntie, I'm not as young as you think," Ignatius said. "I finished secondary school. I saw children younger than me traveling alone on the train."

"Sit down and rest. I can't send you home, because nobody is there right now. *Ewoh!*"

A customer interrupted her and ended up buying a whole fish.

"Your uncle is in his stall and won't be ready to go home until the market closes," she explained. "I usually wait until the offices close and the workers come to the market to buy food before going home. Sit down and try to rest. If you're hungry, we can get you something when the hawkers come around. How is your mother?'

"She's well, but business hasn't been good. You know how it is." Aunt Regina nodded. "How is my brother, Kanu?"

"He's in Form Two at the local secondary school, where he's a day student."

"I understand Cecelia is a boarder at Queen's College in Enugu."

"Yes. We miss her, but we're happy that Kanu is around. He helps his dad after school. He must be there now. You'll have to hang out here either with me or in your uncle's stall until the market closes."

Customers constantly interrupted their conversation.

"If you don't mind, Auntie, I can leave my things with you and rush to my uncle's stall to tell him I'm here."

"That's good," she said between sales. "You'll need directions to find him. It's a bit far. Let's see who I can ask to direct you. Are you hungry? You must have been traveling all night."

"No, Auntie. I ate, but I could do with water or juice." The dust floating in the breeze left his throat dry.

Regina rummaged in a sack nearby and took out a bottle of Fanta, which she handed to him. He drank it quickly. Her stall swarmed with flies, and she had difficulty keeping them away, even though her fan was in use constantly.

"Why are there so many flies?" he asked. "It's not like this at home." "Oh, this is the fly season. Have you forgotten this is cattle country? The flies follow the cattle." "How do you stand it?"

"What can I do? We have to make money to stay alive, and competition is too stiff in the south. Don't you notice that all the women in the market are Ibos? Northern women stay home once they marry."

"Yes, I noticed."

"We're all struggling to put food on the table for our children."

Finally, Ignatius left for his uncle's stall in the manufactured goods section. His uncle seemed glad to see him, but he was very busy. After loitering for an hour, Ignatius returned to Regina's stall to help her carry her wares home.

The first day in Kaduna passed quickly. Ignatius left the market with his aunt, and they proceeded toward the Sabon gari residential area where most of the non-northerners and Christians lived. When they arrived at the street where his family lived, Ignatius was shocked to find his uncle sharing a home with total strangers, far different from their residence in the village. It reminded him of his father's house in Aba, where his father lived while starting his business and before he started his second family. His mother, in her wisdom, resisted leaving the village for town and raised him in a single-family house. Even though he slept on a mud bed, he could play outside, and he never felt as if he and his family lived on top of other people.

His uncle's place consisted of two rooms, one of which doubled as a parlor and bedroom, the other as a bedroom and storage area. At the back of the house, a small shed functioned as the kitchen, shared with other families. The rest of the shared conveniences were also out back.

Regina bustled around the shared kitchen, calling out to Ignatius to get things from the back room. As she laughed and joked with the other women doing household chores and tried to make Ignatius feel at home, his fears dissipated.

His uncle's attitude toward him seemed no different. In Ignatius's mind, he compared their acceptance of him with his father and felt total gratitude toward his new family. These people, who could have easily regarded his presence as a burden, accepted him without reservation.

At nightfall, given the small living space, Ignatius worried about the sleeping arrangements. He felt his presence added a burden to his uncle's family. His mother probably thought her brother lived in a palace, judging by the beautiful home he built in the village. Ignatius vowed to minimize the burdensome effects of his visit by pulling his weight as much as possible, getting a job, and moving out.

By the time his aunt finished in the kitchen, the rest of the family was home. His uncle went to the communal bathroom with a bucket of water to wash away the day, then they sat together and enjoyed a meal of *gari,* fried cassava flour, *egusi* stew made from melon seeds, and fish. Before settling down to listen to the radio, they talked about their day, Ignatius's journey, and the condition of people at home. Finally, they discussed his situation and his hope for employment.

Ignatius made excuses for his father. "My father said times are hard, and he had trouble putting food on the table for his growing family. Besides, Mama Adora is expecting again. It's a difficult pregnancy. She's always sickly, and she can't be expected to work like before. He also felt I've had enough education, which is more than he had, and I should be able to take care of myself. After all, he started looking after himself when he was half my age."

"That's true," Regina said, "but that was then. The situation has changed, and children need help nowadays to progress."

"True, Auntie, but you know my father. He never helped with my education, and his relatives were totally unwilling."

"My dear, your mother has been the mainstay of our family. If we, her kinsmen, don't help, who else will?"

The first three months in Kaduna, Ignatius volunteered to coach his cousin for his exam, helped his uncle with bookkeeping, and sometimes managed the stall when his uncle went on a business trip. Every night he returned to the little house, where he ate with Aunt Regina, his cousin, and his uncle, if he was home, then he helped his cousin with his homework. On Sundays, the family went to the Anglican Church, where they socialized with other Ibos.

Ignatius gradually became acquainted with every part of the market. His uncle sometimes sent him to the meat market to buy beef or goat, something Ignatius hated because of the muddy passageways and the smell of burned flesh and rotting garbage. On Sundays, besides attending church, he also attended town social meetings. The venue rotated among the members' homes, with each host expected to provide food and drink for the participants. Those social gatherings provided an opportunity to exchange information on the political situation and possible job openings. Ignatius saw the relationship between the southerners and the northerners deteriorating. Little socialization occurred between the easterners and the northerners.

Ignatius enjoyed meeting other families from his area who lived in Kaduna, and he gradually made friends with other young men in his situation, who were sponging off relatives while waiting for an opening either in civil service or the private sector. Together, they bemoaned their circumstances and discussed job prospects. From his new friends, he learned ways to improve his skills to become more marketable. For a minimum fee, some enrolled in the British Council evening classes to learn English language, literature, and history. He hoped to enroll, too, once he no longer depended on his uncle financially.

As Ignatius walked down the same road Ejituru had walked earlier, he wondered what his life would have been if his mother hadn't decided to send him to Kaduna. Two months after Ignatius had arrived, Okoro sought help on his behalf from Emeka, an acquaintance who held an important position with the Northern Public Service Commission as a recruiter for the junior civil service administrative cadre. Okoro set up a meeting for the following Sunday.

Throughout the week, Ignatius remained upbeat. Surely, a man in such a position wouldn't have any trouble bypassing government procedures if he wanted to help. He could hardly wait to meet the man. He rehearsed the spiel he would make regarding his ability and willingness to assume any position available, no matter how menial.

On Sunday, they arrived at Emeka's home, a furnished three-bedroom government bungalow in a residential area reserved for senior civil servants. They noticed the beautiful yard, which they later learned was maintained by a gardener.

Okoro brought a bottle of cognac and a bundle of stockfish as an offering. After presenting the gifts, he turned to their host and said in a soft, timid voice, "*Oga,* this is our child who has done quite well in the school certificate examination. As you know, competition is fierce in the south, and he's already spent a year at home without any hope. We would like your help. We don't want you to go out of your way, but if you could just let him know about possible openings, we would be grateful. He's looking for anything to wet his toes. A beggar has no choice."

"My brother," Emeka looked sorrowful and scratched his head, "the civil service is out of the question, given the recent employment policy decree. Non-northerners can only be employed if there is no northerner qualified for the post.

"It's easy to waive or override that policy for a senior position, because it's obvious there are few northerners with the requisite qualifications, but not for lesser positions. However, I heard from an acquaintance in the USIS that the American government is opening a USAID office in Kaduna. They now have a skeleton office on Dawiki Road and are looking to expand. I'll find out what the situation is and get back to you. I hope to see you next Sunday. By then, I should know. Thank you for the gifts."

He called for a servant to bring refreshment to his guests, and they spent another hour discussing politics before departing.

As they walked home, Okoro said, "*Nna,* calm down. I don't want you to be disappointed if nothing comes of this. I tell you, that man is different from other Ibos, who keep good things only for their families. He tries to help others."

"I understand, Uncle."

Emeka immediately arranged an interview for Ignatius at USAID with Mr. Tom Russell, a tall, slim redhead with broad shoulders. Ignatius expected a black man, and it took him a moment to adjust to that turn of events. Surprised that Emeka acted so promptly, Ignatius felt nervous, because he had no time to prepare. Mr. Russell tended to speak slowly to Nigerians, enunciating every word clearly, as if he wanted to make sure his listeners understood. Ignatius noticed that his tone of voice changed depending on his audience.

The interview went smoothly. When Mr. Russell asked Ignatius about his previous work experience, he said he had mainly worked as his uncle's bookkeeper. At the end of the interview, Mr. Russell asked Ignatius to check back within a fortnight.

Ignatius continued visiting USAID to inquire about the outcome of his interview. After a month, he began to wonder if he should return home, so he went to see Emeka for advice.

Emeka was sympathetic. "When I was transferred to the north, Okoro, your uncle, was very kind to me. He helped me adjust to life here. I'll do my best to repay his kindness. I'll call Mr. Russell to inquire about the outcome of the interview."

The call paid off. Five months after he arrived in Kaduna, Ignatius became a messenger at USAID. His duties consisted of delivering files to offices and occasionally filing non-sensitive letters. On slow days, he sat in the mailroom with the other messenger and talked about their lives, or they practiced typing in the hope of landing a clerical job. Working at USAID was the best thing that ever happened to him.

When he first started work, he often asked himself, "Is this all there is in life?" In an attempt to make the most of his spare time, he enrolled in English language and literature classes offered by the British Council, which had offices in Kaduna's commercial area, a short walk from the USAID office. With classes mainly geared to adults interested in selfimprovement, most students held clerical positions in either the civil service or the private sector. Mr. Russell, Ignatius's boss, supported his efforts, gave him books to read by American authors, and encouraged him to visit the USIS library.

During dead times at work, Ignatius lost himself in those books. He loved his classes and enjoyed the interaction with other students and the chance to discuss the films they saw in class. He often daydreamed about living in American, a place that overflowed with milk and honey, where just by asking a person could make as much money as he wanted. He learned a lot about America from the videos he saw.

He sent news of his job to his mother, which helped elevate his uncle's stature in the village and within the family. During Ignatius's first Christmas home after his new job, his mother treated him like a king. It was as if he ran USAID instead of working as a lowly messenger. Unemployed friends asked how he managed to get such a job and whether he could help them find jobs. He felt good, and his mother treasured the little gift he gave her during the Christmas season. Ironically, the current visit reminded him of the awe his relatives held him in for achieving the impossible—striking out on his own and succeeding.

As he entered his mother's house, Ignatius again thought of the planned outing with Ejituru. *Is she looking forward to it?* he wondered.

CHAPTER SEVEN

Ejituru left the kitchen in tears after the altercation with her cousins. Alone in her bedroom, she wept, refusing to leave the room. In her mind, she went through everything she had heard earlier, trying to find something she could understand. Why did her father want to marry her off? From the snippet of information she had from her parents' quarrel, it appeared he wanted to pass on her further education to that man. Why? Was he worried she'd be too old to marry by the time she finished at university? What was his rationale?

She heard it said that many rural parents would rather marry off their daughters at eighteen than bear the burden of further education. She knew many examples of girls withdrawn from secondary school because their parents found suitors for them. Was that to be her fate? She and her friends in school often discussed that legitimate fear. She heard that several highly educated women who remained unmarried offered to pay their own bride price for any man who expressed interest in marrying them, especially if he couldn't afford it. Some even agreed to become second wives, as that would enable them to have children legally. Was that what worried her father?

Discussing her feelings with her father was out of the question. He didn't tolerate disagreement. Fathers were to be obeyed. They were always right. Any argument with him would be regarded as an insult. She could only hope her mother would refuse to give in to such nonsense.

Why hadn't Nkechi mentioned this to her? She probably thought she was protecting her daughter from worry.

If she mentioned this when I first arrived from school, I'd have known how to handle it, she thought. *I should've stayed in the village longer, and I wouldn't have met this man. Now there's no escape.*

Perhaps she could send a messenger saying she couldn't meet Ignatius as agreed, but that would mean her father would lose face in front of the elders and be seen as a man who couldn't control his daughter. Everyone would talk about it, ascribing whatever reasons they could think of for her bowing out of such an outing. She would provide the villagers with fodder for more gossip. Nwada would probably spin quite a tale out of it for her fellow gossipmongers.

Ejituru thought of her friends, of the vows of friendship thy made on the last day of school, and of their hopes and dreams. For the last six years, they'd dreamed of leaving childhood behind and beginning their adult lives. Some had dreams as prosaic as just getting married and having a rich husband who bought them lots of clothes and a big house with servants, a car, and a driver. They wanted husbands who would take them overseas for shopping every six months. Others wanted to go to college, preferably overseas, to acquire a professional certificate and become rich. All their dreams, however, had one single outcome—being rich.

Many of the girls came from homes where they were the first in their family to attend secondary school, and it was drummed into their heads that their parents made huge sacrifices for them by paying for their secondary education, because that was the only avenue for success in the modern world. Rich men wouldn't marry uneducated women. They needed women they could be proud of.

If a woman couldn't land a rich husband, the next best thing was to have a good career and make her own money. Most evenings in the third year of secondary school, groups of girls spent time comparing the salaries attached to several occupations and deciding which paid the most, since they needed to choose the subjects that would lead to a career in the most-lucrative fields.

They often discussed past students, tracking what they did and sniggering over those who got pregnant immediately after finishing school, thereby ruining their lives. Their heroes were those who married well or held responsible government jobs. One alumnus struck it big and was appointed a government minister. She became enormously wealthy from collecting the usual 10 percent of the contracts awarded by the ministry and from contributions from job seekers. That made her their hero.

Ejituru dreamed of studying medicine. If she couldn't get into the Faculty of Medicine at the university, she would try for the next best thing—being a nurse. She heard that nurses stood a better chance of getting work abroad, and she knew one nurse was recruited to work in Saudi Arabia.

Ejituru knew Nkechi would like her to get a science degree and teach, because she hoped to establish a school with her gratuity once she received it. Her hope had always been that Ejituru, on getting her degree, would take over the management of the school at an appropriate time. Nkechi's mantra, one that Ejituru knew well, was that one needed a professional career to succeed in the modern world.

Ejituru wept, beating her breast repeatedly until she no longer had tears. She lay in bed, refusing to come out of her room.

Some of her friends wouldn't understand her anger. After all, she left school and within three days was presented with an offer of marriage to a rich man from the US, along with the promise of an American education. "Wow!" they would exclaim, urging her to accept the offer and telling her that the age difference wouldn't matter. They would point out the many women who had married men old enough to be their fathers and went on to lead rich, successful lives. None of them would understand her argument—it wasn't what she wanted.

She would like to go to Nsukka, study, and get a good job. Marriage meant children, and she wasn't ready. She didn't want a loveless marriage like her mother's. Nkechi always regretted not having the opportunity to go to secondary school and university. Ignatius, at thirty-five, was too old for her, and more experienced. Her father probably regarded the age difference as an advantage.

He probably thinks Ignatius will take good care of me, and I'll be well provided for. Who wants a marriage where one person is the dominant partner? She would prefer to marry someone her own age and grow with him. She thought of her parents' marriage. What would they have done if those sons had never come? Would Nwakama have divorced Nkechi? Would Nkechi have any grounds to complain if Nwakama brought another woman into the house? Ejituru could count on both hands several families like that. The husband presented his second or third wife to his first wife as a *fait accompli.*

Nwakama couldn't support himself financially, but in their traditional society, lack of financial wherewithal never prevented a man from marrying, because women were responsible for the support of their children. Wives were quite content if the children received small gifts from their fathers during major festivals. In her parents' case, though it was quite well known that her mother was the major breadwinner, she always deferred to her husband in public, giving him his due respect and treating him as the head of the family.

Thinking about those things sent her back into convulsive crying. Weeping, she must have fallen asleep. The next thing she knew, she opened her eyes to the morning light. Ignatius would come for her at eleven.

She got out of bed, bathed, and dressed carefully in a short, pleated skirt and matching white blouse. She carefully made up her face, using dark-red lipstick and lining her eyes with kohl in defiance of her mother. She put on gold earrings, a gift from her mother the previous Christmas. She scrutinized her face in the mirror, trying to smooth out any evidence that her eyes were puffy from crying.

The house was unusually quiet, which meant her parents were out. Her mother probably was running errands, and her father would be at the village meeting with the elders.

Downstairs, she found a tray with a covered plate of pawpaw, a flask of hot water, some packets of tea, and a tin of evaporated milk. She assumed it was for her and began eating.

She heard a car horn from the front yard. A little later, one of her cousins ran in to announce Ignatius was waiting for her.

She took her time to finish her breakfast and told herself Ignatius should be able to handle a delay of five or ten minutes. She rinsed her hands and returned to her bedroom to collect her handbag and put on her sandals. She didn't want to give him any hope she liked him. The only reason she was going out with him was in deference to her father.

Ignatius drove a light-blue Peugeot salon car, which he hired at the airport in Port Harcourt. Though it came with a driver, he drove himself. He wore a long-sleeved, light-blue shirt and stonewashed jeans, a jeans cap, and a pair of loafers.

"I dismissed the driver," he told her, "so we could be alone and have the opportunity to get to know each other."

In your dreams, she thought, though she conceded that the blue shirt suited his coloring.

"Where would you like to start?" he asked.

To her own surprise, she said, "Nduka Secondary School."

"That's where I went to school. I haven't seen it since I returned. That's a good starting point."

He drove down the main road, past the district offices on the outskirts of town, and on toward the school.

"I'm surprised to see so many new office buildings compared to when I left," he said, continuing past the hospital with its dilapidated buildings and unkempt yard. "Here, at least, nothing seems to have changed. It's just as I remembered it. Wow, there are a lot of new houses on this road. When I went to school, there was nothing here but cassava plants. We would cut through the farmland to get home after school."

Finally, they arrived at the school. Ignatius was surprised by the changes. A guardhouse stood at the entrance, and the dormitories and classrooms were rebuilt as two-story buildings instead of the long, onestory building of his time. The soccer field had benches for the fans.

"I wonder if I would recognize any of the teachers?" he asked. "Do you want to go to the classrooms to see?"

"No. I don't want to intrude." He pointed at the new teachers' houses in the distance.

"Some of the teachers live in the villages," she explained.

He saw TV antennas on the roof of the new auditorium and joked, "Times have changed. The students are now allowed to watch television."

Ejituru let him do most of the talking, without offering comment. He turned to her. "Did you have television in your school?"

"Oh, no, but sometimes we saw films, mostly classical English plays."

"Good for you. I didn't know we had a teacher-training college here now."

"I've never been to this area before, but this is one of the colleges built after the war. Some of my friends are in training here."

They left the school and drove past several large estates.

"Fancy that," he said. "The farmland has been taken over by houses. My mother once had a cassava plot along this road. I wonder whether any land is left for farming. The road is as I remember it. Why haven't the owners of the houses bothered to improve the roads that lead to their homes?"

"Perhaps because they spend only two weeks a year here."

"It looks as if the owners produce their own electricity and water supply."

"Don't you have generators in the US?" she asked.

"In the US, utility companies supply homes with power and water. Except on the rare occasions when there are problems with the power lines, there's a constant supply."

"I often wonder what they do with garbage in the US. They must produce an awful lot."

"Speaking of garbage, I was surprised at the mountain of rubbish on the streets of Aba. Before I left for America, it was cleaner than it is now."

"How do they dispose of rubbish in America?"

"It's collected from houses once a week in containers put out by the homeowners. In my apartment building, we put our rubbish in chutes provided on each floor. It's removed from there. Nothing is free in the US. Garbage collection is included in our taxes. I wonder where the owners of all these big homes put their rubbish."

Ejituru laughed. "It's probably festering in their backyards. Look at the villages. There's no place set aside for physical or human waste."

"That's a shame," he said sadly. "It creates the impression that the whole area is one big rubbish park, and nobody seems to mind. I understand that the government is trying to clear Aba of the rubbish in the streets."

"The problem is that it awards contracts, and the contractors take the money and don't carry out the tasks. They probably pay bribes so they won't be held accountable."

When they stopped at a roadside market in the next town for something to eat, Ejituru checked to see if the bar was clean. "Typhoid is endemic in our area. I try to avoid unhygienic places. Let's look for a clean one."

They settled on a crowded bar at the corner with inside benches. The bar offered mostly *suya,* chicken or beef on skewers with hot tomato sauce. The walls had several calendars featuring important people from the area from the federal and state governments. They ordered and watched the man prepare the meat. They had difficulty conversing over the loud music, the hum of the generator, the clatter of plates being served, and the loud voices of other patrons.

Ignatius expected her to be dazzled by the attention he paid her, but she didn't act like it. The chiefs raved about her beauty and intelligence, as well as her family background. Ignatius had reservations. Would she fit into his life in the US? She would want to complete her education. Was he willing to pay for that if her parents demanded it? Her father had apparently been very coy about his demands, while her mother's intense dislike of Ugo Chuku clouded her judgment.

"I'm curious about the universities in the US," she shouted over the din, her eyes bright with interest. "I've always envied people who were able to afford to go to university abroad, because there's no textbook shortage. It would be exciting to study medicine in the US and be able to have all the medical instruments at one's disposal."

"I've learned that, unlike when I went to secondary school, textbooks are hard to come by and are very expensive."

A couple of men entered the bar, laughing loudly, distracting Ignatius's attention.

Ejituru continued talking excitedly about her plans. "I hope to study medicine at Nsukka University. I should hear within the next two months if I've been accepted. I scored very high on the General Certificate Examination."

It became increasingly obvious to him that she was only interested in universities, not him.

"What do the college residences look like?" she asked. "Did you share a room with other students, or did you have a single room? What was the food like?"

Humbly, he replied, "I was a day student. I know nothing about the accommodations at the university." It was an opportune time for him to confess his deception, but he refrained, telling himself they'd never meet again once he left for the States, so why compromise himself?

Instead, he said, "I'll be traveling back to the States tomorrow, but I hope to keep in touch. I'd like to know what you're doing."

As they waited for their food, he took out his camera and asked a patron to photograph them. She took several shots.

"I'll send you a copy of each when I'm back in the States," he said. When their food arrived, he remarked on the tenderness of the beef, saying he never expected that, and ordered another portion. He also ordered Star beer to wash down the meat and offered Ejituru a Fanta, since she said she didn't drink beer.

He set up the outing as a way of getting to know her, but, as they ate, he felt she hadn't opened up to him. He carried most of the conversation, with Ejituru either nodding or saying very little. When he asked her a personal question, she managed to avoid answering. She showed greater interest in knowing more about life at American universities than anything else. She seemed uneasy, but all his attempts to make her feel at ease failed.

Though he felt drawn to her, he had no idea how she felt about him. She must have known he was interested in her as a wife, but he refrained from asking outright whether she would consider him as a suitor. What was the point of getting her hopes up if, in the end, her parents turned down his proposal?

Eventually, he ran out of conversation and decided to end the trip.

After they finished eating, he drove her home as fast as he could.

Once the car reached the house, Nwakama rushed out to greet Ignatius.

"I hope the outing went well," he said.

Ignoring her father, Ejituru went inside to change out of her good clothes. Relief washed over her. She managed to hide her feelings during the outing. She felt nothing but anger at Ignatius for appearing in her life, as well as anger at her parents for even considering marriage. All things considered, she felt she behaved well, listening to him talk about the disposal of rubbish and the loss of local farmland.

He tried to ask how she intended to spend her time before going to college, but she deflected the question, thinking it was none of his business. He asked her about boyfriends, and she refused to answer. How could he even think of such a thing, since she was too young for boyfriends, and where would she even find one at boarding school? It was a thoughtless question, and she felt she was right not to answer.

Let him think what he likes, she thought.

She wished she could tell her friends about the outing, but her closest friend from school was in Enugu. She'd never discuss the outing with her village friends, because they would gossip about it to all their friends and relatives.

She still had to face her mother, who she knew was anxious to speak with her. She vowed not to tell her anything about the trip. Her mother would have to imagine what transpired.

Ejituru looked out the window of her room and saw her father still talking with Ignatius, whom she felt would be anxious to return to his uncle's house or wherever he stayed. He said he was leaving the next day to fly out from Port Harcourt for the US. He had promised to send her copies of the photo they took. To that end, she gave him her mother's post office box number.

Instead of going immediately to see her mother in the outer room of the kitchen, Ejituru decided to visit her mother's aunt in her maternal grandfather's village. After making sure Ignatius had driven away, Ejituru left the house, taking the path opposite the main road, walking in the opposite direction from her father's compound.

Along the road, she passed a group of young people returning home from secondary school and others of her acquaintance. She chatted with them, comparing schools and gossip. When she finally reached her destination, she missed her great aunt, who had apparently left to visit her mother.

Ejituru wondered if her mother would confide in her aunt, then dismissed the thought. Her mother wouldn't do that, because she would be afraid her aunt would inadvertently tell someone when she reported on her visit. Ejituru cursed herself for avoiding the kitchen area, because that would have saved her from missing her great aunt and would have also prevented her mother from asking for details of her outing. At least the walk had reduced her anger.

When she finally returned and found her mother in the kitchen, Ejituru remained calm and acted as if nothing happened. They talked about their plans for the following day, the period before Ejituru had to leave for university, relatives on her mother's side, and her friends, who were expected back from school at any time. Ignatius was the elephant in the room that both ignored.

Ignatius drove home lost in thought. Was he prepared to have Ejituru live with him in the US as his wife? What would that entail?

He thought back over his life. The offer to work for Mr. Unegbu in the US came at a time when life as a messenger had lost its allure. Mr. Russell, his mentor, had moved to a different post in another country, and Ignatius had little chance of promotion to an administrative position. He couldn't save any money. His salary, though better than his contemporaries in the civil service, barely covered his rent, and he gradually reverted to eating at his uncle's house.

He started looking for another job within the civil service, particularly in the Department of Veterinary Medicine, hoping that would lead to a scholarship to study abroad. USAID advertised for Nigerian applicants to study veterinary science in the US. He believed his science grades were good enough to snag one, though he hadn't qualified for a scholarship in Nigeria. He didn't realize that applicants had to be nominated by the northern Nigerian government.

Then he met Mr. Unegbu, a fellow student in his British Council classes and an agricultural officer in the federal civil service, a post he held since graduating from Ibadan University, having served in that capacity in various parts of the country. He had been in Kaduna for four years, and within the last year had become chief agricultural officer.

A self-effacing man, Unegbu was the most highly qualified person among students in the classes Ignatius was taking. Ignatius found him a joy to have in class, since he had the knack of finding connections between the world of books and the lives of his fellow students. As chief agricultural officer, he kept in constant touch with foreign-aid donors who were looking for project opportunities to assist Nigeria in its development. Ignatius made friends with him, visiting his home and meeting his wife and family. His wife taught at the girls' secondary school.

At the end of the summer session in his second year, Unegbu announced that he was offered temporary employment with the United Nation's Development Program and would be leaving for New York. He hoped to get permanent employment with the World Bank, after which his wife would join him. The class was happy for him, but Ignatius felt sad, because he hoped his friendship with Unegbu would lead to employment with him at the Ministry of Agriculture.

Sorting letters as usual in the office one day, Ignatius, to his surprise, came to one addressed to him in care of USAID. The return address indicated that Mr. Unegbu sent it. Ignatius tucked it into the pocket of his khaki uniform, hoping to read it later away from the prying eyes of his fellow messengers.

After a busy day at the office, he attended his British Council classes and forgot about the letter until he got home. Remembering it just as he went to bed, he quickly got up and relit his candle. NEPA, the National Electric Power Authority, imposed a blackout day on Kaduna, something it did frequently and unexpectedly.

In the letter, Mr. Unegbu, after the usual inquiry about Ignatius's health, came to the point—would Ignatius be interested in coming to the US to work as his house help?

My wife was very impressed with you, and appreciated your help prior to her joining me in the US. I need someone reliable to look after the children, particularly after school. My wife has decided to pursue a graduate degree at the local university and will be quite busy, so we need someone to help her with household duties.

In addition, my job requires constant travel. As a rule, my wife will need help managing the boys when I'm away. We can't think of a better person than you, whom we know. We will provide you with a room equipped with a television, and a separate bedroom. You'll be paid five dollars an hour for working eight hours a day, Monday through Friday. You'll have a free half day on Saturdays and a full day off on Sundays.

I thought of you because you're already familiar with us, and I know you're looking for an opportunity to improve your situation. We have no close family relatives in Nigeria, since, unfortunately, we're the only children of our mothers, and we both lost our parents very early in our lives.

You would be a member of our family and would have the opportunity to pursue your studies during your spare time.

Many Americans work and go to college at the same time. That's what's really good about this place. Since your food and lodging will be provided, you'll be able to save a lot of money to send to your mother. If you accept this offer, we'll send a contract through a friend of ours who'll help with getting a passport and visa.

Go to America? he thought in shock. He was unable to sleep, because so many thoughts fought each other in his mind. *Could this really be true? Is this the opportunity I've been praying for?*

Upon hearing of the offer, his uncle shook his head. "I don't think you should accept it. It doesn't sound right. Why didn't he consider his relatives first? You'll be too far from home. There are many avenues for making money here for a hardworking young man. If you don't like what you're doing, there are other opportunities. There must be a catch. I've heard stories of people stranded in America, unable to raise the money to come home or ashamed they didn't succeed like others have."

"But, Uncle, this is the opportunity I've been waiting for. I'll be able to further my education. I'll help the Unegbus during the day and go to school in the evening. I inquired at the office and learned many universities have evening classes. You say there are many opportunities here, but look at you. You've worked all your life and are barely scraping by."

"It might appear so, but I've been able to build a good house, and my children go to good schools."

Since Ignatius met his uncle at the market, their conversation was frequently interrupted by customers.

"I have friends and family too," his uncle added. "You'll be all alone in America and dependent on this Unegbu. If life is so rosy, why doesn't he take someone from his own family?"

"I wondered about that, but perhaps his wife doesn't want to have to deal with relatives," Ignatius countered. "My mother always said that bringing your husband's relatives into your house spells trouble. Think of it, Uncle. You never sent for anyone from your family to live and work with you here. You didn't send for me. I just arrived. Perhaps Mrs. Unegbu would rather not deal with relatives. Moreover, she knows me, and I'm sure she knows what to expect. Besides, Uncle, this may be a way I can finally give back to my mother for her sacrifices."

Okoro felt he had lost the argument. The only part of Ignatius accepting the offer that made sense to him was that Ignatius would be in a position to help his mother financially.

Ignatius left Kaduna very late on a Friday night in a lorry carrying cattle to the east. By daybreak, he was in Aba. For a split second, he thought he should consult his father, but the memory of the last visit flooded back. He decided his father's advice would be unhelpful, since Ugo Chuku only cared for himself. Besides, he would probably be hustling in the market and would regard Ignatius's presence as a distraction. All the time Ignatius was in Kaduna, he never heard from his father.

Even when Ignatius went home at Christmastime, Ugo Chuku showed no interest in him. They barely spoke. The preparation and serving of food to Ugo Chuku and whichever children he brought, since his other wife was never there, fell to Ada Ngwu. That infuriated Ignatius, and he implored his mother not to subject herself to such abuse. She constantly urged him throughout the holidays to get closer to his father and tell him about Kaduna, but Ignatius was adamant that he didn't want anything to do with the man. He busied himself with his age group and never discussed anything substantive with his father. As far as Ignatius was concerned, Ugo Chuku forfeited his relationship with him when he refused to pay his college education.

"Have you lost your job?" Ada Ngwu shouted in shock when Ignatius arrived at her stall. However, she got up and embraced him, introducing him to her customers, who fussed over him, telling him to visit his mother more often. "Here's the key. Go home and rest. Give me time to close up. Are you in trouble?"

"No, Mama. I have news I want to discuss with you. Uncle and I disagreed over what I should do, so he suggested a frank discussion with you before making up my mind."

She became agitated and started packing up her stall.

"Don't pack now," Ignatius said. "We'll have enough time to talk when you come back. I have to start back for Kaduna on Sunday morning, so I won't miss work on Monday."

"*Odimma.* Okay, but I'm coming home in an hour and a half. I have to buy produce and goat meat. I need to cook something special for my son to eat tonight."

He was asleep when she came into the house. She let him sleep for a while, but she reminded him a couple times that he would have trouble sleeping that night if he slept much longer.

Finally, he got up, washed sleep from his face, changed clothes, and brought out his dirty pants for her to wash the following day. "I'll wake up early tomorrow to fetch water from the spring for you."

"No, no. Haven't you noticed the water tank for storing rainwater in the back? I have enough water."

After that, villagers began dropping in to get news of their relatives in the north, often interrupting Ignatius's conversation with his mother. It was until much later that they found some privacy.

Ada Ngwu prepared a special vegetable soup with goat meat, and served it with pounded yam and a jug of sweet palm wine. They ate in a desultory manner, savoring their food and drink, talking about kids he went to school with, and village events.

"How is your work going?" she asked.

"Okay, Mama, but it leads nowhere. I have what I think is a better offer." He paused, swallowing a ball of *fufu*. "Perhaps my uncle has mentioned my friendship with the Unegbus to you."

"Yes. We were very concerned about it at the time, but I thought he said they're no longer in Kaduna. He went to America, and his wife stayed in Umuahia."

"That's true, but now she's joined him in America."

"Oh. I'm glad for her. I thought maybe he found another wife and abandoned her."

"No. He'd never do that. He's a good family man. However, what I want to discuss with you concerns the Unegbus."

"My brother told me you were at one point almost living with them. While I wouldn't see anything wrong with that if I knew it would help you advance in life, I was a bit worried that the wife used you to run errands for her."

"I know that's what my uncle thought, but I knew what I was doing. Unegbu has offered to send for me to live with his family in America. I'll help look after his children, since his wife is studying at the university, and I can take college classes in my spare time. Most

Americans work and go to school at the same time. He'll pay me every month. I'll amount to something and be able to help you too. My uncle thinks there must be a catch, because the offer wasn't made to any member of Unegbu's family. You know how the Ibos take care of their families first."

"Okoro Ngwu is right. Why didn't this man first offer the job to a member of his family? It sounds like a great opportunity, one that should be reserved for family members."

"You're right, Ma. I knew I needed to find out more about his family. Don't worry. I was careful. Here is what I found. He and his wife were indeed the only children of their respective mothers, who died in childbirth. All the time I visited them in Kaduna, I met only one member of the wife's family.

"He said he would pay me, provide me with room and board, and I'll get spare time to study if I want. He knows I'm interested in pursuing my education. We met when I took classes at the British Council."

"I trust your judgment, but I'm sad that you're going to a faraway place and I won't be able to see you. Promise me you'll come home, settle down, and marry a village girl."

"Of course, Mama, but don't tell anyone about this, especially my father."

The two of them knelt and prayed, conscious it might be the last time they were together for many years. Ignatius felt happy.

He returned to the present and sighed. *I'm at this crossroad where I have to keep my promise to her,* he thought. *What would she think of Ejituru? Should I worry that her mother chose not to meet me?*

CHAPTER EIGHT

At Port Harcourt International Airport the following day, Ignatius held number seventy-one in the check-in line, having arrived at the airport at noon for a flight scheduled to depart at 6:00 p.m. He had until two o'clock to wait for the counter to open. He had been warned to expect the delay, since it was difficult to confirm a flight or assigned seat from the village. Many of those standing with him held their positions in the queue for actual passengers, and he felt he should have kept the driver for that purpose. However, there was nothing to do at the airport. The terminal was noisy, and the air-conditioning didn't function properly. Occasionally, a passenger asked his neighbor to watch his luggage while he took a bathroom break.

Standing there leaning against the wall, he remembered when he first left to go to the US. The day before, he traveled from Kaduna to Kano to catch his flight, and spent the night with distant relatives who were contacted by his uncle to put him up. Nervous over his first airplane ride, he didn't want to use the bathroom, thinking he would be sucked down and die.

He had difficulty eating the food he was served and watching the movies. When they ended, he couldn't remember any of the scenes.

The plane landed at Gatwick Airport in London, and he had to take a bus to Heathrow to catch his flight to America. He remembered the long bus ride and his fear he would miss his Washington flight, but the transfer went smoothly, and soon he was off to Washington. This time he would go through Charles de Gaulle Airport in Paris.

He thought of Ejituru and wondered what she was doing. What was her opinion of him? What did she tell her parents about the outing? Her father appeared to like him, but her mother had everyone concerned. Was Ejituru as totally indifferent to him as she appeared? Thinking of her helped pass the time before he boarded his Air France plane.

When his Dulles-bound flight landed on the first trip to the US and he emerged from customs, he had stood for a moment as passengers swarmed around him.

A man had walked up to him. "Ignatius, my name is Nkem Uba. Mr. Unegbu asked me to pick you up. He's at work. I hope you had a nice flight." He eyed the suitcase. "Is that all you have?"

"Yes." He lifted the case and followed Nkem to his taxi. "Where are you from in Nigeria?" Ignatius asked the driver. "Umuahia."

"Have you been here a long time?" "Twelve years. I came as a student." "Have you been home since?"

"No," the man said in a tired voice. "It costs money to go home." "Twelve years! Is it true that one can work and go to school at the same time?"

"Yes. It's hard, but it can be done. I know several who have done it. I gave up, because I needed to support my wife and children."

"Is this your car?" "Yes."

Ignatius was impressed and felt he came to a good place. If that man could buy his own car, nothing would stop Ignatius from making something of himself.

As he stood at passport control in Dulles, Ignatius chuckled at the memory. *I was naïve.*

As the taxi took him to his apartment in Thirteenth Street NW, he remembered how mesmerized he had been at everything he saw on the drive from the airport that first time. The houses seemed taller than anything he ever saw.

The driver had chosen to drive into Washington, and he had pointed out the Lincoln Memorial and the Capitol, telling him that the president lived nearby. The streets were filled with people and cars, and the cars actually stopped at cross streets for pedestrians. The traffic lights fascinated Ignatius, as did the patience of the drivers who stopped and waited for a green light even when no other cars crossed.

The Unegbus lived on upper Sixteenth Street NW, an affluent area of Washington, DC. They'd been in the house for six months before Ignatius arrived. Mr. Unegbu confided to Ignatius his worries about privacy, since, unlike Nigeria, the house had no separate servants' quarters, but his wife waved away such doubts.

Like most middle-class Nigerian women, she was accustomed to having servants to take care of the house and look after the children. The six months before Ignatius's arrival had been very difficult for her, according to Mr. Unegbu. She had to look after the house, cook for the family, and care for the children. He helped with driving, but he could do so only when he wasn't traveling for his work. Several times during Ignatius's stay, Mrs. Unegbu moaned about the constant demands on her time. She longed for her old life in the north of Nigeria, where the driver was responsible for dropping off and picking up the children and running errands, leaving her free for other things.

She looked forward to Ignatius's arrival. "Life is hard in the US," she told him.

The taxi driver halted in front of the most beautiful house Ignatius had seen in his entire life.

When the driver rang the bell, the youngest of the Unegbu children opened the door and shouted, "It's Ignatius!"

Everyone rushed out, and Mrs. Unegbu came to welcome him. She paid the taxi driver and thanked him for his help.

In a daze, Ignatius quickly removed his sandals, fearing to step onto the carpet. Mrs. Unegbu led him down the stairs to a small room in the basement with a toilet down the hall and across from the utilities. Ignatius couldn't believe his luck. He had a shower and toilet to himself. Mrs. Unegbu showed him how to use the toilet and shower and explained the layout of the house, so he wouldn't be disoriented after his rest.

"The family bedrooms are on the second level," she said, leading him upstairs to the kitchen.

Ignatius pinched himself to make sure he wasn't dreaming. He'd never been in a house with so many rooms and indoor plumbing. The kitchen alone was twice the size of his mother's house, and he saw there were many new gadgets to master. Mrs. Unegbu demonstrated how to operate the stove, dishwasher, washing machine, and dryer.

Mr. Unegbu must earn a lot of money to afford a house like this, Ignatius thought.

He decided it must be true that everyone in America was rich, if people lived in such houses, especially after having been in the country such a short time as the Unegbus.

The first week went well, with not much expected of him. Mrs. Unegbu cooked. After she and her family ate, Ignatius ate, washed dishes, cleaned the kitchen, and tidied the rooms. After that he could retire to his basement room to rest or watch TV. She forbade him to leave the house, in case he got lost or ran into some difficulty.

Mr. Unegbu, when he returned, was very glad to see Ignatius and said he hoped he would be happy living with them. They talked about the British Council classes, and he asked if Ignatius had taken other courses after he left. Mr. Unegbu seemed genuinely happy to see Ignatius, but it wasn't the same friendliness they had in Kaduna.

The weekend after his return, Mr. Unegbu met with Ignatius in the formal dining room to discuss his position in the house. "Give me your passport for safekeeping."

Ignatius handed it to him.

"Madam has already told you what your duties are, so I won't want to repeat that. Washington is a dangerous place. I must insist that you remain in the house at all times. You must not leave without permission. After completing your duties this evening, you should retire to your room, where there is a television for your entertainment. I'm saying this for your own safety. I know you want to go to school, but first you must get used to life here."

And I believed him, Ignatius thought. *What a trusting boy I was.*

"America is different from Nigeria. You have to be careful. Perhaps in six months we can start thinking of classes you can take."

Ignatius thanked him. "Oga, I've been here two weeks, and I need the salary you promised."

"I don't have it now. What do you want to buy?"

"Nothing, sir, but I need stamps so I can send letters to my uncle and brother."

"Why didn't you ask? I can give you those. After writing, you can put the letters in the mailbox."

On Mr. Unegbu's return from his trip, Mrs. Unegbu was aloof, preferring to talk to Ignatius through her husband. She gradually shifted the cooking to Ignatius, which he didn't mind at first, but it soon became a source of conflict, because she constantly criticized his cooking. She complained he used either too much oil or too much salt. She also found, not surprisingly, fault with his ironing, since he'd never worked as a servant in Nigeria.

Mr. Unegbu's failure to pay Ignatius became another source of conflict. As summer turned to fall and winter, Ignatius's lack of funds preyed more heavily on his mind. He needed warm clothes. More importantly, he needed to send money to his mother. Several attempts to get Mr. Unegbu to pay him what he was due came to naught.

Their conversations about money always involved Ignatius timidly approaching Mr. Unegbu after dinner and saying, "Oga, it has been six months, and I haven't been paid. In your letter, you said you'd pay me five dollars an hour. I've worked for four months, and you haven't given me what I'm due."

Mr. Unegbu scratched his head and stared at his feet. His wife usually left the room.

"Have you forgotten that I paid your airfare?" Mr. Unegbu asked. "I have to subtract that from your salary before I can start paying you. Times are hard for me just now. I can only afford fifty dollars, so here it is. It costs money to run this house, pay for food, for the children's school fees, and madam's education. Why are you asking for money?

You don't have to pay for your accommodations or food. What do you need money for?"

"Oga, if you pay me, I can send some to my mother to help her."

"Send her the fifty dollars I just gave you. She'll be happy."

Ignatius wanting to take classes also became a bone of contention between them. In the spring of his first year, though the Unegbus didn't want Ignatius to leave the house, he began taking short walks to explore the neighborhood. He met Mr. Clark, who lived two blocks away. A retired widower, Mr. Clark always walked after his lunch, and that was when Ignatius was out too. They looked forward to meeting each other. "Where are you from?" Mr. Clark asked when they first met. "Where do you live?"

"Nigeria. We live over there." He pointed at the house. "Are you a student?"

"No, but I intend to register soon for classes. I have my school certificate."

"What are you interested in?"

"Engineering, but for now I don't have the money to be a full-time student."

"I suggest you take GED classes at the high school so you can qualify for admission to the university. The classes are basically free and are offered in the evenings. I can get you an application. You won't have far to go."

Mr. Unegbu learned of the meeting from the children, who saw Ignatius talking with Mr. Clark when they came home from school. "When will you have time for school, and how will you get there?" he asked angrily. "Besides, in winter it will be difficult for you to get around."

"The high school is within easy walking distance. The classes are only in the evenings. I promise it won't interfere with my duties to you, Oga." "I don't think that'll work. My wife sometimes has evening classes. If you take evening classes too, who'll look after the children when I'm away on business? After all, that's why we paid your airfare and went through the trouble to bring you here."

Frustrated and upset, Ignatius vowed he would go to school no matter what obstacles the Unegbus placed in his way. Meanwhile, he decided to follow the rules of the house.

The restriction that he stay close to home irked him. At first, he thought the Unegbus were concerned for his safety in a strange environment. Later, he felt it was odd they never included him in any of their outings, whether to the supermarket or anywhere else. The family went to church each Sunday and never invited him. When colleagues dropped in on occasional Sundays, the Unegbus treated him as a houseboy and asked him to serve them. They never allowed him to speak with their visitors, unless it was superficial. As spring turned into summer and school holiday time, Ignatius's duties increased. The children were at home and needed more supervision. When they played outside, Ignatius had to make sure they didn't leave the yard.

Ignatius wished he could return to Nigeria, report his failure, and make a fresh start. He thought of his contemporaries and how they would envy his good fortune of being in America, the paradise all of them dreamed about. What would they think if they saw he was a virtual prisoner in the United States, with no money or ability to leave? He knew when they thought of him, they would assume he was enjoying life. How could he not? He was in Washington. He had seen the White House, the Lincoln Memorial, and all the city's beautiful things they saw only in films.

Without money, he couldn't return home. If he did, what would he say he had achieved during his two years in the US? Who would believe the story that Unegbu never paid him except for a few dollars occasionally? Unegbu was a highly respected man at home. The papers reported he had snagged a job at the World Bank, and he received high praise for that. Would anyone believe Ignatius? He needed to make plans to leave, and he needed to be very systematic about it.

Thinking back on his early days in Washington, Ignatius wondered what he could have done differently. Would anyone from his hometown believe what he endured for two years before finally breaking away?

He thought of his present situation. What would Ejituru make of that part of his life if she knew about it? Would she sympathize with his predicament at the time, or would she think he was simply an ignorant, weak man who could have left the house earlier and struck out on his own?

No one in his village would ever believe he'd been a houseboy in America.

CHAPTER NINE

Nsukka accepted Ejituru, much to Nkechi's elation, who proudly broadcast the news to all. It seemed like only yesterday that Ejituru had boarded the lorry that took her to Aba, where she changed lorries to reach Ikot Ekpene and on to Ibiaku. That was the first time she left home unaccompanied. Ejituru remembered clutching her suitcase when the lorry stopped in Aba while the driver found the lorry to Ikot Ekpene. At the car park, she met many girls bound for the same school, and they quickly bonded.

She remembered how green she'd been. Her elementary education was at a village school where she knew everyone. Now, for the first time, she was away from the comfort of home in the midst of girls from different parts of eastern Nigeria and different tribes. Ejituru felt lost and afraid, but her mother had told her that the other new girls would also feel afraid in their new surroundings and be unsure how to act. Nkechi urged her to overcome her natural shyness and make friends.

As the first girl in her family to go to a secondary boarding school, Ejituru didn't know what to expect, and the first few weeks were difficult. Some of the girls had relatives in the higher classes or classmates from primary school. The girls from the townships seemed experienced and confident compared to the rural girls. Ejituru wondered how she would stand academically against the township girls.

The first term was very hard, but she adjusted and made friends. Unlike girls from the townships, she had no opportunity to exchange visits with her friends during the holidays. As an only child, she knew her mother would be very upset if she suggested that part of her vacation be spent with her school friends in the towns. Nkechi expected her home during the holidays. Ejituru sometimes dreamed of visiting her friends in the towns, going to movies, perhaps swimming in the Presidential Hotel's pool in Enugu. She longed for the time when she would be free to be her own person.

After she completed secondary school, Ejituru looked forward to a new life. With her admission to Nsukka, she would finally be able to spread her wings and could hardly wait for the term to begin.

Nkechi thought Ejituru would be bored during the interlude between boarding school and university, so she suggested Ejituru apply for an internship at the local government office. Though at first Ejituru thought the job would involve running errands for big shots or just loafing around, she decided an office job would be better than sitting at home doing nothing.

She had an interview and learned she could start any time she wanted, because it was an unpaid position. She was glad to be helpful, knowing full well she'd only be there until it was time to go to university. Her work in the district office exposed her to the problems village people faced and the attempts by civil servants to solve them. She met the heads of various ministries, and sometimes she listened in on the meeting of the chiefs with the district office. When she had nothing to do, her mind drifted to Ignatius, wondering what he was doing. Sometimes she daydreamed about attending an American university.

At home, Nkechi made talk of Ignatius taboo. "Dismiss that name from your thoughts. You're going to Nsukka, and you'll be a doctor. That's your future."

But with Ejituru's village girlfriends, it was different. They wanted to know if she had heard from him. She always answered in the negative, saying he wouldn't want to write to a little girl. In her room, though, she admired the Eiffel Tower card Ignatius sent from Paris on his way back to the States.

On the last day before departing for Nsukka, Ejituru received a letter from Ignatius, telling her he had arrived safely and was back at work. He asked if she had heard from Nsukka, and urged her to be sure to give him her address so he could keep in touch, which made her glad. His letter intimated that after having visited home he found himself homesick, and he wondered how her plan of snagging a scholarship to study abroad was going.

On reading that, Ejituru laughed, thinking he was dreaming. She had six years of study ahead. Since Nigeria had medical schools, there were no scholarships for students to study medicine overseas. Her parents couldn't afford sending her to the US, no matter how she might wish for it. She put that thought out of her mind and went to Nsukka to start her first year of medical school.

At the end of her second semester, Ejituru went home for a few days. One day, her father summoned her to his room, saying he had something very important to discuss. Immediately, Ejituru thought of the relationship between her parents. Was he asking her to move from the house? Had her mother finally cut him off without any money?

When she entered the room that served as Nwakama's office, he sat in an easy chair near the window. Casually dressed in only a wrapper and no shirt, he motioned her to the opposite chair. "Have you heard from Ignatius recently?" he asked.

"No."

"Do you remember the pleasant outing you had with him?" He didn't wait for a reply. "I received a letter from him today, Ejituru. I won't force you to do anything against your will, but I want you to know that he wrote to ask me for your hand in marriage. Ignatius said that if the family approves of the marriage, he'll apply for a visa for you upon completion of the marriage ceremony. What do you think of Ignatius? What are you feelings for him?'

Dumbfounded, she couldn't believe what she heard.

"I want you to know that your mother is totally against this idea. I'm convinced that marrying him would be good for you. Ignatius said you can continue your studies there and will pay your fees. That's a good thing. You could begin as soon as you're there. I know you weren't expecting this now, so think about it. It's an honor. This is an honor."

He again didn't give her a chance to reply. "This isn't for your mother. It's what's best for you. What is there not to accept? You'll be in America. *America.* Maybe you'll invite us to visit you sometime."

Ejituru never really thought of Ignatius in those terms. She just settled in at Nsukka and began making friends, and now she was asked to think of going to the US? She felt torn. Her Nsukka friends would envy her and would wonder why she didn't jump at the chance.

Ejituru was raised to consider the pros and cons of everything before making decisions. The idea of going to America intrigued her, but she never entertained the thought she would go there as some man's wife at that point in her life. Ignatius was a much older, experienced man. She would have preferred marriage to a young man she could grow with.

The marriage was clearly her father's wish, and how could she deny him? On the other hand, her mother would want her to finish her education first. She needed to talk with her mother, but she knew what Nkechi's answer would be. How did Ejituru feel about the whole thing? Would she want to leave her current life for a foreign country with someone she only met, someone who was several years her senior?

Turning to her father, she spoke in a shaky voice. "Papa, I want to complete my education before getting married. I've only just started at Nsukka. I like it there. I've never thought of Ignatius as someone I might marry. In fact, marriage has never entered my mind. I have to think about what you've said. I'll give you my reply in a day or two."

As an afterthought, she added, "I have several things to work out in my mind. Besides, I need to learn more about what Mama thinks of this proposal. I don't want to go against her wishes."

She left unsaid that at the university she had met a young man named Nduka whom she liked a lot. She was sure that he, too, had strong feelings for her, though their relationship was just in its initial stage. He came from a very prominent family, and her college friends considered him a good catch. She would be foolish not to return his feelings. Ejituru had intended during her visit to seek Nkechi's advice before encouraging him. She knew her father wouldn't like it that the young man wasn't from her ethnic group, but her mother always said she would prefer her only daughter to marry from anywhere other than where they came from.

"Ejituru!" His eyes were filled with concern. "Remember, this is a great honor."

Not knowing what to say, she stood to leave.

"Visa approval can take a long time," Nwakama said. "We still have to set the date for the wine and marriage ceremonies, so it might be at least several months before you can travel."

Ejituru rushed to her mother's room and sat on the bed, where Nkechi lay resting. Ejituru narrated the discussion and asked Nkechi's advice.

"Your dad isn't thinking about you," Nkechi said. "He's only thinking about the honor that he would gain from his association with rich people and having a daughter in America."

"You're too hard on him, Mama. He said he has my best interests at heart. You're right to think that the marriage is very important to him, but I honestly don't believe he would sacrifice me for that. He said if I don't want to marry Ignatius, he'll gladly suspend all talk on the subject. He knows Ignatius has written to me a few times. In Enugu, I met women who have lived in America. I think I know basically what to expect, if I were to agree."

She wanted to confess about her boyfriend but didn't say anything, because that would just complicate matters. Her mother would jump to conclusions and worry that Ejituru was being sexually active, thus ruining any chance of a marriage.

Nkechi gave a hollow laugh, determined to press her point. "I need to tell you why I'm opposed to your aligning yourself with that family." She made herself stop before saying anything derogatory about Ugo

Chuku and Ignatius. Instead, she poured out her frustrations about her own marriage.

"I want you to finish your education before thinking of marriage. We've talked about the importance of education in the modern world. Getting married means having children, because our men expect nothing but children from our women. Once you're married, you'll have no option but to produce babies. Can you study while breastfeeding a child or while expecting your second or third child? My dear girl, that will happen to you in America, where there will be no one to help you. You'll be all alone.

"You need to think hard and consider the consequences of marriage. It sounds wonderful to go to America, wearing beautiful clothes we see in movies and living in a house filled with everything imaginable, but I'm frightened for you. Things might not be what they seem. What do you know about this man? You know only what he writes in his letters."

Ejituru listened to her mother with a heavy heart. She didn't want to marry Ignatius, but it was her father's wish. Maybe by marrying and going to the US, she could spare her mother the expense of paying for her studies.

After a pause, Ejituru said, "Mama, I'm not as foolish as you might think. I believe I know what I want in life. I share your hopes and ambitions for me. I've thought about this. Going to America may be a way to achieve my life's ambition. You see, I'll no longer feel guilty that you're denying yourself so much to ensure I get a sound education. I've heard that in America I can get a job as long as I don't care what it is, and make enough money to pay for my own education. It might take longer than being here with your help, but I won't let anything stand in my way.

"I'm your daughter, and I won't disappoint you. I've told Papa I won't agree to the marriage without your consent."

"Oh, Ejituru, you say those things, but fate has a way of interfering with our plans and changing them from the path we plotted."

Like all young women of her generation, Ejituru discussed Ignatius with her friends. She gave them the impression he was just an old relative, nothing more.

Deep inside, she felt she'd like to go to America to study. Who wouldn't? Why then was she returning the attention of the young man always at her side in Enugu where the medical school was? Living in Enugu, they constantly met people who emigrated to America and came home to visit their parents. Those women looked great and appeared very rich. Critical of Nigeria, they talked incessantly about their American experience.

When Ejituru met a nurse who worked in a hospital in Houston, Texas, she asked if she knew about Washington. Unfortunately, she knew nothing, since she had never visited the East Coast.

"Houston and Dallas are the places to be," the woman said. "The weather is warm."

The nurse went to America as a bride, but she was able to study nursing.

"Nurses earn almost as much as doctors," she added. "I was married once, but he had no ambition and exploited me. The only good thing from my marriage is my handsome son, who's in high school."

"I have a relative living in Washington, and I might go stay with him," Ejituru said.

"Going to America could be a good opportunity, and it's worth risking marriage to whoever takes you there, whether you love him or not. Once there, if the marriage isn't suitable, you can always leave him. That's what many of us do. You pretend you love the man, but your objective is to better yourself."

Surprised by the flippant talk of marriage, Ejituru asked, "But divorce isn't always easy for couples from the same family group."

"Nonsense. You'd be surprised to learn that it's the so-called relative husbands who are the most abusive. Make your decision based on what you want from life, my dear. I was as green as you are when I met my exhusband. I thought he would keep his promises, but it didn't take long in America to discover my mistake and learn from it. Don't take my word for it. Follow your heart."

At a party Ejituru attended on the outskirts of Enugu, she met another woman visiting from Boston.

"I'm thinking of going to the US to study," Ejituru explained. "A relative living in Washington is interested in me, and perhaps you could tell me about life in America."

The woman turned toward her. "If you're thinking of going there as someone's wife, that's not my experience. I met my husband while in college over there. We dated for a while before we married. There's no doubt that America offers many opportunities for personal advancement, but be warned. It's very difficult to combine childbearing and education there. Day care is expensive. Women often have to choose between deferring childbearing or deferring their studies. In my case, I completed my education and had a good job before I married. With two incomes, we could afford to start a family."

The woman's story impressed Ejituru, because it was a different take on the subject.

"I'm confused," Ejituru confessed to a girlfriend, Stella, sitting in the common room of their hostel. "I've spoken to two women visiting from the US, and they gave very different accounts of their experiences."

"You, of all people, should know that everyone's experience is unique," Stella said. "All marriages aren't the same, even here. Besides, there are always two sides to a story. Are you seriously thinking of marrying that old man you told me about?"

The question remained unanswered, but Ejituru began wondering what her own experience might be like. Would Ignatius allow her to finish her education before starting a family, if she agreed to marry him? That was another subject she couldn't discuss with Nkechi.

❧

Back in the present, she looked at her mother, wanting to be more open with her. Instead, she said, "Mama, listen to me. I need to get back to Nsukka immediately and buckle down to my studies. Papa said that even if I agreed there would be a knocking-at-the-door ceremony and a wine ceremony. I don't have to come back for that."

She left her mother's room determined not to give her father any reply during the near future. She felt that going against her mother's will wouldn't augur well and would probably have unintended consequences. If things went wrong, as they inevitably would, her mother would never forgive her father, and would blame her for pandering to him. Ejituru had to be certain what she wanted out of life. She wouldn't rule out Ignatius.

CHAPTER TEN

"Hey, is that you, Ignatius? Where have you been all these years?"

Exiting the McDonald's on Georgia Avenue, Ignatius turned to see who addressed him. It had been four months since he had returned from Nigeria, and trying to make up for lost income kept him busy. The encounter came as a surprise, since he still assiduously avoided those places where he might meet people he knew during his dark years.

Uche had tried to advise him during that period. They had met at Howard University, where Ignatius went to sell drugs. All of his acquaintances knew what he was doing, but they pretended otherwise, except for Uche, who constantly urged him to leave the drug business and get some education. At the time, Ignatius didn't think he could do anything else, and he was too ashamed to ask for help. Most of his so-called friends predicted he would be caught and end up in a DC jail or be deported.

Since he had decided to become a cab driver, Ignatius stayed away from his former Nigerian friends, even when he worked for McDonald's on Fourteenth Street NW. He had lost touch with Uche during that time. "Imagine running into you here," Uche said. "I'm glad to see you looking so well."

"I'm glad to see you too." He embraced Uche after his initial shock. "I've been busy trying to make something of myself."

"I see you're a cab driver." Uche seemed genuinely glad to see Ignatius and find out he had a legitimate job. Uche had completed his own education, and worked as a real estate appraiser in Montgomery County. "I recently got married, and I now live in Silver Spring, Maryland. You should come and meet my wife. Come this weekend. I want to hear what you've been up to."

"Did you marry a girl from here?"

"No way. I made the arrangements at home. My parents found a suitable girl, and I went home, met her, and liked her. I came back and started the process. Now she's here. We're having our church wedding in two weeks at Our Lady of Mercy in Silver Spring. The reception will be at the Marriott there. You're invited. It'll be mostly people from my area, but you're welcome."

"How'd you manage to get a visa for her to come here?"

"It wasn't easy, because the American government wanted so many papers, but we were lucky that we had photographs taken together during my visit to prove we knew each other. The chiefs and her parents testified we were properly married according to traditional law and custom. Photographs of the ceremony were required too, and my company provided evidence that I could support her."

"Thank you for inviting me. I'll come to the wedding. Please send me the invitation and count me in. I have to run." He looked forward to the event as a way of being integrated into the community.

Since Ignatius had returned to the US, his uncle and father wrote him often asking about his intentions. They wanted to proceed with the marriage arrangements, and they needed the green light from him. Ferrying customers from one place to another, he contemplated his response. If he were to initiate the arrangements, he had to do several things. He would also need to keep better account of his finances and make sure he paid his taxes.

He would also need to look for accommodations. He couldn't bring Ejituru to the apartment he had on Thirteenth Street NW. He needed a good explanation why he had lied about his profession during his visit too. On second thought, he felt that was the least of his worries. He could always justify it by saying he lost his job because of his Nigerian vacation and hadn't found another, so cab driving was just a temporary measure.

His uncle estimated the amount of money he needed to send home for the ceremony if he wanted to proceed with the plans. His father told him not to worry about the expenses related to the marriage, since he would be happy to cover them. That was the least he could do for his son. Ignatius didn't want to owe his father. If he went ahead, he wanted to cover his own expenses.

Ignatius had never been to such a lavish affair in Washington as Uche's wedding. The women wore expensive Nigerian lace, and the men wore the traditional white *agbada* with expensive jewelry. A Nigerian woman who lived in Lanham catered the reception at the Marriott. Ignatius knew that because she passed around her business cards. The disc jockey played Nigerian music, and everyone enjoyed drinks at the free bar. Most of the Nigerians present, like Uche, were professionals who used the time to make contacts with each other and show off their qualifications. They were lawyers, doctors, accountants, and business owners. At the wedding, Ignatius met a Nigerian immigration lawyer who could handle Ejituru's application.

At the reception, Ignatius caught up with news about his former acquaintances. Some had returned to Nigeria either to work for the government or start businesses. Many had moved from Washington to Houston, where employment opportunities were better. A few still in the area held responsible positions or had started their own import/export businesses.

Nine months after his return from Nigeria, Ignatius had written a formal letter to Ejituru's father. Although he corresponded with her, he hadn't directly proposed to her in any of his letters, restricting himself to inquiries about her education and leaving it up to her to deduce his intentions. Her letters mentioned her progress in college, the shortage of textbooks, and her classmates buying mimeographed copies of the texts from the professors.

Ejituru liked being at university. Enugu, where the medical school was based, was a big city, and life was very different from that in the village. She occasionally wrote about going home during a short break and told him news about the village.

In one of his letters, he flippantly mentioned he was very lonely. He spent days regretting having written that, because it might be misconstrued as a marriage proposal.

When Ejituru came again to her and asked her views regarding the proposal, Nkechi's first thought was to pour out her soul to her daughter, to tell her all of the frustrations she suffered in her own marriage, but she wisely decided she had already said enough. Telling her more wouldn't be the right approach.

"You know that when you marry," Nkechi said, "and your family accepts the bride price, you will belong to your husband. However, you never give up your membership to your clan, since that is matrilineal. I've often wondered about the origin of clans, and I'm convinced it began because, in a polygamous household, the wife's only security is from her children. The first woman made sure that other women and their offspring would belong together for eternity.

"The clan I belong to stretches from here to the hinterlands. It's said that in the past, if one entered a strange village, the first thing he did was name his clan and ask if he had any kinsmen there. If he did, they would identify themselves and offer him hospitality that befitted a kinsman. I, Nkechi, your mother, belong to the most numerous of all the clans in our place. Other clans are jealous of us because we are many, and we have a sense of belonging and affection for each other. We help each other, recognizing we share the same blood.

"Your father's clan, I'm sorry to say, is the worst. The members distrust each other and wouldn't hesitate to sell each other into slavery. They speak with two tongues. You're never sure whether they're telling the truth or if they mean whatever they say. They're usually carried away whenever the wind changes direction.

"Look at the lack of unity within the village. In that clan, even brothers distrust each other. Look how they fight and sell each other out over land claims! There's no love in the family. The only love and respect they know is derived from money. As long as you give them money, they love you and pay lip service to you. Once you close your bag, they forgot how you helped them in the past and will turn against you."

Nkechi paused, blew her nose, and wiped it with the end of her wrapper.

Ejituru held her hand, wondering what the tale of the past had to do with her.

After a pause to catch her breath, Nkechi said, "When your father's people approached my father for my hand, my mother opposed the marriage, citing evidence of bad treatment of other women from her clan who married into your father's clan. She argued that your father's clan had been our mortal enemy, and she didn't think your father's promise of protection would be enough to overcome the concerted hatred of his family members, who believed that I, as a member of my clan, would produce many children who would automatically overshadow them."

She laughed bitterly. "Little did they know my fate would be different.

I was destined for only one child.

"My mother saw them for what they were: forked-tongued serpents who laughed at you while gradually killing you from behind. I know you're wondering what all this has to do with you and the young man, Ignatius. You'll probably say times have changed and many of society's rules that applied when I was younger are no longer valid. Yes, you're right, but I can assure you that deep in the hearts of our village people, the old traditions remain and are guarded. My dear daughter, I'm afraid for you."

By then, tears poured down Nkechi's cheeks, and she couldn't stop. She knew she hadn't yet explained her innermost objection. How could she tell her daughter of the trials and tribulations a woman suffered in a bad marriage? How could she tell her that she didn't stand a chance, given that Ignatius was far more experienced than she was, and he would hold the upper hand in the strange land where he lived? Ejituru wouldn't have her family to fall back on. She would have to flounder alone in a strange country.

She blamed her husband for giving in to the idea so easily. Why couldn't Nwakama have said he wanted Ejituru to complete her education in Nigeria? Why was he enticed by the promise of another person taking over the responsibility for educating his daughter? Why couldn't he stand up to the chiefs and argue forcefully against the proposal?

Nkechi supposed it seemed right to him because his trusted friends approached him, and he saw the thousands of *nairas* and gifts that would flow to him from Ugo Chuku. She didn't believe he ever thought how Ugo Chuku made his money, just how the marriage would give him the resources to develop the little land he inherited from his father. He always said how he wanted to make an oil palm and rice plantation beside the Cross River bank.

"But I know these people," Nkechi whispered, clinging to her as if to ward off evil. "Once they get what they want, will they keep their promises?"

Ejituru had never seen her mother in such pain and held her tightly. As tears streamed down her own cheeks, she said, "Mama, one thing I promise is that no matter what, I'll complete my education and will make something of my life. I'm aware of the problems you've had with my father's family. I know you've been the mainstay of our family. You sacrificed to make sure I had a good life to this point, and I have no doubt you'll continue to sacrifice so I can reach the highest possible level of education. I promise that whatever I decide, it will be a decision that will let me attain the hopes and ambitions you have for me. *Ezigbo nnem,* my dearest mother. You raised me. I'm your daughter. You taught me well, and I promise I won't disappoint you."

She lay beside her mother until she stopped crying, then she got up and went to help with the evening meal.

The next morning, as soon as Ejituru left, Nkechi walked to her father's village. Several days had passed since she had visited or sat with anyone there to discuss anything important. True, her kinsmen and women dropped in when they heard she wasn't feeling well or when she failed to show up during church services or important village events. She stayed away from them and her special relative, Kanu, because she knew they'd remark on how sad she looked and would try to dig out the truth about what worried her. She felt events were moving quickly, and she needed sound advice on how to handle the situation.

Her thoughts drifted to Kanu. They had known each other their entire lives. As young children, they had played together when she visited her grandparents. He waited for her early in the morning to wake up so he could walk her to the stream. When she became a boarder at the girls' primary school outside the village, he had waited outside the gate on market days to bring her gifts of food from her grandmother.

He became the brother she never had, and sometimes he wished their blood relationship hadn't existed, because he would have liked their relationship to be different. He talked to her about every event in his life, and she depended on him for impartial advice. When he chose a wife, he went to Nkechi for guidance. He never demanded anything from her but love, respect, and loyalty, and she expected the same from him.

At one time, Kanu's wives were jealous of Nkechi and Kanu's relationship, reading more into it than existed. Nkechi managed to allay their fears and won them to her side. Both wives realized she wasn't in competition with them and accepted the fact that she and Kanu were bound together in ways that couldn't be explained in normal terms. He was part of her, and she was part of him—two people who cared for each other enough to lay down their lives for each other.

Nkechi valued Kanu's advice. As she regarded him as the brother she never had, he regarded her as his most-trusted sister. He would do anything for her, even if it meant harming someone, but she never demanded that from him. She desperately needed impartial advice, so she decided to take her problems to him and would abide by whatever advice he gave.

As she approached the village square, where many disputes in the villages were settled, she thought of her grandparents. She saw the house they had lived in, the first one anyone saw upon entry to the compound. Her heart beat fast as memories of her grandfather flooded her mind.

I loved it here when I was growing up, she thought.

She remembered the many times she was carried to and from the mission compound where her parents lived before her father built the current house. Her grandfather loved her. She insisted on being taken to visit the grandparents. Sometimes in the middle of the night, she cried out for the room in the mission compound where she usually slept, and her grandfather lifted her up to make the journey back to her parents' house. As she grew older, she spent two or three days in the compound, helping by fetching water from the spring or cleaning the hearth, doing any odd job assigned to her.

Sometimes she had sat outside the house while her grandmother made a big pot of soup to be eaten between market days. How she had enjoyed those evening meals with her grandparents! A smile came over her as she recalled the many times they ate from a communal pot. She always had to resist breaking off a piece of the fish or meat in the pot while eating. Everyone in the family had to wait for her grandfather to divide the fish and give each person a portion. The rest of the fish in the soup would be reheated and kept for another evening.

It was so different from her father's house, where her family didn't practice communal eating and each one had their own plate. Perhaps that was what bound her so tightly to her grandparents that, even though it had been years since they died, her heart broke when she thought of them.

As a child, she loved sitting outside, greeting people who came in and out of the compound in the evenings. They always sat around to chat with her grandparents, passing along information about happenings in the village. It was a happy time in her life. She remembered that even when she went to the mission boarding school her grandparents were more present in her life than her parents, because the school was near their village. Most late afternoons, her grandmother came to the gate, asking someone to get Nkechi so she could take small packages of peanuts or fruit, such as bananas or oranges, to share with her friends.

Nkechi would have to go in and say hello to her aunt, who still lived in the old house. When she knocked, her aunt bade her enter. Nkechi helped her get out of bed and asked if she had anything to eat. Since her retirement, she usually sent food to her aunt. Then she noticed the maid had already delivered the *akara* balls with *gari* for her breakfast. Nkechi watched her aunt eat, talking with her for a few minutes.

"I have to go now, because I have something to discuss with Kanu," Nkechi said.

Her aunt nodded. "Please stop by on your way home."

As Nkechi walked toward Kanu's house, she reflected on all the times she had run to him for advice on her marriage and how to deal with her husband's relatives. That she remained married all these years was because Kanu was there for her, advising her how to deal with events as they unfolded. She was sure that her kinsmen heard the rumor about Ejituru and the proposed marriage, but none of them dared mention it to her, because if there was any truth in the rumor, they felt she'd share it with them. Such was their love for her and confidence in her. No one in her grandfather's compound ever thought ill of her.

Nkechi entered the compound and greeted the men and women standing outside their houses. Some invited her inside to share kola and bitter nuts, so it took longer than normal to reach Kanu's door.

When she knocked, Kanu had just finished his morning bath and was preparing to make his customary round of visits to his acquaintances. He greeted her warmly. "Whatever it was that brought you out of your house so early in the morning must be very important."

"It is, Kanu."

They walked into his meeting room, and he asked his wives not to disturb them under any circumstances. Nkechi sat down and began crying.

"Stop weeping, *Ada Nnem,*" he said. "My sister, if you tell me what the problem is, I'm sure the two of us can find an answer."

She explained how Nwakama had handled the marriage proposal to Ejituru, how he hadn't listened to her objections, and then placed her in the position where it seemed as if she stood in the way of her daughter's future if she objected.

"Under normal circumstances," Nkechi said, "I would be rejoicing that my daughter had the chance to go to America. She would have a wonderful experience, the kind I never dreamed of. I just wanted her to go to university and become a doctor, as she wished, before getting married.

"How can I allow her to marry an older man, someone who's a stranger? True, he grew up here, but apart from that we know nothing of his life since he left the village. To tell the truth, I don't want her married into that family. Why can't Nwakama understand that? What happens to her if the marriage doesn't turn out well? How will she come back? I'm worried, Kanu, my brother.

"Nwakama said it's up to Ejituru to refuse the offer, but how can she? I can sense she's excited about the whole thing. When they first met, I knew she was upset with me for not telling her the purpose of the meeting. How could I, when I was opposed to the whole idea? She went out with him, driving around, and I'm sure he filled her head with stories about life in America. Since then, he's written her letters, I'm sure telling her how wonderful everything is and how easy it would be for her to go to college there.

"How can that be? If they get married, what if she becomes pregnant? How will she complete her studies and manage a child simultaneously? Oh, my brother, I'm beside myself with worry."

As the words rushed from her mouth, her tears continued unrestrained. "Stop crying and slow down," Kanu said calmly. "Ejituru is your daughter, and she's in a difficult position. She wants to please you *and* Nwakama, and she's probably worried how to do that. Does she want to drop out of Nsukka, where she is now?"

"Not yet, but Ugo Chuku wants to begin the wine ceremony next week. She's been corresponding with Ignatius, and he's been filling her head with all the wonderful things that will happen to her once she joins him in America. You know no girl can resist the offer of going to America, and she wants to go. There's no doubt about it."

"*Odimma.* Okay. If that's the case, this is what you should do. Don't oppose the marriage directly, but try to influence Ejituru indirectly. Tell her you have no objection, but you want her to concentrate on her studies and do well, because even if she goes to America, she needs to show she's done well in school so far. My sister, between now and when she goes—*if* she goes—your daughter will realize the importance of education. Make her understand she has to finish her education so she has something to fall back on if the marriage fails.

"Under no circumstances must you oppose the marriage on the grounds that it won't succeed. Tell her that, for you, the important thing is that going to America will enable her to have a good education and be able to stand on her own two feet. By your example, you've been able to support your family, and you didn't depend on your husband. If she knew that you were really thinking of her best interests and weren't opposed to the marriage based on perceived poor judgment by your husband, she will open up to you and will share her thoughts. Then you'll know what this young man has told her. Nkechi, my dearest sister, this is my advice. Think about it. Wipe your tears. Let's talk about something else."

He asked one of his wives to bring food and mineral water for their guest. Nkechi wiped her eyes and was able to converse calmly with Kanu's senior wife about her children's education and their progress. They talked a little about her aunt's health, and she laughed at their jokes. They made arrangements for future meetings. By the time Nkechi was ready to leave, her spirits were lifted.

In that same spirit, she decided to spend the day at her aunt's house. Her aunt readily agreed, and they walked back to Nkechi's house later.

Throughout the rest of the week, Nkechi laughed and joked with everyone. She treated Nwakama exceptionally well, and peace reigned in the house.

Nkechi decided to visit Ejituru in Enugu.

CHAPTER ELEVEN

"Mama, what are you doing here?" Ejituru asked.

Nkechi had waited until Ejituru came out of the lecture hall to greet her.

"I didn't know you were coming to Enugu. Where are you staying? How long will you be here?"

Nkechi's heart nearly burst with pride when she looked at her daughter. Ejituru wore a navy-blue skirt and white blouse, and as she rushed forward to embrace her mother, her face glowed with excitement.

So many questions swirled in Ejituru's mind. Were her parents separating because of the marriage talk? What would her father do? Why wasn't the visit planned?

Nkechi had come to Enugu to personally tell her daughter that she had changed her mind and wouldn't oppose the marriage if that was what Ejituru wanted.

Not expecting her mother's consent, Ejituru had banished thoughts of America from her mind and didn't take Ignatius's letters seriously. She liked being a medical student and was engrossed with her studies and friends at Nsukka. Apart from the power outages at inconvenient times and the hustle for textbooks, she felt she was learning a lot. Being a medical student, she didn't have time to participate in many student political activities. She hated the various strikes organized by student organizations, regarding them as distractions from the university's main function.

Ejituru had lab work during the evenings and had to prepare for midterm exams, so she found her mother's visit inconvenient. She would have to excuse herself from her study group to spend an afternoon with Nkechi. Her mother stayed with friends at the girls' secondary school near the medical school, and Ejituru knew her mother expected to see her in the evenings after classes.

She couldn't imagine what had led to her mother's change of heart. She was about to ask when Nkechi said, "I told your father to waive the bride price, but he said that he should realize the other side would consider you worthless. In the end, we compromised. We'll ask for only the traditional twenty-one guineas or the current equivalent in *naira*."

"So, Mama, when will this happen?" she asked, her eyes brimming with tears.

Nkechi continued without looking at her daughter. "During your Christmas vacation. I don't want to interrupt your studies." Nkechi seemed excited and happy.

Ejituru had the impression her mother was in full control of events. She felt trapped, but felt she could do nothing but make the best of the situation. With Nkechi's consent, she could no longer use her mother's objection as an excuse for her indecision. She had hoped her mother wouldn't give in, thereby giving her a reason to either stop writing to Ignatius or write and say she had a boyfriend at the university. Her relationship with Nduka had progressed, but with Ignatius in the picture, Ejituru wasn't able to commit fully to Nduka. She was honest with him and told him about Ignatius, intimating perhaps nothing would come of it, given Nkechi's strong objections. It seemed the decision was out of Ejituru's hands.

"I don't want you to drop out of college," Nkechi said. "Many things remain to be decided, and the visa situation can drag out a long time. A bird in the hand is worth two in the bush."

Ejituru wished she could interpret that to mean she shouldn't give up her college boyfriend, but she knew Nkechi didn't mean it that way, because she didn't know about the young man in her daughter's life.

Ejituru welcomed her mother's decision to continue her studies during the visa-processing period. Otherwise, she envisioned herself staying in the village, waiting for a visa, and missing out on an important part of her life—college with her friends. She wanted to tell Nkechi about Nduka, but the trust and openness she shared with her mother was broken during the time her parents fought over Ignatius. Ejituru began restricting the information she shared with her mother, out of respect for her feelings. She needed time to process what was happening, and she couldn't do that until Nkechi left.

Ejituru set aside her fears and resolved to enjoy her mother's company for the two-day visit. At the Presidential Hotel, they went to the pool and looked for a secluded spot to sit and watch the swimmers, since neither mother nor daughter could swim.

"Perhaps I should take up swimming," Ejituru said. "I heard somewhere that all white people know how."

"Do you want to learn that before you go to America?"

"I don't know, Mama. It just popped into my head while we sat here, watching all the rich white children swim. I just realized there are many things I don't know how to do."

"Don't be silly. You can run if you put your mind to it. You can dance, sew, and knit. You can do many things, and what you can't do, you can learn. You're a very clever girl."

"Mama, I feel so inadequate. I'm afraid of the unknown."

"That's not like you. You're usually very confident. Has something happened you don't want to tell me? Has Ignatius said something in a letter?" "No, no, Mama! His letters never say anything useful. He just talks about being lonely."

"In that case, if he thinks you won't fit into his life, he could have told his family not to pursue the engagement. Why do you feel inadequate? He obviously will help you adjust to life there. You should remember that you're going for a better education."

"Mama, do you really think this marriage will work out? You've always worried that we know so little about Ignatius since he left."

It was an opening for Nkechi to tell Ejituru what led to her change of mind. Instead, Nkechi lied. "I changed my mind because I realize that marrying Ignatius will result in your getting a better education than you would have in Nigeria. I've been able to compare doctors trained abroad and those trained here. I'd rather be treated by those trained overseas. Some of our local doctors have been known to mistake appendicitis for stomach pain."

That wasn't the answer Ejituru expected, but she didn't press her mother further.

"This evening, I'll take you to dine here at the Presidential Hotel." "Why, Mama? Do you know that the cost of meals here would feed the family for a week at home? Let's eat at your friend's house. I'm sure she expects you back for dinner."

"No, my child. I want you to start eating the kind of food you'll get in America."

"We still have to visit the market to buy the clothes you talked about for the wine ceremony. You'll be short of cash."

In the end, Nkechi got her way.

Nkechi wore her best wrapper and matching lace blouse, along with an eighteen-karat gold necklace and matching earrings. On her head was the latest head tie with images of playing cards. On her left wrist sat two broad ivory bangles, a gift from a friend who was a delegate to the teacher's convention in Nairobi. Her high heels, half a size smaller than normal for her, pinched her feet, making her walk down the hall with difficulty. Ejituru, with braided hair pulled back in a tie, wore a below-the-knee pink dress and gold-toned necklace with matching earrings. In defiance of her mother, she added bright-red lipstick.

As they approached the *maître d'*, Nkechi whispered to him they would like to sit where they could observe the other diners without being seen. She wanted to be able to free her feet from the tight shoes.

Throughout the meal, Nkechi, unaware of the turmoil in her daughter's mind, prattled on excitedly. "Oh, my! Look at what that *Oyibo* woman is wearing! I wonder where the woman sitting in the corner with the fat man bought that beautiful gold necklace and matching earrings." Her eyes roamed to another corner where a young woman dined with an elderly man in a wine-colored eyelet shirt. "Do you think they're married?"

"Mama, I don't know. Many rich men treat their girlfriends to an evening at the Presidential Hotel." Ejituru tried to join the conversation, but her mind wasn't there.

It was a relief when the evening ended. Since it was too late for Ejituru to return to her dorm, she accompanied her mother to the place where she stayed.

Ejituru tried to resume her life at the university, but it wasn't the same after her mother dropped the bombshell. Not as driven as before, Ejituru went through the routines of class and lab work, and her friends began to notice. She rarely saw Nduka, and when she did they just talked about studies. His requests for her to accompany him to social events at the college were ignored. She gave an excuse of too much work, telling her friends the same thing, then spent most of her evenings in bed or at the library.

She had no social life, and her friends wondered about the change in her since her mother's visit. She knew they were talking about her, but she couldn't bring herself to tell them the truth. It was none of their business. Disappointed that her mother assumed her willingness to marry Ignatius without bothering to ask her, Ejituru nevertheless gave her mother the benefit of the doubt and rationalized that the matter had been discussed so many times that her mother must have assumed Ejituru was in favor of the marriage, with the only stumbling block being Nkechi. If Ejituru wasn't willing, why had she continued corresponding with Ignatius?

Ejituru couldn't concentrate on her studies. Her thoughts flitted to America, and she wondered what kind of life she would have there. Ignatius said very little about his own life. Hers was an open book, and apart from writing about her studies, she had very little to say in her letters. She hoped he would tell her what to expect once he was certain the marriage would go through. She hoped for a formal proposal, but none came. Wasn't that what should happen, according to romance magazines she read? His next letter mentioned the wine ceremony and the requirements for a visa, but he didn't mention love. The letter sounded as if he were merely fond of her and expected to marry her according to native law and custom.

Stella, Ejituru's best friend, was also considering marriage problems. She and Stella had met at boarding school when they were both selfconscious first-year students and quickly bonded. They knew everything about each other, and she knew Stella was under great pressure from her father to marry a young man from a socially prominent family in her area. Her father would rather spend the money for education on her brothers than waste it on a girl with no benefit to the family. Stella's school fees were paid by a scholarship fund set up by a prominent man in her area to benefit indigent students who had the potential for secondary education. It was a great honor, and one she was proud of.

At secondary school, Stella was very studious. Like Ejituru, she was determined to go to university. She won a government scholarship to study at Nsukka. To maintain her scholarship, she had to keep up her grades. Both girls competed to see who could earn a 4.0 average at the end of each semester.

One day, Stella came to Ejituru. "I need to talk to you. You've been elusive since your mother visited. What's wrong?"

Ejituru remained quiet.

"Okay. You don't want to talk about it. I have a problem I'd like to discuss with you."

She turned and looked at Stella, who wore slim jeans and a blouse that molded her body and accentuated her breasts. She looked so vulnerable that Ejituru's heart melted. Her dear friend was hurting, and Ejituru felt that she hadn't been paying attention to her. They were always able to discuss their problems together. Ejituru realized she'd been selfish.

"I'm sorry, Stella. Tell me what's worrying you."

"I'm in love with Dr. Ogbu. You know he's from my area." "The lecturer? You should be happy."

"I should, shouldn't I, but it isn't like that. Custom forbids us to marry. He's from the Osu social class, one my father would never let me marry into. I don't know what to do. He's pressing me to tell my parents and allow him to carry out the wine ceremony. The taboo is such that nobody has ever tried to break it, at least in my area."

Stella's face clouded. She couldn't face the wrath of her father and resulting excommunication from her family. "Ogbu feels that it's incongruous with his doctorate and rich parents to be prevented from marrying the girl of his desire simply because his great-grandparents came to the area as slaves. His father is a very rich man who made a fortune from transportation. The whole taboo on interclass marriage is nonsense, he says. I agree, but I don't want to marry without my family's consent."

Ejituru felt that Stella's problem was nothing compared to hers. Stella obviously loved her man, and it was clear the man loved her. They had been seeing each other since Stella completed her secondary education. "Tell your parents and try to convince them to agree. They may see the value of the marriage if you present it to them as being financially beneficial. Tell him his parents should be the go-between and gradually negotiate the issue."

"But, Ejituru, he's afraid to tell his parents. They too might be against the marriage."

"You both have a problem then. You should both stop being cowards. If he really loves you, the burden is on him to ask his parents to open the discussion with your parents. If he refuses to talk to his parents, he isn't serious." She shook her head emphatically.

Stella agreed. "I've been thinking the same, but I'm afraid to stop seeing him. I love him very much. I'm thinking of marrying him, whether or not my parents agree."

"Whatever you do, make absolutely sure he won't disappoint you. You know there are many girls at the university who would be willing to displace you. You also know men are treacherous and don't always show their true feelings. He might get you pregnant and desert you."

"I'm well aware of that. My only fear is leaving university without getting engaged. You know how hard it is for overeducated girls to get married. Let's talk about you. Why have you been so sad since your mother visited, my friend? You've been keeping secrets from me. Are your parents breaking up?"

Ejituru had confided in her friend over the years that Nkechi was the family breadwinner and held her husband in low regard. She also told her friend about the conflict between her parents over Ignatius, and that Nkechi despised Ignatius's father. Her description of some of Ugo Chuku's antics amused both of them. If they saw a man accompanied by a group of sycophants, both exclaimed "Ugo Chuku!" and laughed.

"No, no," Ejituru replied. "That's not it. In fact, they appear very united. My mother has given her consent to Ignatius's proposal. She came to tell me about it and help me buy things for the ceremony."

"Then what's the problem? You should be happy. You gave me the impression you'd like to study abroad. This is your chance."

"Well, I'd like to study abroad, but the marriage part is frightening. I don't want to be like my mother and marry someone I don't love or who I've known for only two days. I'm afraid I don't know Ignatius, and his letters don't help. I'm afraid of the future.

"You're lucky that you know your boyfriend, what he likes to do, what he eats, and when he's sad or unhappy. You can talk over your problems. You can hold his hand and look into his face. That's not how I envision my marriage. I'll get married without the groom. He'll be represented by a go-between. My parents won't be there either. I have difficulty processing it all."

"Look, many girls would be jealous of you. They'd jump at the chance to go to America. I'm a little jealous too. I wish it were happening to me. I wouldn't give it a second thought. Just think! You'll live in America! Oh, my God. Does it matter who takes you there? You might even grow to love him. Think of the many women with arranged marriages who didn't have the luxury of falling in love. The couple grew in the marriage and learned to accommodate each other's feelings.

"But seriously, my friend, I know how you feel. We're modern girls who expect to fall in love and marry our lover. I understand what you're going through. The important thing, however, is that your parents are united in the decision. Does that mean you'll terminate your studies here after this semester?"

"No, I don't think so. Apparently, Ignatius will apply for a visa for me. That'll probably take months to materialize. Meanwhile, my mother wants me to continue my studies at university, and I'm grateful for that. I'd hate to leave here and sit in the village, biting my nails and waiting for a visa. Whenever it arrives, I'll ask for copies of my transcript, in the hope I can finish my studies at an American university."

"What does Ignatius say about your studies?"

"Believe me, he's said nothing. One would have thought he would at least mention it or send me an application form to complete. I could begin the admission process into a university, but he's never said a thing about it. My parents and his family have assumed my studies won't be interrupted."

"Have you said anything to him about your interest in continuing your education?"

"No. How could I? Until my mother's visit, I didn't think I would be joining him. I was quite sure my mother would stand her ground and reject the proposal. That was why I began a relationship with Nduka, the one you all think is my boyfriend. Now I don't know what to do. I've been avoiding Nduka, because I don't want to tell him my mother has consigned me to Ignatius."

"Oh, dear, don't look at it that way. You have options. If you really hate the idea of marrying someone you don't know very well, you should tell your mother."

"You know I can't do that. My father would lose face in the village. He's already regarded as someone who's controlled by his wife. My refusal would mean he also can't control his daughter. I'm afraid events have progressed past that. My only hope now is that the visa won't be granted." "Listen, Ejituru, there must be something you can do. I overheard my boyfriend talking to a student who was interested in pursuing further studies in the US in a very esoteric area. He told him to go to the library and research possible schools offering such courses. Armed with that, he got to the United States Information Service and asked how to get the application forms. You should do the same. Quite frankly, it would be easier if Ignatius helped you obtain the application forms. Being there, he should know the process."

Confiding to her best friend lifted Ejituru's mood. Barring unforeseen circumstances, she would go to America to study. Marrying Ignatius would let her fulfill her dream. She decided to shape events to her advantage. She would, immediately after the wine ceremony, start researching universities and their requirements.

"Can you keep my secret?" she asked. "I wouldn't like the news spread throughout the university. I don't need the distraction. I promise I won't breathe a word about yours."

CHAPTER TWELVE

As he picked up and dropped off passengers every day, Ignatius couldn't help but think of the trajectory his life had taken. It had been ten years since he'd left the Unegbus, and so much happened. First, he enrolled at Howard as a science major, but he never completed his studies, because it wasn't easy being a student and working full-time. He had been accosted by the police more than once for minor drug infractions and was lucky they had released him with a warning. Always one step ahead of the law, he was never actually convicted. He managed to get a green card with refugee status during the Nigerian-Biafran War. Thanks to sheer luck and one minor connection, he got a job as a cab driver for a well-known company in DC. He transferred to Montgomery College, because it was easier to work and attend classes there, but he still couldn't keep up. It was a struggle just making ends meet, but he persisted.

He picked up a Nigerian woman at the World Bank office on H Street. She reminded him of Ayo, his first serious girlfriend, the woman who had made it possible to leave the Unegbus. He met her through Mr. Clark, whom he asked for assistance when Unegbu failed to honor his contract. Ayo found a lawyer who sent a threatening letter to the Unegbus, suggesting that Mr. Unegbu could be reported to the authorities if he didn't hand over Ignatius's passport immediately. She provided emotional support during those early days of uncertainty, and helped him adjust to his new status as an undocumented immigrant before he obtained his legal papers.

When her husband threatened to send their children to Nigeria, Ignatius convinced her that her child would be better off there, living either with her parents or the in-laws, instead of being in a house where the parents fought constantly. Besides, that gave her peace of mind to pursue her studies. She took his advice.

At that time, Ayo and her husband lived in a quiet neighborhood called Somerset, off River Road in Montgomery County. With her children back in Nigeria with her husband, who was often away on assignment for the International Monetary Fund, she sometimes invited Ignatius to her house. He was there most weekends, and they had an affair. He went everywhere with her, and she taught him how to navigate the different customs in America. The relationship lasted for nine months before being cut short by her husband's death, when he died in his sleep. Ignatius planned to meet her at Howard, but she never came. Afterward, she sent a message giving him the news, as well as telling him of encounters with the police and the personnel officer from the agency that employed her husband. She asked Ignatius to refrain from coming to her house, because her husband's relatives from Houston were visiting.

The next time she called, she told him she was accompanying her husband's body home and would contact him on her return. The in-laws in the US took charge of all the arrangements, including handling her husband's estate in America.

Ignatius was devastated by her departure. His only friend was no longer there for him. He couldn't discuss the situation with anyone, because most of his Nigerian acquaintances were disgusted with him for carrying on with a married woman. He would have offered to marry her if he were in a position to do so, in the hope of stopping her from returning to Nigeria, but how could he propose to her with her husband's body in the mortuary? He couldn't meet her to say goodbye, because of the situation in her house. He expected her to keep in touch once she was in Nigeria, but she didn't. He subsequently learned that her parents forbade her from returning to the US.

For some weeks after Ayo's departure, Ignatius was depressed. He stopped showing up to work at the gas station that employed him, and he was let go. He realized he'd been emotionally and financially dependent on Ayo since he'd left the Unegbus. He got involved with drugs to alleviate his pain. At first he accepted only a small amount of marijuana to get him going in the morning. Gradually, he eased into buying and selling small bags of it. It was easy money, and he didn't have to pay taxes. His clients were mainly university students.

Soon, he progressed to crack. He tried to keep clean, but he needed to eat, pay rent, and look good. His friends worried about him. He tried to stop selling drugs, but it wasn't easy, especially since he had few marketable skills. Jobs at fast food places paid very little. Only during the last three years had he found a steady job driving for a cab company in DC, but after rent, insurance, and gasoline, he barely made ends meet.

Before his departure to Nigeria, he had temporarily sold drugs on the side to make extra money for the trip, careful to make sure no drugs were ever found in his cab. He knew he had to train for another trade eventually, but that wasn't an immediate concern. He was happy to receive US citizenship, since none of his infractions were recorded. His lawyer warned him his application would be in jeopardy if he didn't get his act together, which was the wake-up call he needed. It was ironic that his father was said to be the biggest drug dealer in Nigeria. Ignatius finally had something in common with his father. What would Ugo Chuku say if he knew?

He's so proud of my achievements, Ignatius thought. *Little does he know.* Ignatius looked forward to Ejituru's letters, because they were his main contact with home. The decision to visit Nigeria wasn't easy. Apart from his uncle and his uncle's wife, he had nobody else there. He wasn't close to his father, and he didn't know his half-brothers and sisters. He had no knowledge of the current number of other children in the family, though he knew his father had left his second wife and was on his fourth. His uncle had passed that information along in a letter.

The letter informing Ignatius of his mother's sudden death had come as a shock. He had no money at the time, and he couldn't leave the country, because his citizenship application was pending. He couldn't relay his problems to his uncle either, so he used the application for permanent status as the reason he didn't return. He would go as soon as his situation stabilized.

Again, he blamed his father for his problems. The man never owned up to his responsibility to his son. As soon as Ignatius's citizenship was approved and he had an American passport, he started saving small sums of money each month for a trip home. He felt apprehensive, knowing he had to prove he did well and was in as good a position as any of the friends he left behind in Nigeria.

Some of his friends back home held important government jobs or made money in their own businesses. Many had enough money to build substantial homes in the village, where they spent their weekends with their wives and children. Ignatius hadn't achieved anything. He expected his uncle to pressure him to secure a piece of land for a house, as befit his stature as a been-to, and to get married. He resisted that. Going home entailed having enough money in one's pocket to pretend he had made it in America. By his own reckoning, he needed two or three thousand dollars.

He couldn't tell anyone he was a cab driver. His uncle would exclaim, "With your education, you're driving a taxi? Whoever heard of such a thing? *Fiah!* What's wrong with you?"

His family, like most Nigerians, didn't understand why any Nigerian who went to America would become a taxi driver. What was the point of spending all that money to get to America, when taxi drivers worked for someone else and barely earned minimum wage. A taxi driver couldn't afford the fare from America or Britain to Nigeria. Nobody in his village could imagine that during his long absence in America he gained no useful qualifications. If he wanted to be a taxi driver, he could have apprenticed with another driver in Nigeria. Why go to America to become one? Ignatius decided to maintain the myth regarding his education and qualifications during his stay in the village.

The decision to marry proved especially difficult. Marriage briefly entered his mind when Ayo said she had to leave the US with her husband's body. On his first visit back home, Ignatius was pushed by everyone to get married. On one level, he understood the concern over his single status. Marriage was the norm for young men in his ethnic group, whether or not they could afford the cost of a wife and children. On the other hand, living in the US, he had to carefully consider if he could afford a family. His married friends, especially those with working wives, were always grousing about the cost of maintaining a family, given the cost of day care. Could he afford to take the plunge?

However, as the pressure from the chiefs, his uncle, and his father intensified, he succumbed. One of the deciding factors was the belief that his mother would want him to marry to ensure continuity of her lineage. All her letters to him during her lifetime bemoaned the fact that he might be tempted to enter into marriage with an American. She greatly feared he would marry a white woman. There were cases of men from his village who studied in England and returned with white women, but such marriages floundered under relentless cultural pressures. Little did his mother know that he never spoke to a white person except as a cab driver. He lived in a predominantly black city, but he wasn't drawn to black American women, or they to him, because he had no money.

Letting down his reserve, he agreed to consider marriage if the family found a suitable girl from a nice family. Skeptical, he went ahead with the arrangement to meet the girl. Having met Ejituru and driven her around in the car, he felt the least he could do was treat her as a friend while he was in Nigeria and forget her once he left.

Having made the decision to ask her father's consent, Ignatius sent money to his uncle and made an appointment with the immigration lawyer to initiate the visa application. Before he could proceed further, he needed to hear from his family that Ejituru's family had agreed to the proposed marriage. It pleased him to learn that Nkechi withdrew her opposition. He asked for personal information, as well as photographs of the ceremony, which would confirm that Ejituru was his fiancée. He needed those documents for the visa application.

He was concerned about his proof of income, since he was selfemployed and owed back taxes. After reviewing his case, the lawyer informed him he could bring Ejituru to the US under the fiancée exception if he could show proof of income and produce a tax return to verify it. The lawyer gave him a list of the required documents and the schedule of fees. It took him a few months to assemble all the necessary documents, because of how long it took to receive things from Nigeria and to file his tax returns. Finally, he filed the visa application and the wait began.

The lawyer agreed to be paid in installments over eighteen months. The last of those payments would be made after Ejituru arrived in the US. For it to work, Ejituru would be given prepared answers to the questions she would be asked at the consulate during her interview. She had to make the consulate believe she had known Ignatius for a long time. The lawyer told Ignatius that US law required the two of them to marry once Ejituru arrived in the country.

Ignatius needed Ejituru's cooperation, but he wasn't sure how to get it. Both he and the lawyer had written to her explaining the plan. The lawyer wasn't sure how long the wait for approval would be, but he estimated six months. Ignatius should be ready at that time to send Ejituru an airplane ticket, and Ignatius needed to find better accommodations and the money for the lawyer's fees.

Reflecting on his visit home, Ignatius felt ashamed that he had lied about his profession. True, he had enrolled in college and attended a few classes, but he wasn't able to keep up with his studies while working odd jobs. He was lucky that because of the Nigerian-Biafran War he could claim refugee status and receive a green card, which he got just before the war ended.

He lived in a crappy, one-bedroom apartment on Thirteenth Street Northwest, in a building he shared with several Latino residents who barely spoke English. He wasn't sure who the tenants were, because his job demanded that he leave home early in the morning and return late at night. He constantly feared someone would steal his cab. Several times, he woke to find the cab had been vandalized by neighborhood drug addicts looking for money or something to sell. Insurance covered the repairs, but that led to higher premiums.

In the last six months, he had arranged for his cab to be parked in a garage owned by an older cab driver who took pity on Ignatius. The man lived in Prince George's County, just over the DC line, so

Ignatius could easily retrieve his cab in the morning and return it at night by using public transportation. He offered to pay rent, but his friend generously refused.

Ejituru went home at the end of the semester and arrived one week before Christmas. All the villagers expected to have their kinsmen and women united with them for the holiday, and the area population would triple. The throng of arrivals wouldn't abate until Christmas Day, when those who had transportation difficulties would finally arrive. With each newcomer, welcome shouts and rejoicing would ring from the houses, alerting neighbors of joyful news, and the whole compound would come out to welcome the person.

Abuzz with activities, the week between Christmas and New Year's Day was always a busy time. People assembled to discuss social issues affecting the community and to settle intrafamily disputes. Age group meetings and other social activities took place, and each village assigned days to perform a masquerade dance.

The holidays also served as a time to look for future partners, with the young girls parading in their finery in an attempt to attract appropriate suitors. Families that missed having their daughters married during the New Yam Festival could take advantage of the presence of so many family members to arrange the wine and marriage ceremonies for their sons and daughters.

Ejituru always enjoyed the Christmas period, when she saw relatives and friends whose parents lived and worked in different parts of Nigeria. She enjoyed watching the masquerade performances in different village squares with her friends. Whenever there was a betrothal within her kin group, she enjoyed participating in the dances and resulting merriment. This year, it would be hers. How different that would be from the ones she had attended in the past where the groom had been present. In hers, he would have a substitute.

Happy to see her, her father spoke to her shortly after her arrival and confirmed that since Nkechi withdrew her objection, both families agreed to the marriage ceremony taking place on the last day of the year. Ugo Chuku wanted it to coincide with his New Year's Eve party. With her engagement to Ignatius generally known in the village, many people, on hearing she had returned home, visited to congratulate her on her good fortune.

Ugo Chuku sent several pieces of gold and coral jewelry to welcome her as his son's bride. He wanted her to wear them during the ceremony. "He should have waited until the ceremony to present those things," Nkechi said, extremely irritated. "We have to return them immediately." "Nkechi, let's send them back with Ejituru," Nwakama said. "Da Erimma will accompany her, and she'll explain our family customs."

He dispatched a messenger to fetch Da Erimma, who had fully recovered from her illness and was again her acerbic self. Happy to spend time with her favorite aunt again, Ejituru hoped to discuss her feelings fully.

The visit to Ugo Chuku began badly.

"What do you want?" the Hausa man at the mansion's gate asked. "The master has many people with him right now. Wait here. Let me send someone to ask the master if you should be admitted."

He double locked the gate, set down his gun, and shouted for someone to come from the back of the house. It took ten minutes of shouting before a young man appeared and was sent to ask if Ejituru and her aunt could be allowed into the compound. By then, tempers frayed, and Ejituru and her aunt were ready to stalk back to their village. Finally, one of Ugo Chuku's bodyguards appeared and gave the required permission.

Someone ushered Ejituru and her aunt into the biggest parlor they ever saw. It was the size of a university lecture hall, but the walls were completely bare. At least fifteen people were in the room.

When Ugo Chuku saw Ejituru, he said, "*Oko!* Oh! I wasn't expecting you. Our wife, when did you return? How is the university? I hope you'll be home for a while." He led them to a separate room with sofas and chairs grouped together.

"I tell you, our in-law-to-be," Da Erimma said, "I don't like the treatment we were given at the gate. One would have thought we were here to steal all your gold." She shook her head. "I'm an old woman, and I don't normally go where I'm not wanted. I have to tell you we will be hard on you when you come for the marriage ceremony. You'll pay for the way we were treated."

"*Da Anyi,* forgive me." He genuflected. "The man doesn't know you. Next time you come, I promise it will be different. We're about to be joined together. What a wonderful occasion."

Ejituru noticed he wasn't wearing any rings and necklaces. "I'm sorry we came without warning, sir. I came to thank you for the gifts."

"But we must return them," Da Erimma said. "It's best to give them during the ceremony."

"Let me offer you something to eat and drink, since this is the first time you've been in my house."

"Next time," Da Erimma said. "We're in a hurry. We have many preparations to make before the event. Besides, you're very busy right now."

Once they left the compound, Ejituru burst into tears, as if a dam broke. Her frustration finally came out.

Da Erimma turned to her. *"Ada Anyi,* why are you crying? We should have expected such treatment. This is how big men treat ordinary people. You're marrying into this family, so you'd better start getting used to it." Ejituru wept more. Da Erimma made her sit on a fallen tree trunk alongside the road to talk. She felt the despair Ejituru showed wasn't justified by what had just happened. Something else was troubling the poor girl.

"Tell me, my child, what's worrying you? You're about to get married, and I've been told you'll live in America. You should be happy. Has something else happened you aren't telling anyone?"

"Auntie," Ejituru said between sobs, "nothing has happened." As if reading her aunt's mind, she continued, "I'm not pregnant, if that's what you think. I know many people think we sleep around at the university, but that's not true. I'm still what I was before going to Nsukka."

"Then what's the problem, my daughter?"

"Auntie, I don't honestly know. I feel sad that I'm supposed to marry someone I don't really know. Going to that house reinforced the feeling that I know so little about the family. I can't talk about my feelings with my parents. Everyone expects me to be happy at the prospect of going to America to join my husband, but I'm not."

"It's normal to be afraid. Every woman has the fear of the unknown as she approaches marriage. Even those of us who knew the men we were marrying experienced periods of grave doubt." She turned toward the young woman. "I too entered into an arranged marriage with someone I utterly disliked. Believe me, you aren't alone. In your case, the doubt is more intense, since you saw each other only briefly, and you're going to a country you don't know without any family to run to. Who am I to advise you?"

"Auntie, promise me that none of this discussion will be passed on to my parents."

"Ejituru! You know you can always rely on me to keep your secrets. Even if you told me you were pregnant, I wouldn't divulge your secret to them. I would help you solve your problem."

"Auntie, I'm not even sure I want to marry Ignatius. I know nothing about him. In his letters, he hasn't said anything to me about my education. I really want to finish my education here."

"Have you spoken to your mother?" Erimma asked, concerned.

"No. I hoped she would withhold her consent, which would give me the opening I needed to tell my father I didn't want to get married. Now that she gave her consent, I feel I'm forced to go along for my father's sake."

"Oh, Ejituru, you're right. Events have proceeded too fast. If you now say you won't go ahead with the marriage, everyone loses face. You want my advice? I hear there's a possibility your papers won't be approved. If that happens, no one will expect you to stay married, because you two can't live together."

"Thank you, Auntie. That's my hope too." She hugged her aunt.

By the time they returned to Ejituru's parents' house, she seemed her usual self again.

The marriage ceremony took place in Nwakama's ancestral compound. The women wore colorful head ties. Ejituru sat among the family, facing Ugo Chuku's family, feeling as if she were on display. The women of the compound spent most of the day preparing vats of goat stew, pounded yam, and *ngwo ngwo,* traditional pepper stew made from goat entrails. By the time the groom's family arrived, the women had everything ready to welcome them.

Haggling for the bride price turned out to be the easiest part of the business, though the rest of Nwakama's and Nkechi's families weren't happy with the amount. To appease them, Ugo Chuku agreed to meet all the additional demands of yard goods and various requests to furnish Ejituru's kitchen with a fridge, paraffin lamps, and assorted kitchen utensils.

The negotiations left Ejituru a nervous wreck. She felt as if she were being sold to the highest bidder. *Why did I agree to this?* she wondered.

Merriment continued until midnight, when it moved to Ugo Chuku's compound.

CHAPTER THIRTEEN

Ejituru was instructed by both Ignatius and his lawyer about what to expect during her interview at the US consulate in Lagos. During the time it took for the visa to be approved, they followed through on her plan to research universities in the Washington area and their requirements for transfer students. She also wrote to Ignatius, requesting information that could help her decide which university to choose. She realized she might need time to acclimatize, but she hoped once her visa was approved she could time her arrival for summer and be ready to resume her studies at the beginning of the college year.

Rather than address her educational concerns, Ignatius wrote about his impending move to his new apartment and the preparations he was making for her arrival. He told her what clothes to bring and said food would be the least of her worries, because common Nigerian items like yams, manioc, and plantains were imported from Latin America. Stores like Red Apple and many Caribbean stores carried Nigerian food. He said such information should make her happy.

Ejituru remained preoccupied with ways to ensure her continued education. She learned that if she completed her medical education in Nigeria she would be required to take only the qualifying examination for foreign medical candidates. If she passed, she could enter a residency program. Knowing that, she felt she would rather complete her studies in Nigeria before going to the US.

Each time she went home, her father worried about how long it was taking to get the visa approved, but Ejituru acted nonchalant. She hoped it would be denied so she could finish her studies in Nigeria. She wondered why Ignatius said he wouldn't contribute to her education while wanting her to lie and pretend he would. The lawyer instructed her to say that during her interview. On the other hand, she was pleased not to be beholden to Ignatius, because that would make the situation easier if she decided not to go to America. She felt quite sure the embassy would see through the lies and deny her visa.

To her dismay, eighteen months after the marriage ceremony, she received her visa approval.

Ejituru's letters had become more demanding. Ignatius expected her requests would be for money to spend on clothes and shoes. He wasn't happy when she returned to university rather than stay in the village and wait for her visa approval. He mentioned that to his uncle, who said Nkechi wanted to continue her education, since no one knew how long visa approval might take. Estimates ran from six months to three years.

It would have been easy for Ignatius if Ejituru had demanded money. He could understand that, because she was his wife and he was supposed to take care of her needs. Fortunately, her family never asked him to assume responsibility for her university education after they were married, and he never offered. He made that clear to his uncle, who told her parents when the issue of her return to Nsukka was raised that Ignatius would prefer she stayed in the village to wait for her visa approval. If her parents felt otherwise, the responsibility for her fees should be theirs.

In all her letters, Ejituru seemed interested only in obtaining information that would help her pursue her education once she arrived in America. She demanded to know when she could expect the prospectus and application forms for entry into one of the local universities. Ignatius could have called any of the area universities to send him the information, but he didn't want to do that, because he felt Ejituru was under the illusion that he had enough money to pay for her full-time education in the US. He never gave her the impression that he would just because her family made it a condition for the marriage.

Ignatius assiduously avoided saying anything about American universities, but he did at one point send her a hundred dollars through Western Union.

Though grateful for the money, she said she would really like to begin the application process for a university before her arrival. In addition to her requests for forms and information on universities, Ejituru asked if her credits at Nsukka were transferable and wanted Ignatius to inquire about that.

He hoped she would write about other issues and stop hounding him about admission forms. He began to dread her letters, knowing what they would contain.

He sought the advice of a Nigerian friend while they were both waiting at a taxi stand in front of the Hilton Hotel in Washington, DC. His friend laughed and said, "You'll have a hard time with that one."

"What do you mean? I already did the wine ceremony, so we're married by native law and custom."

"She sounds like someone who's coming here to go to school, not to get married. I don't think she'll be a docile wife. If you want one like that, she isn't the one for you. She'll make your life a living hell unless you find a way she can pursue her studies."

"I have no objection to her pursuing her studies, but she has to find her own way to pay for it. I can't pay for her education. Besides, what happens when she has a child? If she goes to school too, then I'll have to pay for day care."

"I doubt she's even thinking about babies right now. If you're determined to bring her here, you need to find a way to pay for her education, or I see nothing but trouble in your future."

"I can't stop now. I already applied for a visa for her. Besides, stopping would upset both our families, and I'm obligated to carry out the process of bringing her to this country and marrying her in the courts here."

Ignatius tried to forget the conversation, because he had other problems. Finding an apartment he could afford was difficult. In addition to high rent, he had to overcome the stumbling blocks of a security deposit and the one month's rent in advance required by many apartment managers. How could he pay those when he had to stay on schedule with his payments to the IRS and his lawyer?

Eighteen months after his return from visiting Nigeria, he finally moved into an apartment off New Hampshire Avenue in Langley Park. He chose that apartment because he knew some other Nigerians who lived there, and he felt their wives would provide company for Ejituru when her visa application finally came through. He hoped that wouldn't be soon, though, because he needed to buy a minimum of furniture for his one-bedroom apartment. He also needed to look for affordable health care insurance to cover Ejituru.

Meanwhile, he continued driving his cab. Because of the anticipated change in his status, he worked longer hours to earn more money. He resumed setting small sums aside in a savings account so whenever Ejituru joined him he would be able to buy her warm clothes.

"What brings you home, Ejituru?" Nkechi asked as her daughter entered the courtyard after being dropped off by a taxi she caught at the motor park. "I thought your holidays were a month away."

Sitting in the anteroom of the kitchen gossiping with female friends, Nkechi stopped in the middle of a comment about the latest head tie craze to address her daughter. She wondered what brought Ejituru home, because although Ejituru loved her parents, she made it clear that she enjoyed the hurly-burly of town life rather than spending time at home. After Nkechi's friends left, she didn't have long to wait before Ejituru blurted, almost in tears, "Mama, the visa has been approved. Going to America is inevitable now."

Nkechi had always known that time would come, but she didn't expect it only eighteen months after the marriage ceremony. "Oh, my child, come here." Her eyes filled with tears too. "Let me hold you. I always assumed you'd complete your studies before joining Ignatius. From what many people say, visa applications for a wife to join her husband normally take at least two years. This one is much shorter than normal. The lawyer must know his stuff, eh?"

"Did I hear that the visa is approved?" Nwakama shouted, coming from the main house to the courtyard on his way to the bathroom. "Oh, my child, I'm so happy for you. When will you go to America? Has Ignatius sent a ticket? We should send someone to his uncle immediately to ask him to tell Ignatius to send the ticket. I hear his father is in Aba. This calls for a celebration, Nkechi."

Ignoring him, Ejituru and her mother went inside to Nkechi's bedroom to talk undisturbed.

"Mama, I don't want to go." Ejituru sweated profusely, and her cheeks were damp with tears. "I want to finish my education here. If I go now, I'll lose two years of college and will have to start from scratch."

"Ejituru, what's happening? Here. Wipe your eyes. You told me Ignatius would send you application forms. By this time you should know which university in America you could transfer to."

"That was the plan, Mama, but he never sent the forms. Since then I've learned that no college in the US will accept me into medical school unless I have an undergraduate degree. Even with that degree, there's still no guarantee of acceptance into medical school. I've wasted two and a half years! I don't want to go to the US now."

"It appears you have no other option. You're his wife, and we've given our word."

"No, Mama. I don't want to go. You'll have to bind me and shove me onto that plane. I wrote to Ignatius and told him it wasn't my wish to join him immediately, because I want to complete my studies here. I'm prepared to join him later during my residency."

"That's in three years, assuming you finish this year?" "Yes."

"Hmmm. I don't know how that will play with the in-laws or the embassy. Wouldn't it mean starting the visa application process over again?"

"I don't care. The man appears uninterested in my educational development. He's done nothing to help me get the basic information from those colleges."

"Ejituru, you know I agree with you. I want what's best for you, but in my view you're young. Three years is nothing. What you've studied here will help you there. You'll find that studies will be quite easy, and you'll catch up quickly and fulfill your dreams.

"Come here. Let me hold you. My suggestion is that you complete this term at university and travel during May. Let's agree to this between us. To the outside world, including Ignatius, we'll insist you aren't ready to forego your studies at the university. Perhaps that will push him into doing something about getting you into an America university."

On hearing Ejituru's change of heart, Nwakama said, "But why? The man's willing to pay for your education. Besides, didn't I hear that one can work and study? He did that. He spent money getting you a visa, and you said he's found an apartment. You should be happy and anxious to go there and enjoy the good life. I don't understand you. I thought you wanted to go to America."

Visibly upset but knowing he couldn't push her, he went to visit Okoro, Ignatius's uncle, to relay the new development.

The meeting between the families took place at Ugo Chuku's house. Okoro wanted it held at his house, arguing that Ada Ngwu, Ignatius's mother, would have wanted that. Unwilling at first to be seen at Ugo Chuku's, Nkechi allowed herself to be persuaded to attend, because her daughter's future was at stake. She had never entered that house before and felt uneasy about it, refusing several mineral drinks and kola nuts that Ugo Chuku offered.

"Ejituru," Okoro said, "we want to hear your reasons for this decision. Why didn't you say anything before Ignatius went through the visa application process? Why did you suddenly change your mind now that the American government has issued you a visa?"

Ugo Chuku said angrily, "It's Nkechi who put these ideas into her daughter's head. She's been against the marriage and will do anything, even now, to stop it."

To Nkechi's surprise, Nwakama sided with the in-laws.

In response, Ejituru said, "I've tried to get information on colleges from Ignatius during the months I've been waiting for the visa, but he hasn't been forthcoming."

"He's a busy man," Okoro said. "Do you want him to stop working and go looking for colleges?"

"Uncle, show me the letter from him stating he'll let me continue my education in America."

"While we have nothing to show you in writing," Okoro said, "we know Ignatius wants you to continue your education as his wife. From our perspective, the only thing that might prevent you from fulfilling your dream immediately is pregnancy. Are you pregnant? Is that the reason for your change of heart?"

Ignoring the implied insult, Ejituru said, "Nowadays, Uncle, there are ways of preventing pregnancy, so I can assure you that isn't my reason. I want to complete my studies in Nigeria. I have only three more years to go after this semester. I want a profession I can rely on if this marriage fails."

"Are you already assuming it will fail?" asked one of the chiefs present. "Whoever heard of that?"

"There must be another reason behind this," Okoro's wife said. "Have you met someone better than Ignatius at university and you're expecting his baby?"

Aghast, Nkechi stood to leave and called Ejituru to follow her. When Nwakama stood in support of his wife and daughter, the chiefs restrained all of them, saying that Ignatius should be informed. Since he hadn't yet sent a ticket, nothing was lost. It was, after all, up to him to make the final decision.

It took longer than Ignatius anticipated to get the visa. Slightly more than three years after his first meeting with Ejituru, a letter arrived from his uncle giving him the news that the visa was approved. He wondered why he hadn't heard from Ejituru, since she had been in contact with him immediately after her interview. Now that she had a visa, he had to plan for a small wedding for when she arrived.

While preparing to send the ticket money, he received a bombshell. Ejituru wanted to complete her studies in Nigeria before coming. She had heard that in the US she had to complete a bachelor's degree and take the Medical College Admission Test, MCAT, before applying to medical school. Even then, there was no guarantee she'd be accepted at a school. Under those circumstances, she didn't want to come. She had already spent over two years in medical school out of the six needed for completion and hated the thought of starting over. Was it possible the consulate would grant an extension on the visa?

He felt betrayed. He already spent a large sum of money he could barely afford for the visa. His family fed into his feeling of betrayal by suggesting that Ejituru hesitated because she had another suitor. It must have been difficult for her to feel married to someone she barely knew when there were many eligible young men at the university, they said. His family needed guidance from him about what steps to take. He wondered why Ejituru allowed the visa process to continue if she never intended to join him.

Taking matters into his own hands, he sent an express mail letter to Ejituru to call him at a specific date and time to discuss her fears. He was reluctant to provide her with information about universities because he didn't want her to presume he would pay for her education in the US immediately upon her arrival. He wanted her to settle down first, have children, then go back to school. At that time, he would be able to fund her further education. It seemed she was forcing his hand. He hoped, with reason, she would understand.

When they spoke on the phone, Ignatius said, "Of course you'll continue your education once you're readmitted to college here. We can't postpone your coming. If we fail to use the visa now, there's no guarantee that our next application will go through. The university forms will be waiting for you here when you arrive."

Anxious to go to the US, she allowed her doubts to evaporate. "Ejituru, my dear, I'm really looking forward to your coming, even though we've known each other only a short time. You should have faith that I won't disappoint you. Don't let anyone tell you that I'll behave like my father. I'm myself. I promise I won't knowingly hurt you. Have faith in me."

Sitting in his car in the Sheraton Hotel's taxi stand in Washington, DC, Ignatius reflected on the phone call. Ejituru agreed to arrive in May. *What Nigerian girl would give up the chance of coming to the US?* he wondered. If she merely wanted to complete her education in Nigeria, she wouldn't have changed her mind on the basis of one short phone call. It must have been a ruse to force him to agree to bear the burden of her education in the US. That he would never do.

He had high expectations of their marriage. He didn't want what his mother and father had, with each party making independent decisions, nor what his friends had, with endless bickering over money and children. He thought of the Unegbus' marriage, or what little he saw of it while living with them. Mr. Unegbu was the head of the family, and his wife couldn't make any decisions without his approval. Mrs. Unegbu had a good job in Nigeria and agreed to accompany her husband to the US on the condition that he help further her education, so when they returned to Nigeria she would have better job prospects.

Luckily for her, Mr. Unegbu's employment enabled him to keep that promise. Ignatius couldn't emulate him, and if Ejituru's happiness depended on his ability to send her to college or pay for her education, then perhaps his marriage to her wouldn't be the same as that of the Unegbus.

Ejituru's youth appealed to him. He felt she'd take direction from him, since she had no other experience besides village life. He hoped she would grow to love him and would become his friend and confidant. He wanted children, and he hoped she did too. Together they would plan their future. He looked forward to embarking on his new life. He hoped Ejituru looked forward to a life with him too.

As he busied himself driving clients to their destinations on the Mother's Day of his fourteenth year in the US, his mind went to his own mother. She was why he decided to marry a girl from his village. He had kept his promise to her. The idea that there would soon be a little child in the apartment calling for their mommy or daddy made his heart race. Located off New Hampshire Avenue, half a mile from the East-West Highway in Prince George's County, Ignatius's new accommodations were in a development of high-rises containing two hundred rental apartments. He furnished his one-bedroom on the second floor of the middle apartment building in the complex with secondhand furniture bought from a thrift store. It had a sofa bed and two matching chairs in the parlor, a small dining table with two chairs in the corner space beside the kitchen, and a double bed, dresser, and stool in the bedroom. For the kitchen cupboards, he bought unmatched pots and pans, assorted plates and bowls, and mismatched cutlery. The walls were bare of decorations.

From his living room, he could almost look into the living room of the apartments on the opposite building. For privacy, he kept his blinds drawn all the time, keeping out any natural light. Still, the apartment seemed fine, a big improvement over his DC efficiency, despite a couple of drawbacks. Lack of soundproofing meant he heard what was happening in the adjacent apartment. Often, the aroma of cooking filtered into his bedroom.

He wondered how Ejituru would react to hearing the neighbors flush their toilet or play music loudly, or breathing the pungent smell of stale food wafting into the bedroom. None of that bothered him, since he stayed there only at night. He hoped she would become accustomed to any inconvenience. As soon as financially possible, he would find a moresuitable apartment in the same complex.

CHAPTER FOURTEEN

Ejituru arrived on an unseasonably warm day in May. Washington came alive, with all the spring flowers blooming. Even in Ignatius's neighborhood, the forsythias and daffodils planted between the buildings were in full bloom, and maintenance men kept busy planting annuals at the entrance to the development.

Glad for spring's warmth, Ignatius stood outside the United Airways arrival gate at Ronald Regan Washington National Airport, awaiting Ejituru's arrival. The weather would make it easier for her to transition from the heat of Nigeria to that of the Northern Hemisphere. When he booked the flight, he decided that National was more convenient than Dulles, since he could easily pick up a client leaving for the airport from one of the taxi stands and still arrive in time for Ejituru's arrival. Fortuitously, Nkechi found a distant relative of hers in the Foreign Service who was traveling to New York on business and was able to change Ejituru's flight so she could travel with him.

As Ignatius stood with others expecting their loved ones, he wondered what would be the best time to tell Ejituru about their civil ceremony. He decided against a church wedding, on practical and financial grounds. He and Ejituru had no relatives in the US, and he deemed a church wedding too expensive.

As passengers disembarked, he tried to imagine what Ejituru looked like. What would she wear?

The sophisticated, poised young woman who got off the plane appeared totally different from the shy girl he met three and a half years earlier. He would have missed her were she not the only black young woman among the disembarking passengers. She wore tight jeans, a white blouse under a jean jacket, and black pumps. Her braided hair was tied with a band at the back. Bright-red dangling earrings and a matching necklace completed her ensemble. He rushed to hug her, but she stepped back to avoid the contact. Instead, she offered her hand.

"When did you arrive at JFK?" he asked. "You seem to have made your connection in time."

"Immigration took a long time," Ejituru replied, "but I was an hour early for my next flight. I'm here now, am I not?" She followed him to the baggage carousel and to the parking garage where his taxi sat.

"Where's the driver?" she asked in confusion as he opened the cab to put in her suitcase.

"I'm driving. I'll tell you about it when I get home," he said firmly.

Excited by the scenes before her, Ejituru asked lots of questions about the places they passed. "What's that tall building? Where does the president live? Do you live near the White House? What films are in the theaters now? I brought some Nigerian videos for us to watch sometime. Do any of the film stars live in the Washington area?"

She prattled on excitedly, twisting and turning and not giving him time to reply.

He opened his mouth to answer, but she was already asking her next question.

"I'm dying to see where all the film stars live," she said.

When she finally paused, he said, "I don't know if any live here." He hoped that answered her current question. He had difficulty keeping up with her conversation, and felt as if she were a broken tap. He assumed she was nervous.

"Take it easy," he said. "You must be very tired from your journey." He turned to study her profile. "I told you in my letter that I moved. I hope you'll like the apartment. I'm off work for two days and will be able to show you around. We'll go shopping to buy you a few things, although just now the weather is warm and your Nigerian clothes will do. We'll get winter things for you in September."

When she stepped out of his taxi, she cringed at the filth in the neighborhood. A few minutes later, she walked into his dark, second-floor apartment and stared in shock at the secondhand furniture. The blinds were drawn, and the strong smell of the neighbors' cooking wafted through the room.

She stared at the meager space in dismay. She had expected him to live in a big house, similar to the ones she saw on TV. She expected a beautiful garden with lawn furniture, several bedrooms, and a separate dining room. After all, as an engineer, he no doubt earned a good income.

Coming in behind her, he apologized. "I'm sorry. This isn't much. I lost my job, and this was the only vacant apartment I could afford. I would prefer to live on the seventh floor, but there weren't any available units. As soon as our situation improves, we'll move."

Ejituru stepped to the window to let in some fresh air. When she opened the blinds, she came face to face with a half-dressed man in another apartment staring straight into her living room. She quickly dropped the blinds and turned toward Ignatius.

"The top floors are safer," he explained. "There's little danger of breakins." He went to the door and showed her the double lock. "Keep it locked at all times, whether or not you're in the house."

Stunned, she stared at her husband, who refused to look her in the eye. She couldn't believe she was in America only to live in a dump like this. She swallowed hard. It was clear she had a lot to get used to with her new husband.

"Why don't you sit down?" he asked in a small voice. "Are you hungry? I picked up some fried chicken and fries before coming to the airport. Living alone, I don't normally cook. I eat at fast-food places. The only time I cook here is to microwave leftovers. I'm really looking forward to some home-cooked meals."

He handed her a can of Coca-Cola. "I remembered you like sodas, so I bought some. You may wish to rest. The bed is freshly made."

Ejituru gave a monosyllabic answer and fell asleep on the sofa with Ignatius still talking.

When she woke a minute later, he said, "You must be very tired. I realized you weren't listening to me. I was telling you that we'll be married in a civil ceremony. I didn't see the need for a church wedding, since our families won't be present."

Ejituru couldn't believe it. *Another blow!* she thought. She'd been looking at wedding dresses in the magazines at a newsstand at the airport and wondered how she'd look in them. Clenching her teeth, she didn't answer. "We're getting married the day after tomorrow," he continued. "My lawyer will be present. You don't have to dress up too much. A simple dress will do." He saw her disappointment. "We can go out tomorrow to buy a dress if you think you need one."

"No. I think I have a suitable one." She became preoccupied with their sleeping arrangements. She noticed there was only one bedroom, which contained a double bed. She was determined to sleep on the sofa.

During the first three months, Ignatius had trouble adjusting to married life. They encountered several unexpected expenses. Ejituru had to see a dentist when she had an impacted tooth. Soon after that, she had a severe recurrence of malaria. Ignatius had had no medical or dental insurance since he'd come to the US. He had intended to get some as part of his preparations for her arrival, but he never followed through, so he had to pay for those unplanned expenses out of pocket.

Ignatius worried about Ejituru while at work. He introduced her to the Nigerian wives in the building, hoping they would look in on her and perhaps include her in trips to the supermarket. He worried, however, that they would inadvertently tell her that he drove a cab and didn't even own the one he had but rented it from the cab company. All that added to his stress. He had no fixed work hours. Sometimes he didn't return to the apartment until seven o'clock at night. By then, Ejituru had already eaten and would be watching TV when he came through the door.

After the novelty of living in America wore off, Ejituru felt very lonely. She didn't know what to do with herself. Unlike in Nigeria, where she never lacked company at any time, in America she was alone in the apartment during the day. In Nigeria, she could knock on any door whenever she felt like it. She met some Nigerian families in the complex, but most of the women had outside employment and weren't available during the day for company. Afraid to venture out on her own after having read so many stories about crime in America, she turned to TV as her only companion during the day and the only way to combat her loneliness.

Sometimes she read through her old textbooks. As time passed, she memorized many of the pages. Some days, she overcame her fears and walked up New Hampshire Avenue to the shopping center where Red Apple was located, wandering from shop to shop, looking at the variety of goods on display. Ignatius gave her spending money, and she occasionally bought something at the dollar store. Most times, she ended up crying and wishing she were back in Nigeria.

As the weeks stretched on, her loneliness became overwhelming. One day, she asked Ignatius, "Is there a church nearby? I'd like to go to church on Sundays."

"There are many churches," he replied. "I thought of joining a Nigerian church in Lanham. It was just a thought, because I work some Sundays and don't have the time. I presume we could go one Sunday if it'll make you happy to meet a wider circle of Nigerians other than those in the complex." Slightly irritated, he saw no point in widening his circle of acquaintances.

The following Sunday, he took her to the morning service at the church, which didn't yet have its own premises but met in the hall of a local high school. The congregation sat on folding chairs arranged in rows facing the makeshift altar, and behind the altar was the choir and church officers. The format was evangelical, with the congregation shouting "Amen!" or "Alleluia!" whenever the preacher said something they agreed with.

At offering time, the congregants sang and danced to the altar to present their offerings. Ejituru, who attended a mainstream church in

Nigeria, found the service unsettling and too long, but she was happy to be among so many Nigerians. The service lasted from eleven to three, with a social hour afterward.

"My name is Cece," a feminine voice said behind her. "Are you new here?"

Ejituru turned and saw a beautiful, tall black woman in an aquamarine suit and high-heeled black shoes offering her hand to shake. As one of the very few Nigerian women wearing Western clothes in the church, Cece stood out.

Taken aback at being addressed, Ejituru said, "Yes, this is my first time. I came here six weeks ago to join my husband. He's over there, talking to the light-skinned man." She pointed.

"I see. My husband's the one talking to the man in a blue cap. He's a doctor at the hospital in Lanham."

Ejituru saw a professional-looking man in a dark-green suit and white shirt, in contrast to Ignatius, who wore a short-sleeved shirt over jeans.

"I attended medical school in Nigeria," Ejituru said. "I completed three years. I'm hoping to get back to the university here."

"Hmmm. It'll be hard for you. I'm a lawyer, though right now I'm taking maternity leave. Perhaps we can talk about it another time. I see my husband beckoning."

That was how Ejituru made friends with Cece. She learned Cece was the daughter of one of the ministers of the old eastern Nigerian government and was educated at the prestigious Queens College, a girls' secondary school in Lagos. From there, she went on to read law at Lincoln's Inn in London. During the Nigerian-Biafran War, she came to the US as a visitor and met her future husband, who persuaded her to continue her education in the States. She studied law at Georgetown University, where her husband attended medical school. She and Ejituru became close friends and met regularly during the week to go shopping or hang out at Cece's house in Lanham.

Having Cece as a friend was the best thing that happened to Ejituru. Cece and her husband lived in a new development in Prince George's County, with big houses and beautiful lawns. That fed into

Ejituru's idea of America. Cece's kitchen, with its granite countertops, lovely mahogany cupboards, and expensive-looking kitchen appliances, overlooked the backyard where Cece and her husband liked to entertain fellow professional Nigerians on weekends. The beautifully decorated house had four bedrooms and an equal number of bathrooms. That was what Ejituru had expected her life with Ignatius to be. She loved the family room where Cece and her friends hung out and watched movies.

Cece told her that before they bought the house they lived in an apartment on East-West Highway. That big building had a doorman at the entrance, and every visitor had to be announced before entering the building. Mary, a friend of Cece's, still had an apartment there. Cece took Ejituru to visit her. Ejituru fell in love with the apartment, and wondered why Ignatius chose to live in such a crummy place when he was making lots of money as an engineer.

With Cece's mother-in-law visiting from Nigeria, Cece sometimes left the children with her while meeting Ejituru. Ejituru couldn't imagine her own mother visiting her apartment off New Hampshire Avenue. She could just see Nkechi sniffing the air and trying to open the windows wide to let out the stale smell.

When Ejituru next met Cece, she asked for advice about where to look for employment.

"It's really hard here, especially if you don't have qualifications," Cece said. "Your only option may be to work in a fast-food place or a drugstore or supermarket, but those are dead-end jobs."

"What I really want to do is go back to college and complete my education."

"Is your husband willing to pay for your education?" "He said he would, but not now."

"Perhaps you can start on a part-time basis, depending on your financial situation. You could take one or two courses and get a job that enables you to fit in the hours you go to school."

Ignatius had difficulty adjusting to the girl he knew for only ten hours when he was home for a visit. Though she treated him with respect, he felt like an older brother, not a husband, and she prefixed every sentence with "sir." While he appreciated the respectful way she addressed him, since he was at least fifteen years her senior, he felt uneasy. He finally had to tell her to stop calling him sir and use Ignatius.

"I'm your husband, not your employer," he said in a bemused voice on several occasions. "Ignatius will do."

Always deferential toward him, she answered only when spoken to and appeared unwilling to express her opinion.

Three months after Ejituru's arrival, Ignatius began to tire of her constant requests for prospectuses from colleges. She seemed preoccupied with finding a school where she could pursue her education. To placate her, he rashly promised he would pick up a prospectus for her whenever he dropped a customer at any of the nearby universities. He maintained the fiction that he drove taxi for a living temporarily, having lost his job just before she came. It was a throwaway promise, one he never intended to keep.

Ejituru wouldn't let it go. She ragged him over the issue every day. As soon as he came into the house each evening, she asked the same question: "Were you able to pick up a prospectus today?"

"No," he always replied. "Unfortunately, I wasn't near any university today. I'm sorry. Perhaps tomorrow."

She then lost interest in whatever he had to say.

Tired of the question and irritated beyond measure, he finally lost his temper one day. The moment he came inside and saw her expectant face, he lashed out.

"Don't think I'll forego my clients just so you'll get your precious prospectus. Do you realize that if I miss a customer, I'll give money to my competitors? Taking my customer to their destinations is what puts food on the table and pays our rent. This isn't Nigeria. Here you have to work for every penny. Besides, we have what is called a phone in the apartment."

He pointed at it for emphasis. "You could use that and ask the universities to send you the information you want. If you don't know how to use the phone, you can ask me. If you find it difficult to ask me how to show you how or help you use the telephone directory, your friends, especially your rich friend Cece, can teach you."

Pausing, he looked at Ejituru, who stood in the kitchen, her mouth open in amazement. "Come to think of it, they can also take you to any college to pick up the forms. Don't expect me to do everything for you. Try to use your brain. After all, you've been in college for three years."

The next morning, he regretted talking to her that way, but he had to stop her constant nagging. He remembered that in order to get her to agree to travel, he said a prospectus would be waiting for her upon her arrival. He was too busy preparing for her to carry out that promise. Frustrated, Ignatius stormed from the apartment and drove to work.

Sex was another major issue between them. Ejituru refused to share the same bed with him, preferring the sofa. "I don't want to get pregnant now. I want to finish my education first."

"Nonsense, Ejituru. We're married. Part of marriage is sharing a bed." "No, I won't sleep in the same bed with you."

"If you're afraid of pregnancy, I can use protection."

"Sir, there's no guarantee I won't get pregnant. It's not foolproof." Tears welled in her eyes.

Not having any benchmark of what a marriage should be, he didn't know how to handle the events. His father never lived with his mother as husband and wife, though he visited the home where Ignatius lived with his mother. Throughout Ignatius's childhood and adolescence, his father was a distant figure who appeared now and then during important festive occasions. Ignatius couldn't remember his parents sharing the same bed and planning a future together, the way couples did on several TV shows he watched in Washington. He wanted neither kind of marriage.

Whatever he learned about marriage came from his uncle. He wanted a wife like his aunt, pliant and submissive, someone with whom he could share his thoughts and plan a future.

He remembered during his stay in northern Nigeria with his aunt and uncle that they ate together in the evening and discussed their respective days, planning for the coming day. He recalled the congenial atmosphere in the house, with his uncle and aunt joking and jostling each other. That was the kind of marriage he wanted.

When he remembered his relationship with Ayo, he regretted how it ended. He spent very little time with her before her husband died, then she had to leave abruptly for Nigeria. He wished the situation had turned out differently.

When he could no longer bear the lack of intimacy with Ejituru, he said, "Ejituru, you're being silly. You're my wife, and you must submit to me." He pounded the table for emphasis.

Ejituru didn't answer.

"Ejituru, come on," he pleaded. "When you marry a man, you're expected to have sex with him. I've looked forward to your coming for a long time, and you're withholding the most important part of our marriage. Come on, Ejituru. Give me a break." He held out his hand to take her to the bedroom.

"Sir, I have no intention of getting pregnant right now, with my future so uncertain." Turning away, she slammed the bathroom door hard and locked it.

"What future?" he shouted through the door. "Your future is with me. We're married. As my wife, you're expected to sleep with me. I don't like this nonsense of sleeping on the sofa in the living room. Enough is enough. Come on, Ejituru. Open the door. Come into the bedroom!" He pounded on the bathroom door.

"Sir, I know that as my husband you're right to expect to sleep with me, but I need to protect myself. Nobody else will do it except me. I have no intention of becoming pregnant. If you want to force me to have sex with you, I'd rather go back to Nigeria. I won't let anything stand between me and that certificate."

As she unlocked the door, he thought how hopeless it was. She didn't understand that a few innocent words spoken with requisite warmth would have been enough to make him try to understand her point of view so they could work out a solution. It wasn't working the way it was supposed to.

He expected her to behave like other girls in his village who knew nothing about protection, but Ejituru was a medical student at Nsukka

University. Who knew what she did during those three years at the university? She must have been using protection, which was how she learned about it. In desperation, he stopped that train of thought. He couldn't jump to conclusions. After all, prevention of pregnancy must have been taught in her biology classes.

How long would he have to wait before having a child? He wasn't a young man. Having a family was the primary reason he married her. In desperation, he said, "Listen to me, Ejituru. You're young. You can have children and still go to college to fulfill your dream. That's what I'd like." "Sir, is that why you never stopped at the universities to get the forms for me?" she shouted. "You don't want me to continue my studies. You want me to become a mother right now. That won't happen, I assure you. Send me back to Nigeria. I'll resume my studies. I can be readmitted. It's not too late."

She cried inconsolably, and Ignatius felt like an ogre for frightening a little girl.

Exasperated, he said firmly, "If you think I'll work and send you to college, you should have your head examined. At the rate you're spending money, where do you think your university fees would come from? If you want to study, you'll have to find a way to pay for it yourself."

"I will!" she shouted through the door. "You'll see."

Rather than listen to her desperate crying, he stormed out of the apartment, slamming the door behind him.

Ejituru admired herself in the mirror, turning to see her back, as the door opened and Ignatius entered with a bag of groceries.

Shrugging off his jacket and removing his shoes, he watched her from the corner of his eye. "Did you go shopping again today? I haven't seen those shoes and clothes before."

Ejituru constantly needed money to buy things.

"Oh, I went to the shops with Cece. You remember her? We met at church. Her husband's a doctor at the hospital. She picked me up and we went shopping. I bought this to wear to church."

"What happened to the one you wore last week or the clothes you brought from Nigeria?" he asked, feeling distraught. "After all, it's summer and you can still wear them."

"I can't wear the same dress every Sunday," she said, removing the dress and folding it. "We aren't poor. Cece said many people form impressions about you based on what you wear. I need to look as if I'm not a new arrival."

"Ejituru!" he shouted in frustration. "Her husband's a doctor, and I'm not in the same league as him! I'm a cab driver who can't find another job. I lost my other job shortly before you came. We can't afford ninety-dollar dresses and shoes. I was hoping to take you to K-Mart to buy your winter coat and boots later. What's wrong with you? Have you no sense of money?"

"I saw some really nice winter coats when I went out with Mary and Cece," she said, ignoring his anger. "I was going to ask for money to buy one I liked."

"We can't afford to buy such expensive items."

"You're joking, aren't you, sir? What do you want me to wear? Cece is my friend, and she's picking me up tomorrow to take me to her house. I told her I'd ask you for the money to get the coat I liked."

Coming as Ejituru did from a relatively wealthy family, she had no idea how to manage money. She expected Ignatius to provide her with whatever she wanted. She grew up pampered by her mother, who bought her anything she asked for. Ejituru was still under the impression that Ignatius was rich and was just hiding his money from her. She saw how her friends from church and the people living in the complex dressed and spent money, and she wanted to be like them. Whenever she went shopping at the mall, she always gravitated to the most expensive items of clothing, and Ignatius had difficulty restraining her.

"Listen to me, Ejituru," he said sternly. "I forbid you to go shopping with her again. The money I give you is for you to buy small feminine items you may need. No more shopping! Do you hear me?"

"Why can't you look for a job in your field? Engineers make a lot of money."

He winced. What did she know about job hunting?

Ejituru, like a petulant child, moved on to the next set of grievances. "You want me to stay home all the time? Please, sir, I would be so bored. I'm learning so much about America from Cece, and the information will be good for me once I resume college. I won't stop seeing my friends."

Living with Ejituru hadn't turned out at all as Ignatius imagined. He had looked forward to her arrival. She would be his confidant, someone he could plan a future with. She would enjoy hearing stories about his customers, and she'd have interesting comments to offer.

So far, their lives together hadn't turned out that way. He tried to make her feel comfortable with him by telling her funny things that happened to him during the day. He sometimes came home during the day to see if she wanted anything, but she wasn't home. If she was in the apartment, she would either be watching TV or reading some of the textbooks she brought with her.

He made sure she had money at all times to buy whatever she needed within reason, but he soon learned she preferred expensive shoes and clothes and often asked for more money. At the rate she spent, he wouldn't be able to save anything. She hadn't bought her winter clothes yet either. If he gave her money, it barely lasted a week, then she wanted more. Her wardrobe bulged with expensive shoes and clothes, and he wondered where she intended to wear them.

After battling with Ejituru for several months about sex, Ignatius decided to consult his married friends, who proved sympathetic.

"How old is she?" one friend asked.

"Let me see. She was eighteen when she went to university, so she must be at least twenty-two. She's just the right age, in my opinion, to produce a beautiful, strong son for me."

"Remember, she isn't a village girl. The educated ones want love, whatever that means, before they give themselves to you. You must have given her the idea you were rich. That's why she gravitated to the high-class Nigerian women in church. You didn't know her that well in Nigeria before you married her. From what you've said, I must say that I'm surprised that she agreed to come here and marry you. She must've felt a spark, my friend. You just have to be patient and hope you two will develop a relationship."

"How will I convince her to have sex? I don't want to use protection." "I wouldn't either," another friend said. "Perhaps you should send her to a doctor who can prescribe birth control pills. Unfortunately, you may not have that child you're dreaming of for some years."

The others sniggered.

After mulling over the advice and still feeling bitter toward Ejituru, he realized she held all the cards. He made an appointment with the doctor, in the hope that at least the most important aspect of marriage would be satisfied.

CHAPTER FIFTEEN

During Ejituru's first months in the US, Ignatius had introduced her to Esther Okorie, who lived on the fourth floor of their apartment building, as someone she might turn to for help. She had married a man who came to the US on a USAID scholarship, but the marriage broke up after five years and three daughters. Although the couple hadn't divorced, they lived apart for almost two years.

Esther's husband made a new home with another Igbo woman, who had a son by him, while Esther remained in the apartment with her children. She accepted the fact that her husband had another life, and as long as he gave her a sufficient monthly stipend to cover her expenses, she was fine with that. She justified the arrangement to Ejituru and her customers by saying that back in Nigeria having a second wife or concubine wouldn't be a cause for divorce. Why would it be otherwise in America? Her husband wanted a male child, and the other woman gave him one.

Ejituru went to visit Esther in the large corner apartment. In contrast to Ejituru and Ignatius's quarters, that apartment had three bedrooms, a full kitchen, and a fairly large dining area. Esther used an alcove off the dining area for her hair-braiding business. The tastefully furnished parlor had photographs of her children on the walls showing their various stages of development.

Esther constantly sprayed her kitchen and dining area with deodorizer. "The walls of these apartments are so thin that I have to neutralize the smell of other people's food as well as mine. I don't want my clients coming to a smelly place."

Once when Ejituru visited, she met two other women slightly older than her. Ejituru's visit interrupted their conversation. One of them sat in a chair, having her hair braided.

"You're the new arrival Esther mentioned," she said. "Are you getting used to living here?"

"I'm Ejituru. It's different, but I'm getting used to it, except for not having people around me all the time."

"You'll get used to that. At least you have Mama Esther upstairs."

"I told her to come up any time she feels like it," Esther said. "I'm always here. I don't go out to work."

Esther had a graduate degree in economics from the University of Nigeria at Nsukka. Unable to find work in her field after a year of interviews and rejections, she gave up. With three children and a husband willing to support two households, she no longer had the urge to work outside the house. She didn't want to give her husband any cause to reduce his monthly stipend, so for the last two years she merely supplemented her income with the hair-braiding business she ran in her apartment.

"I can't imagine going out to work, battling traffic and snow," Esther told Ejituru. "Besides, this way I don't need to worry about taxes."

Her business depended on word of mouth. Satisfied customers ensured she had a steady stream of people coming to her apartment each day. If anyone asked, she could always say it wasn't really a business. She was just helping friends who needed to have their hair braided and couldn't afford the fees of professional hair salons.

"What did you do in Nigeria, Ejituru?" asked the other women in the apartment. It was her day off from the hospital, where she and her companion worked as nurses.

"I went to medical school. I'm getting tired of staying home, and I'd really like suggestions for how I should get work."

The woman dismissed Ejituru's concern. "If you were a nurse, it would be easy to get a job." She turned to Esther. "I didn't see you last Saturday at the Emekas' wedding, Mama Esther. Weren't you invited?"

"I was, but I didn't want to run into my husband and the other woman."

"You should have come," said the woman having her hair braided. "Our women really know how to dress. So do the men. The gold earrings and necklaces were fabulous, I tell you. I found out that the Indian shops on University Boulevard now carry the best batik from Holland, and other gorgeous laces. That was also where one of the ladies I met at the wedding bought her eighteen-karat-gold necklace and matching earrings. She said they allow you to buy on time." She gestured with her arms and swiveled in the chair.

Esther tried to keep her client still. "Auntie, the Emekas really spent money on the wedding. They provided a free bar and delicious food nicely presented. The highlife music was out of this world. The whole place was pulsing, and we danced past the time the hotel allotted them for the reception. It was great."

"Who did the catering?" Esther asked.

"Mrs. Ojukwu. You know her. She lives with her daughter and husband in Bowie. That woman is making a lot of money, eh?"

Turning to Ejituru, Esther asked, "Why don't you help me with my braiding business? I could really expand if I had help."

"Thank you, Auntie, but I'm not good at it. I'd drive away your clients."

They laughed.

Ejituru sat quietly, listening to the women talk about their lives, clothes, and the latest gossip in the Nigerian community. She couldn't tell them about her current problems, which were nothing compared to what other women went through. She couldn't just say, "Ignatius wanted to have sex with me because I'm his wife. It's his right and he's ready to have children, but I refused to have sex without protection. He said I spend too much money on clothes and I should stop. He won't give me money to buy what I want."

Those women would think Ejituru was in the wrong, and Ignatius would be branded as a weak Nigerian man who couldn't control his wife in bed. She would be ridiculed too. Besides, she felt she needed to keep what happened in the apartment to herself. If she confided in Esther, she would spread the story to every customer. It would very quickly become common knowledge among all the Nigerians of their acquaintance.

No, she thought. *I'll keep my own counsel and deal with this my own way.*

In a heart-to-heart talk with Cece, Ejituru said, "I never expected when I left Nigeria that it would take me so long to get into a university."

"What's the problem? Why haven't you applied?"

"Ignatius doesn't seem to have time to collect the forms from the university. It looks as if I'll have to pay for my education myself, since he doesn't show any enthusiasm."

"I worked to finance my husband's education when he was in medical school. Now that he's qualified, we agreed I should take a rest while having children and return to work when the children are of school age. I don't understand why Ignatius won't pay for your education. The sacrifice while you're studying will be worth it once you graduate and start earning. Why don't you talk to him about enrolling in a few classes first? The fees would be much smaller than for a full-time student. It seems a waste for you to stop your education at this point."

As an afterthought, Cece added, "I never could understand why he chose to live in such a place, except to save money. Couldn't he find something nice?"

Ejituru had no answer. She agreed with her friend.

Ejituru had difficulty adjusting to life with Ignatius. She thought the visa would take much longer to obtain, and she saw him as an older, distant relative from her village, not as a husband. True, he had been kind to her since she arrived, but the lack of progress in helping her find a suitable college made her doubt the veracity of the many promises he made to her and her family. At the same time, she realized he made it possible for her to achieve her cherished hope of coming to America. She didn't know how to respond to him. She'd been raised to respect her elders. That was why she insisted on prefacing his name with sir when she first arrived. When he told her he didn't like to be addressed that way, she was at a loss, so she avoided addressing him directly.

As a couple, they had no social life. Often, he said they'd been invited to an event at someone's house. Once she had her hopes up, he would shoot them down in the next sentence.

"We aren't going. I don't have time. I have to work to pay off my debts."

What those debts were, he never said. At the end of the month, he told Ejituru, "The phone bill for this month was high. Don't use the phone unnecessarily. You should stop giving out our number to everyone. I don't like all those phone calls when I come home to rest."

"How do you expect me to stay in touch with my friends?" she asked, lashing out. "Don't expect me to obey that rule."

Since the fight over her college application, Ignatius knew nothing of her intentions. Their conversations always centered on events unrelated to their problems. Sometimes he told her about his days.

"What a rough day I had today. I had to drive one man all the way to Fairfax, Virginia. That was difficult, because at one point I had no idea where I was."

"What did you do?" she asked.

"I stopped at a gas station and asked for directions."

Sometimes she said, "I had a letter from my mother today. She sends her greetings."

"Did she give you news about my uncle? I haven't heard from him in a long time."

Both of them avoided mentioning their differences.

Ejituru had very little to say about herself or her activities. Ignatius assumed she had learned the expenses associated with a college education and realized it was beyond his means. He tried many times to tell her indirectly that he wasn't in a position to pay for a university education. He still had debts from her visa and resettlement. He had the impression that, for some reason, she thought he was worth more than he said. He hoped she would realize he could barely make enough to keep her fed, housed, and clothed.

The marriage so far hadn't turned out as Ejituru expected. She asked herself what had she expected by agreeing to marry a man she didn't know. She never wanted a marriage like her parents. She wanted a man she could rely on, one who would provide for her, not the other way around. Her father never held paid employment and depended totally on her mother for financial support.

Ejituru didn't want that kind of marriage. One of the reasons she had agreed to come to America as Ignatius's wife was because of her hope for a man who would support her aspirations. Ignatius turned out to be the opposite. The one thing she wanted him to give her, he was unwilling to do. She believed he married her mainly because he wanted children.

At the beginning of her stay in the US, Ejituru felt totally dependent on Ignatius. With her mother so far away, she had no other emotional support. Having Cece as a friend provided her with someone she could share some of her problems with. The women she met at Esther's weren't really interested in Ejituru and couldn't offer what she wanted. They didn't care about furthering their education and were mainly concerned with making money and living a good life.

Some weeks after the sex quarrel, Ejituru sat watching TV and applying toenail polish while waiting for Ignatius to come home. She spent the day watching TV and going through her textbooks to keep current with her studies.

When Ignatius came into the room, he stood at the threshold, one foot behind the other, in his work clothes, sweating profusely. His hair was damp from rain. Her heart skipped a beat, as she looked at him expectantly. He carried a paper bag, which she hoped held university catalogs, and an envelope in the other hand.

"Ejituru, this is your lucky day," he said. "I made an appointment for you to see a doctor. This is her address. The appointment is for tomorrow at eleven in the morning. The office is only one block from here. It isn't far. If you like, you can call a taxi to take you. I can't, because I have to take a client to Baltimore. The doctor will talk to you about your fear of getting pregnant."

Disappointed, she murmured, "Sex is the important priority, eh?" Ignoring her comment, he walked pensively toward the bedroom. While changing clothes, Ignatius thought about his financial problems.

He'd been renting the cab he drove, and with three hundred thousand miles on it, the cab was constantly breaking down and often was in the garage for repairs. With his weekly income reduced by half because of that, he contemplated owning his own cab instead of renting. That seemed a more-profitable route. The company had a few licenses for sale, and he was promised one. He had barely enough money for a down payment on a car, and he intended to finance the balance. Whenever his car was in the garage, he made the rounds at car dealerships to compare prices. That week, he made his final decision and was in the process of finalizing the purchase and licensing arrangements with the company.

The amount he had to pay was almost three times what he paid to rent a cab, but he felt good about his decision. In a good month, he made at least three thousand dollars before taxes. He hoped to be able to repay all the money he owed the lawyer by the end of the year. He also planned to buy a piece of land back home, and sent money each month to his uncle, who helped him arrange the land purchase. He felt there was no way to pay for Ejituru's education, and nothing would change his mind.

He came out of the bedroom and looked at Ejituru, who was bent over examining her toenails. She looked very vulnerable in that posture. He saw her long neck stretched out, and noticed that her hair was freshly braided. He assumed she'd been to Esther's.

His heart skipped a beat. He wanted to hold her and drag her into the bedroom, and he had difficulty restraining himself. Instead, he said, "Ejituru, I've made arrangements to buy a new cab. It will be my own. I'm tired of making constant trips to the garage."

She hadn't known he was renting his cab, and she didn't know what to make of his news. "Hmmm. That's good," she said in a bored voice.

He waited for a further reaction.

She hid her thoughts and said, "I thought you said we had to be careful with money."

If that's the case, why did you suddenly splurge on a car instead of keeping the old one? she wondered. She didn't ask. She felt he'd been lying to her about how much money he had, and the fact that he would spend it on a car upset her. Why couldn't he defer his purchase and send her to school?

"The old car wasn't mine," he explained. "I was renting it. I was losing too much in repairs, so I decided it would be cheaper to own my own cab."

No longer listening, she hardened her thoughts against him. He would probably say he needed the car for his business, but why wasn't he making any effort to find an engineering job? Did buying a new car mean he intended to be a car driver forever? He never once mentioned trying to find a job in his profession. All he talked about were his clients, not job interviews for engineering.

As with most nights, that night she lay on the sofa and saw her life at Nsukka University flash before her eyes. Again, she felt she made a big mistake coming to the US. Her contemporaries would be getting ready for their exams and beginning hospital rotation. Nduka, the friend she left behind, had probably forgotten her. Her letters to Stella left out the difficulties she faced, and only mentioned Cece, her beautiful house, and the movies Ejituru saw with Cece and her other friends.

Ejituru went through her options many times. She had no idea of Ignatius's financial situation. From her experience, no husband ever told his wife his income. It wasn't done, and she was in no position to ask. Her only option was to get a job and earn money for her education. Cece and Esther promised to make inquiries among their acquaintances on her behalf, but nothing substantive came up.

Every night, she cried herself to sleep. By the time she woke in the morning, Ignatius was already at work. She wouldn't let anyone know of her problems. That was one lesson her mother drummed into her head.

"Be careful what you tell strangers about what's happening inside your home," Nkechi said so often it became a mantra. That bit of wisdom served her very well.

CHAPTER SIXTEEN

D r. Washington saw a beautiful, healthy young black woman in her early twenties watching her nervously as she entered the examination room. Most of the patients in her practice were elderly women on Medicare or Medicaid. This girl wore tight jeans with a snug woolen top and platform shoes. Her black eyebrows were plucked, and she wore bright-red lipstick. Cornrowed hair framed her face.

Ejituru hoped that visiting the office of Dr. Washington, a pleasant, light-skinned African American woman, would solve two immediate problems—how to prevent pregnancy, and how to continue her education.

As Ejituru sat on the examination table in the small room, she spoke frankly of her hopes and fears. "I'm afraid of getting pregnant, because it would prevent me from completing my studies." She broke down, weeping inconsolably.

Dr. Washington touched Ejituru's arm and patted her gently. "You have no immediate health problems then?"

"No." She looked up, tears smudging her makeup.

The kind doctor handed her a tissue. "I want to tell you that I spent a year after my residency in a hospital in Lagos. I have great admiration for Nigerian women."

Ejituru wiped tears off her cheeks and looked into the doctor's compassionate eyes.

"I'd like to learn more about this," Dr. Washington said, picking up a file, "but given the limited time for your appointment, we'll have to do this outside office hours." She chuckled. "This is kind of impulsive, but you can either wait outside in the waiting room until lunchtime, or go home and return at one o'clock. I'll treat you to lunch, and we'll have more time to talk."

It was Dr. Washington's half day, so after she finished with her last patient, she took Ejituru to a restaurant in a nearby mall. For the first time since coming to the US, Ejituru felt she could open up to someone and try to find a solution to her predicament. She sat in the restaurant with someone she just met and poured out her innermost thoughts, crying frequently.

Dr. Washington tried to restrain her. "We aren't alone here, and people are staring. They probably think I'm telling you off or hurting you. Please stop." She began to wonder if she'd taken on too big a task, but she also saw that the young woman before her felt completely alone, so the doctor wanted to help. "How old are you, Ejituru?"

"I just turned twenty-two."

"Let's break down your concerns. As a medical student, you should know you have options to prevent pregnancy. The doctor you're seeing tomorrow will discuss those with you and advise you on the one that best meets your needs. It seems to me that there's more to it than not getting pregnant. When you agreed to marry your husband, I'm sure you knew he would want to be intimate with you. You say you don't love him, and, because he reneged on his promise to help you continue your education, you dislike him intensely. Have you ever thought he might not be financially able to fund your education?"

"This marriage wasn't my wish. It was arranged, and I went along with it because I wanted a better education than I could get in Nigeria. Yes, I knew an intimate relationship would be part of it, but I hoped he would understand my situation and would wait until I finished college. He promised my parents he would pay for my education. If he doesn't have the money, why did he make that promise? Nobody forced him to agree to marry me. I was the one who was forced." Her words tumbled out without any particular order.

"Have you discussed your concerns with your husband?"

"No, Doctor. It's difficult for me to talk to him about it. He treats me like a little girl who doesn't know her own mind. He told me he lost his job as an engineer, and since he can't get another job, he drives a taxi. Whenever I mention my education, he changes the subject."

"Ejituru, you need to separate having sex from having children," Dr. Washington said firmly. "Not all sexual activity results in pregnancy. As a medical student, you should know that. I believe that if you love your husband, you'll learn to enjoy intimacy with him without worrying about pregnancy."

She paused as waiters removed the dirty plates from the table and inquired about dessert and coffee. Once the clatter of plates stopped and coffee was poured, she continued, "You say he's been very kind to you. Pregnancy could be avoided. Think of it. I would advise you to discuss your concerns with your husband. You should tell him how you feel."

Ejituru watched, stone-faced.

"He made the appointment with me for you. That shows that he too wanted to find ways of changing the situation between you."

Ejituru winced in disagreement.

Ignoring her, the doctor said, "Your education concern could also be dealt with in time. If you're bent on furthering your education, you should take responsibility for it. First, you need to find a job. Your husband probably doesn't have enough funds to support a wife at the university. With a job, you can save some money. By the next academic year, you could enroll in one or two courses and eventually earn a degree.

"I came from a poor family, and during my undergraduate years I worked in the college cafeteria, because my financial aid didn't cover my living expenses. It's not unusual for students to work and pay for their education."

As they left the restaurant, Dr. Washington turned and took Ejituru's hand. "I see you're a very resolute, thoughtful person. It's refreshing to meet a girl so determined to better herself. It just happens there's an opening in my office. The receptionist is taking maternity leave in a fortnight. You might consider applying for the position. It would be a temporary appointment for the duration of her maternity leave.

The duties aren't defined, and you'd be required to take on several responsibilities.

"Ejituru, think about this carefully. Discuss it with your husband. Come back to the office to drop off your résumé and be interviewed by the outgoing receptionist and the nurse. The office is small. I need to make sure any temporary staff fits in. If you're a good fit, you'll need training by the outgoing staff. It's not highly paid, but I regard it as an important part of my office. You're very lucky you came at this time, because I was just about to contact a temp agency to ask them to send candidates to interview."

"Thank you, Dr. Washington, for your kindness. I'm very grateful."

"When your husband calls, I'll tell him to use protection, okay?"

"Cece I have news!" Ejituru was beaming. She sat in Cece's kitchen eating fried fish and fries Cece had brought back from a fast-food place.

"Either you have a job or you've enrolled at the university. Which one?"

"First, I have to tell you that Ignatius and I had a fight over sex."

"Mmmm." Cece laughed.

"It's no laughing matter. I've been refusing to have sex with him since I came, because I don't want to get pregnant."

"Did he beat you up and force you to have sex with him?" Cece was still laughing. "You can report him to the authorities if he did."

"Seriously. He's been quite good about it. He found me a doctor who has referred me to a specialist who can discuss my options, but I don't want him to know what birth control I'll be using."

"I presume that means you won't let him know you've been referred to a specialist." Cece watched Ejituru closely. "When is the appointment?"

"Tomorrow."

"I can help you with the payment. It'll be our little secret," Cece replied without thinking about it.

"Thank you, my friend. I may be able to repay you, since I might have a temporary job at the doctor's office."

"You don't have to pay me back, okay? I'm glad about the job news."

Cece paid the cost of Ejituru's appointment with the OB-GYN and for the intrauterine device Ejituru chose. The doctor assured her it would hold for at least a few years, but she would need yearly check-ups. She was glad that her immediate problem had a solution Ignatius wouldn't know about. He would think she was resigned to starting a family, because she wouldn't have any birth control pills around.

Ejituru was elated, not only about seeing the doctor, but at the prospect of a job, something she had always dreamed of but never thought would materialize so soon. She saw the job as a step toward achieving her educational objectives. She made up her mind to impress Dr. Washington so that at the end of three months she would recommend Ejituru for a similar job at another office.

Of course, it all depended on Ignatius. How would he take the new information?

Very cheerful that evening, Ejituru restricted her conversation to what the doctor had said about birth control, but she didn't tell Ignatius what she chose to use. He had already received that information from the doctor and hoped Ejituru would change her mind about having a child.

Ejituru also didn't tell him about the job, though she had begun working at the doctor's office by the end of her sixth month in the US. Once the employee on leave taught Ejituru what to do, she was able to handle the job easily. She was happy to have somewhere to go during the winter, and was always glad to return to the apartment after work.

She wrote to her mother, telling her she took the first step in her quest for education and was certain she would make it. She talked about her new boss, a doctor, and how much she looked forward to going to work at the office each day. She hoped to learn about the functioning of the office, because one day she wanted to have one of her own. Glad that she had something to talk about with her friends, Ejituru sometimes took the bus to Silver Spring to meet them after work. On weekends, she was at Cece's house, playing with the children and sometimes shopping with Cece.

When Ignatius learned Ejituru found employment, it took all his selfcontrol not to storm into the apartment and confront her. What upset him most wasn't that she had a job but that she had hidden it from him for so long. She remained an enigma.

Deep in his heart, he was glad she showed initiative in getting a job. He never intended to marry a woman who expected him to bear the total burden of the household. His mother never depended on his father for financial support. He'd been hoping Ejituru would show initiative and find something to occupy herself, instead of lounging around the apartment, moaning about what she left behind in Nigeria, or roaming the malls with her friends.

Ignatius hadn't set out to spy on her. He had dropped off a customer near his home and decided to surprise Ejituru at the apartment, but she wasn't there. He wondered where she'd gone and guessed she was either on the fourth floor gossiping with the ladies, or went to the drugstore to pick up something. As he drove off, he happened to pass the doctor's office, when he was flagged down by a prospective client, who turned out to be chatty.

"Where do you come from?" he asked. "Are you a student, and is this a side job?"

"I'm from Nigeria and not a student," he replied truthfully. "This is my trade."

"The receptionist at the doctor's office is from Nigeria. Do you know her?"

"I don't think so, but if you give me her name, I can tell you where she came from."

"She's called Ejituru."

He hid his shock. "She's from my ethnic group. I'll have to call the doctor's office and meet her." *It has to be her,* he realized.

Ignatius blamed Esther, the Nigerian woman on the fourth floor, for Ejituru's treachery, though he had difficulty believing Esther would advise Ejituru to refrain from telling her husband about such an important event in her life. At first, he wanted to barge into Esther's apartment and confront her, but reason prevailed.

As it happened, he learned the truth from Esther without a confrontation. He came to the apartment to pick up some documents he needed for his license renewal and ran into her on her way to her children's school. After the initial greetings, Esther inquired after Ejituru, accusing him of forbidding her from having anything to do with Esther.

"What do you mean?" he asked. "I never did such a thing. If Ejituru said so, she's lying. I encouraged her to make friends with you because she needs someone who knows how things are done here."

"It's been more than a month since I've seen her. She used to drop by in the afternoons, and she occasionally came with me to pick up the kids. I knocked on your door to find out what was wrong, but she never answered. What have you done to her?"

"Mama Esther, now I remember," Ignatius lied. "Maybe you went to visit on the day she was out with her church friends or went to see the doctor. She saw him last month, and she was advised to get some rest to get over the flu. I've been coming home each day to check on her. I promise to tell her to drop by and see you this evening."

So, she hasn't told anyone she's working, Ignatius thought. *Why? I can't tell this woman what's happening. It would be the talk of the whole Igbo society here. I must protect our privacy. I must warn Ejituru to choose carefully what she tells people.*

At the end of three months, the doctor confirmed Ejituru's permanent appointment as the receptionist. The person on maternity leave had decided not to come back. That evening, Ejituru felt she could no longer hide her job situation from Ignatius. She suspected from his behavior and small hints he dropped that he knew she wasn't spending full days with Cece or roaming the shopping centers.

As she carried plates to the sink that evening, she scrutinized his face. "I found a job."

"Good," he said innocently. "Where and when do you start?"

"You know the doctor you sent me to some time ago for advice? She needed a temporary receptionist. I applied and had to be trained before I could be sure of the job. I didn't want to tell you until it was definite I had it."

"Ejituru, I know you've been working, but I wanted you to tell me yourself."

"Who told you?" She was aghast.

"Nothing is hidden under the sun. I noticed you weren't home during the day, and there are some new things in the house. I wondered where you got the money for them, since you haven't asked me for money in a while, nor have you asked to be taken to shops.

"One day, I came home during the day, but you were nowhere to be found. As I drove off, I picked up a customer who just saw the doctor, and he heard I was from Nigeria, so he asked if I knew the nice receptionist in the office who was also from Nigeria. He told me her name was Ejituru. Your friend upstairs, Esther, saw me shortly afterward and mentioned she hadn't seen you for some time. She wondered if something was wrong."

"Why didn't you say anything?" She was almost in tears. "I wanted you to trust me enough to tell me."

"You didn't trust me enough to ask, so don't lay all the blame on me!" "Ejituru, it's not the same!" His voice rose with anger. "You had something to tell me and never mentioned it. I'm your husband. I'm responsible for you here. You shouldn't have hidden such important information from me. Don't you know I'll have to declare your income at tax time?" "Someone told me I can file as a single person. You have nothing to worry about. I'm glad we have this in the open, because I was afraid of your reaction."

"How did you think I'd react?" He slammed his hand against the table. "You don't know me." He stood and walked back and forth, scratching his head in frustration. "I'm glad you have something to do. I've been worried you would spend too much time with the ladies upstairs and from church, and they would fill your head with all sorts of things."

"Oh!" She didn't know how to respond. "I never really liked going upstairs. I felt they weren't my type. I'm not into gossip, and I had nothing to offer in return for what they said. I get bored easily. I like Cece and her friends. There's nothing stopping me from seeing them when I'm off work. Cece is happy for me."

"So you told her before you told me?" he shouted. "That shows your priorities."

She didn't reply, taking his anger as an indication he was against her working outside the house.

"Look, Ejituru. I'm glad you are working, but I'm upset that you hid information from me for a long time. Now that you're working, I need to know how much they pay you and whether we can afford a two-bedroom apartment so we'll have room for the baby."

Ejituru, ignoring his comment about the baby, focused on the apartment. "Mary, another friend, lives in a beautiful apartment in Silver Spring. They have a doorman. Her apartment is huge. You can't hear what's happening next door. If we have to move, we should go there. If not, this is all right. We spend very little time here anyway. I don't want to move within this complex. This apartment is enough. I can walk to my job. Besides, I'm saving my money for my education."

"Oh, that!" he spat. "We should be thinking of a child. I'm not that young." Having been an only child, he wanted a big family, and he had taken that into consideration when he married Ejituru. Like most Nigerian men, he wanted to perpetuate his lineage. The pressure to start a family came from his uncle, who felt that was what Ignatius's mother would have wanted. What was the purpose of marriage but to have children who would care for you in your old age and close your eyes on your deathbed?

"I'm not that young," he repeated. "This is the right time for us to have a child."

"Sir, I've told you that I want to finish my education before I have children."

"Ejituru, if we wait until you have your professional qualifications, I won't have the strength to run after little children, especially in this country where day care is very expensive. I'll be too old."

"Forget it." She stormed out of the room into the bathroom.

"Come on, Ejituru," her nurse friend said on one of her half days. "Let's run to the shop or the 7-Eleven to pick up a sandwich." Sometimes she invited Ejituru to her home for a quick lunch.

"The kids are in school, and I have nothing in particular to do until they're home." She lived on University Boulevard in a neighborhood of older houses. She told Ejituru the house was built in the 1930s and was given many additions.

"You should have seen the old kitchen," she said. "The brown counters and cupboards were depressing. We modernized the old bathroom and added a new one. Can you imagine four people sharing a bathroom? The mornings were nightmares before we had the addition."

Ejituru made complimentary noises while comparing the house to Cece's fabulous one with several bathrooms, each as large as Ejituru's father's parlor.

As they sat down to eat a pastrami sandwich during one of their visits, the conversation became personal.

"We've considered moving from this house, but with the children going to college in a couple years, we're seriously thinking of retiring to Florida. My parents live there, and it would be nice to be near them. What are your plans, Ejituru? Will you continue working with Dr. Washington? If you are, you should think of training as a nurse at the local college."

"My aim is to become a doctor. Right now I need to save money to pursue my education."

"When will I meet your husband?"

"Soon." Ejituru's tone brooked no more questions on that issue. She assiduously avoided answering questions about Ignatius, preferring to discuss clothes or colleges.

CHAPTER SEVENTEEN

Eighteen months after Ejituru joined Dr. Washington's practice, she gave her staff notice that she needed to close for two reasons: she had been offered a position at Howard University Hospital, and the practice was losing money due to cuts in Medicaid reimbursement. Her staff suspected something was up because she had stopped taking new patients, and the nurse already found a position and gave notice by the time Dr. Washington made the formal closing announcement. Ejituru, hoping the day would never come, hadn't begun looking for another position.

The month before the formal closure, Dr. Washington took her staff out to lunch. As they waited for their orders, she asked Ejituru, "What are your plans?"

"I expect to enroll for fall classes at Strayer University." "Have you considered Howard?"

"Not really, since I can't afford the tuition."

"Have you started looking for another job?" Dr. Washington had to strain to make herself heard over the din. "I didn't expect this place to be so noisy at this time of day."

"Not yet," Ejituru replied. "I was waiting for a good time to ask for your suggestions."

"May I make one? I know the man in charge of hiring at the hospital in Howard, and I'll see if they have an opening for a receptionist. Did you know if you're employed at Howard, you can take classes at a reduced rate? Let me see what I can do."

Ejituru nervously fiddled with her napkin as Dr. Washington continued speaking.

"If you get a job there, you should apply for admission in the spring semester and start by registering for a few classes. I'll let you know whatever I find out. I don't want you to feel like I'm abandoning you. We don't want any more tears."

"Thank you, Doctor. When can I see you to pick up an application?"

"I'll get in touch soon."

Ejituru rushed to Cece for advice, because Dr. Igwe, Cece's husband, had recently moved to Howard University Hospital. Dr. Igwe came home late from work that day, and by the time they discussed Ejituru's situation, it was too late for her to go home. She phoned Ignatius to let him know where she was.

"Why didn't you leave a message for me earlier?" he shouted. "You knew I'd worry. I'm responsible for you. Who will people at home blame if anything happens to you? Tell me where you are and I'll come get you." "I'm at Cece's. I lost track of time. She'll bring me back tomorrow. I'm sorry I didn't tell you beforehand. It just happened."

"Is that all you have to say?" He was irritated at hearing Cece's name. "I warn you, nothing good will come from the way you're behaving."

She ended the call, anxious to hear Dr. Igwe's advice.

"Come to the office tomorrow," he said. "We'll visit the personnel office together. You know, some of your Nsukka credits are transferable. Do you have any of your transcripts?"

"Yes." She felt relieved that she might finish her undergraduate studies in less than four years.

Hugging her, Cece added, "My friend, if you're working at Howard, we can sometimes have lunch together. I've decided to return to work. My office is near Howard."

In the fall, she had returned to work at the same law firm she was with before her pregnancy. Her mother-in-law was granted permanent residency and would look after the children. The older Mrs. Igwe, in her late fifties, had been in the US since Cece had had her second child. A retired principal of a girls' secondary school in the Enugu, she couldn't bear to live apart from her grandchildren, since Dr. Igwe was her only son. A capable woman, she had embraced life in the Washington area and recently bought a small car, which enabled her to visit her many friends. With the help of the two doctors, Ejituru secured a job at Howard University Hospital and registered for two classes. Throughout the summer, she waited for an opportune time to tell Ignatius about her new appointment and the beginning of her college education. She had one month of free time between the closure of Dr. Washington's office and the start of her new job. Lately, Ignatius was covertly watching her every night while she sat on the sofa reading, but he never said anything to her directly.

With free time on her hands, Ejituru decided to visit Esther to catch up on the gossip. "I hope this isn't a bad time," she said when Esther answered her door.

"No. I'm between clients, and I was relaxing on the sofa when you rang the doorbell. I see the doctor's office has a closed sign on it. What's happening?" She handed Ejituru an orange drink.

"The doctor now works at Howard University Hospital. I have another job at Howard."

"Really? You're one lucky lady. Will you be studying there too?"

"I'll register for a few classes this fall. I might apply to be a full-time student in the spring."

As Esther stood to get something from the kitchen, she asked, "What does Ignatius think?" and looked hard at her.

"I have yet to tell him." Anxiety showed on her face.

"*Mwam mwayi,* my dear child, you have to talk to him about it before you start. Come with me to the car. I have to pick up the kids."

"I know." She followed Esther out the door. "What's the point? I already know he won't be in favor of it." Her voice rose with emotion. "He wants me to get pregnant and stop all this nonsense about completing my education."

"Take my advice and don't listen to him. If you can manage to pay for your education, you should take whatever opportunity you have before having children. Once you have a child, it won't be possible for you to finish your education for quite a while, unless you're married to a man who can pay for child care. On the other hand, you can decide to have children now and go to college later when they're in school. It's your choice."

"Mama Esther, that's exactly the advice given to me by Cece's motherin-law. I knew you'd understand. I want to finish my medical education. If I can manage to complete four years of college and take the MCATs, Dr. Igwe said I can get loans to pay for the rest of my education. I recently got my driver's license, thanks to Cece, who introduced me to a fairly inexpensive driving school. I'm looking for a cheap car to buy."

"Try, eh? How will you know you can make it if you don't try?"

"How should I tell Ignatius?" Ejituru's face clouded.

"Just tell him you were offered a job at Howard University, and it's a great job because you might get reduced tuition."

"Mama Esther, I'm afraid. He really wants a child now, and I can't give in on that. I'm very grateful that he brought me here, but I can't get pregnant."

Esther always suspected the younger woman wasn't happy, but she hadn't pried, leaving it up to Ejituru to say something when she was ready and trusted her. "Don't worry. I won't tell Ignatius what you told me, but I beg you to go to him and discuss it before he finds out from another source."

Often during that month, Ignatius came home midday and found Ejituru in the apartment reading or watching TV. "Are you unwell? No work today?"

"I'm taking the day off," she muttered.

On one of her visits to Howard University, she met a colleague from Nsukka who was doing his residency at Howard, having taken the United States Medical Licensing Examination (USMLA) while a student in Nigeria. Through him, she met other Nigerian students at Howard who were taking summer classes. On the days when she met with her new friends, she felt less uptight, and Ignatius wondered at the change in her behavior. She never mentioned the new friends, fearing Ignatius would disapprove, because he never approved of any of her friends.

One evening that summer, Ejituru was in good spirits and felt she needed to talk to him. "Ignatius, I have something to tell you," she said demurely.

It was a hot evening in June, and she discarded most of her clothes for a wrap tied under her armpits. With the air-conditioning not working, Ignatius sprawled on the sofa in shorts and no shirt. Ejituru noticed a sprinkling of white hair on his head and chest.

"I hope, Ejituru, you have some good news for me." He was surprised that she addressed him by his name. "My uncle has been inquiring after your health."

Ejituru felt she should tell him the news without further hesitation. He probably assumed she was pregnant. "Dr. Washington closed her office, so I won't have any money this month, but I found a new job that starts at the beginning of next month. When I start, I'll have more expenses, such as bus fare and lunch, since the new office is farther away. I'm also thinking I'll probably need a car. Would you consider helping me get a cheap car?" She glanced briefly at him before staring at the floor.

"I noticed her office was closed, but I assumed you moved to her new office with her." He tried desperately to be polite and calm.

"Dr. Washington accepted a position at Howard University. She was kind enough to introduce me to the personnel office and the registrar at the university. That's where I'll be working. I've also registered for classes at Howard. When they resume in the fall, I might be coming home late sometimes. That's why I need a car."

"Isn't that a bit too much? I can understand about the job, but I don't think you should take classes immediately. When does the job start again?"

"I have to start at the beginning of August, because that's a very busy period for the department I'm working for."

Conflicted, he didn't know what to say. The money wasn't the problem. He was angry because, once again, she had made a decision without asking his views. He wanted to hit her or pack up her possessions and throw her out of the apartment. He couldn't understand why she refused to discuss her plans before taking action. It seemed to him that even though she lived in the same house and was technically his wife, she didn't feel obligated to talk to him.

Why is she so unwilling to discuss anything that pertains to her? he wondered, his mind in turmoil.

He turned to look at her, sitting calmly as if she didn't have any cares. His inner fury came loose and he demanded, "Why did you marry me? It seems to me you've used me as a ticket to the US. I'm supposed to be your husband. You should have consulted me before making a decision that affects us and our relationship. We talked about this when you got the first job, because you hid it from me for months. I never asked you to give me your money or to pay half of the apartment expenses. I've been patient with you."

Getting up from the sofa, he went into the kitchen for a drink of water. Sipping it, he said more calmly, "As your husband, I forbid you to work at Howard and take classes simultaneously. This action will affect my relationship with you. I might as well not be married, since I can't see you after a long day's work or depend on you to keep me company. You say you'll be taking classes, which means you'll need time to study. When would I be able to see you?"

Although taken aback by his anger, Ejituru was determined to be in control of the discussion. She laughed and asked, "Sir?"

"Don't call me sir!" he shouted.

"All right then. You can't stop me from doing what I want," she lashed out. Emboldened, she looked him in the eye. "I'm not your slave. We don't have a child to look after. You managed with your food when I wasn't here, and I'm sure you can do it on those days when I return late. I don't see how working and studying would badly affect you. I'm not asking you to pay for my tuition. I know you're paying for the place where I live, but you can regard that as payment for sleeping with me occasionally."

Ignatius was shocked. He'd been paying for sexual favors? Was that how she regarded their relationship?

"Ejituru, look at what you just said! You're my wife, not someone I picked up on the street. Nobody is paying for any favors." He had the sudden urge to add, *I no longer want to be married to you. I need you to move out immediately.*

In a quandary, he pondered what to do. What would people at home think if he ordered her from the apartment? He could do it, but he had no idea who her friends were or what advice she was getting. He couldn't afford a court case. He just wanted to carry on with life. How could a simple girl from home, whom he expected to be a nice, humble wife, do this to him? His big mistake had been taking her to church and letting her work for that doctor. He should have gone directly to the doctor and told her that, as Ejituru's husband, he didn't want his wife working there. Such an approach would've worked at home, but in America, with all its talk about equality and individual freedom, he knew the doctor would have laughed in his face and told him to leave. She might even have called in the police. By going to her in that fashion, Ignatius would be acting as if he owned Ejituru.

He couldn't order her out of the apartment, because that would give her an excuse to ask for a divorce and financial support. Convinced that Cece, a lawyer, was giving Ejituru advice, he thought about how such a decision would be perceived at home. He could almost hear people saying, "What did you expect from Ugo Chuku's son?" They would smile knowingly, and his uncle would become embarrassed and cast out.

Needing to keep a cool head and consider his next move, he decided he would let Ejituru destroy herself. She would learn from experience that it was too much to hold down a job and go to school.

His conversation upset Ejituru too. She knew that Ignatius could easily put her out of the apartment; that was within his rights. She shouldn't have made that comment about his paying for sexual favors. He'd been good to her and very considerate of her feelings. He had never demanded she contribute toward the household expenses. He had paid her airfare and continued, or so she was told, to pay for lawyers' fees. He never complained either. She felt she had hurt him by not discussing her plans beforehand, but he would have just told her why she couldn't carry them out. The ensuing argument would have been pointless.

Ejituru was at a point of no return. It was the opportunity she dreamed of, and she wasn't about to let it go. She wanted her plan to succeed.

Weeping, she turned to Ignatius and said, "Sir, you've been good to me, but this is what I want to do. You can't stop me. If you want me to move out, I will."

He felt she just read his mind.

"You need to give me time to find an apartment. I'll look for one closer to work. Once I find it, I'll move. It isn't right that you should support me when I'm doing something you don't approve of. You're already done too much by paying my air fare and supporting me all these months."

Too upset to answer, he left the room. A few minutes later, he walked out of the bedroom fully dressed and stormed out of the apartment. Nothing was resolved, and each knew it was only a matter of time before the situation came to a head.

For several days, he tried very hard to understand the situation. He had underestimated the class difference between them. Her family might be relatively poor, but they were regarded as the most culturally sophisticated family in the town. While other people might feel education wasn't for them, Ejituru was raised to accept education as a right. From the time she was born, it was instilled in her that she must attain the highest-possible educational level. She was doing what she'd been raised for. Why couldn't he accept that?

He was the first in his family to complete secondary education, and he barely made it. After fleeing from the Unegbus' home, he had enrolled at Howard University, only to find he was socially unprepared for college. His experience there was disastrous. He stayed with the Unegbus as long as he had only because he lacked the courage to set out on his own in a strange land.

Then there was Ejituru, who didn't allow any obstacle he placed in her way deter her from her objective.

In retrospect, he felt his own naïveté kept him bound to the Unegbus, even after he realized they wouldn't honor their agreement with him. Ignatius accepted whatever the man said at face value and had difficulty understanding the reality of the situation. He had no money when he left them. Since he wasn't accustomed to the American work ethic, he had trouble coping with work at a gas station as his first job. He was unprepared for life outside the Unegbus' protective environment.

His life spiraled out of control when Ayo left for Nigeria with her husband's body. If he were able to rely on her continued support, he would have survived better, and his life would have been vastly different. He couldn't stand the constant barrage of advice from his acquaintances after her departure, and he didn't know how to handle money. Hence, he tried a quick fix through dealing drugs.

His thoughts returned to the present situation with Ejituru. He was frightened for her. She was protected all her life and attended a secondary boarding school with other privileged girls. What did she know of the dangers awaiting her at Howard University?

The next day, Ignatius sat in his cab in the suffocating heat, waiting for the dispatcher's call to pick up passengers. He laid his head on the wheel, overwhelmed with grief for his lost youth and opportunities, and wept. He cried for his absent mother and other losses. Unable to finish the day, he wanted to go home, but that wasn't an option. If Ejituru was there, he would have to face her, and one look at his expression would show his distress. He couldn't afford to let her know how much she hurt him, nor was he prepared to discuss their situation rationally.

Ojike, a friend and fellow cab driver, knocked on the windshield, wondering what was wrong.

"Enyi, can you take a short break and talk to me?" Ignatius asked. "I'm hurting too much."

One look at Ignatius's face showed Ojike that his friend was in trouble and needed to talk to someone. They drove to the nearest McDonald's, finding it almost empty. Cups of soda in hand, they huddled in a corner to talk, and Ignatius unburdened himself. Starkly honest, he gave an unvarnished version of what transpired between him and Ejituru.

His friend was aghast that Ejituru said Ignatius was paying for sexual favors. "These Nigerian university girls! I don't know what has come over them. They're full of shit! I've heard many stories of the way they treat the men who helped them come to the US. You're lucky she hasn't taken you to court yet."

"My friend, I never regretted marrying her. We're practically related. I saw her as a very nice, well-brought-up girl when we met. I don't even blame her for wanting to continue her education. What worries me most is that I'm not young, and I need to have children. I don't want to wait until I'm an old man. She isn't prepared to have children now. She wants to wait until she finishes her education. Who knows when? She won't discuss her plans with me. She just assumes I'll agree to anything she says. Her excuse is that I didn't keep my promise to her family that I would make sure she completes her education, so I should just accept her decisions.

"You know how expensive university tuition is. I can't afford to send her to college now. I might in the future, if she's prepared to wait.

"She says she'll work and go to college. You know what college is like, my friend. Howard! Can you imagine? Who knows what will happen to her, since she'll come home late every night. She won't take advice. What will I tell her parents if she endangers herself? She's made friends with some highly sophisticated Nigerian women married to doctors and lawyers, and they're her confidants, advising her on what to do." He burst into tears again, and Ojike had trouble consoling him.

"Control yourself, my friend. People are looking at us. Calm down. Let's discuss the problem rationally." To give Ignatius time to calm down, he added, "Let me tell you about the latest Nigerian scandal. One of the politicians was caught trying to dig up a bag of money he buried in his backyard."

As he gave Ignatius the details, he couldn't help laughing.

Ojike had lived in the area for twelve years. He came to the US under a student visa and worked through the university, taking six years to complete his bachelor's. He had registered for an MBA course at American University, but he had to give it up. With a wife and four children, he couldn't find time to study. His wife, who sponsored him for permanent residency, was African American and a nurse. Between them, they made a comfortable living.

Sympathetic to Ignatius's plight, Ojike offered two suggestions on ways to deal with Ejituru to contain any possible fallout from their disagreement. "You should ignore the situation and let her find out for herself the difficulties of studying and working. One of the reasons I gave up on my MBA was because my wife was also trying to get her nursing degree, and one of us had to be home to care for the children. My wife was taking evening classes at the time. *Oga!*

"I'm not sad I dropped out of college, because it turned out to be a good decision for my family. With a nursing degree, my wife has a good salary. Even though she works odd hours, I can now afford to take the weekend off to take the children to their extracurricular activities. I was fortunate that my wife and I could plan our lives together. I urge you to work toward gaining Ejituru's trust.

"But *Nna,*" he continued, "I anticipated this when you asked me if you should pursue this marriage, remember? I told you that the success of such a marriage depends on the motive of the girl for accepting the marriage proposal from someone she's known for only a short time. I won't say I told you so. It's happened. You need to find a way to make it work." "My friend, I agree with you," Ignatius said, "but she's here now, and I have to find a solution to my current problem with her. It's killing me. She wants to force me to pay her tuition, and I can't because I have too many financial obligations at home and here.

"I should let you go home," Ignatius said, ending the discussion. "Thank you for listening to me. You're a good friend. I'll tell her that since I'm not a party to her decision, she should be able to get whatever she needs for herself. I won't buy her a car or pay for her clothes. My obligation will be limited to paying for food and the apartment. I'll try to avoid more conflicts with her."

"I hope you'll be firm. I know she'll cry and weep, and you'll be tempted to give her money."

Ignatius felt as if a great load had lifted off him. At least he had someone to talk to.

At the taxi stand, when asked about Ejituru, he confessed the marriage wasn't going well. Even though his friends commiserated with him, they were united in advising him not to escalate the problem by forcing her out of the apartment. Some of his friends predicted she'd leave him eventually, but that would be the best solution if he could endure living with her until it happened. At an opportune time, he would tell Ejituru she could do what she wished, provided she exercised caution when traveling at night.

Ejituru wished her mother was nearby, but she was thousands of miles away in Nigeria, so she couldn't seek her advice. She had a surrogate mother in Mrs. Igwe, who tended to advise her to meet Ignatius halfway— advice she didn't want to hear. The situation demanded a face-to-face discussion with her mother.

What she wouldn't give to sit on her mother's bed and look into her eyes while she communicated her problem. She imagined her mother holding her hand, wiping her tears, and telling her to calm down. Letters were no good. She couldn't express her emotions on paper. Besides, by the time Nkechi replied, the situation would have changed and the advice would be irrelevant. Her mother would know the best way to handle the situation.

Oh, what have I done? Ejituru wondered. *I should have stuck to my views and rejected the marriage offer. I was weak, unable to withstand the pressure from my father. He should have been the one who married Ignatius.*

That brought a sad smile to her face. Though not a satisfactory method of communication, she decided to write anyway, giving her mother a full account of the situation and swearing her to secrecy. Her mother would certainly be agitated. Ejituru could see her hurriedly dressing and rushing off to her paternal village to discuss the letter and seek advice from her own confidant, but at least she would do so without telling Nwakama.

Two days after posting her letter, Ejituru met Esther at the complex as Esther returned from dropping off her children at school.

"Hi, Ejituru. What's up? Have you talked to Ignatius? What did he say?"

"He's very upset." Ejituru's legs were bare, and her flip flops protected her feet from the rough warmth of the concrete courtyard. "We can't discuss anything without shouting at each other. He might ask me to move out eventually. I said I wouldn't mind if that's what he wanted. In fact, I wouldn't blame him."

"Ejituru, why don't you reconsider your decision and meet him halfway? Drop the classes for now."

"Definitely not," she said firmly. "I won't give in on that." She turned to walk away.

"You're a very determined girl," Esther called after her. "I've met quite a few Nigerian girls like you, so I'm not surprised. I wish you well."

At the beginning of the fall semester, Ignatius told Ejituru of his decision. She could stay in the apartment, since she was still his wife, and he had no intention of divorcing her. He stressed the need for openness on her part.

Ejituru was relieved, but she was also suspicious. *Why did he suddenly change his mind?* she wondered. She felt he would ask her to move out eventually.

CHAPTER EIGHTEEN

At twenty-four, Ejituru's life revolved around Howard University. In the spring of the next year, she became a full-time student, juggling work and her studies. She had little spare time and went to the apartment only to sleep, though she kept up with her friends on weekends. Single-minded in pursuit of her education, she took summer classes and availed herself of any opportunity to improve her financial position and skills, unconcerned about the impact on her home life. All she could think of was the goal she set for herself.

Those three years were difficult for Ignatius. He didn't know what to do. Should he act like a man and put his foot down, give Ejituru an ultimatum to limit the hours she spent outside the home or move out? He couldn't ask her to find another apartment. He considered that possibility earlier and rejected it. Given his limited options, he accepted an offer to work part-time for a limousine company. The money was good, and the company took care of his board and lodging whenever he went outside the area. He regularly sent money to Nigeria to finance a business venture with his uncle.

"Stranger," Ignatius said one evening when he waited up for Ejituru to come home.

"I'm not a stranger," she said. "You are." She hung up her coat and set her backpack on the table.

"Ejituru, we need to talk. We can't go on like this, with you hardly in the house even on weekends."

"What do you want me to do? I can't study here, because the place is too noisy. I prefer to study in the college library." She removed her shoes and put them away.

"Why can't you find time to spend with me?" he asked, trying to be reasonable. "I don't know how to contact you during the day, nor do I know who your friends are."

"You know Cece. My other friends are university students. You aren't home much yourself." With a vacant, worried air, she tapped lightly on the table with her fist. She wasn't prepared for an argument.

"Ejituru," he said, his voice rising in anger, "I have to work to pay for the apartment and your clothes. Since we hardly see each other, you're always leaving me notes asking for money to buy clothes. I won't be able to pay for them anymore. You don't contribute anything to the running of this place."

"Is that what this is about? You want me to contribute money toward the household expenses? I can't afford it. You promised my parents you'd pay for my education. Your contribution toward it is allowing me to share the apartment with you." She looked at him belligerently.

"I'm not asking much of you. I just want to know where you are when you fail to come home at a reasonable hour."

"I can't tell you, because my hours change every day. I need time to spend with Cece. The weekend's the only time I can see her and Mrs. Igwe. I won't give that up."

"Watch it, Ejituru," he said angrily. "You're pushing me to the breaking point."

Ejituru was angry too. He expected her to spend all her free time in the apartment, even when he wasn't there. She hated the apartment and hoped for a chance to move out. Her friends advised her not to initiate the move, because that would give Ignatius cause to divorce her for abandonment. She wasn't about to give him any such excuse. She wanted a divorce that would force him to contribute to her upkeep in the US until her studies were over.

Given Ejituru's hours, she and Ignatius spent little time together in their apartment. He was usually asleep by the time she came in, and she had begun to relax about the possibility of pregnancy. She sometimes stayed the night at Mary's apartment on the East-West Highway rather than make the journey back home late at night. The couple never went anywhere together.

"Hi, Ejituru," Dr. Washington said, opening the door of her home at the beginning of the spring semester in Ejituru's final undergraduate year. "I was surprised when you called and asked to see me privately."

The three-bedroom home was situated in the upper northwest section of Washington, DC, in a very lovely neighborhood of beautiful old houses and gardens. Dr. Washington lived there with her only daughter.

"I've been very busy," Ejituru said. "I'm sorry I haven't kept up with you, but as I'm about to graduate, I need advice on medical schools."

She followed Dr. Washington into the parlor decorated with family portraits and paintings of scenes of the historic neighborhoods of Shaw, the H Street northeast corridor, and Columbia Heights. "I love these old photos and paintings."

"The paintings are of scenes of the historic black neighborhoods before the 1968 riots, painted by a Washington artist," Dr. Washington explained. "At the end of legally mandated racial segregation, the ready availability of jobs in the federal government in the early 1950s and '60s attracted middle-class African Americans to Washington. These historic neighborhoods became the centers of African American commercial life. Following the assassination of Dr. Martin Luther King, there were five days of widespread riots in the city, starting on April 4, 1968. Many businesses on Fourteenth Street, where my grandfather owned a small restaurant, were destroyed and looted. I bought the paintings to remind of how the area looked before the riots."

Ejituru enjoyed the short history lesson. "The scenes are beautiful. What happened to your grandfather?"

"He's no longer with us. Now, come into the kitchen with me while I make tea, and we'll discuss your problem."

As they sat down to sip their tea, Dr. Washington said, "Normally, I'd advise you to apply outside the area. Emory in Atlanta has a good medical school. As a married woman, however, you can only go out of state with your husband's consent or if he's willing to move. Is everything okay between you two?"

"Yes. We get along, but I'm not sure he would approve of my applying to colleges outside the area."

"I'll tell you that medical school is very stressful. You have to be sure of your husband's full support. If a marriage is shaky, the pressure of medical school will exacerbate the problem. Think carefully whether you really want to pursue a medical degree. Have you considered a teaching career or any other job that would give you time to repair your relationship with your husband?"

Why is she asking about my husband? That has nothing to do with this. It never occurred to Ejituru to factor her marriage into the equation. She wanted to apply to out-of-state universities, just like many of her college fellows.

"If you're determined to go to medical school, consider Howard. Many schools give preference to applicants from other colleges to dilute their student pool, but with your very high scores on the MCAT and high GPA, you should qualify as a credible candidate for Howard Medical School. Send your applications to various medical schools if you wish, but let me see them before you send them out."

"Doctor, before I make my next move, I'll make sure my husband is fully consulted and in agreement. I don't intend for him to pay for my medical school expenses. I was hoping to get a part-time job in a lab and to finance my schooling through loans, if that's possible."

"My concern isn't related to your method of payment for medical school, though I know that's your primary concern. I'm worried about the emotional cost for you and Ignatius, since you're still married. You need to make absolutely sure he's onboard. Stress in your marriage and stress from medical school would auger badly for your mental health."

"Thank you, Doctor. I appreciate your advice."

When Ejituru left the house, she had a lot to think about.

At Cece's house the following day, Ejituru sought out Mrs. Igwe, her surrogate mother. "I want to apply to medical school, but I'm not sure how to approach Ignatius to get him to understand that this is my wish." "Send in your application and wait until you know for sure you've been accepted first." Cece agreed.

The day Ejituru received her acceptance letters, she wept for joy. Unable to keep the news to herself, she rushed upstairs to Esther, hoping to get her thoughts on the matter. Esther was more in tune with Ignatius's way of thinking.

Esther was in the midst of braiding a customer's hair when Ejituru arrived, but she finished quickly and invited Ejituru to accompany her to pick up her daughters from school.

After chitchat about their common acquaintances, Ejituru said, "My big news is that I've been accepted into medical schools at Baltimore, Howard, and VCU in Richmond. I don't know how Ignatius would feel if I decided to go to a school outside the area. I haven't discussed any of this with him yet. Mama Esther, I'm afraid it will cause another rift between us."

Surprised at being consulted, Esther asked, "How will you pay for medical school, given the cost? I know he wouldn't agree to take on such a heavy burden, even if he could afford it."

"I've given it a lot of thought. I've been advised to finance it through student loans. I also applied for a few scholarships and a few hours' work in a lab."

Esther was amazed at how capable Ejituru had become over the years. It seemed that she considered all her options or had a really good college advisor. "You'll have a lot of debt to repay when you graduate. How would Ignatius feel about that?"

"Other people manage to pay off their loans over time. I presume I can do it too. I don't intend to return to Nigeria immediately after graduation. I'm quite sure I'll manage. I'm just glad I've reached this stage. My mother will be happy to hear I finally can start medical school. My contemporaries in Nigeria finished a long time ago."

"It'll be difficult to persuade Ignatius to agree to further education," Esther said. "He wants children, and your plan would mean postponing his need for a family even further. You should consider the effect of this decision on your marriage."

"I know he wants children, but I'll finish my studies when I'm at an age where I can still have them, if we're still married. I'm only twenty-six." Esther and Ejituru hadn't seen much of each other over the past three years. Whenever they met, Ejituru was extremely cordial and passed on some information about her activities. Esther saw Ignatius more frequently and knew he occasionally drove for a limousine company.

Esther turned to Ejituru. "I have one question." "What is it, Ma?"

"Do you love Ignatius, and do you want to continue to be married to him? I often wonder about that."

Taken aback and somewhat irritated, Ejituru tied and untied her braided hair. "I can't answer that. Why else would I still be living with him? I'm married to him, aren't I?"

The question set Ejituru to thinking. In her mind, Ignatius was just a distant relative who brought her to the US. She had long since ceased thinking of him as her husband. Her studies were all that mattered, and everything else in her life was peripheral. She was ready to start the mostimportant stage of her academic career, and she needed to plan her course of action.

Did she have any feelings for Ignatius other than gratitude to him for helping her get to where she was at that point? Was she being fair to him? What had he gained from their marriage? He might have some prestige at home and an occasional bed partner. Why else did he put up with having her around?

She never tried to get close to him, and if she were asked, she couldn't list his likes or dislikes. She knew nothing about how he spent his days or who his friends were. She never confided her innermost thoughts to him. Cece and others of her friends in college knew more about Ejituru and her plans than Ignatius. If he asked her to defer starting medical school for one year, would she agree?

She spent several days pondering those and other questions, arguing with herself. She decided that her only concession, if Ignatius asked, would be to choose Howard Medical School and hope for a residency outside Howard. She was ready to tell him that.

Three weeks before graduation, she and Ignatius were in the apartment, and he asked about her day.

"Ignatius, I have some news," she said, getting up from the sofa to stretch her legs.

His ears perked up. Was this what he'd been hoping for? Her next sentence shattered such thoughts.

"Graduation is in three weeks," she said. "I'm hoping you'll come. I'll invite Cece, of course, and Esther. I think Mrs. Igwe said she'd come too. She's been like a mother to me here, so it would be really nice if she came, but it depends on her finding a sitter for the children."

Thinking that they could finally plan for the future, Ignatius let the rest of her words wash over him. "Congratulations. I was expecting it to be next year. Of course I'll try to come, but you have to tell me when it is so I don't take any assignments on that date. I guess now you'll try for a better-paying job. Perhaps we can visit Nigeria together, so your parents can see you."

"I'm not looking for a job." She stopped stretching to look at him. "I've been accepted by several medical schools. Two are out of state, but I wanted to talk with you before choosing one."

Agitated, he fought to control himself, not liking the way she parsed the information. *Why is she doing this?* he wondered. *I'm sure she's saving the knife for last, when she'll plunge it into my heart and finish me.*

He wiped his face and suppressed his irritation. His gaze wandered toward her, standing in a neutral manner. He didn't want to succumb as usual to violent anger, which he found degrading.

She broke the silence. "The choice is between Richmond, Baltimore, and Howard. I want to discuss them with you. What you want will decide where I go."

"I'm glad for you, Ejituru, but personally I don't care for any of them. I want to start a family. I won't wait another four years for that to happen. I was hoping you'd get a job and we could finally begin living like husband and wife, planning our lives together."

"I'm sorry, sir. *O ihe, N'choro.* I have to do this."

"Then why'd you ask me if you've already decided? What do you want to do about our marriage? Do you want to be married or not?"

"I don't know. I haven't thought about that. I'll do whatever you want me to do. If you want me to move out, I can. Perhaps I should live closer to the school."

"How do you expect to pay for medical school? I've been told it's hard to work and attend school simultaneously."

"As part of the medical school requirements, I had to state how I intended to pay for my fees. I said I would apply for student loans, and I already submitted the application."

Ignatius felt as if he'd been hit by a locomotive. He sat down and wrapped his arms around himself, feeling so much pain he couldn't speak for a moment. When he found his tongue, he said, "I thought banks asked for the husband's signature before making a loan to a married woman."

She ignored his remark. "I'm willing to consider Howard if that's your preference. I'm very grateful to you for putting up with my weird hours these past three years. You know I've always wanted to be a doctor. I deferred my dream by marrying you when I did, and I won't put it off again. Sir, medical school will require a lot of my time, especially when I have to work late in the lab to make extra money. I haven't accepted any of the offers yet, but the deadline is in three days. I have to make up my mind this weekend. I'm sorry I'm disappointing you again with my decision, but I'm afraid there's no other option."

He listened carefully to her explanation, then he calmly replied, "Ejituru, you've already made your decision. What option do I have? I'm no longer young. I need a family. When would be the best time to have one? Have you included that in your decision? In all your decisions, you never thought of what's right for our marriage. Believe me, I'm happy you've worked so hard to get where you are in your career, but I'm more convinced than ever that you have no intention of continuing this relationship. I'm not sure how to respond. This has come as a surprise. Go ahead and accept whichever school you wish. That's not my decision. It's yours. You'll be the one who has to live with it."

Saddened to see him in such pain, she wished she could ease his hurt and make the discussion less painful. "I'll go to Howard University Medical School to accommodate you. I also have many friends here, and I'd rather not start over in a new city." She saw the calm, clear, sensible look in his eyes, the slight droop of his lips, and his generally pleasant features, but she remained emotionally detached.

Ignatius gave a hollow laugh at the thought of another three or four years of sharing an apartment with a ghost. He couldn't go through that again, but he wasn't about to announce his plans either.

He stood from the couch where he'd been sitting during their discussion and left the apartment, slamming the door behind him. He had a lot to think about. Questions swirled in his mind, seeking answers.

If he asked her for a divorce, what grounds would he use? She had to be fully informed of her rights, because her best friend was a lawyer. Should he refuse the invitation to her upcoming graduation? He didn't want to see Cece or Cece's husband. Who knew what Ejituru had told them about him?

I'm not young. My contemporaries in Nigeria all have children in secondary school. Who am I working so hard for?

He was glad she had completed her studies in record time and admired her tenacity, but he had hoped she would stop there and get a job that would enable them to resume their marriage. He hoped for normalcy in his married life, but Ejituru, as usual, dashed any hopes he had.

He decided not to attend the graduation and would plead a heavy workload at the company, but he would offer a small celebratory dinner for her with Esther and one of his friends. In his anguish, he called his uncle just to hear a familiar voice. In the process, he told him that Ejituru had finished college. His uncle was elated and promised to pass on the information to the in-laws, even though he was sure they must have already heard.

"I hope there's further good news in nine months," his uncle added. "I do too."

"Why don't you come home for a few weeks before you start college again?" Nkechi asked Ejituru during their next phone call.

"Mama, I don't have the money for the fare. I have to work during the summer to save money. I won't be able to hold a full-time job when I'm in college." She wished she could visit.

"In that case, daughter, if I see anyone from the US who is willing to carry a small packet for you, I'll send something. I wish it were possible for me to see you receive your certificate. Those round-trip tickets are expensive. I waited for Ignatius to send me one, but he never offered."

"Mama, don't put yourself out. I don't need anything, really."

The conversation left Ejituru feeling sad. What she wouldn't give to have her mother present for the graduation. How could her mother think that Ignatius, who wouldn't contribute one penny to Ejituru's education, would offer to bring her mother to America for a visit? Even if he offered, would Ejituru want her mother to see the dump where she lived? Her situation with Ignatius was becoming unbearable. She wanted to move out, but she resisted that out of consideration for her parents.

The dinner to celebrate Ejituru's graduation took place at a Chinese restaurant in Silver Spring. Many of Ejituru's friends and a few of Ignatius's were there. Dr. Washington wasn't able to come, but she sent a card indicating her pleasure at the choice of Howard, which also offered the best financial package.

Ignatius was quiet throughout the meal, wondering what those present would think if they knew the truth. He didn't want a brilliant wife. He wanted a woman who would give him children.

Esther was more bubbly than usual, covering up for Ignatius.

CHAPTER NINETEEN

Ignatius sat in his cab opposite the Inn at Cambridge on the eastern shore of Maryland, waiting for a client. He called his friend Ojike. Throughout the previous night, he kept having the thought, like the vestiges of a degrading dream, that it would have been better if he had never married Ejituru. He wanted the comfort only a best friend could provide.

"Man, to what do I owe this honor?" Ojike asked.

"I know I've neglected you. It's the nature of my new job. They work you to death. How are you anyway?"

"Everything's fine. The children are doing well. My wife is fine. We're thinking of visiting Nigeria in August before school starts. My senior brother at home has been beating me up for not bringing the children to Nigeria."

"I'm glad I caught you. I thought I'd visit you next week, perhaps after work. I should be free Monday evening. Would that be convenient?"

"I always knock off at six o'clock during the week. Would you prefer to meet for drinks? Perhaps not. Why don't you come to the house? I'll try to get home early. My wife and children will be happy to see you. I'll call my wife to tell her I'll bring home some Chinese food. How's Ejituru? She still has a year to graduate I presume."

"My friend, you're behind the times. She graduated last week. I'll tell you about it when we meet. My client is beckoning. We're about to head home."

He hung up quickly, not wanting to give a client any cause to complain.

He needed the job. It was the best-paying job he could hope to get.

Ignatius looked forward to meeting with Ojike. He suddenly realized how much he missed the camaraderie at the taxi stand. Buoyed by the conversation, his spirits rose.

<hr>

He drove out to Takoma Park in Montgomery County where the Ojikes had bought a four-bedroom house on a quiet street full of old, owneroccupied homes. Many of the families had lived there for years, but the population was changing as young couples looking for inexpensive homes discovered the area and started buying houses the moment they were available. Ojike and his wife had rented previously, but two years earlier they decided to buy and renovate the house, conveniently located near his wife's job at the Adventist Hospital and their children's school.

Ignatius envied his friend for having achieved what he always wanted— a family and a nice house. Ojike's three children talked excitedly about their planned trip to Nigeria.

"Why do we have to take so many malaria pills and get so many vaccinations?" one complained.

Ignatius enjoyed being with the family. After eating the Chinese food Ojike ordered, the two friends retired to a quiet corner of the backyard to talk.

"My friend, what a lovely yard," Ignatius said. "Do you have anyone helping you?"

"I'm afraid the yard is my responsibility. My okra and pepper did very well this year. I can give you some jalapeno peppers to take home if you wish." He proudly led Ignatius around the garden. "In addition to this small patch, I've rented some space in the country where I can plant more things."

They sat on a bench at the far side of the garden.

"What's happening with you?" Ojike asked. "When will we see Ejituru?"

"She has her bachelor's degree."

"She must have worked hard to complete her studies in three years. I'm glad for you."

"I tell you, my friend, these past three years were awful. We lived in the same house, but we were like ships passing in the night. We had nothing to say to each other. She worked and studied all the time. There was no time for me. I bore it because I knew it would end and we could resume a normal life. For three years, I let her come and go as she pleased. She spent most Saturdays with her friends or at school, because she had lab work or had to study with her team. She always had a reason why she couldn't be home on weekends. Even when school recessed, she was out on Saturdays either to meet a girlfriend at the mall or to start studying for the next session. She took summer classes. It never stopped."

Ojike shook his head and looked at his friend with pity. "Did you tell her how you felt?"

"Yes, when I saw her, which wasn't often. Do you know that in those three years I hardly knew any of her friends? She never knew what I was doing either. I know of Dr. and Cece Igwe, but that's because I was with her in church when she met them. Believe me, I've regretted my decision to let her continue living in the apartment as my wife."

He slumped and his eyes lifted to Ojike's face. "Do you know the latest? She's going to medical school. She sprang that on me at the same time she said she was graduating early. She was planning to go to a school outside Washington, but she said she'd attend Howard Medical School in order to accommodate me. To *accommodate me!*"

He shook his head, clasping and unclasping his hands. "Have you ever heard anything like it? On the baby front, I don't honestly know why she hasn't become pregnant. As far as I can make out by searching the medicine cabinet, she doesn't have birth control pills."

"Calm down, my friend." Ojike stood to get Ignatius a beer. "I'm sorry things haven't worked out for you. I feel bad for you. Believe me, I know how much you worry. She probably uses another kind of birth control that you don't know about. Remember, she was a medical student in Nigeria, so she must be familiar with such things.

"The question now is what you want to do. You and I know that after medical school she must enter a residency program. That might last two to four years, depending on the program. Furthermore, she won't have much choice about the location. She might have to leave Washington. You might have to move to another city if you want to stay married." "That's what I'm here to talk to you about. I'm truly happy for her get-

ting into medical school. Make no mistake about that. I just wish it wasn't at the cost of our marriage. I've been thinking about going back home. My uncle needs me. He isn't young anymore, and he's been dropping hints about his diabetes getting worse. I might have to go back if something happens to him, since I have no other reliable person there.

"I've been sending money to him to pay for a project we're supporting, but to complete it I have to stay here and work. It's the only way I can pay for it. I also need to reconcile my uncle with his son-in-law who lives in Lagos, but that's a long story.

"I don't think I can continue to live with Ejituru. We aren't helping each other. I feel she's staying with me out of a feeling that if she hadn't married me she wouldn't have come to America. I'm tired of hearing that. I don't need her gratitude.

"On the other hand, I can't tell her to pack up and leave. What would the people at home think of me? They'd think I was jealous of her success or that living in America made me selfish and uncaring. I don't want to wait for Ejituru to decide what my future will be. I need to choose for myself."

"Ignatius, my friend, there's a strong possibility that both of you are in the process of determining your futures. Medical school is no joke. It will consume her—that is, if she wants to do well and get into a good residency program. I know quite a few of our people who studied to become doctors, and I know what they went through. She is, I suppose, paying for her education through student loans. She'll come out of school with so much debt that it'll take years to pay off before she can live comfortably.

"I don't know how to advise you. Whatever advice I have might not work, since we don't know Ejituru's plans. The best advice is to do whatever is best for you."

Ignatius looked lost.

"If I were you, I'd sit down and work out the pros and cons of being married to Ejituru," Ojike said. "Remember that in the future she'll make a lot of money, and that could be a reason to stay in the marriage. On the other hand, it seems you don't have any home life right now, and I see someone sitting in front of me who longs for a family to love and be with. You only knew your mother. From what you said, your father never acknowledged you until he saw you during your short visit home. I know you feel time is passing you by. Perhaps you should cut your losses and tell Ejituru you want a separation. Then you can find a woman who'll love you as you deserve to be loved and will give you the family you're longing for. If it's a girl from home you want, there are many looking for husbands. If not, there are many suitable black girls who'd jump at an opportunity for marriage here. All I can say is to decide what you really want."

Ignatius sat in the apartment waiting for Ejituru to return from wherever she was. As he waited, he absentmindedly watched TV, thinking what to say about their marriage when he returned to Nigeria. He packed his suitcase and had all his travel documents ready, but he still had to tell Ejituru he was leaving for Nigeria the following day. He would face questions from her parents, and he mulled over his approach to the inevitable question about when to expect a grandchild.

Finally, the door opened and Ejituru appeared. He wrenched his thoughts from Nigeria back to the present. "I'm glad you're back. I'm going to Nigeria tomorrow. My uncle's in the hospital and my aunt needs me."

"What?" She was genuinely shocked. "I hope it isn't serious. Where is he?"

"At the hospital in Aba." "Will you go to the village?"

"No. I'll be away for two weeks, but I'll stay in Aba."

For a long time, she watched him rock his head back and forth, and she finally asked, "When did you get the news? My mother never said anything about your uncle being ill when she called."

"My aunt called last week. I've only just now gotten the money together for the trip."

Though upset she didn't have a chance to get a gift for her mother, Ejituru said pleasantly, "Please give him my best. I hope he's being well taken care of at Aba. My thoughts will be with Aunt Regina. I'll scribble a letter for you to send to my mother, if you don't mind. Please explain it was a sudden decision."

It would be the first time Ignatius went home since they met. He had missed the traditional wedding and was represented by a distant cousin. Given the strained relationship between him and Ejituru, would he bother to meet her parents? Under normal circumstances, he would be expected to present them with gifts. He would be excoriated for not bringing Ejituru with him. No doubt, he would have a good explanation for that lapse.

The next day, Ejituru stayed in the apartment until Ignatius left. Feeling relieved, she went to spend time with Cece and tell her about Ignatius's departure.

"What will you do about him?" Cece asked.

"I need to make sure that whatever I do he will maintain me until after medical school."

"Do you think he'll discuss your problems with your parents?"

"He's not going to the village, so I doubt he'll see them. I'm sure he'll talk to his uncle. If he does, my parents will hear about it, then my mother will call to check the facts."

"Why don't you move out?"

"I can't. I don't have the money for a security deposit and rent. I'm looking for a student who might need a roommate and is willing to take me on. Then I'll tell Ignatius I'm moving out."

"Be careful you don't give him any excuse for a divorce on the grounds of abandonment."

"I'll try not to. Thanks."

Ignatius was met at the baggage carousel in the Lagos airport by Ajao, his cousin-in-law and a high-ranking officer in the Nigerian Army. Outside the customs area, they met a huge crowd waiting for the arrival of their loved ones. Ignatius had booked a room at the Sheraton in Ikeja, but Ajao insisted he should stay in his house, since it was the first time Ajao met a relative of his wife's.

Ajao had met his wife when he was stationed in Enugu shortly after the end of the Nigerian-Biafran War. Young and unsure of herself, she was one of the girls soliciting for favors in front of the army barracks. Ajao befriended her. His offer of marriage was rejected by her parents, Regina and Okoro. When Ajao was transferred to Lagos, he took her with him and made her his wife. Regina and Okoro disowned her.

Ignatius's letters to Ajao and his cousin stressed the need for reconciliations, given his uncle's health and age. His constant harping paid off, and the couple would accompany him to the east. Ignatius hoped that after the initial visit his uncle would accept the offer of a bride price, which would legalize the marriage.

While fighting the crowd in an attempt to keep pace with Ajao, Ignatius heard someone call his name.

"Can that man be Ignatius?" asked an elderly Yoruba woman. "Surely it can't be."

Ignatius stopped to see who was talking.

"I'm sorry," the woman said. "You remind me of a friend I had a long time ago in Washington. His name was Ignatius."

"Madam, that's my name." Looking at her carefully, he recognized Ayo, his lifeline from twenty years earlier. She had gained weight, but it was well hidden by her *bubba* and wrapper, which set her apart as one of the rich Nigerian society women he saw in Lagos society magazines at Esther's apartment.

Surprised and shocked, she rushed to hug him, reminding him of her love of Chanel No. 5. "What are you doing here? Where are you staying? You look well."

"Ayo, it's nice to see you," he whispered, overcome with emotion. "You look well too. Age agrees with you. I came in on Air France a few hours ago, and it looks like I'll stay with my cousin at the army barracks in Lagos." He wanted to know what had happened to her during the intervening years.

"I'll come to Ajao's house tomorrow in the barracks," she said. "Perhaps we can talk then."

They exchanged addresses, and Ignatius, still shaking with emotion, reluctantly followed Ajao to the motor park. Ayo had been on his mind so often that he didn't want to let her go without learning what had happened since they parted.

The drive to his cousin's house was uneventful. Lagos had changed since he'd left years earlier to get his visa and join the Unegbus, but the streets were as crowded as ever with pedestrians and cars. The noise was deafening, and the heat would have been unbearable without the airconditioning in the car. The new bridge and many recently developed areas were impressive. Ignatius noticed that there were traffic lights, though nobody stopped when they turned red. The lights were just another hazard the government added to the woes of daily existence.

"Welcome," Ajao said when they reached his three-bedroom flat in the Army barracks. "I'm happy to have my wife's relative in the house for the first time. I've prayed for this day."

The children, who stayed up late to see their uncle from America, excitedly inspected the gifts Ignatius brought them.

"I'm happy to be here," Ignatius said, "but especially happy that we'll be going to Aba to visit the family so we can end this rift. Thank you for doing this for me."

When they sat down at breakfast the following day, Ignatius told his cousin, "Mary, I'm surprised you never made an effort to reconcile with Uncle and his wife, especially since you're their only child."

"I tried at the beginning, but they didn't want anything to do with me. They wanted me to return to the village. How could I? No one would marry me with my history. Ajao offered me kindness and love. His family accepted me without question and helped get me assimilated."

"What has your life been like?"

"Good. Ajao gave me the capital to start petty trading, and I've done very well. We're relatively better off than most people of his rank. What else can I ask for? My children have a family who loves them."

Ignatius was impressed.

"We'll travel with you tomorrow," Mary said. "I hope my parents will grow to love Ajao. He's been very good to me."

As promised, Ayo came to visit the following day.

"Hi, Ayo," Ignatius said. "You found the house. Come in. I'm alone right now."

They sat in Ajao's little parlor in the army barracks. Over drinks of Fanta and lemonade, they talked.

"What were you doing at the airport?" Ignatius asked.

"I was seeing my daughter off to London. She was home for a short holiday."

"Why Britain, when you could send her to the land of her birth?"

"It's a long story. You know British education is valued more by the Yoruba elite."

"Where are you sons?"

"One's here in Nigeria. Both studied first in London, then went for further education in the US. One has his own business here and is doing well. The other lives in San Francisco, where he works. I'm sorry I never contacted you. I planned to return after the funeral, but there was so much *wahala* with the in-laws that my family decided I should stay in Nigeria with the children. I've done fairly well since the creation of Lagos State. I had a paid position in the government, and now I have a political appointment. Tell me about your life since we parted. You must be relatively well off to make the journey home."

"My life took a downward spiral after you left. I drifted from job to job and dropped out of Howard. At one point, I used and sold drugs, but I now have my act together. I have a steady job as a cab driver and own my own cab. I'm in an arranged marriage with a girl from my village who's very ambitious and is in medical school.

"She's unaware of my past and believes I couldn't get an engineering position, which is why I'm a cab driver. I would have learned to love my wife if she showed any feelings for me, but she's very inconsiderate. She married me as a passport to pursue a US education, and she tried to get me to pay for her studies, but I refused. I hope to use this separation to think about my relationship with her."

"I'm so sorry, Ignatius." She placed her hand in his and looked at his sad expression. "I understand how you feel. I too was a victim of an arranged marriage, but my husband was also abusive. I never wished him to die the way he did, but his death freed me from further suffering."

"In my situation, I'm the abused husband. I don't expect anyone to understand how I feel, because I'm only now beginning to get a handle on it myself. I quite liked my wife and would have no difficult loving her if I was sure the feeling was mutual. The only thing I won't do for her is pay for her education.

"Seeing you at the airport was a gift from God. I often wondered what direction my life would have taken if you hadn't returned to Nigeria when you did. I hated and blamed you for my problems, but I now feel differently. No one person can be the cause of another's failure to cope with what life has to offer."

"Have you ever considered returning to Nigeria?"

"Yes, but I'm not qualified for anything. I bought a piece of land in Aba, and my uncle's trying to help me develop it. We intend to build rental properties. Perhaps if I had several of those I might consider it, but right now I need to be in the US where I can make good money to send to my uncle."

Her eyes full of emotion, Ayo said, "I'm sorry I wasn't there when you needed me. I hope you can work out things with your wife. Promise you'll call and tell me when you're going back to the US. We should meet again."

CHAPTER TWENTY

Ignatius left Lagos for the east the following day. The twelve-hour drive, which for an ordinary person under normal circumstances would have been difficult, was relatively stress free because of Ajao's position with the army.

On arrival in Aba, Ignatius left his companions at the rest house and went to the hospital to tell his uncle he arrived. His uncle lay in a men's ward of twenty beds. Ignatius saw his aunt sitting on the side of the bed, because there were no chairs for visitors. Her shout at seeing Ignatius walk in woke his uncle, who tried to sit up.

"Uncle, no!" Ignatius said quickly. "You'll hurt yourself."

"Oh, Ignatius, I never thought I'd see you again in this world," his uncle said. "Welcome, my son. You've made an old man happy. If I die today, I'll die a happy man."

"What nonsense! Your doctor said you're getting better. He plans to discharge you next week."

After some desultory talk, his uncle calmed and became his usual self. They discussed the project, and he assured his uncle he would make sure he had the resources to complete it.

"Uncle, you shouldn't worry about the management of the project. If anything happens to you, I'll take care of it."

"Ignatius, you said you weren't thinking of coming home for another four years. You wanted to be financially secure before you return."

"I know what I said. As far as I'm concerned, that's still the plan, but plans change according to circumstances." He changed the subject. "I have something to tell you, Uncle. I brought two people to Aba who would very much like to visit you in the hospital. I want you to promise you won't refuse to see them. They're very important to my plans."

He didn't explain further.

When evening visiting hours arrived, Ajao and Ignatius's cousin appeared. After the initial shock, Ignatius's aunt hugged her daughter, overwhelmed with happiness.

"I never expected to see you again," she said repeatedly. "Thank you, Ignatius."

More restrained, his uncle confined his questions to the state of the road from Lagos to the east, and whether they were stopped by armed guards along the way. Then he realized he was talking to an officer in the Nigerian Army, who probably had an easier time than civilians navigating the checkpoints. The family talked about grandchildren and shared photographs.

"I know I should have made more effort to overcome your anger toward the marriage," Ajao apologized, "but, sir, forgive me. I hope to make amends in the future. My wife is the most important person in my life. Reconciliation with her parents has always been uppermost in my mind. I didn't know how to accomplish that. I'm grateful to Ignatius for his part in effecting this meeting. I promise my family will visit frequently. I have to return to Lagos, but my wife will stay a few days and will return with Ignatius."

"That's all in the past," Okoro said. "I'm glad to meet you. You should know that according to our custom, the children aren't yours until you have performed the marriage ceremony and paid the bride price."

Over the years, Okoro's initial pain had faded, and as he and his wife grew older, they regretted how they had handled the rift with their daughter. The meeting allowed them a way to save face.

"That I'm willing to do," Ajao aid. "My parents will come for it. They love Mary very much and will do anything for her. We should agree on a date as soon as possible."

Happy with the outcome of the visit, Ignatius decided to stay in Aba with his aunt and cousin until his uncle's discharge. He felt his aunt and uncle needed time to get to know their daughter and hear about their grandchildren, though Ajao had to return to Lagos. The time Ignatius spent in Aba gave him the opportunity to discuss his project with his uncle, while the two women caught up on their lost time.

Convinced that Ajao was trustworthy and a loving husband and father, Ignatius was happy he had accomplished something during his visit. Even if his uncle died that day, his aunt would have the comfort of her daughter and son-in-law.

Ignatius thought of his own marriage. It met all the customary rules, but how successful had it been? *If Ejituru had been less ambitious,* he thought, *we would have succeeded. My cousin did what she must to survive the war, and it was sheer luck that she married a man who cared for her, loved her, and was willing to forgive her for selling her body during that time. Ajao recognized the jewel in her. From what I've heard, he has never referred to her life before they met. She's been a loyal wife just like her mother, and they have three lovely children.*

Ignatius was happy that his aunt and uncle would soon meet their grandchildren. He thought of his own mother who would never know her grandchildren. Even if she were alive, Ejituru's ambition and unwillingness to consider children would prevent that.

During a visit with his uncle, Okoro asked, "Ignatius, I thought by now we'd be carrying kegs of palm wine to Nwakama's house to welcome a new addition. What happened?"

After the initial shock of hearing the question, Ignatius said, "It isn't God's will yet."

"You know Nkechi also had trouble carrying a child to term. I hope that's not Ejituru's fate."

Among village people, infertility was the wife's fault, never the man's. It was natural for Okoro to blame Ejituru for the unfortunate situation. "Uncle, we should give her time. She's too young for the responsibility of motherhood in America." He spoke in a voice that brooked no questions.

"Nkechi would like to see you," Okoro said. "She asked about you last week when she visited. I told her we expected to see you sometime, but you said Ejituru wouldn't come due to her studies."

"No, Uncle, I won't be seeing her family. I came specifically to see you, since you were in the hospital and you're my only relative. I've given Auntie the little gifts I had for Nkechi and the note from Ejituru."

Ignatius changed the subject. "You told me you found a tenant for my mother's house. I'm glad for that. Our project is progressing. I've been to the site, and I believe what you said about my mother's house. I have no reason to visit the village."

"Okay, Ignatius, the women aren't here. You have to tell me the truth. Whenever we mention Ejituru, your face clouds over. That tells me there's something wrong."

Ignatius sighed. "Uncle, you must promise that you'll keep whatever I say to yourself. She has her own life, and I have mine. She does what she wants. She only tells me when she thinks something will impact my life and she needs my endorsement for her actions."

"What do you mean? I don't understand. She's your wife. You should control her. Both of you should plan your life together."

"Uncle, remember that in order to get Nkechi's consent I said Ejituru could continue her studies and that I would help pay for that?"

"Yes, I remember. You must have helped her, or she wouldn't have graduated from university by now."

"In a way, you can say I helped. She lives in the apartment and has food to eat, but I'm not paying any of her fees. I can't afford to pay for her education. I asked her to give me a little time, to postpone her education until after we have children. She refused. She's working and uses her own money to pay for her classes.

"We never really sat down to discuss our plans. She comes in and announces what she intends to do, and she expects me to agree and shut up. She doesn't want children. I think she's using birth control to make sure of that. She only talks to me when she tells me her next plan."

A nurse came in. "Is it all right if I send in the next visitors? You asked us to hold off while you two talked."

"Can you wait a little longer, please?" Ignatius asked. Once the woman left, he said, "Can you believe it, Uncle? Ejituru will be in medical school for another four years, and this time I'm not sure if she'll still live in the apartment. She hasn't discussed her plans with me. I don't even know if I'll see her when I go back.

"Believe me, Uncle. She's ambitious and obstinate. She won't let anything stand in the way of her objective. I feel she agreed to our marriage so she could study in the US. Since she arrived five years ago, she's never shown any interest in me or how I make my living. It's always about her education and why I should pay for it, since I promised. Can you believe it? She even said that sleeping with me occasionally is her way of paying for the roof over her head and her food, so I shouldn't complain. The awful part of it is, I really care for her."

He began crying and quickly wiped his eyes. "I can't believe I've admitted all this."

"How can you allow a woman to use you that way? Why do you allow her to treat you like that? I don't understand you. She's more like her mother than I thought. Have you told her how hurt you are that she's using you in this way?"

"You should lower your voices," the patient in the next bed said softly. "The whole ward is straining to hear this discussion."

"Uncle," Ignatius said more softly, "it isn't that simple. America isn't like home. I can't tell her to move out, because she has advisers who tell her what to do. She could take me to court. I keep hoping she'll move out, then I can ask for a divorce. That's what my lawyer advised. I respect her for what she has achieved. She's very smart. I just wish she also had a heart. One thing is certain—she has no love for me. I'm just someone she's using."

"Shouldn't you discuss this with her parents? They need to know."

"I'm sure she's told her mother of her plans. She telephones her mother to talk from time to time. You'd think her mother would want to talk to me, but I've never heard from her."

"This is really hard for me to bear. I honestly thought the girl would make a good wife. She looked humble, and everyone at home thought she'd be the right wife for you. My dear son, I'm so sorry. You deserve to be happy. What do you want to do?"

"For now, nothing. I'm thinking over my options. I want a family, and I feel time is passing me by. When I get back to America, I'll decide."

Ignatius spent a few more days in Aba before returning to Lagos. Most days, before setting out for the hospital, he visited old schoolmates who lived and worked in Aba. He also went to Port Harcourt, an hour's journey away, to see some of his acquaintances.

One day, he lingered over breakfast in the dining room of the rest house, reading the local newspaper about the shenanigans of the successful businessmen and politicians in Imo State. He thought of his father and how he wanted to prove to him he could succeed in life without the man's help. All his business ventures with his uncle were undertaken to show his father he could build a legitimate, successful business that would make him even richer than his father. He just needed a few more years in the US. Hopefully, the Almighty would grant his uncle longer life. He vowed to see that his uncle had the best available medical care to control his diabetes and blood pressure.

Lost in thought and oblivious to his surroundings, he was shocked when a waiter approached and whispered, "Sir, you have visitors."

"Who can they be? I'm not expecting anyone."

"Oga, they didn't give us their names. They just said they're here to see you. It's a young man and girl. They look like college students."

Ignatius was taken aback. He'd been in Aba for a week without any visitors. *My father must've sent emissaries with an order for me to appear before him,* he guessed, then he dismissed the thought. Okoro told him that his father only came to Aba at the end of each month to pay his workers.

My in-laws must've found out I'm here, he thought, hyperventilating, *and they sent relatives to spy on me.*

He searched for a way out that wouldn't bring him face-to-face with the visitors. The kitchen seemed the only option, but the staff would sneer at him if he slipped out that way. They would assume he was running from his creditors.

Ignatius, taking his time, carefully drank the last drop of his tea, folded the newspaper, and calmly walked into the foyer. When he looked around, he saw only strangers staring at him, so he surmised the visitors were people he didn't know. He debated whether he should just walk to his room and ignore them.

Curiosity won out. He approached the counter and asked the receptionist where his visitors were.

"Look outside near the croton bush," the receptionist said, "on the opposite side of the yard. They're near some hawkers selling fruit and vegetables."

He looked and saw two people staring at him. One was the image of his father, and the other was a smartly dressed young woman, who he surmised was either a sister or cousin of the young man.

He walked toward them. "Were you looking for me?"

"Yes. My name is Isaac. This is my sister, Mary. We're sorry to worry you, sir, but we've waited a long time to meet you. We're your half-brother and half-sister."

"How'd you know I was here?"

"Dede Ume came to our house to look for you. He mentioned you were in Aba to see your uncle, who's in the hospital. He thought you were staying with us. We went to the uncle and saw your aunt, who told us where you were staying, so we decided to come to see you. We've waited many years to meet you, and we're very glad we finally succeeded."

They accompanied him to a quiet spot in the rest house lounge, and he ordered soft drinks for them. He told himself they weren't responsible for their father's behavior the last time Ignatius went to Aba, and he couldn't blame them for it. Still, they were strangers, and he felt no connection to them.

"We've gained admission to college, and we hope to start at the beginning of the term," Isaac said.

Mary interrupted. "We're hoping you'll pay for us to study in the US." He was taken aback. Didn't they know that Ugo Chuku used them as an excuse to deny paying for *his* university education? How dare they come to ask help from him?'

"Is Ugo Chuku not prepared to send you to college?"

"Oh, he is," Mary said, "but not to America where he sent you. Education in Nigeria isn't that good. We want to go to America. Since you're there, we thought you could help. You're our rich brother, and our maternal uncles aren't in a position to help."

Aghast, he couldn't believe those children were under the illusion that Ugo Chuku paid for Ignatius's US education. He didn't feel right to disabuse them of their misunderstanding, but he had to make it clear that they couldn't depend on him for financial assistance.

He glared at them and said carefully, "Why do you expect me, who you've never met until now, to send you to the US and maintain you there, assuming I even have the money?"

"You're our brother," Isaac said. "You owe it to us. Who else will help us if you don't?"

"I owe it to you?" he shouted. "I owe you nothing." He fought to control himself and stood up. "Thank you for the visit. I don't have the money to give you or to send you to the US. You're lucky Ugo Chuku will pay for your university education. You should be thankful for that."

The incident preyed on his mind all morning. He lay on the bed in his room, fuming, asking God to forgive Ugo Chuku for his lies. He was angry with his father, and recalled the way the man treated him when he met him in Aba to ask him to pay for his university tuition. How could the man claim he had educated Ignatius? He thanked God that he had no intention of visiting his father in the village, but if he met him in the street, he would spit on him and curse him.

As Ignatius entered the hospital foyer, the receptionist remarked, "Oga, your uncle's room is like a motor park today, with many visitors coming and going. I hope some of them will leave now that you've arrived." She was under the impression that the visitors were there to see Ignatius, not his uncle.

"Perhaps I should return later," Ignatius said. "I really want to spend my last day in Aba with my uncle."

She laughed. "You're be denying the visitors the very reason for traveling to Aba. Besides, he's looking forward to your visit. Perhaps you'll force some of the visitors to leave so you can spend time alone with your family."

He prayed Ugo Chuku wasn't one of the people waiting in the room, and walked slowly down the hall.

The first person he saw when he opened the door was Nkechi, who looked very elegant in her caftan with matching head tie. He laughed and cursed himself for wishing such a thing accidentally. *I must have conjured her when I thought she was at the rest house,* he thought.

Nkechi immediately began berating him for not visiting home. "You know you could have stayed with us, since your uncle's in the hospital. You can't use him as an excuse. We would have been happy to have you stay with us, even if just for a day. We got the gifts you sent through the driver, but they don't make up for not making an appearance. You weren't at home during the wine ceremony, and since then we haven't seen you. Many people in the village even doubt the legitimacy of the marriage."

"Nkechi, that's not true!" Okoro said. "You know Ejituru is truly his wife. Didn't he send her to college as he promised? Even now, she's going to medical school. I won't let you say anything bad about him. He's an in-law to be reckoned with."

"I only said that people will think there's something wrong with the marriage since he hasn't been home to visit his in-laws," she said more calmly. "Let's not fight over words. I hear you're returning to tomorrow," she said to Ignatius, "so we won't even have time to talk. How is Ejituru? When will she start medical school?"

"She has already started. That's why she didn't come with me."

He saw immediately when Nkechi raised her eyebrows that she was toying with him. She came to meet him so she could pretend she knew nothing about his problems with Ejituru.

Ejituru had called her mother to tell her about Ignatius's visit and urge her not to mention her marital problems if she met him. Nkechi assumed Ignatius would make the trip home to see her, but after waiting ten days without a visit, she decided it was time to go to Aba to see him. She had a few gifts for Ejituru, which she hoped he would agree to carry. Given the tension between the two young people, Nkechi wasn't sure how well she would be received. She knew Ignatius opposed her daughter's education and wanted her to have children before continuing her studies. Ejituru confessed that Ignatius wasn't happy she was going to medical school and would rather she started a family immediately.

Nkechi supported her daughter's decision to defer parenthood, but she wasn't about to start an argument with those two illiterates. She came to the hospital just to find out where Ignatius stayed, hoping she could intercept him there.

"My son-in-law, when are you and your wife planning to make me a grandmother? Now that she's finished her first degree, I'm hoping it won't be too long." She planned to inquire about the couple's plan for children as a way of ensuring Ignatius wasn't aware of her collusion with Ejituru in that issue. Meeting Ignatius in the presence of his uncle suited her plans.

To Ignatius's chagrin, his aunt and cousin joined in, saying it had been several years since the marriage ceremony. By that point, there should be at least two grandchildren.

"Tell us," Regina said, "what are you waiting for? Are you like the *Oyibos,* who put off having children until they're too old?"

Ignatius felt cornered, but he said calmly, "You should ask Ejituru. I'm doing my part. We'll have one when God wishes."

Nkechi had to return to her village. Ignatius offered to take her to lunch first, and they went to the one of the few decent fast-food places that had recently become popular in Aba.

As they ate, Nkechi said, "Very few men would do what you're doing, Ignatius."

He wondered what she meant. "Mama Ejituru, what am I doing?"

"Ejituru said you've been very supportive of her educational aspirations and you could have asked her to contribute more to the upkeep of the apartment, but you didn't. She's very grateful. God will reward you."

As I thought, the two of them are in collusion, he realized. *There's no doubt.* "Ejituru deserves to be congratulated on her achievement."

Nkechi plunged into the topic that was on her mind. "I don't know when you'll come again, and I know that until Ejituru qualifies to be a doctor she won't be able to come home, but I'm hoping you'll invite me to visit. I see many parents with children in America going to visit them. I'd like to be present to see my child holding that diploma."

I'll bet you would, he thought. *Even if she isn't still married to me.* "Mama Ejituru, it'll be in four years. During that time, many things can happen. I'm sure Ejituru hopes you'll be present at the ceremony. I know she was unhappy you weren't there in May when she graduated and was awarded several honors. She gave me very short notice, so there wasn't time to invite you."

"My son-in-law, I'll hold you to that promise." Nkechi left.

Ignatius returned to the hospital, where Okoro was being discharged. There were drugs to buy and bills to settle. His aunt wept with gratitude, thanking him repeatedly for what he did during his visit. She clutched her daughter's hand desperately, asking when she would see her again.

His aunt now had a cell phone, and Ignatius taught her how to use it and to charge the battery. He programmed the daughter's number into the phone so they could be in easy contact. He added his own number and showed her how he was only a call away.

Ajao had called many times and told his in-laws to set up the date for the wine ceremony so he could arrange the accommodations for the relatives who wanted to accompany him. They chose a date in September. Ignatius assured her that the event, only three weeks away, was something to look forward to. He was sorry to miss such an important occasion, but he hoped they could send him photographs taken with the new camera he gave his cousin.

After arriving in Lagos the following day, Ignatius called Ayo. They agreed to meet as soon as he returned from the east. He knew his cousin would be busy, having been away from home for two weeks, so he told her that a friend was showing him around during his last two days before flying to America.

Ayo was happy to see him again. They decided, since he knew little about western Nigeria, she would take him sightseeing.

He spent his evenings at his cousin's house, where he got to know Ajao well and discussed his real estate plans. Impressed, Ajao advised him to start looking into possible investments in Lagos, because he could make serious money there.

On the flight back to the US, Ignatius reflected on the visit. He was happy to have united his uncle with his daughter and son-in-law, and he felt Ajao was a good addition to the family and would prove very dependable. His cousin was a good businesswoman, wife, and mother.

Most of all, he was glad he found Ayo, whom he still loved very much, who would be a part of his life as the sister he never had.

He arrived at Dulles the next day, determined to have a more-positive attitude toward life. He felt ready to face whatever Ejituru could throw at him.

CHAPTER TWENTY-ONE

Ejituru and Ignatius had no contact while he was away. In his absence, she completed her orientation and began classes. She had no contact with Esther either, because Esther would invariably pry into her marital situation. Ejituru felt she had told her friend more than enough.

"My friend," Cece warned her, "you must avoid discussing your business with people like Esther, who has a salon and trades gossip."

Esther inevitably lectured Ejituru on her failures. To Ejituru, Esther's life wasn't a good example, no matter how much she liked to tell others how to live. No longer prepared to tolerate Esther's preaching, Ejituru restricted her visits to Esther's busy period, when they could gossip about acquaintances or talk about fashion and cars.

Esther regarded Ejituru as the younger sister she could lecture at will. On one visit, she asked Ejituru, "Why are you so determined to deny Ignatius the one thing he really wants that would make him happy?"

Taken aback, Ejituru asked, "What's that?" "A child." Esther laughed.

Ejituru looked at her pleasant face, her head wrapped loosely with a square tie-dyed cloth, and shook her head. "Oh, no. That's the one thing I'm not prepared to give, Auntie. I thought you knew what a child would do to me. I want a child, but not when I'm about to start medical school. Besides, I don't think I want one with Ignatius."

"Why not? He clearly wants one with you. Please understand, I'm not trying to tell you what to do. I just want to be sure you know what you want."

Ejituru rubbed her face with her hands and bit her lip, then she said heatedly, "Auntie, I'll tell you because I've grown to like and perhaps trust you. I'm a product of a loveless marriage, and I wouldn't want my child to have that kind of life. All my life, I tried to please both my parents. I married Ignatius because I wanted to please my father. I'm going to medical school to please my mother. Fortunately, medical school is something I really want. It would be awful if I were studying and was pushed into this because of her.

"I would hate any child I had now, because every time I looked at it I'd blame it for my frustrated life. I can't do that. My parents stayed together because of me. They weren't strong enough to face the outcome of a decision to end their marriage. I feel as if I'm in my mother's shoes right now. I don't know if I'm strong enough to make a decision about my marriage. The only decision I feel confident in making is to prevent bringing a child into the mix."

"Ejituru, my child, forgive me. I didn't mean to open wounds. It's my firm belief that if you had any feelings for Ignatius, you would have found a way to get what you both want. You would have been more willing to defer your dream, and you would still have made that dream come true. I now know what's lacking in your relationship.

"Who am I to say if you're right or wrong? I have a co-wife I've never met, not because I don't want to, but because she feels threatened by me. It's also because accepting her into my life would mean stating that I approval of polygamy. My dear girl, we all have burdens we bear. There's a saying that God gives you the burdens he thinks you can bear. I want to say that you aren't your mother. You're a strong person, and I'm sure you can come to a decision that will be good for you. Look at how far you've come from the little girl I met five years ago."

"Thank you, Auntie Esther." She hugged the woman.

The discussion helped them understand each other better, but still, Ejituru felt it was a mistake to share so much.

The time Ignatius spent in Nigeria led to a reevaluation of his relationship with Ejituru. He came to terms with her lack of affection for him. He couldn't force her to love him or consider his feelings. If he could think of her as a co-tenant of the apartment, his hurt would lessen. He could tolerate her occasional presence if he focused on an imaginary date when the tenancy would end.

Of course, he knew they both had to choose such a date, but meanwhile he drew comfort from knowing the current situation wouldn't last. He decided to focus on work, in an effort to raise the capital he needed to complete his project at home.

A life-changing event that was totally unexpected occurred on the way home, though Ignatius wouldn't have labeled it as such at the time.

On the plane from Charles de Gaulle in Paris to Dulles in Washington, he sat beside a good-looking Nigerian woman. She had the window seat, while he was on the aisle. At first they were both reserved, but as the flight attendant served drinks, Ignatius introduced himself.

"What's your name?" he asked. "Ndidi."

"Are you from the east?"

"My parents are from Owerri, but I was born in Silver Spring when they lived and worked in the US. On retiring from their respective jobs, they decided to resettle in Nigeria. I've been visiting them for the past month. I'm their only child."

"Were you on the plane from Lagos to Paris? I didn't see you at the airport."

"My plane left from Port Harcourt."

"Your parents must miss you. Why'd you stay when they left?"

"I decided not to follow them to Nigeria and stayed to work in the US. I value my independence. I'm a physiotherapist in a group practice in an office off Democracy Boulevard in Bethesda."

"I think I know the place."

Their food arrived.

"I'm a taxi driver," he continued. "Is your husband traveling back later?"

With some difficulty, she opened the bottle of wine she ordered. "I'm not married. I'd like to, but I haven't met the right man yet." She shrugged. "My parents are desperate for grandchildren, but without a husband, I haven't been able to give them any. This visit was very stressful, because they paraded a group of men during the visit they'd like me to marry, but I had no feelings for any of them." She paused to sip her wine.

"I'm surprised you aren't married. You're a beautiful woman. I'm married to a girl from my village. We met during my last visit."

"Thank you. I've decided I don't want to be married just to give my parents what they want. I have a good job and can support a child, so I'm thinking of artificial insemination. That way, I don't have to deal with men or think of divorce." She turned and looked him defiantly in the eye. He blinked and turned away, busying himself with eating. Her attitude was shocking. Who could believe a Nigerian woman would talk so casually about becoming a single mother? What was the world coming to? In his village, an unmarried pregnant girl was subjected to ridicule. She would be hounded and regarded as a free gift to every man. Many parents who faced such a situation would immediately arrange a secret abortion.

Others would send the girl away until the baby was born.

Looking at Ndidi, he wondered why a beautiful woman could nonchalantly say she'd like a child by artificial insemination and it didn't matter if she was married. As the food trays were removed and the cabin lights dimmed, he wanted to argue with her about the virtue of having a baby within a marriage, but he held his tongue. Her lack of reservation must be because she knew he was married. He felt drawn to her. Under normal circumstances, he would have grown to like her.

At Dulles, he asked for her business card and promised to call. On the way home from the airport, he thought of Ndidi, who, unlike Ejituru, would spare no expense to become a mother.

In a hurry to meet Cece and friends in Adams Morgan, Ejituru rushed from the building with her book bag on Friday of her second week of medical school and bumped into a doctor who was coming in from the parking lot.

"Ejituru!" the doctor exclaimed.

"Nduka? What are you doing here?" She was shaken.

"I should ask what you're doing here. The last time I heard, you were married to someone from your village and living somewhere in the US." He had filled out and added weight since they'd last met. When she knew him, he'd always taken good care of himself.

Her mind in turmoil at seeing her ex-boyfriend, she remembered how she often regretted never saying goodbye to him before she left to marry Ignatius. Nduka was the last person she expected to run into at Howard. Tongue-tied, she lowered her eyes to hide her tears.

"This is a shock," he said. "Can we sit outside on a bench and collect our thoughts?"

She agreed and sat beside him. "I'm a first-year medical student. What are you doing here? Are you visiting from Nigeria?"

"I'm completing my surgical residency and will go on to George Washington University to do a plastic surgery fellowship in the fall."

Ejituru glanced at her watch. "I have to go. I'm meeting a friend at a restaurant in Adams Morgan, and I'm late. I'm sure we'll run into each other again."

As she turned to leave, he said, "Ejituru, at least give me your phone number. We have unresolved issues."

They exchanged numbers.

Ejituru thought of Nduka all the way to meet Cece. *I can't believe it. Fancy running into him! How will I handle seeing him again? Why now?*

She thought of all the years she had wasted. If she continued at Nsukka, she would have finished her degree many years earlier. She assiduously avoided thinking of her Nigerian contemporaries or where they were in their chosen professions, preferring to put the past behind her.

I'm a first-year medical student. Many of them, like Nduka, will be finishing their residencies and moving on to something better.

When she finally met with Cece, she looked distraught and agitated, constantly gnawing at her lip.

"What's the matter?" Cece asked. "You look like you've seen a ghost." "I ran into my old boyfriend from Nsukka. He's a surgical resident at the hospital. Can you believe it? He's been here three years and I never ran into him before. I don't know if I can handle seeing him again. I've thought of him all these years and wondered what would've happened if I stayed at Nsukka and married him. He was very keen on me, and I broke his heart by leaving without saying goodbye."

"Tell me about him. What's his name?" "Nduka Oji."

"Oh, my husband knows him. I understand he's led a very tragic life, but nobody has been able to get him to open up. His previous residency was in Russia. He's repeating it here, like everyone else who studied abroad."

Feeling sad, Ejituru became quiet and unresponsive.

On the way home, she had trouble controlling her thoughts. *Is Nduka's wife in Washington with him? Am I setting myself up for a major disappointment?*

She couldn't keep calm. Stella, her Nsukka friend she was still in touch with, had mentioned that Nduka married a fellow student immediately after graduation.

As Ejituru approached her apartment, her cell phone rang. It was Nduka, wanting to know when and how they could meet. Not realizing Ignatius was landing at Dulles even as they spoke, Ejituru arranged to meet him the following day.

Ejituru sat in her apartment, wondering how to handle the situation with Nduka and having second thoughts. Should she keep the appointment or put it off?

As she set down the book she was trying to read and got up for a bathroom break, the door opened and Ignatius stood in the threshold. He carried one suitcase and had a bag slung across his shoulder.

After the initial shock, Ejituru took a deep breath. "I didn't know you'd be back today. How was home?"

Nkechi had already called to say she'd met Ignatius in Aba and reported her discussion with him.

"I saw your mother. She sent gifts." Ignatius tried very hard to be civil with her. He carried his suitcase into the bedroom and began pulling out the presents from her mother. One way of being in control, he decided, was to treat Ejituru as he would an acquaintance.

He carried the presents into the living room. "Here are the things your mother wanted me to give you."

"How is Uncle Okoro?"

"He's been discharged. He was on his way home when I left."

Ejituru busied herself with opening Nkechi's gifts of red pepper, crayfish, melon seed, and dried bitter leaf. "What a lot of things! We hardly need them. Esther and Mrs. Igwe will be happy to get some of them."

If you were the wife you're supposed to be, he thought, *we'd enjoy delicious soup made from those ingredients for a long time.* "Your mother wanted to send stockfish, but I told her I couldn't carry that, since the smell would linger on my clothes."

"Look at these!" Ejituru said, admiring the multicolored caftans. "I love them, but I can only wear them in the summer."

"She'll be pleased that you like them," he said politely. After a pause, he asked, "How's Esther?"

"She's good. She told me about a police raid in the complex last week, where some people were arrested."

"You need to be careful who you talk to in the complex. You don't want to be guilty by association."

The conversation dried up. Neither knew what to say. Questions about school, he decided, were out.

In the end, he confined himself to telling her about the political situation in Nigeria and the little news he had of village events. As far as he was concerned, nothing had changed in their lives.

The next day after classes, Ejituru met Nduka as arranged, and they left for his apartment where they could talk privately. They sat on his sofa bed in the beautifully furnished top-floor efficiency in Foggy Bottom, which overlooked the Kennedy Center.

"How is your mother?" Ejituru asked. "Is she still traveling to Dubai to buy jewelry?" His mother was a big trader plying between Dubai and Nigeria. His father had died during the Nigerian-Biafran War.

With a sad voice filled with emotion, he said, "She died during surgery. Because of the circumstances of her death, I decided to do a fellowship in plastic surgery. I was very angry with you when you left. You should have at least said goodbye." He handed her a can of Coke, while he drank beer and caught her up with news in his life.

After Ejituru left Nsukka for the US, he became distraught and angry. He devoted himself totally to his studies and avoided a social life until the year before graduation, when he began a relationship with a social science student. He didn't want to have anything to do with female medical students.

On graduation, he was one of the students selected for a surgical residency in Russia on a Soviet Union scholarship. He spent three years in Kiev at the premier medical institute there. On his return, he had a surgical practice at the University Teaching Hospital.

"What happened?" Ejituru asked. "She died on the operating table."

"My God, Nduka! Were you operating on her?"

"No. The surgeon was a friend of mine, the best surgeon in Enugu. I assisted. I'd like to think I'm a competent surgeon, which is why what happened to her was one of the most painful experiences of my life."

"What happened?"

"It was a senseless death. It was elective surgery to remove a keloid. She didn't need it, but she felt it was a nuisance and was very irritating. She was one of those people who scarred easily, and the scars would form a keloid. Her scars were large, and she had a lot of discomfort from them. "I suggested she have the keloid removed, after which she could undergo radiation on the spots to stop it from returning. She agreed. Unfortunately, the surgeon cut an artery and wasn't able to stop the bleeding. She died on the table. It was a terrible tragedy."

"I'm very sorry to hear this. I wonder why Stella never mentioned it to me."

"I lost touch with our group at Nsukka when I went to Russia for my surgical residency. When I returned, I held a position at the teaching hospital and never reconnected with my former classmates. By then, they'd gone their separate ways."

"Stella mentioned you married. Is your wife planning to join you at some point?"

His face clouded. "When I came back from Russia, I connected with an old girlfriend, someone I met during my last year of medical school. She was a teacher at one of the secondary schools in Enugu. I liked her a lot. My mother was happy I didn't marry a Russian girl, as many of our students in Russia did. The girl I married came from my area. We had a lot in common and moved in the same social group. I wish she were joining me, but unfortunately I killed her. That's the cross I have to bear."

He looked so sad and downcast, Ejituru moved closer and held his hands. "What do you mean you killed her?"

"She died in a car accident. I was driving." "What happened?"

"We were returning from my mother's funeral. It was raining very hard and it was dark. I didn't see the lorry coming toward us. When I realized what was happening, I swerved and crashed into a tree. She died instantly."

"Oh, my God, Nduka. I'm so sorry. I shouldn't have brought up such painful memories." She stroked his hands to calm him.

"For about a year, I couldn't do anything. That was partly why I decided to leave Nigeria and come to the US. I decided to intern in plastic surgery because it's a specialty that doesn't exist in Nigeria. First, I had to repeat my surgical internship. Howard gave me that opportunity. I'm glad I chose plastic surgery, because I can help many deformed people back home who can't currently receive assistance. If it were another specialty, I might not have been able to gain admission to the program at GWU.

"We've talked about me. Now tell me about yourself."

Ejituru felt reluctant to discuss her own life. "Tell me about your time in Kiev. How does interning there differ from here?"

He frowned. "Apart from the cold, which I had difficulty getting used to, I learned a lot during my internship. Foreign students spend three months of intense immersion in the language before beginning classes. I made friends easily, and my professors liked me and were very kind to me. They often commented on my surgical stitches. It seems my mother's insistence that I learn to mend my own clothes paid off. I was allowed to do rudimentary surgeries under supervision.

"At first I did nothing but study. To overcome my loneliness, I learned how to play the piano and attended many recitals and operas. I found I enjoy classical music and the opera. I actually missed it when I was back in Nigeria after the end of my residency. Here, I can indulge my passion for classical music and see some of the best operas during the season.

"When I went back to Nigeria and found out that pianos were expensive, I sought a church with an organ in Enugu and to assist the organist sometimes."

He lifted his gaze, which had been on the floor. "Now it's your turn. I know you married someone named Ignatius." He looked at her expectantly. "Are you still married? He must be a good person to be able to withstand the stresses of a medical education."

"We're still married, though we hardly see each other. He came back from Nigeria yesterday, where he visited his uncle in the hospital. Really, there's nothing to say about our marriage. In hindsight, I realize I married him under false pretenses. He was my ticket to America. I realized early in our marriage that I wanted to become a doctor, and I refused to compromise on that. Nothing will stop me from achieving my objective.

"Once I realized I couldn't depend on him to pay for my education, I lost whatever respect I had for him and started thinking of ways to achieve my goal. I was lucky in my first job. My boss at the time, a doctor, was very supportive and steered me toward the path that led to my being able to achieve my life goal.

"My husband wanted a family immediately. I wasn't willing to give up my dream for that. It's just a matter of time before he finds someone willing to provide him with a family, so that's that."

"Are you both thinking of divorce?"

"I am, but I have to find an opportune time and reason."

He nodded, pondering her words. "I often go to the concert hall at the Kennedy Center to hear great music. Perhaps you'd like to come with me sometime. I'm quite lonely."

"I have to tell you, Nduka, that I know nothing about classical music. I've done nothing since I got here except study and watch TV. Going to listen to classical music would be a new experience for me. I have to be careful. I don't want to give Ignatius cause for divorce, though at this stage, I really don't care."

She changed the subject. "Do you know Dr. Igwe? His wife, who is a great friend of mine, said he knows you."

"Yes. I've met him. He's an administrator at the hospital."

"She helped me bear the loneliness of my marriage, and she's been like a sister to me."

"Ejituru, I'd like to see more of you when you have the time. I've been lonely here, and I still have strong feelings for you, as you know."

"I too have strong feelings for you," she confessed, "but we can't allow that to be an issue with Ignatius. We'll have to see what develops."

Ignatius was home when Ejituru returned to their apartment, still feeling the glow from the time she spent with Nduka. Both were very polite with each other.

For the next few weeks, Ignatius thought of Ndidi and wanted to call her. Ejituru gave him the excuse he needed. Her absence from the apartment had become very noticeable. At first she called to say she was working late, but gradually she stopped informing him where she would be spending the night. Some evenings, he saw evidence of her presence during the day, but she didn't return home.

Ignatius was lonely and needed to connect with someone other than his coworkers, even if it were just on the phone. Going through the stack of cards he collected over the years, he found Ndidi's and called to see how she was.

"Have you found a donor?" he asked.

She laughed. "Not yet. I'm looking into it."

He arranged to meet her at the California Kitchen in the Montgomery Mall near her house. Ignatius often dropped clients off in that side of Bethesda, but he hadn't been in the mall. It was a new experience for him.

They met outside the restaurant.

"This is my first experience of a restaurant of this type," he said. "I often eat at fast-food places."

"I'm not surprised, given your type of work," she replied as they waited to be seated.

In the beginning, Ignatius and Ndidi were careful not to place any emphasis on their relationship, but they often met at her apartment on Westlake Drive in Bethesda, and he spoke of his past.

"I have to tell you my life in the US has been rough," he said one day. "I came here as a houseboy. Friends helped free me from what was virtual bondage."

"I've heard of such things, but I never actually met anyone who experienced it."

He told her of his relationship with Ayo and of meeting her again in Lagos after so long, explaining how the separation from Ayo affected him. At one point, he mentioned in passing that he once sold drugs. She listened without judging.

One day, he said, "I'm surprised to be telling you aspects of my life I would never dream of telling my wife. I lied to her about my professional qualifications. When I was ready to correct her assumption that I was an engineer, I couldn't do it, because she would've felt my objection to her pursuing her education was because I was jealous. On the contrary, I'm happy she persisted and is doing what she wants."

"I have to admit, Ignatius, that my life has been nothing like yours. Both my parents were educators. They have a boarding school in Owerri for Nigerian children whose parents are abroad and who wanted their children to be conscious of their Nigerian heritage. The curriculum is slanted toward the American school system, with the objective of getting the children either to an American-accredited high school diploma or the international baccalaureate. When my parents left, I was in the midst of my professional education at the time, and I decided I'd rather be in the US than Nigeria.

"My parents are US citizens, so they come to visit every year. I have dual citizenship, which is great given the high cost in time and money it would take to get a Nigerian visa whenever I wished to see them."

Later in his apartment, Ignatius berated himself for baring his soul to Ndidi without thinking of the consequences. *What do I know of her, except that I don't want her to have any illusions about me? I want her to want me for myself, not because of any preconceived ideas. What would her parents think if they found out she had anything to do with me? Am I setting myself up for another disappointment?*

Grateful to Ignatius for sharing his story with her, Ndidi continued seeing him. After they'd been visiting each other for six months, she allowed him to make love to her for the first time. It was a landmark in their relationship.

Ignatius was convinced Ndidi would regret her rash decision and would sever all further contact. It was unthinkable that a well-educated, highly paid Nigerian woman from a high-class family would want to have anything to do with him, a former drug dealer and a lowly cab driver. It didn't matter that he'd been straight for years and had a good income at his trade. That was why he had never confessed the truth to Ejituru.

With Ndidi, it was different. Older and more experienced, she didn't come from his village and clan. She was no longer under her parents' thumb, so she had the freedom to make her own decisions. If she were to decide not to see him again, he would understand. Ignatius decided to give her enough space to allow her time to make up her mind about their relationship.

Ndidi felt that events were moving too fast for her. She never had a long-term relationship with a Nigerian man, despite her parents' numerous attempts to hook her up with the sons of their acquaintances. Most of the men she went out with were Americans, but she never felt a strong emotional attachment to any. Friends said she was too picky. As years passed, she began to think she'd never meet anyone she could think of marrying. It didn't help that during her last visit home, her mother had harped on her wish for a grandchild, and her father sat down with her and enumerated the difficulties of growing old without a child.

"You're an only child," he said. "It wasn't our wish, but, as you know, everything happens for a reason. We tried to have more children, but it wasn't ordained. Ndidi, you're getting older, and you should be thinking of giving us a grandchild. We won't force you to marry someone you don't love, though I believe you can grow to love someone even if at the beginning of the relationship you don't have strong feelings for him. Look at all the successful arranged marriages here. Why don't you let us find you a good man who'll take care of you? We'd hoped by now we'd have a bunch of grandchildren running around."

What he didn't say was that he hoped for a successor.

Ignatius and Ndidi sat together, eating dinner on the small patio of the house overlooking Democracy Boulevard. Ndidi had grown up in that house and occupied it since her parents left for Nigeria.

"My mother's arriving next week," she said.

"For how long? I presume we can't see each other during that time." He looked glum. "I'm sure she would disapprove of our relationship."

Ndidi sensed his concern that her mother would disapprove because of the perceived class difference. "My parents' views have nothing to do with our relationship. I want you to meet her." She hoped she could reassure him that her parents' attitude wouldn't affect their relationship.

"When is she arriving? Perhaps I can pick her up at the airport. I presume it'll be Dulles."

Ndidi was touched. She felt guilty for not sharing the news with him after he had shared so much with her. He confessed he was thinking of filing for divorce, but his lawyer said he needed a good reason.

Ndidi felt her mother would assume Ignatius knew about her pregnancy and was abdicating his responsibility. The woman would stamp her foot and mutter, "Typical Nigerian man!" It was only right she tell Ignatius before her mother arrived.

As she put away dishes into the dishwasher in the kitchen, she turned to him. "Ignatius, I have something to tell you. It will soon be common knowledge, and I don't want to hurt you."

He braced himself for another rejection.

"You're already been hurt so much, so I want to tell you something. Please don't feel you have to stay with me because of what I'm about to say. The reason why my mother's coming so soon is because I'm pregnant and she wants to make sure I look after myself and the baby. Please don't feel you have to stay with me because of the baby. As I told you long ago, this is what I wanted. I don't need your financial support." Tears filled her eyes.

Ignatius was stunned. He knew she'd been feeling unwell lately, but he never expected her to become pregnant. He assumed she was using protection. He had to handle the situation carefully to avoid giving her any wrong impressions. He wanted the baby, but what if she didn't want him in her life now that she had what she wanted? If Ejituru learned he fathered a child with another woman, she would have the bargaining chip she needed to extract money from him. Nkechi would waste no time broadcasting the news to the village, either. He could imagine her telling her friends, "My poor child, married to a philanderer just like his father." Her friends would reply, "What else can you expect from that family?" His silence hung in the air. Ndidi, fearing he was upset, left the room.

He recovered himself and followed. Catching up to her, he held her hands. "Your news took me by surprise. I never expected this. I thought you wanted to tell me to stay away during your parents' visit. Ndidi, you can't imagine what you've given me. I've dreamed of having a family for such a long time.

"I'm my mother's child. I have no immediate brothers and sisters. I have half-brothers and half-sisters, some of whom I recently met, but I couldn't relate to them. I've longed for a family of my own for years.

I know I can't offer you marriage because I'm not divorced. Besides, I don't know how you feel about that. I can only say that the child you're carrying will be loved by me. I would like him or her to bear my name, but I know your parents won't allow that because we aren't married. Please, let us raise the child together. Perhaps there will be more. I promise you, our situation will change in due course, if . . . if you so desire." He broke down and began crying.

His long speech gave her a lot to think about. "Of course you'll be an important part of the child's life when he's born. I'm fairly certain my parents would insist on not using your surname because we aren't married, but that's all in the future. Please don't worry. You have too many things on your plate."

CHAPTER TWENTY-TWO

September of Ejituru's third year in medical school proved to be a busy period for Ignatius. There were several international conferences in Washington, and he had a busy schedule transporting international leaders to their various appointments. Assigned to the Nigerian delegates to the World Bank/International Monetary Fund meeting in Washington the second week in September, Ignatius drove in and out of Foggy Bottom during the day and late into the evening.

One day as he drove along New Hampshire Avenue on his way to pick up clients at a reception at the Kennedy Center, he thought he saw someone who looked like Ejituru walking with a young man he didn't recognize. He stopped to make absolutely sure, and saw them enter a nearby building. Making a note of the number, he drove on.

The next evening, after dropping off his clients at the IMF, he stopped at the four-unit building to see if he recognized any of the inhabitant's names. He planned to ring the bell and pose as a taxi driver answering a call, but from what he could ascertain, none of the occupants had a Nigerian name, or any name that might be associated with a black person. Thinking he'd been imagining things, he gave up on the idea.

On the last day of the conference, Ignatius picked up one of his clients outside the IMF building on Nineteenth Street NW. "We've been invited to a reception in Lanham," the man said. "Would it be possible to take us there? We know it's against the rules, so if you can't, perhaps you can get us a cab. This is our last chance to see our relative before flying back to Nigeria. The reception's being held at her house. She immigrated to the US to stay with her son, who's a big doctor at Howard University. We're really looking forward to the reception, because many people from our area have been invited. The party will start quite late, and we aren't sure when it'll end."

"I can take you in my cab after I've dropped off the limousine," Ignatius said. "How will you find your way back?"

"That should be easy. Our relative will arrange for a cab. It's no problem."

Driving on the Beltway toward Lanham in his cab, Ignatius eavesdropped on the conversation.

"I can't understand why the Igwes, living so far away, didn't arrange for a car to pick us up instead of making us pay for a cab," one person said. "This Lanham is too far from our hotel."

"Don't blame him," another replied. "I thought the limousine would take us, so I told him it wouldn't be necessary."

It dawned on Ignatius that he was taking them to Cece's house, and one of his clients was related to Cece's mother-in-law.

When he arrived at the house, Ignatius was ready to drive off when one of the men said, "Wait! I want to make sure a car will be available to take us back to our hotel. If not, we might have to ask you to come back for us."

As he waited, another car drove up and out stepped Ejituru, smartly dressed in a short skirt and patterned blouse tucked in at the waist, accompanied by a young man Ignatius didn't recognize at first.

Why hadn't he expected her to be at an event at Cece's? Who was the young man? Not wanting Ejituru to see him, Ignatius hunched down in the cab and stared at them with one eye. He realized it was the same young man he saw her walking hand-in-hand with on New Hampshire Avenue in Foggy Bottom.

Don't jump to conclusion, he told himself. *Things aren't always what they seem. There must be an explanation. Avoid making a scene in front of big shots from Nigeria.*

Talking to himself helped him curb his natural instinct to get out and confront Ejituru. Instead of waiting for his clients to be ready to leave, though, he drove off, furiously determined to investigate fully before confronting Ejituru.

Ejituru didn't return home that night, but she called to say she was at the hospital. He wondered if she would be expected to be on night call, since she was a third-year medical student, but he didn't want to know. If it wasn't true, it would be too painful to find out.

Ignatius needed to plan his next move carefully. First, he had to know who he'd seen her with. He knew where the man lived, so he decided during his time off he would drive up there, ring every bell, and ask for a man who wanted a cab.

Each evening for the following week, he drove to Foggy Bottom and followed through on his plan, hoping to learn the name of the individual he sought and maybe catch Ejituru with him. He was becoming a nuisance, though, and the tenants who answered threatened to call the police. For the next few weeks, he did nothing that would further his investigation. Busy at work and preoccupied with Ndidi, he bided his time. As it turned out, the answer was surprisingly easy.

One day as Ignatius left work, instead of visiting Ndidi, he drove to Foggy Bottom and saw Ejituru with the same man, walking back from the Kennedy Center. He waited until they were in the building. Since none of the four occupants had a Nigerian name, he decided to ring all the bells one after the other. On his second try, a young man with a Nigerian accent answered, giving his name and saying he hadn't called a cab.

"It must be someone else in this building," he told Ignatius.

Ignatius drove home with the man's name ringing in his head. He had to think how to handle the situation. Should he march up to the apartment, call his name, and accuse the man of cohabiting with his wife? Should he wait for Ejituru to come back home and confront her? She could always say he was mistaken, that she was visiting a friend and did nothing wrong. He needed to catch them in action before he could accuse him of anything.

Deciding to seek advice, Ignatius went to the taxi stand at the Sheraton Hotel to meet with Ojike. They drove to McDonald's on Connecticut Avenue NW to have lunch.

"My friend, what's eating you?" Ojike asked.

"I think Ejituru has a boyfriend. I've seen them together several times.

I need to be certain, so I can file for divorce, since Ndidi's pregnant."

"You mean the girl who wanted a child by artificial insemination?"

"Same girl, but I'm the father of the child. The baby's due soon. I want to be present in his life."

"I hope it's a boy and that she allows you to see him." Ojike bit into his Big Mac. "Tell me why you're suspicious of Ejituru."

Ignatius narrated the events of the last few months, how he saw Ejituru with a young man named Nduka several times. "He's a medical doctor living in Foggy Bottom. I've seen them together more than once."

"My friend, you can't conclude they've done anything bad. He might be her medical advisor."

"She goes to Howard University. If he's her advisor, couldn't he advise her there?"

"My friend, why are you so furious? It's not as if you didn't expect this. This gives you the reason you need to divorce her, unless you still harbor some hope she'll change and start caring for you. Do you want to continue the relationship? Make up your mind, my friend. You're talking like a man who wants to stay married to Ejituru. I thought you said you were past that and you have a strong relationship with Ndidi."

"She's still my wife, and I tried not to give her cause for divorce. You know how it is in this country. The man's always wrong. I don't want to have to pay alimony. I need to know if she's sleeping with him. That would give me the grounds I need to divorce her. Besides, I don't want people at home blaming me for the failure of my marriage. They'd say it was just like my father."

"Can you hire a private detective?"

"I don't want to. There must be a way I can catch them together. I want to look her in the eye and say, 'See? I know what you're doing. You think you're better than me, but you're just another village slut.'"

"Is this Ndidi willing to marry you?"

"I told you she isn't interested in marriage. If she were, she wouldn't have been paying attention to me. She knows I can't marry her since I'm married to Ejituru. We're just good friends and nothing more. She helps me overcome my loneliness." Sweating profusely, Ignatius wiped his face with his napkin.

"Didn't you say her parents visit every summer?"

"They're due to arrive soon. She's agreed that I meet them, which is a big surprise. She usually tries to compartmentalize different aspects of her life."

"She sounds like a high-class woman."

"She is. Her mother's the daughter of Iheba, the transport magnate. I'm sure you've heard of him. His lorries ply the routes between Lagos and the east. Although he had only a rudimentary education, he wanted his children to excel and take advantage of his ability to buy them the best possible education, so he sent them to private schools in Britain. He sent Miriam, Ndidi's mother, to an English public girls' school at the age of eleven. She went on to study mathematics at Oxford. She came to the United States for her graduate degree and met her husband here. Miriam, I'm told, is very conscious of her social standing and qualifications, and she looks down on those she considers her social inferiors. That's why I don't think Ndidi will marry me, even if I'm free."

Ojike patted Ignatius's back and stood. "Well, my friend, look on the bright side. Things will soon come to a head between you and Ejituru."

Ignatius felt unsettled. He needed to know what Ejituru was doing, but he bided his time. Whenever he ran into her in the apartment, he looked for any perceptible difference in her behavior. From all appearances, she was the same—still preoccupied with her studies, but less confrontational.

One evening when Ejituru didn't return or call, Ignatius drove to New Hampshire Avenue and rang Nduka's bell. Traffic was heavy at that time of night, and it took thirty minutes to drive from his apartment to Sixteenth and K Street. He passed the Hilton, where he saw some of his friends working late at the taxi stand, but he drove on. Winding around Washington Circle and heading toward New Hampshire Avenue, he noticed the Kennedy Center crowd just coming out. A few people looking for a cab at that late hour tried to hail him, but he didn't stop.

Parking outside Nduka's building, he considered his next move. He was rash to run over there, thinking Ejituru would be in the man's apartment. What if she wasn't? What if she was really at the hospital?

He called the hospital, asking for her, and was told she wasn't in, so she had to be with Nduka. *Where else could she be?* he wondered.

He got out of the cab and walked toward the building. He rang the bell he used previously when he flushed out the young man.

The same man answered with a sleepy voice. "Who is it?"

Without thinking, Ignatius said, "Nduka, let me in or I'll wake all your neighbors and tell them what kind of man you are."

Shaken, Nduka replied, "What do you want? Who are you? I'll call the police."

"Why don't you open the door and let me in? I'll tell you who I am. I'll keep banging on the door until you do."

Not wanting to cause a ruckus and fearing what his neighbors would say, Nduka opened the door.

Ignatius shoved past Nduka and didn't immediately see Ejituru. "I know you're in here!" he shouted.

He moved past the bed to the bathroom and threw open the door. Ejituru, in tears, was hiding inside. He lifted his hand to slap her, then, seeing her tear-streaked face, lowered it.

"You slut! This is your medical school? You won't get a penny from me!

Make sure you move all your things out of the apartment."

He stormed out in shock, ran down the stairs, and went out the front door to his cab. It was what he expected. He had proof of her infidelity. Finding her in another man's bed obliterated whatever respect he had left for her.

He sat in his car, collecting his thoughts, then drove like a madman to his apartment and lay on the bed fully clothed. The whole evening, his mind replayed his life with Ejituru. It flitted from the first time they met to their rocky relationship and his hope for the marriage. He saw the future he hoped for. Without a father figure in his own life, he hoped to be a constant presence for his own children.

In his mind, he saw the future he'd dreamed of. His children ran in and out of the house he built near Ejituru's clinic. Ejituru returned from work, and the family enjoyed their time together. The children happily jostled each other. Gradually, he realized his dream had no basis in reality. He'd been living a fictional life.

By morning, he was worn out and could hardly get out of bed. He never believed Ejituru would nonchalantly sleep with another man. He always took her at her word that her education preempted everything else. If anyone would stray, it would be him, and he couldn't imagine her doing the same.

He asked if he could honestly place all the blame on her. Hadn't he sought the company of another woman to assuage his loneliness? His involvement with Ndidi was Ejituru's fault, because she placed him in an untenable position by refusing to be a traditional wife. Why was he beating himself up? Would he forgive her if she asked?

Home people be damned, he thought. *I'll discuss my options with my lawyer and take it from there.*

Having reached that conclusion, he was at peace with himself.

In shock, Ejituru thought, *It wasn't supposed to happen this way.* She never dreamed Ignatius would discover her relationship with Nduka. What was Ignatius doing in that part of town? He operated in Prince George's County. Had he followed her? She began crying.

Nduka was at a loss for words. The intrusion happened so fast he couldn't think. He tried to comfort Ejituru. "I'm sorry, darling. You can't possibly return to the apartment tonight. We'll figure something out in the morning. You can always stay here. We'll look for a bigger apartment if you want."

"I can't imagine how he found out," she repeated several times.

Luckily, she was in the midst of a short break from classes and intended to spend the following day with Mrs. Igwe at Cece's house.

She and Nduka decided after that, she should move in with another female student who needed a roommate while they tried to resolve the situation with Ignatius.

Ejituru reflected on the events that led to Ignatius's discovery. Having gotten over her shock at meeting Nduka at Howard, she had seen him occasionally. Being busy with her studies didn't leave her much social time. He was her link to a happier time in her life. At the beginning of the spring semester when he transferred to George Washington University Medical School for his fellowship, she occasionally attended musical events with him.

At first it was mostly jazz, but Nduka introduced her to classical music. Her previous taste in music was confined to highlife, which she could dance to, and religious music. At first she found classical music with its various instruments discordant. Gradually, Nduka taught her to distinguish the various sounds and understand the beautiful music created by combining those sounds. He obviously enjoyed it. It gave him relief from the stress of the operating room.

As they sat together during performances, she timed her breathing to his, and it was as if they became one person. That was when she realized she'd fallen in love with him, something she had never experienced before. When she was with him, she felt as if she were drowning, and it frightened her. After being with him, she returned to her own apartment and wondered how she could stand living a double life.

Her studies were still important to her, and Nduka encouraged her to do well. Once she realized she was on love with him, no one else existed. She lived for the occasions when they were together. She tried to plan her time so she'd be free to see him whenever their schedules permitted. She knew she had to deal with her marriage, but she wanted to put that off until she graduated from medical school. She didn't want to pay for an apartment until absolutely necessary.

Once she decided to commit to Nduka, she stopped sharing a bed with Ignatius. She always came home late and slept on the sofa, saying she didn't want to disturb him because he was an early riser. It had been almost a year since they'd shared a bed. With Nduka, she couldn't help herself.

Throughout the day, she debated her next move. First, she needed an apartment. She couldn't move in with Nduka, given her present situation. She would seek Cece's advice. She wasn't a divorce lawyer, but she would know what to do.

She drove to the apartment, hoping Ignatius wasn't there, so she could pack her things and move out. Just as she brought down the last load of her belongings, she ran into Esther, who was returning from picking up her children from school.

"I haven't seen you for almost a year," Esther said. "Come up for coffee."

At first Ejituru was reluctant, but she realized she had nothing to lose, and the woman's prattle might lift her spirits.

After the usual talk of children and business, Esther asked, "It isn't my business, but I noticed a lot of your things in the car. Are you moving out? I saw a suitcase and your books in there."

Ejituru thought for a moment, then whispered, "I think so. It'll be easier living closer to the university." She felt Esther assessing her and wondering why she looked so disheveled.

"Does Ignatius know?"

"Oh, yes. It had to happen sometime. School's getting more intense, and I have to do well to get into a good residency program. We've begun our rotation. I'll probably opt for pediatric residency."

"Ejituru, I'm impressed. I was telling someone the other day that I never met a person as single-minded as you. You know exactly what you want, and nothing stops you. Your mother should be proud of you. Does Ignatius know where you're moving?"

"Oh, yes." Ejituru thought Ignatius would assume she was moving in with Nduka. "I'd better go. I have to meet my roommate for the keys."

"Come by anytime." "Of course."

Her meeting with Cece was different. Cece knew about Nduka and was very encouraging, urging Ejituru to file for divorce. However, Ejituru was unwilling to approach Ignatius because she worried about the repercussions back in Nigeria.

"I'm surprised it took two years for him to discover your involvement with someone else," Cece said, "given the number of nights you were out of the apartment. What do you intend to do? Will you move in with Nduka? If you need something temporary, you can stay with us. We have plenty of rooms."

"You live too far away, but thank you anyway. Nduka and I agreed it wouldn't be right for me to move in with him immediately. I'll share an apartment with a fellow student. It's only one year before I graduate."

"You should call Ignatius and find out what he plans."

"I can't. Judging by what he said last night, I doubt he'll talk to me. I want him to cool off. Perhaps he'll get in touch. I left him a note saying how sorry I was that he found out the way he did. I'll accept whatever he decides."

Ignatius filed for divorce, but didn't tell anyone but Ojike about it. The negotiations with Ejituru were in a critical stage, and he didn't want her finding out about Ndidi. He gave his uncle the full details, but forbade him from discussing it with Ejituru's family. He had already shared with his uncle the good news about the baby, after swearing him to secrecy on that too.

"I met Ejituru the other day to discuss her lawyer's new ploy to extract money from me," Ignatius told Ndidi when they met for a quick drink at Hamburger Hamlet on Old Georgetown Road. "I didn't tell you that I sued for divorce on grounds of adultery. I caught her with a man. She isn't contesting that, but she somehow found out about my past and is trying to use that to get me to agree to spousal support."

Surprised, Nduka said, "That can't be true. You have no children, and she has high income potential. Why is she doing that? From what you said, you've been very good to her."

"My lawyer put his foot down. I told her she can go to Nigeria and say whatever she likes about me. I understand she's traveling back home soon. She can trash my reputation as much as she likes."

Before the case was heard in court, Ejituru learned the secrets Ignatius had kept hidden from her, and she threatened to expose his lies to the people at home if he used infidelity as the grounds for their divorce. She often wondered about his lack of ambition throughout their marriage. As a trained engineer, he should have made more effort to find a job in his chosen field instead of wasting his time driving a cab. The answer came to her by chance as she sat on the lawn at Howard University between classes. The professor sitting beside her happened to be one of the men who, together with Ayo, helped Ignatius when he left the Unegbus' house.

"Hello, young lady. You're obviously Nigerian. What's your name, and what's your specialty, if I may ask?"

"Ejituru. I'm from the Cross River area, but we speak Ibo."

"A long time ago, I met a young man from your area named Ignatius. We lost touch with each other. I went to Boston for my graduate work. I understand he dropped out after two semesters because he couldn't cope with the stress of college life. Do you know him?"

"I'm married to him. He's doing quite well." That explained why Ignatius was so satisfied with his current career choice. Why had he kept that secret? Could it be he was ashamed he wasted so many years in the US without any qualifications?

She learned his other secret from Jesus House, a free medical clinic in Silver Spring where she volunteered. The clinic saw many uninsured Nigerians suffering from hepatitis and other diseases. Her immediate patient was an elderly man with many ailments that stemmed from drug use. He needed to be hospitalized, but without insurance, no hospital would accept him. The clinic offered only temporary relief from his pain.

In the course of the examination, the elderly man said, "I see your name is Ejituru Ngwu. I knew an Ignatius Ngwu some time ago. Is he related to you?"

"It's a common name in our area." She continued the examination, hoping the man would stop talking.

"We were both dealers. Unlike me, Ignatius cleaned up his act, and I hear he's now making good money as a taxi driver. He's married to a nice girl from the village."

In her confusion, she mumbled, "I think I know him."

She quickly finished the examination, her mind whirling. She lived with him for many years without knowing anything of his past. He concocted a new, sanitized biography to impress his relatives and build respect back home. Nigerians had a very low opinion of taxi drivers.

Could she use that information to her advantage? Her lawyer would know.

CHAPTER TWENTY-THREE

At last, I'm in a good place in life, Ignatius thought. *I have a son.* That his son didn't officially carry his name was disconcerting, but it was a mutually agreed-upon decision to humor Ndidi's parents' wish for a male child. Despite his fears, Ndidi's parents appeared to have accepted Ignatius as just one of their daughter's friends.

The divorce from Ejituru was still pending. Ignatius had to find the right time to ask her to withdraw her objection.

Sometimes he thought of his marriage and wondered how he had tolerated Ejituru's selfishness. He recalled their quarrel during her second year of medical school. He had come home tired and dejected after dealing with a difficult client he drove to Baltimore. She came home later, drenched from the rain. She had forgotten her umbrella, and her coat's hood was a poor substitute.

Discarding her coat, she'd said, "I can't do this anymore. We must relocate someplace nearer my school. I found an apartment close by."

Numb, he stared at her, wondering, *Couldn't she ask me first how my day was?*

Unconcerned by his silence, she removed her wet clothes and shoes. "I saw an apartment in Adams Morgan today we could sublet. It isn't very expensive, and it's near Howard. Moving there wouldn't affect your work, would it?"

He stared at her silently, wondering how she could assume his opinion wasn't necessary and he had no say in where they lived. She had to be the most selfish person he had ever met. How could she think he would consider moving? She decided what was the most convenient address, given his job. If he agreed, he wondered where else she'd want him to move later. She thought he would follow her wherever she decided to go because he was just a cab driver.

He told himself to remain calm and act in a way she didn't expect. In the past, their discussions predictably ended in his shouting at her and walking out because he was too angry and she had managed to push all his buttons. That time he would surprise her with his indifference.

Feeling her eyes on him, he knew she was watching him. Finally, he said, "I'm sorry, Ejituru, but I have no intention of moving. Even if I were to consider it, apartments in the DC area are very expensive, and I can't afford to spend more on rent right now. I have other things I want to use my money for."

"Like not helping with my tuition?" she retorted.

He had expected that answer and wondered what she'd do if he agreed to move with her to the District.

Ejituru already had an alternate plan in case he refused. She didn't want to continue living in the apartment, so she said, "There's a girl from Nigeria who's also a medical student, and she's looking for someone to share an apartment with. I was thinking that if you agree, I could do that. I could always come here on weekends. Would you prefer that? It's not my intention to hurt you in any way. It's just that it's very dangerous for me to come here in the dark during the winter months."

"Do that then, Ejituru, but you needn't feel obligated to come back to see me. It looks like we've reached the end of the road. When do you think you'll be finalizing your arrangement? I hope you don't expect me to pay part of your rent too."

Ejituru looked confused, and he chuckled. She hadn't expected the conversation to go that way. She'd been dreading his expected show of anger and another outburst from him all week. "Oh, no, Ignatius. My scholarship funds and the student loan cover most of my expenses. I hope you aren't annoyed with me. I don't want you to take this the wrong way. You agreed to my going to medical school, and you were happy for me, so why are you behaving like this? You appear indifferent to my well-being."

"Like what, Ejituru? You expected me to get annoyed and storm out of the apartment. You've trained me well. I passed all my examinations, and now I'm an obedient dog. Why are you surprised? You're free to do what you want, and to hell with what I want. Just let me know when you're moving in with your friend."

He left with a bag of laundry. In the end, she didn't move, and he never knew why.

Ejituru also recalled that quarrel. It had been four years of hard work, but she was finally about to become a doctor. Her relationship with Nduka had progressed further, and they planned to marry once her divorce was final. Glad she was finally graduating, he encouraged her to apply for residency at George Washington or Georgetown University. She had to pinch herself often to be sure she was the same woman who left Nigeria almost ten years earlier. She was accepted into the residency program in pediatrics at Georgetown University Hospital. Since her parents couldn't come to her graduation because of her father's heart condition, she would travel to Nigeria before the start of her residency. She looked forward to that visit.

Her thoughts turned again to Ignatius. They had lived apart for two years since that fateful day when he found her in Nduka's bathroom. He had served her with divorce papers, but they had to wait for a cooling-off period, during which they tried for reconciliation. Both parties never felt like it, but they had to obey the judge. She hadn't heard from him or seen him during that time. She visited Esther a few times, but both refrained from mentioning Ignatius.

As she sat in her sublet apartment, Ejituru reflected on his life. During her second year of medical school, she worked as a research assistant to one of the professors. She had very little time and was often absent from her apartment, particularly in winter.

At the end of the year, some of the students planned to visit Mexico City to volunteer in one of the slums, but she couldn't go because the professor reached a critical stage in his research and needed her help. Busy working the whole summer, she hardly noticed that Ignatius wasn't in the apartment when he should have been. The fact that she didn't notice his absence told her their marriage had reached a critical stage and something needed to be done. She hoped he would be the first to provide her with grounds for divorce. Unfortunately, she gave him a reason.

If the facts were known in the village, everyone would demand Ignatius forgive her. Then he would be a hero. How would her parents feel? Would they be required to return the dowry? She tried to ignore such thoughts. The rift with Ignatius had occurred during her third year in medical school. She never allowed personal problems to affect her studies and persevered. The move to her shared apartment was a good one because she no longer ran into Ignatius. She concentrated on her studies and her relationship with Nduka. She made friends with other students, too, which wouldn't have been possible if she stayed in the apartment, since she couldn't socialize with them outside the classroom.

She discovered the Smithsonian and the summer festivals around Washington. She acquired a taste for classical music and traveled once to Williamsburg with Nduka. She was happy. She felt guilty about Ignatius, but she realized that many of the new things she was experiencing wouldn't have been possible if she lived with him.

Every time during her final year when she thought of Ignatius, she couldn't help remembering what she'd learned of his past. She knew of many men with bogus, unsubstantiated degrees who returned from the US, either because they were deported or they were running from a crime they committed. They got away with it because no one came forward to discredit their claims. Unlike the claims of bogus doctors, Ignatius's claim to be an engineer did no harm, and she felt if it became public knowledge back home, it would ruin his reputation. She would keep his secret, though she would confide in Nkechi if she promised to keep the secret too.

Ejituru received a call from Ignatius, requesting they meet at a popular restaurant on Georgia Avenue at a time convenient to her, and she agreed to be there during happy hour. The request took her by surprise, since they hadn't spoken since their separation.

It would be their first meeting since she had left the apartment, and she didn't know what to expect. Nervous, she set out for the restaurant, trying to imagine various reasons for his call and to come up with answers for anything he said. Technically, since the divorce wasn't yet final, she was still his wife, so he could ask her to move back into the apartment now that she had graduated. She knew she couldn't do that, and that was one of the things she planned to discuss with her parents.

She wanted a separation that would allow them to be friends, considering that Ignatius was instrumental in helping her come to the US. True, he fought against her going to school, refused to pay for her studies, and opposed her moving out. She wondered if he had heard she planned to visit Nigeria and wanted her to agree on what to say about their situation. She decided not to talk badly about him in front of the families.

Ejituru blamed herself for not carrying out her decision to move out during the winter of her second year. If she had, Ignatius would never have learned about Nduka. She chose to attend Howard University because she felt bound to Ignatius. She had other advances from her fellow students, but she felt bound by her marriage vows.

Falling in love with Nduka was inevitable. It never crossed her mind that Ignatius might find out. She planned to travel to Nigeria upon graduation, and then, when she returned to the US, she would move out and ask for a divorce. Cece advised her she could file on grounds of incompatibility.

Ignatius said many times during their quarrels that he cared for her. She was the one who found it difficult to accept her spouse, even though they were married in an American court. She always felt he wouldn't let her down because he'd lose face at home. From his reaction, he seemed to be willing to release her without a fight. There was no turning back.

She still wondered why he had asked to meet with her.

In the restaurant, Ignatius and Ejituru exchanged greetings. "Would you like something to drink?" he asked.

She chose a Fanta, and they placed orders for appetizers. They talked about events in their town. It was very surreal, as if there was never any tension between them. Ejituru still wondered what was going on.

Toward the end of the meal, Ignatius said, "I understand you've found out things about me that you want to use to your advantage in the divorce."

"Being at Howard, it was inevitable I should meet your past friends." "How are they? Did they tell you about my involvement with drugs? I presume you know I didn't graduate from the university and I don't have an engineering degree. I said that to impress the home people. It impressed you enough to marry me.

"Do you plan to use those things to fight for spousal support? If so, I can assure you that you won't get anything from me. We don't have children together. Your future financial prospects are good, thanks to me. I caught you in an adulterous relationship. I understand you don't want your boyfriend's name mentioned in the divorce papers. You think telling people at home about my past will justify what you did? Ejituru, I don't care. Our divorce will happen, and you and your boyfriend are the guilty parties."

"In that case, there's nothing to discuss. I intend to make sure that people at home know what kind of person you are."

"Yes, tell your lawyer this new ploy won't work. Neither of us wants to remain married to the other. You have your boyfriend, and I want to be free to marry someone else. I came here today to tell you I don't hate you. We're practically related, and I want what's best for you. It's better that we part in peace than in anger. If you want to spread rumors about me, that's up to you. I don't owe anyone an explanation for the failure of our marriage, except to say we didn't get along and each of us deserves someone else. I want you to petition the court to finalize our divorce."

Distraught, she couldn't believe the cold way he presented his case. He was so different from the man she thought she knew, the one who once would have lashed out at her for citing his past. He seemed untroubled that she knew about his lies. She needed to think about her answer carefully. She would discuss it with Nduka and Cece.

Graduation was coming soon, so she would visit Nigeria to see her parents. Nduka was attending a medical conference in Nigeria, and they agreed to meet in Lagos and travel back to the States together.

Feeling dejected, Ejituru left the meeting and went to visit Esther, who, based on her past experiences, might have some insight into the situation. When she arrived, though, Ejituru found Esther in a very bad mood. One of the children was ill, and Esther had spent the whole day at a free clinic near the apartment. She tried to settle the child in bed, and Ejituru helped by distracting the other ones.

When they could finally talk, Ejituru said, "Ignatius and I met to discuss the terms of our divorce. He's refusing to pay spousal support, and his coverage of my medical insurance will stop once we divorce."

"How generous of him."

"What do you mean, Auntie? I have evidence that he lied to my family about his qualifications and his past indiscretions. Those should count for divorce. He needs to give me spousal support."

"Do you want me to tell you what I think? Your marriage has been dead a long time. You moved out of the home, but he didn't push you out. I know many men would have done so, given the lack of communication between you. You said many times you didn't love him, and it's obvious you married him as your passport to America. Why are you now trying to continue the charade?"

"He lied to me about his job. He told me he was a qualified engineer, but he never had that degree. He has always driven a taxi. He should have told me about his past."

"Did you ask him about his past?" "No."

"Then why are you trying to use that to extract money from him? He paid your fare here, got you a green card, and supported you while you were an undergraduate and for two years of medical school. If he had money, I feel certain he would have paid your tuition. He was extremely besotted with you, as everyone with eyes could see.

"My dear daughter, you have no leg to stand upon in this case. Don't prolong the inevitable. I know you have three years of residency before you start making good money, but even during residency you'll have enough to support yourself. Sign the papers and get on with your life without Ignatius. That's my view."

"What will the people at home say?" Ejituru asked angrily. "My father won't hear of a divorce. That's why I never initiated it." She stood. "I'm surprised to hear you blaming me for the breakup of the marriage. As far as all of you are concerned, Ignatius is an angel. I broke his heart and he deserves to be free of me. Why doesn't anyone consider my point of view? He broke his promise to my family that he would pay for me to complete my medical qualifications. He knew medicine was what I wanted to do with my life. He lied to us about his qualifications. If he told us he was a taxi driver, my parents would have thought twice before consenting to the marriage. Surely, those things count."

Esther ignored her complaints.

"What about his past with drugs? He's no different from his father. My mother would never have agreed to the marriage if she knew. Why is everyone trying to gloss over those important facts and blame me for the whole fiasco?" She gestured to emphasize her points.

Fuming, Esther shouted, "Look, Ejituru! Did you think of your father when you moved out? Have you told him you aren't living with Ignatius? You're behaving like a foolish girl. You're a doctor now and can support yourself. You don't need Ignatius, and to hell with what your father might say!

"I'm sorry, Ejituru, but I can't believe what I'm hearing. Grow up, child. Give Ignatius his freedom so he can enjoy his new friend and perhaps have a child. I saw him the other day. He looked so different from the way he was when you two were dueling every night. I remarked on it, and he said it was because he was in a very good place in his life now. He told me he has met someone recently he hopes to marry once he's free."

Ejituru felt chastised. Visiting Esther was a big mistake, since she would discuss everything with her clients, and each would have an opinion about how Ejituru acted.

When Ignatius first filed for divorce, Ejituru visited a free legal center in Adams Morgan to seek advice, but she was told that since

Ejituru had proof of her infidelity, she had very little grounds for fighting the divorce. The lawyer advised her ask forgiveness if she wanted to continue the marriage. Ejituru said she didn't love her husband. It was an arranged marriage, and she was trying to buy time before ending it.

Cece found an inexpensive lawyer who tried to arrange alimony for Ejituru, but Ignatius and his lawyer remained adamant that Ignatius wouldn't pay any, and that Ejituru's medical coverage would end once the divorce was permanent. Ejituru's lawyer didn't want a protracted divorce and urged her to negotiate for an amicable end, especially since Ignatius didn't seem to care about his reputation at home. Finally, Ejituru agreed. Citing other pressing matters, Ignatius refused to come to her graduation from medical school. That hurt more than Ejituru was willing to admit, especially since her mother couldn't make it either, given her father's ill health. She was grateful to Ignatius for keeping her on his health insurance. Most of her calls to him were about that.

Following the meeting with Ejituru, Ignatius went to Takoma Park to see Ojike so he could vent. He'd arranged the meeting with Ejituru, fully expecting her to jump at the prospect of freedom, and was blindsided by her insistence to fight for spousal support on the grounds that he deceived her about his past.

"How's the divorce going?" Ojike asked.

"My friend, you haven't heard the latest. I just came from a meeting with Ejituru. I thought she'd be anxious to get rid of me, but you know women have twisted ways of doing things. The first thing she said was that I deceived her into marrying me because I didn't tell her about my drug use and that I lied about my educational qualifications. She and her lawyer wanted to use that information to fight for spousal support."

"What?" Ojike shouted. "Are you serious?" He slapped his thighs and rolled his eyes. "I can't believe this."

"Yes. She said she'd met people from my past. If I refused to give her spousal support, she intended to broadcast the news in the village, since it would prove I'm worse than my father. Quite frankly, I don't know who's giving her legal advice."

"I don't think she has a leg to stand on. Didn't you tell me that you caught her in an adulterous situation? Look what you've done for her and how she treated you throughout the marriage. I told you she'd be trouble. None of our men would tolerate what she did to you. What will you do?" "I told my lawyer I won't pay for spousal support. I don't care about my reputation in the village. She's free to do whatever she likes. I've kept her on my health insurance all these years, and I offered to pay her legal fees. I feel I've been overly generous."

"Does she know about Ndidi's pregnancy?"

"I doubt it. I was afraid if she knew she'd countersue for divorce and it would drag on for a long time. At this stage, I don't care about Ejituru's intentions. We'll be divorced whether she likes it or not. I told my uncle about my problem with her and her moving out. It appears she said none of that to her mother."

"How'd the visit with Ndidi's parents go?"

"Her father was concerned about my lack of educational qualifications."

"I have an MBA and look where it got me. I'm also a taxi driver." They laughed.

"Do you intend to marry Ndidi?"

"I don't know if she'll marry me once I'm free. She once said she wanted a baby out of wedlock, and she'd never force the father to support her or the baby. The problem is, I've fallen in love with the baby and with her, so I want to marry her if she'll have me, but I'm not sure she'll agree. "I suspect her parents don't think I'm her social equal, but they've come to accept me as her friend. Toward the end of their stay, her father stopped harping on my lack of education and choice of profession, and he said he was happy Ndidi chose a Nigerian as the father of her son. She wants to baptize the child, but I'm not sure where. I'd prefer to wait until my divorce is final, so I can honestly plead my case over the surname, but on the other hand, maybe I should let it go."

Ojike nodded and waited for Ignatius to continue.

Ignatius paused. "You know they want to take the child to Nigeria with them? I didn't know what to say. I have no legal option. I allowed the argument to be between them and Ndidi. She was adamant in her refusal. In the end, I think she won that battle, because she's started looking for day care places. Her parents are going home soon."

"Once they leave, will you give up your apartment and move in with Ndidi? She lives in a beautiful part of Montgomery County."

"We haven't reached that stage yet. For the moment, I'll keep the apartment. I need my own space. I should have also mentioned I'm taking computer classes. Apparently, I have a knack for them. At first it was just for fun to take my mind off my problems with Ejituru, but I've been encouraged to work toward a diploma. It might be a career for me. I'm keeping that part of my life quiet for now."

"I'm glad for you, my friend. Let me know about the baptism. I'd like to be there. I still haven't met the mother. Come to think of it, I never met Ejituru either."

"You will when the time comes. I still have a long way to go. I intend to tell Ndidi only when I'm ready to propose."

The visit lifted Ignatius's spirits. The two friends were able to discuss many things about their work. They ended up going to eat in a nearby West Indian restaurant on Thayer Street in Silver Spring.

A visit to Ignatius's lawyer a few days later confirmed he could get the divorce on his own terms, though the timing depended on Ejituru's decision.

CHAPTER TWENTY-FOUR

Ejituru's plane landed in Port Harcourt early one June morning. A light rain fell, drenching passengers on their way to the passport-control area. Getting through that took an hour, and customs took longer. By the time Ejituru appeared, Nkechi had been waiting almost five hours.

When she saw her daughter, she burst into tears. "I haven't seen my daughter for almost ten years! *Ewoh!*"

The men and women around her, knowing she wept for joy, supported her.

"This is a joyful occasion," one said. "We rejoice with you."

They laughed and applauded.

When Ejituru emerged from the gate, she was welcomed by a happy throng. She hugged her mother and cried with her, sharing her joy.

Ejituru too felt overwhelmed at seeing her mother. She didn't expect her to travel the long distance from home to the airport, and planned to hire a taxi to take her to a relative's house in Aba, but Nkechi had hired a minibus to bring her to the airport and take both of them home.

The trip had left Ejituru exhausted. There had been a six-hour layover in Charles de Gaulle in Paris before the Nigerian flight departed, and she'd been traveling over twenty hours.

It took three hours to reach her parents' home. Her mother talked incessantly on the drive to her hometown, pointing out new developments they passed.

The preparations for Ejituru's return had begun three days earlier. Invitations were issued and women were hired to prepare the food. They'd been hard at work since early that morning.

As soon as the bus arrived, exuberant shouts rang out. *"Ayooh, blessed daughter! Ayooh!"*

Villagers welcomed Ejituru with dancing and joy.

When her father appeared, Ejituru was shocked by how gaunt he was. He could barely walk. One hand hung at his side, the result of a stroke he had suffered some time earlier. She wondered why her mother had organized such an elaborate welcome, given her father's illness, but when she whispered her concern to him, he whispered back, "My daughter deserves the best."

Everyone wanted to know why Ignatius hadn't accompanied her. They wanted to thank him for keeping his promise to continue her education. Speech after speech mentioned how grateful the families were to him. His uncle and his wife were among the celebrants, and Ejituru paid her respects to them when she saw them. The festivities lasted until late in the evening. Finally, most people went home, talking about how beautiful and grown-up Ejituru looked.

She was glad to be home. In recognition of her status, her parents prepared a room for her. It was the first time in that house that she didn't have to share a room with anyone. A mosquito net covered the bed so she could leave the windows open.

She awoke to familiar sounds—the cock crowing, goats bleating as chickens tried to chase them away, dogs barking to announce early morning visitors, houseboys making noise as they returned from the spring, villagers shouting greetings to each other on their way to and from the spring and farms, and her mother's voice giving instructions to helpers. She missed those sounds while in the US. They made her feel that was where she belonged.

As she lay in bed listening to the early morning noises, she thanked God she had lived long enough to experience them again. She looked around and saw the familiar chamber pot in the corner and kerosene lamp on the side table—an emergency measure in case of power failure. Geckos clung to the ceiling, with one chasing a fly. She was home.

She lingered in bed, thinking of her parents and marveling at how much her mother had accomplished in her absence. Ten years earlier, Nkechi had retired from teaching and started collecting her gratuity and her first pension. Nwakama wanted her to give him the gratuity to start some harebrained venture, but Nkechi resisted. Instead, she invested in several sewing machines, built a workroom in the small space behind her father's house, and began a sewing institute that eventually evolved into a workshop with several stations and a yard-goods store attached to it. Like everyone else, Ejituru thought her mother had made a big mistake, given that the community already had a profusion of seamstresses. Because the majority of the local people could barely afford three meals a day, Nkechi's friends felt she'd never be able to find customers.

Nkechi had proved all of them wrong. The clothes leaving her shop were of better quality than her competitors. She used her contacts to ensure that school principals sent their children to her for their uniforms. Many others tried to cut into her business, but none succeeded. To expand her scope, she employed male tailors and began providing uniforms required by several government offices. Her shop was the first to be approached when events required people to dress in uniform. It was a new cultural trend that began after Nigerian-Biafran War when the Ibos began emulating the Yoruba fashion of wearing uniforms at important events.

"Mama, how'd you get into the funeral business?" Ejituru asked later as she and her mother sat in the anteroom beside the kitchen shelling peanuts and eating a few. "You say it's very lucrative."

"My daughter." Nkechi clasped and unclasped her hands, biting her lips as if about to cry, "I have Kanu to thank. I wrote and told you of his death. That was what led me onto that path. When he died, the news was first broken to me. Together with the family members, we decided how his death should be handled so the family could better prepare for the funeral expenses of such an important person.

"We had the body quietly taken at night to a mortuary in Aba, and then launched a concerted effort of misinformation regarding his prolonged absence from home. We had particular difficulty deceiving his fellow chiefs and cronies, who were accustomed to his daily rounds of visits and presence at all important gatherings. We said, 'He went to Lagos to stay with his son,' or, 'He decided to go to Kano to visit his grandson and family,' or, 'He went to Aba for a checkup.' You know we don't announce deaths immediately."

Nkechi stopped to blow her nose and wipe it with the end of her wrapper before continuing. "Finally, when the family was ready, we delivered the news of his death in the traditional way to all the kinsmen and set the date for his funeral.

"I took it upon myself to prepare the place where he would be laid out for the viewing. First, I asked the wives to produce their best *joji* to be used as a wall covering, and the walls were beautiful. It was a sight! I made a bedsheet with eyelet white lace, which we also used as a dust cover on the mattress and the pleated skirt around the bed. We dressed him with the best *joji* from his wardrobe, a traditional shirt with leopard design and a cap. He looked so handsome as he lay in state.

"It rained the whole week before the funeral." She paused to wipe her eyes. "Everyone said even the heavens mourned the passing of such an important man. For several days I went back to the primary school where I was sent by my parents when I was five, and I stood at the fence to remember him."

Her eyes clouded as she thought about how every market day he had stood there and asked some passing girl to call her because he had a gift for her. It might be a small bag of native pears or some ground nuts, but she always appreciated the offer.

She remembered how her friends teased her. They thought he must have been the person her parents chose to marry her. No matter how much Nkechi denied it, saying she and Kanu were relatives and forbidden to marry by their culture, no one believed her. He was her first love, and in recent years they had discussed it together and agreed their love for each other transcended all other affections they had for others.

Nkechi collected herself. "My dear, you don't really want to hear this story. We should talk of other things."

"No, Mama, I want to hear about it. I'm sorry I missed his funeral."

"You know how it is here. The elders forbade the wives from bathing, and required them to sit on the bare floor opposite the bed throughout the ceremony, as was the custom. That upset me. I argued in the olden days, when there was no cold storage for storing a body, one could understand why the wives were required to watch the body for any sign of decay, since it would have had to be preserved by smoking. That's not the case anymore.

"I felt they should be allowed to sit on the floor in the next room where the family would be, as that would enable visitors to pay their respects to the deceased. To reinforce my argument, I said in the old days a chief of Kanu's stature would be buried with some of his wives and slaves, but that tradition was abandoned. As far as anyone knows, that didn't diminish the stature of the deceased chiefs."

"Did they agree?"

"They did, but we had another problem. They always come in pairs. The son who's a pastor in Aba fought against a traditional burial, arguing that Kanu had renounced the traditional gods and had fully accepted Christ as the only path to the true God. He felt that even though Kanu hadn't been baptized and was a non-practicing Christian, he should be accorded all the rites due to Christians. Busloads of the son's parishioners came for the funeral, and he insisted his father deserved to be accorded a Christian burial.

"Many family members poked holes in that line of reasoning, arguing that Kanu in his lifetime never refrained from participating in traditional rites, and he went to church only on special occasions like funerals or weddings, and then only when he had to. They argued he should be accorded the traditional burial rites as befitted a man of his stature.

"In the end, as a face-saving measure, it was agreed that during the wake that the minister of the church could perform prayers, after which the traditional burial rites would be carried out. The Aba choir would participate fully in the wake. That agreement was made to appease the son, whose church members came to the village to participate in the burial rites for their pastor's father. The choir sang and danced throughout the wake."

Nkechi chuckled. "My dear, I worried during the funeral that the rain would prevent people from attending as befitted such an important man. To everyone's joy, the sun came out, as if it too wanted to pay its respects. There was no more rain, and people sat outside during the wake and the following seven days of mourning. Kanu had a magnificent funeral. We had his corpse placed on a bier covered with leopard skin and carried in procession throughout the villages, with members of the Ekpe society dancing and singing. Everyone thought he looked as if he were merely sleeping, except for the traditional cap on his head, which he normally wouldn't have worn in bed.

"Twelve cows, along with several goats and chickens were slaughtered to feed the mourners. Everyone congratulated the family for giving Kanu a magnificent funeral, one befitting a chief of his stature, and they praised me for the room decorations and beautiful uniforms worn by the relatives of the deceased. As a result, I began getting requests to decorate parlors where the deceased would be placed for the wake."

A shrewd businesswoman, Nkechi tailored her charges according to what the families could afford.

"How'd you get into catering, Mama? I see so many big pots and basins stored in the back rooms."

"My dear child, I also have Kanu's funeral to thank for that. I've witnessed so many fights within families after any large family event that required serving food. Since the preparation and serving of food is left to volunteers, many snafus happen, with no one taking responsibility for the failure. Instead, they point fingers at each other for the resulting chaos. I didn't want that to happen at Kanu's funeral, so I persuaded the family to do away with volunteers. All the food preparation and cooking would be done by paid people.

"I hired good cooks and butchers from among the people who normally volunteered at such occasions who were very willing to serve, since they would be paid for their services. I assigned each one a task and made sure they all understood what was required. The result was a very orderly reception, with every attendee going away satisfied and the family members happy in their role as chief mourners. I found a niche and took advantage of it."

"Mama, I'm amazed. How did you keep track of everything?"

"I have a list of possible people I can use. At first I catered for small funerals where the guest list was about fifty. Suddenly I was being asked to provide food for weddings and other events. People say I'm overextended, but I don't think so. My cooks are only hired when I have an event. Recently, with funerals confined to Fridays and Saturdays, my cooks and waitresses have started regarding themselves as full-time employees. The beverage business is also an extension of my catering. My contacts with parents as a headmistress of a primary school have paid off. Many of the parents hold responsible positions, and I've been able to obtain the sole dealership for beer, Coca-Cola, and soft drinks in this area. My clients recognize that I'll give them wholesale prices for any drinks required during any occasion."

"I'm very impressed, Mama. Papa said that before his illness he was helping you with the beverage business. What do you do now?"

"I've hired a young man as manager."

An important client interrupted their discussion. Always busy, Nkechi delighted in showing off to her daughter. It was difficult to find private time to have a discussion with all the demands on Nkechi's time.

During Ejituru's absence from home, her maternal and paternal families had lost family members, so she had to make the rounds to pay her respects. Her saddest loss was Da Erimma, who had died three years earlier. Ejituru always believed Da Erimma would live forever, and she wept inconsolably when she went to her paternal compound and found one of Erimma's daughter occupying the house. She was led into the room where Da Erimma was buried, so she could visit and be comforted. Her stepbrothers, who had returned specifically to welcome her, accompanied Ejituru on all the visits to the families of those she lost.

On the fourth day of her return, Ejituru had an unexpected visitor. Her Nsukka University friend, Stella, visiting relatives in a nearby town, unexpectedly stopped by. Happy to see Stella, Ejituru invited her to the upstairs parlor to talk about their student days and share a meal of fried plantains, rice, and chicken stew.

Stella had married her professor boyfriend, despite the disapproval of her parents. "I won them over by producing a male child." She laughed. She completed her medical degree and was currently practicing in Enugu. "My husband has been invited to serve as a visiting professor at a university in Atlanta. I have a very lucrative practice, and I'm not sure I want to leave for the US. On the other hand, the children are very excited about the prospect. I need your advice. I'd like to do something while I'm in the US, but I don't want to repeat my residency just to practice there. What do you think?"

"Consider a course in public health administration to counteract the boredom, if you want. I wish you were coming to Washington so we could see each other."

"Congratulations on slugging through medical school there. When is your residency starting?"

"As soon as I get back."

"How is Ignatius? Are you happy? I tend to forget that not all marriages are like mine. I married someone I knew very well. I often wondered how it went with you. Your letters never dwelt on that aspect of your life." She looked at Ejituru expectantly.

Ejituru's face clouded. Staring at her hands, she considered how to answer. "Well, there's nothing really to say about it. We never agreed on anything. In fact, he's asked for a divorce."

"Oh, Ejituru! Are you sad? I know you used to be against divorce. I remember you talking about your parents and saying you always admired your mother for not separating from your father, despite his indiscretions."

Instead of answering immediately, Ejituru called the servant to remove the dishes. Turning to Stella, she said, "I'm still against divorce, but now I know there are circumstances that make it necessary. I have to say in retrospect that in this case I feel partly responsible. I was so determined to get my professional qualifications that I didn't care whose foot I stepped on. I didn't give my marriage a chance. Ignatius was set in his ways and had difficulty accepting what I wanted. I haven't yet had any discussion about the divorce with my father. His health is precarious, and I don't want to make it worse. My mother's busy. I keep trying to find a suitable time to talk with her. She knows my marriage hasn't worked out, but I haven't mentioned the divorce."

"Oh, I'm so sorry. I know how you agonized over getting married, and you only acquiesced because your father thought it was the best thing for you."

"I know. In hindsight, I shouldn't have listened, but what's done is done. Now I have to think of a way to tell my father I'm about to become a divorced woman. Let's talk about your children. I'm so proud of you. I think not having any grandchildren is something that preys on my father's mind. Since I've come home on holidays, he had asked me several times when I plan to start a family now that I've got my degree. He's worried my biological clock is ticking, and he can't understand why, having been married for several years, I have no child."

She stopped and debated whether to tell her more, then decided to go ahead. "Do you remember Nduka?"

"Of course. He was very fond of you at Nsukka. You were almost inseparable until Ignatius came around."

"Well, we're together again. My relationship with him precipitated the divorce."

"I knew he went abroad after his mother and wife died, but I didn't know he went to America."

"Honestly, I didn't set out to fall in love with him. It just happened. He kept me sane during my medical school years. Ignatius caught us in a compromising situation, and he filed for divorce. I actually planned to ask for a divorce once I finished medical school, but it happened during my third year."

"You never said anything in your letters."

"It wasn't the kind of thing I wanted to write. We're planning to get married once the divorce is final. I don't know how to approach this with my parents. I have to tell them before I return to the States. They're unaware of the whole drama, though I think Ignatius's uncle knows."

"Where is Nduka now?"

"He's completing his fellowship in plastic surgery. He's attending a conference in Lagos. We plan to meet there and travel back together."

"I don't envy you. All hell will break loose when you tell your parents. You should leave out Nduka. Simply say that ending the marriage was a mutual decision between you and Ignatius."

Ejituru had a nice visit with Stella, and she felt good after discussing what had been on her mind since she'd returned. She resolved to have a heart-to-heart talk with her mother and to discuss only the divorce with her father on the last day of her stay.

When Ejituru and her mother finally found time to sit down in Nkechi's bed to talk, Nkechi asked, "What's happening with Ignatius?"

Ejituru debated whether she should tell Nkechi about Ignatius's past, because Nkechi would use that to justify the separation. "You know, Mama, despite what everyone believes, Ignatius didn't pay for my education. I worked my butt off to pay for it."

"What they believe doesn't matter. The truth will come out one day, so forget about it."

"Mama, I've been living apart from him for two years. It wasn't my wish, but he wasn't willing to move closer to my college. I decided to study in the Washington area to give us time to jump start our relationship, even though I didn't love him." She paused to let her mother absorb the news.

Thinking she might as well tell her everything, she said, "I have a boyfriend now. He's a doctor, and he's the reason why I quickly agreed to divorce Ignatius. Ignatius found out about us."

"Don't let your father know about this. Do you hear me?" Distraught, Nkechi stood and began pacing. "Never let him know! I wonder whether Ignatius told his uncle. It will become gossip in all the villages. If anyone says anything about this, I'll threaten to take him to court. I'm sure if

Okoro knew, his wife would broadcast the information. Keep it under wraps, Ejituru. Let's say to anyone who asks that you left your marriage because Ignatius refused to pay for your education.

"What you told me explains the snide remark Okoro made during your reception when people congratulated him for Ignatius having kept his side of the bargain." Hyperventilating, Nkechi flapped her hands and constantly picked up and set down small objects in the room.

"Mama, please sit down. Listen to me. I was so intent on getting an education that I never really worked on our relationship. I felt I married for the wrong reasons. I didn't like him, and I wasn't physically attracted to him, and that made things difficult. Before he caught me, I was already thinking of a way to ask him for a divorce, but he beat me to it. Have you heard anything about this? Has his uncle or his uncle's wife ever said anything about our marriage to you?"

"I heard a rumor of a pregnancy, but since you never said anything, I assumed it was false. A lady from his uncle's compound let it slip that she overheard the cousin and her mother talking about the baby and wondering if it would resemble Ignatius. She thought they were discussing your child, so she asked me if you were expecting. I never mentioned it to anyone."

"I never heard that. Ignatius sued for divorce on the grounds of adultery. I agreed not to contest it. I know he wanted us to part as friends, but that won't happen. He hates me. I heard he met a Nigerian woman recently, and he wants to tell his uncle to visit the woman's parents as soon as possible to confirm his intent. He never said anything about a child."

"What do you want to do?"

"At first I wanted to contest the divorce to get spousal support, since I have too much education debt to pay off. It will take years. My lawyer advised that since I was at fault and left the conjugal home voluntarily without cause two years ago, Ignatius could argue I left him with no option. My lawyer got him to agree to pay the court fees, and it would be an amicable separation.

"At first I didn't want to do that. I wanted to fight on the grounds that he lied about his past, saying he had qualifications he never had, and he glossed over his drug involvement. I wanted to argue that he forced me, through his behavior, to seek the company of someone else. If we went to court, my lie would be exposed, because I only found out about his past after he sued for divorce.

"If I knew when he proposed that he was just like his father, I would never have married him. I would have to produce witnesses to verify when I found out, and I'm not sure any of the men who spoke to me would be willing to testify against him. I've been advised those aren't grounds for divorce, since I didn't try to learn more about his past before our marriage."

Quieting down, Nkechi said, "Oh, Ejituru, my child, I'm so sorry we forced you into this. The one thing that came out of your marriage is that you're now an American-trained doctor, praise be to God. We're so proud of you. You did what you needed to do to get what you wanted. Get rid of him and find an educated, worthy person. Socially, you aren't Ignatius's equal, which is why I opposed the marriage from the start. Who was the young man he found you with?"

"He's a fellow doctor. We'll get married when this situation calms down. Mama, I hate to tell Father about this. He'll be very disappointed." Nkechi dismissed the thought. "Just tell him that the marriage didn't work. As I foresaw, Nwakama never really benefitted from the marriage. Ugo Chuku never committed himself to any joint business venture with your father. He was very disappointed with Ugo Chuku, and has often complained about what a lousy in-law he is.

"If his family wants us to return the dowry, we can. His uncle must know you two have been living apart. I can't understand why he didn't discuss that with us. When Ignatius visited four years ago, he never bothered to come home. I was forced to see him in Aba. We met in his uncle's hospital room, because no one knew where he was staying. He was very pleasant, but he never said much about you except that you were well."

"That's because we're never able to discuss anything without shouting at each other. Will you talk with my father about this, or should I?"

Nkechi thought for a few moments. "I'd better discuss it with him first.

You can mention the separation on your last night here."

Ejituru turned to her mother. "Mama, I noticed that you've reconciled with Onyeka. When did that happen? You once said the two of you would never live under the same roof again."

"I've learned forgiveness since then. She almost broke my heart, but she learned her lesson. She saw how well I treated her children. One of them is an inspector at the Ministry of Works, and the last one is completing secondary school. Onyeka was living from hand to mouth because your father had no money to support her. It broke my heart. With my businesses taking off, I was persuaded to forgive her. She's quite a good cook, so she's my right-hand person in the catering business."

"I was brokenhearted when she left," Ejituru said. "She was my sister, and suddenly I lost her. It wasn't the same when she came to visit on market days. I'm glad she's a member of the family again. Her children will be happy."

"I don't know about that. The children never really regarded her as their mother, because she never did anything for them. I've been more of a mother to them than she has. When she lived at the farm they hardly saw her, except fleetingly on big market days."

"How does my father feel about it?"

"He's ill, as you can see. His arthritis is really bad. He can hardly move. The painkillers he's taking don't help, and the doctor said that the hospitals here aren't equipped to handle his situation. He needs several joints replaced. We've been to the orthopedic hospital in Enugu, but the wait is long. Besides, he's adamant he doesn't want anything artificial in his body, and he feels he'd contract diseases in the hospital. I think he's happy to know I have a family member helping me, given his situation. He sometimes helps with settling problems with my buyers."

"Mama, I wish I could help, but I still have three years of residency, after which I'll evaluate my position and decide whether to set up practice here or in the US. Now that you're such a busy woman, I hope you'll make time to visit me. When I get back, I'll try to find a small apartment of my own. Whenever you think you'd like to come, I can write the necessary letters required for a visa. As soon as I'm settled, I'll let you know and we can make plans."

"My child, that's like music to my ears. There's nothing I'd like more than to see where my child has been living for the past ten years. I'm glad you're free of Ignatius. I never wanted you to be in a bad marriage. Remember, we're all related in this place. Any prolonged court case between you two, and any reason you may give for fighting the divorce, would have serious repercussions here. Please find a way to settle the problem quietly. Now that I'm well established, if you need my help, I'm in a position to do so."

Time passed quickly, with Ejituru visiting her relatives and enjoying the company of her half-siblings whenever they were around. Most days, she spent time with her father or in the drawing room at the back of the house, talking about her wonderful life in the US or accompanying her mother on errands. Most nights, she was exhausted by the constant visitors and the questions about Ignatius and why he didn't come with her.

"Can you try to persuade him to change his mind and help his halfsiblings go to America to study?" Ugo Chuku asked when Ejituru saw him. "Perhaps you too can help, since you're a doctor now. After all, you're a member of our family. I was disappointed that when he visited he never bothered to see me."

Ejituru said diplomatically, "I still have three more years of study. Ignatius has too many competing demands and is presently in no position to help. I'll definitely talk to him and try to get him to contact you."

"I hear he's building several houses in Aba. I'm surprised he didn't consult me before embarking on such a big venture. Okoro has poisoned his mind against me. Tell Ignatius I feel slighted being overlooked by my American-educated son. He allowed other people to tell me his business. What kind of son is that?"

Ejituru didn't know what to say. That was the first she heard of the venture. "Perhaps he feels you have too much on your own plate and he was trying to spare you. Please, Father, forgive him. I'm sure he has very good reasons for his actions."

When she left Ugo Chuku's mansion, Ejituru felt like an imposter. Ignatius never confided in her about his affairs, and there she was defending his actions to his father.

Ejituru enjoyed her stay at home, but she looked forward to returning to the US and completing her residency. She needed to find an apartment in Georgetown, and for the first time since she arrived in the US, she would live on her own. She had advertised for a one-bedroom apartment in the local shopper, and she wondered if she'd gotten any bites. She and Nduka agreed they'd live apart until their marriage. He wanted to do everything right to negotiate her bride price and marry her in accordance with the customs of her people. She hoped when she arrived home her lawyer's letter would be waiting, telling her the divorce was final. Nkechi couldn't pay her education debt.

All those things weighed heavily on her as she and Nduka boarded the plane for Dulles. When they landed, she turned to him and said, "The first thing I'll do when I get home is sign the divorce papers."

"Now we can make plans for our future together," he replied.

CHAPTER TWENTY-FIVE

It was a very difficult year for Ignatius. A close friend and confidant died at work from a heart attack, and Ignatius had to deliver the news to his family. He also ended up having to arrange the transport of the body to Ghana. Around the same time, a fellow cab driver was shot and killed during a robbery in southeast Washington. What made his death so poignant was that the man had started a lucrative business in Nigeria processing agro products for the US market. To keep his US citizenship current, he had visited every summer and drove his taxi for several months, returning to his Nigerian life in October. Ignatius knew that the five-months' stint as a cab driver provided his friend with the capital to extend his agricultural landholdings and to connect with US clients.

The deaths brought up Ignatius's latent wish to return to Nigeria while he was still healthy. He didn't want to return in a box. The arrival of his divorce papers lifted his spirits.

His relationship with Ndidi was progressing. With his divorce final, there was nothing to stop him from proposing. Her possible response, however, was a mystery. She had stated emphatically many times that she wouldn't have to depend on a man for financial security for herself or her children. He liked being with her and the child, and waited for an opportune moment to persuade her to change her mind.

The time he spent with Ndidi's parents during their visit was good, and he felt comfortable discussing his real-estate ventures with Ben. His uncle had just finished building a duplex, and had managed to rent both sides to an expatriate firm. Ignatius was proud of that. Ben was pleased that Ignatius chose to build in the city, not in his hometown, as that would facilitate a future sale of the property if he so wished. He advised Ignatius to make sure the land lease and the properties were in his name, not his uncle's. He added he should make sure that several years' rent was paid in advance, and the contract should include payment for repairs.

Ignatius mentioned he was thinking of developing a small strip mall on another piece of property he owned. It was on the Aba Umuahia Road, which he thought was a good location. Ben, agreeing that was a good idea, promised to look at the land when he visited relatives in Aba.

As the parents prepared to leave for Nigeria, they suggested Ndidi and the baby should accompany them. They argued the baby would have better care in Nigeria, whereas with Ndidi working, he was left with strangers during the day. Furthermore, that would free Ndidi from worrying about the baby when she was at work. Ignatius could sympathize with that reasoning. In Nigeria, the baby would have a full-time nurse, who would most likely be a family member, under the doting eyes of the grandparents.

Ndidi wouldn't hear of it. She interpreted the request as yet another way for her parents to control her life. They wanted to force her to return to Nigeria earlier than planned, since she couldn't bear to be apart from her son for long. Her parents knew their only way to achieve their wish was through the baby.

Ndidi argued that the baby needed to know his father, and that couldn't happen if the baby was in Nigeria. He would grow up thinking Ben was his father. Ndidi's not being married didn't help. The last week of her parents' visit was tense, and it only abated when Ignatius came to visit.

At some point during the visit, Ignatius felt he had to discuss his marital situation with Ben. He didn't try to paint himself as the victim. He said that he and Ejituru married for the wrong reasons. Ignatius wanted a family, so he chose a village girl to keep his promise to his mother, and Ejituru had fit the requirements.

Ejituru agreed to marry him because he would provide a means for her to come to America and get a better education than in Nigeria. He admitted to Ben that Ejituru had qualified as a doctor. There was no love between them, and that was primarily why the marriage failed. He explained that he had finally caught her in an adulterous relationship and filed for divorce, which would soon be finalized.

During the discussion, Ignatius became aware that Ben, though he never said it, didn't feel Ignatius was the right husband for his only daughter. He saw Ignatius as her educational inferior. No matter how he tried, Ben couldn't shed himself of the Nigerian middle-class mentality that anyone without a university degree was on the lowest rung of society. The exception, of course, was self-made businessmen, but even they were often looked down upon.

In private, Ben told his wife that Ndidi could do better than Ignatius. "I don't understand what she sees in him," he muttered under his breath.

To Ndidi, Ben said, "Remember, this man isn't your social equal. We'll help you find someone who'll accept the baby."

Unaware of that behind-the-scenes drama, Ignatius believed he won Ben over by the time he and his wife returned to Nigeria. Ndidi was happy that Ignatius was on good terms with her father, who gave him valuable advice concerning his Nigeria investments.

Her mother was another story. Ndidi had said recently, "I thought she was beginning to like you when she was here, but it looks as if her opinion of you changed since she went back to Nigeria and learned things about your father. She wants me to stop having anything to do with you. I told her you're the father of my son and I'll do what I think is good for the baby."

"What brought this about?" Ignatius asked.

"Even though she loves her grandson and enjoys showing her friends and family photographs of him, she glosses over my situation as an unmarried woman whenever my name comes up in discussions with her friends. She's slightly ashamed of my unmarried status, and is afraid that to rectify it I might make the wrong decision."

Without the final divorce papers, Ignatius couldn't offer her an answer. Given such strong views, he could only hope that at the appropriate time Ndidi's views on marriage would soften.

She arranged a small party for their son on the weekend of his birthday. He had already had a birthday party at the nursery school, with Ndidi taking time off work to be present. She invited Ojike and his wife and children to the party on the weekend, so she could meet them for the first time.

Ignatius came home early to help Ndidi with the preparation. When her parents called to wish their grandson happy birthday, he was able to speak with Ben. He hadn't revisited the mall site at Umuahia and was unaware of the progress made there, so Ignatius brought him up to date, adding that he planned to visit home next Easter.

Ojike and his wife were impressed with Ndidi. Taking Ignatius aside, Ojike asked, "My friend, why haven't you proposed to her? Why are you holding out? The divorce is final, isn't it?"

"I'm thinking about it, but it's not that straightforward." "Don't think, Oga. Act."

His wife agreed.

A month after his son's birthday, Ignatius proposed. Coincidentally, it was the twelfth anniversary of his marriage to Ejituru. In the intervening years he had aged, and with age came wisdom. He knew what he wanted, but he feared rejection.

"Ndidi, sit down. Hold my hand. I have something to tell you."

They sat on the sofa, with the baby sleeping in the other room.

"I've been divorced for some time, and I want to know if you would consider marrying me."

The question hung in the air. Taken aback, she felt as if Ignatius had read her mind. For some time, she knew the divorce was final, but when he didn't mention it, she didn't pry. Her views on marriage and parenthood had changed, and she felt that children would be better cared for in a two-parent household. Being older, Ignatius would make a good father. He had demonstrated that by the way he fussed over the child and catered to his every whim whenever he saw him. She was surprised it took him so long to tell her of his divorce, which was common knowledge. She concluded that he was afraid to commit himself totally because of the failure of his first marriage to a Nigerian girl. She'd been contemplating asking him outright just what his plans were.

She was under constant pressure to raise her child in Nigeria, and with a second child on the way, that pressure would intensify. Her father often asked about the current status of Ignatius's divorce, implying he'd like to see her situation stabilized. Her mother, once she took a dislike to something, had great difficulty changing her mind. Ndidi realized that Miriam's upbringing and her social consciousness had a lot to do with her initial dislike of Ignatius. Though Miriam had married a man from the lower middle class, at least he had a doctorate. He was able to hold several important posts, culminating in a high position in the Montgomery County government, which made him her social equal. Ndidi didn't quite know how to explain Ignatius's lack of ambition and his occupational status to her relatives, whose sons and daughters married well and maintained their place in society.

Ben, however, was impressed that Ignatius had pulled himself up through his own work and never depended on Ugo Chuku for financial support. He often said that Ignatius reminded him of himself. Ben had come to the US with nothing, taking a menial job in a Midwest town. He put himself through school and managed to get an assistantship that helped pay for his graduate studies. He often said that the difference between him and Ignatius was that he had met a good Christian family in that town who gave him moral support and pushed him to succeed, whereas Ignatius lacked that support. He often told his wife they should be grateful their only child chose a man who was determined to succeed despite the hardships in his past. He never failed to remind his wife that not everyone came from a wealthy family like her father, who was able to support his daughter in the US. He urged her to temper her views about Ignatius.

Aware of the constant argument between her parents regarding her choice of a boyfriend, Ndidi hadn't told them she was expecting a second child. Her mother wouldn't approve if she accepted Ignatius, but Ndidi felt she had to decide what was best for her and her children. She was having trouble in her role as a single mother, despite the front she presented to her parents.

She hesitated and pretended she hadn't heard Ignatius's question.

"Ndidi, did you hear me?" he asked. "Please give me a reply." He felt increasingly desperate.

"Are you sure you want to do this? You don't have to. I told you from the start you needn't feel obligated to marry me because of the child."

"Ndidi, I've been afraid to ask you ever since the divorce came through because I was afraid of your answer. I'm not asking you to marry me because of the child, but because I feel comfortable with you and value your advice. More importantly, I hate living apart from you, because I love you. I know you're financially secure and can afford to care for our child on your own, but I was hoping you loved me enough to agree to share your life with me. I know you're more educated than I am, but I'm hoping that won't be an impediment." He paused to catch his breath. "I'm sure that doesn't make any sense."

"Ignatius, I've wanted to marry you for some time, but I knew you weren't free, or I would have proposed myself. You're the first Nigerian man I can honestly say I'd feel comfortable living with. Most of them are either arrogant or pretentious."

Relieved, he blurted that he wanted them to get married in Nigeria as soon as possible. He planned to visit his home at Easter, and hoped she and their son would agree to accompany him.

"Hold on," she said. "We need to think about this. There's something else happening that you don't know. Besides, we have to consult my parents about the timing."

"What is it? Has someone else proposed to you?" he teased.

"No! If someone else had, would I have just agreed to marry you? No. I'm pregnant. The baby is due in late summer." "You've been hiding this from me?"

"I just found out last week. I would have told you in good time."

He held her tightly. "I'm so happy to hear of this second blessing. You know how much I've always wanted a large family." He released her and held her at arm's length, seeing a beautiful Ibo girl who was giving him the thing he most wanted—a family to call his own. "Have you told your parents? When can we get married? I'd really like to be married before the baby comes."

"I haven't said anything to my parents. You know how they are. My mother will want to jump onto a plane and come immediately. I've been putting off telling them as long as I can. Now that I have more than my pregnancy to tell them, I have an incentive to call them."

However, Ignatius spoke to Ben first, formally asking his permission to marry his daughter. "I waited to ask because I wanted to be single again first. I know you're both disappointed that I lack the educational qualifications you expected from a future son-in-law, but I feel that in my current occupation I could support your daughter even if she wasn't working. I hope, if you agree, that my uncle can visit you, as required by custom, to formally ask for your daughter's hand in marriage."

It was a long speech. When Miriam got on the phone to talk to her daughter, Ndidi restricted the conversation to the impending birth. Miriam immediately asked if she should come to the States immediately to help with the grandson so Ndidi could rest, as befitted an expectant mother.

When Ben got back on the line, they discussed the proposed wedding. Ndidi and Ignatius planned to get married in Nigeria at Easter. Would the timing conflict with Ben and Miriam's annual visit to the US? Her parents felt the Nigerian wedding should be delayed until the baby was born and they returned home from their visit.

Unhappy with that idea, Ndidi and Ignatius agreed to get married in the Rockville courthouse as soon as possible.

CHAPTER TWENTY-SIX

When a rental apartment in the Palisades neighborhood in Northwest DC came available, Ejituru went to see it. Mrs. Fischer, the prospective landlord, said she had lived in Lagos for two years and made some Ibo friends. She wanted to meet Ejituru and hoped she would like the apartment.

Ejituru had never been in Georgetown before, except for her interview. She'd never been inside an American home in her life, and she didn't know what to expect. She heard stories of dogs being set on black people who ventured into the residential areas of Georgetown, so she was frightened.

For the last ten years, her life had centered around New Hampshire Avenue in Langley Park, Georgia Avenue NW, and more recently Foggy Bottom. Her shared apartment was near Howard University, only two blocks from Georgia Avenue NW. She visited the Smithsonian and saw the White House and the Capitol, but she'd never been in a residential area in northwest Washington. After her interview that one time, she strolled along Georgetown's commercial area, marveling at all the different shops, but she never felt at ease. She was glad to return to her apartment. Standing outside the house in the Palisades, she felt especially uncomfortable. The whole situation was beyond her experience, and she wondered what her prospective landlord looked like. As she rang the doorbell, she tried to calm herself.

A tall, slim, gray-haired woman of indeterminate age answered the door of the large, three-story house. Mrs. Fischer, a recent widow, looked flustered. She'd just had a difficult call from her lawyer, and she tried to compose herself as she ushered Ejituru into the living room.

"What would you like to drink?" she asked.

"I had a drink before coming here," Ejituru said nervously.

"Nonsense. Have tea with me."

"Madam, I'd rather have Coca-Cola without ice."

As Mrs. Fischer left to fetch the drinks, Ejituru looked around the living room. She recognized several artifacts from Nigeria scattered throughout and paintings by Nigerian artists on the walls, including one by Ben Enwonwu. In addition, she saw the Akwete cloth covering the throw pillows. Amazed at how beautiful the room looked, she wondered what the rest of the house was like.

When Mrs. Fischer returned with their drinks, Ejituru said, "Your house is very beautiful."

"Thank you. My late husband worked in many African countries with USAID, and we were privileged to be posted twice to Nigeria. He recently passed away. With our children all living their separate lives, the house has become too big for me. Until I can decide what to do with my life, I wanted to share the house with someone nice.

"A friend who works at the Georgetown hospital mentioned the billboard at the university as a possible place to look for a student who needs housing. I went there and found your listing. Since I've lived in Nigeria and have many Ibo friends there, I recognized your name and felt you might be the one person with whom I could share my house."

"How many children do you have, Mrs. Fischer?"

"Two sons and two daughters, all married. The pictures of the children you see over there are my grandchildren. Unfortunately, I don't see as much of them as I should, because none live in the Washington area. Two are in California and one is in Vermont. The closest child lives in New York. So you see, I'm all alone."

"Do they visit you?"

"Oh, yes. We see each other at Thanksgiving and on the holidays. I sometimes visit them, and they also try to visit me. I wondered if your family was affected by the Nigerian-Biafran War."

"I don't really know. I was too young."

"What do your parents do?"

"My mother is the retired principal of a primary school. My father is a councilor to the chief in our area." She felt that sounded better than saying her father was unemployed and lived on handouts from his wife.

"Do you have any brothers or sisters?"

"I'm the only child of my mother, but my father has several other children. My brothers are all younger than me."

"Have you returned home since you came to the US?"

"I've just returned from a visit. I went there after graduating from medical school."

"How'd you find the place?"

"Nigeria has changed a lot. I'm not sure if it's for the better."

Mrs. Fischer offered to give Ejituru a tour of the house, adding she was particularly proud of her Nigerian artifacts and happy that her husband's job allowed her to indulge her love of them.

"We had two tours in Nigeria," she explained. "The first was with Michigan State University in Enugu before the war. That's how I became acquainted with the Akwete weavers. Our second tour was with USAID in Lagos shortly after the war. I was very happy in Nigeria."

She spoke enthusiastically about her drivers, her yard men, and her cook. She had made several trips to Oshogbo, and she was particularly pleased with the paintings she bought there.

"However," she said when they stood before the Ben Enwonwu painting, "this is my proudest possession. I realize he wasn't part of the Oshogbo group, but as you know, he was an important Nigerian artist, better known for his sculpture. I'm happy to have this painting."

"I admired it when I noticed it earlier."

"Do you know anything about the Oshogbo group founded by Susan Wagner?"

"Except for stopping at the airport on my way to the US, I haven't been anywhere in Nigeria, except for the east. Until I came here, I didn't know anyone from the west or north. I've heard of the Oshogbo group of artists, but I know of Enwonwu only because he was mentioned in the papers. By studying in the US, I missed the opportunity of being posted to a different state for my youth service."

"Why'd you choose to study here?"

She wondered what the woman would think if she said she came here to marry someone she only briefly met in Nigeria. "It's a long story. A relative from home was kind enough to sponsor me to study in the US." She knew she'd tell Mrs. Fischer the whole story someday.

"Let me show you the room I'm renting out."

It was larger than her apartment with Ignatius, and to Ejituru's surprise, the furnished bed/sitting room had a kitchen and bathroom to one side. The bedcover was made from Ashoke cloth. Though small, the kitchen had a refrigerator, and the bathroom contained a small washer and dryer.

"You've thought of everything," Ejituru said.

"Yes, I wanted my tenant to live independent of me. I knew how hard it would be to find a self-service laundromat around here, so I thought I'd make it easier for whoever rented the place by equipping it properly, especially since the rent isn't cheap. The rent includes utilities, except for the phone, because I couldn't get separate meters for the basement."

Ejituru hadn't expected the rent to be quite that high, but considering she didn't have to pay for utilities, she felt the amount was fair. She liked the apartment, but she had one small concern. "I hope you won't object to my boyfriend visiting me sometimes."

"He won't stay here during the entire period of your residency?"

"Of course not! He's a very busy doctor. He'll come here only when we both have time."

"That would be fine, provided you aren't too rowdy and he doesn't stay overnight. The apartment has its own outside door, so his visits won't be a problem."

Although the house was four blocks from the university, Ejituru hated walking, and wondered where she could park her car. She had grown fond of that little car, her one prized possession.

"This area is well served by public transportation," Mrs. Fischer said, "and you might want to use that. However, there is ample parking in the alley behind the house. Parking shouldn't be a problem."

They agreed on the terms, and Ejituru happily used her mother's gift to pay for two months' rent in advance, as required. Living among predominantly white Americans would be a new experience, one Ejituru was looking forward to.

As Thanksgiving approached during her first year of residency, Ejituru's mind turned to her relationship with Nduka. He'd finish his fellowship soon and was already looking for a permanent position. He doubted he would stay in the Washington area.

Every time she thought of Ignatius, the memory of her perceived injustice flooded her mind. The divorce was finalized and she had her copy in hand. With the move to the Palisades area and the demands of her residency, she hadn't been in touch with her ex-roommate who called her to come pick up her mail. She was so busy she hadn't contacted Esther since she'd returned from Nigeria, though she managed to stay in touch with Cece and visited her several times with Nduka. Cece totally accepted them as a couple.

Ejituru's thoughts turned to Dr. Washington, who was instrumental in Ejituru's completing her studies. She hadn't seen the woman in months. When she'd attended medical school at Howard, she saw Dr. Washington often, either in the corridors or the cafeteria, and she was always very pleasant. On her advice, Ejituru applied for a residency in Georgetown as a way to widen her experience.

On impulse, Ejituru called Dr. Washington and was surprised when she answered.

"How's it going, Ejituru?" she asked.

"Everything's fine. I just haven't spoken to you for some time. I found an apartment not far from the university."

"Is your husband with you?" "No, we're divorced." "When did that happen?'

"We've been separated for three years, but I didn't tell anyone." "Do you have time to meet? I want to hear all about it."

"I'd really like that. I haven't discussed the divorce with anyone but a few friends."

They arranged to meet at a restaurant in Adams Morgan. Dr. Washington arrived first and chose a quiet corner where they could talk. She had just come from a meeting and wore a business suit. Ejituru had difficulty finding parking and was twenty minutes late. Dr. Washington had almost given up on her when she rushed in looking frantic.

Ejituru, apologizing profusely, sat down. Over the meal, she poured out her grievances toward Ignatius.

Dr. Washington listened carefully and then asked, "Did he ever abuse you?"

"No."

"Did it ever occur to you that perhaps he never paid for your education because he didn't have the money? We seem to have had this discussion before."

"Then why'd he say he would? He shouldn't have said that. I was in medical school at Nsukka and had already completed two years."

"Did he force you onto the plane?"

"No, but he enticed me by saying he'd pay for my education."

"Did he ask you to leave the apartment when you did? You told me you needed to be nearer to the school."

"In a way, he asked me to leave." She debated whether to tell her friend about the night Ignatius found her in Nduka's room, but she decided to skip that. "I asked him when I started my medical school to move with me, but he refused."

"Do you know what I think? I think he was very kind to you. He let you live with him for seven years without asking you to contribute anything. He maintained you under his health insurance. True, he didn't pay for your fees, but most people work and go to school, so what you did isn't unusual. You could have continued to live in the apartment and minimized your education debt, but you chose to move out."

"I admit he was generous in that regard."

"His lying about his past and his educational qualifications shouldn't be grounds for divorce. You didn't marry him for his educational qualifications, did you? Besides, even as a taxi driver, he was still able to pay for your upkeep once you started living with him. On what grounds did he ask for a divorce?"

"He sued on grounds of adultery. He caught me in a room with another man I knew from home." "Did you try to explain?"

"I wanted the divorce, but I wanted him to pay for my upkeep." "Oh! The divorce is final now, isn't it?"

"Yes, but he should have paid spousal support. I wouldn't have incurred all this debt if he agreed to pay for my education."

"Are you happy?"

"Yes. I have a boyfriend, and we'll get married once I finish my residency. We aren't living together because that would be awkward if my mother comes for my graduation. Besides, we're too busy right now to look for a bigger apartment."

"I'm glad for you. You should move past your grievances with Ignatius and look forward to the future."

The women talked about other things. Dr. Washington wanted to know Ejituru's plans for Thanksgiving, and she told the doctor that her landlady had invited her and her boyfriend for dinner.

"What do you think of your landlady and your new surroundings?" Dr. Washington asked.

They chatted for some time. Ejituru promised to think about Dr. Washington's advice. As they stood to go, the doctor shook her hand. "I hope you'll keep in touch," Dr. Washington said.

On the Sunday following her meeting with Dr. Washington, Ejituru decided to visit Esther, who often reserved Sunday afternoons for a quiet time, since her children normally spent that day with their father.

She found Esther in the midst of cleaning and tidying her apartment, but she was glad to see her.

"Hello, stranger," Esther said. "This is a pleasant surprise. What did you do to your hair?"

"I had to cut it short, because having a perm takes too much time. This way, I can wake up, wash my hair, and comb it. I can manage it a lot better during my residency."

"I must say that short hair suits you. I love your outfit. I've often commented on how chic you look, even when you're studying. No T-shirts for you."

"Thank you, Auntie!"

"What brings you here, apart from visiting me?" "That's enough reason. What's been happening?"

Esther brought Ejituru up to date on the happenings in the Nigerian community in Prince George's County. She and her husband had finally come to an agreement regarding the older girl's education. Esther wanted to send her to a Catholic school, but her husband didn't, saying he couldn't afford it. Esther won after convincing him of the merits of a parochial school education.

Esther went on to tell Ejituru that the girl was very happy in her new school and very proud of her uniform. "I worried she might fall under the influence of girls I don't like. They compete to see who has the best outfit. Now she wears a uniform, and she's grown to like it. She's been coming home with a lot of homework, and has no time to hang out with undesirable girls in the complex."

Ejituru was happy for Esther and said so. "Have you been to see Ignatius?" Esther asked.

"No. That's not why I came. I don't intend to. We're divorced now."

Ignoring the petulant tone, Esther said, "I would have suggested you drop in to talk to him, but I doubt he'd be home. He told me Sunday is the day he spends with his little boy. Did you know about that?"

"No! When did it happen?"

"I think he said the child's six months old, but I'm not sure. What have you decided about the divorce?"

"We're divorced. I talked it over with my parents when I was in Nigeria, and my mother agreed it was for the best. I've signed the papers. We're both free of each other."

"Are you happy, Ejituru?" "Yes. Why?"

"You look so sad."

"No, I'm not sad. I've been busy. The residency program is very demanding."

"Are you still rooming with another student, or have you moved?"

"I moved closer to the hospital. I'm renting a basement apartment from a fantastic woman who lived in Nigeria. She saw my posting and sent me a note. I went to see the place and really liked it. You should see the house. It's beautiful, like nothing I ever saw before. She has many paintings and artwork from Nigeria and other African countries. Do you know she had throw pillows made from Akwete and Ashoke cloth from western Nigeria?"

"You mean she cut up the beautiful Akwete cloth and used it for pillow slips? How outrageous! These *Oyibos!*"

"Auntie, you need to see the place. You'd be amazed. The rooms are so beautifully decorated. Even my basement apartment has a stool from Ghana and an Ashoke bedcover. The drawback with living there is that I can't have any overnight visitors, and there are very few blacks. I arrange to meet my friends at a coffee shop on Wisconsin Avenue or M Street. Of course, sometimes I sneak my boyfriend in."

"You have a boyfriend?" She pretended she hadn't heard how Ignatius found Ejituru in bed with another man.

"Yes. We knew each other in Nigeria. It was a surprise to see him at Howard. We've been seeing each other, and we plan to marry in the future. He's gone for an interview in Dallas this weekend."

"No wonder you never thought of poor Esther."

"No, Auntie. That's not true. I've been very busy. Anyway, I really like living in the Palisades. The neighbors know me and call out greetings. The other day I was running for the bus, and one of the men offered me a lift. It turned out he's a doctor at the hospital."

"My, you're coming up in the world. I'm glad you remembered me and are free. In time, I hope you won't feel so bitter. There's no need for you to be mired in revenge. By the way, what are you doing for Thanksgiving? As usual, we'll be having a combined Thanksgiving in the party room at the complex. You're welcome to come, and you needn't worry about running into Ignatius. He'll be with his son that day."

"Auntie, I would have loved to come, but my landlady invited me and my boyfriend to celebrate with her and her family."

"My, my. You're really coming up in the world," she repeated. "Please remember to invite me to your wedding. Better yet, bring your boyfriend for a visit."

Ejituru left feeling much lighter in spirit. She would tell her mother her decision to marry Nduka.

Ejituru looked forward to her first Thanksgiving dinner with an American family. Many of her American colleagues went home for the holidays. Some foreigners, like her, were invited to celebrate with friends.

It was a beautiful fall day, and Ejituru walked to the Safeway on MacArthur Boulevard to buy flowers as a gift for Mrs. Fischer. By the time she and Nduka rang the doorbell, the guests had already arrived.

"Ejituru!" Mrs. Fischer exclaimed. "I thought you had forgotten. I was just about to send Cecelia to your door to see what was wrong. I'm so glad to meet your young man at last. Is this for me?" She accepted the flowers Ejituru offered. "Come in and meet the others while I put these in a vase." Joining six others in the room, Ejituru deduced that the youngest woman must be Cecelia, Mrs. Fischer's daughter. The other ladies were friends of Mrs. Fischer from her days in the diplomatic service and her volunteer work. They appeared happy to greet the newcomers, and soon peppered them with questions about their families and medical programs. Ejituru talked about her mother, telling them that after she retired from teaching she had turned her attention to business and did very well. That led one of the women to comment that Nigerian women were known for their business acumen. "You should see the big mama traders in Lagos. Do you know that some of them travel to Rome each week to buy things to sell in Lagos?"

"Nduka's mother, until her death," Ejituru said, "traded between Dubai and Nigeria."

"Why residency at Georgetown instead of Howard?" someone else asked.

Ejituru explained about the placement process. "I chose Georgetown because I wanted a different social and academic experience."

One woman had been a patient at Georgetown and talked about the kindness of the doctors and nurses and how she valued the treatment she received. "You couldn't have chosen a better hospital. I'm sure you'll get the best training."

"Nduka, what about you? Why are you doing a fellowship in plastic surgery? Will it be useful in Nigeria?"

"There aren't that many plastic surgeons in Nigeria," he replied. "It's a field in short supply. We have conjoined twins and deformed people I can help."

"What will you two do after your training? Will you return to Nigeria immediately? I'm sure the country could use people with your expertise." "I'm not sure," Ejituru said. "I have a lot of student debt. I couldn't have reached this point in my training without loans. While my mother offered to pay for my education in Nigeria, she would have had difficulty supporting me here."

"I hope to get a job in Dallas," Nduka said. "I was just there for an interview, and I hope Ejituru will join me there when she finishes her residency program."

"I worked for USAID," another person said. "I noticed many foreign students preferred to work in the US instead of going home. Those who went home said they were frustrated by the lack of equipment, which they came to rely upon here."

"That may be so then, but the situation is changing," Nduka said. "I was a surgeon in Nigeria before I came here, and I had all the equipment I required. We both expect to return to Nigeria."

At the table, the conversation turned to food, of which there was an enormous variety, and the story of the origin of Thanksgiving, about the early settlers and the Indians.

Ejituru found the conversation brisk and interesting. Someone asked her if there was anything in her culture similar to Thanksgiving. She explained that among her ethnic group they had a festival usually celebrated in September called *Ikeji,* or the New Yam Festival. In the olden days, that marked the beginning of the new year and the end of the old. Girls who came of age were married at that time.

Mrs. Fischer explained the difference between the yam and the sweet potato and added, "When I lived in Nigeria, I had the good fortune to be invited to the homes of my Nigerian friends and was served with pounded yam and *egusi* stew. I quite liked the flavor. Of course, the cooks employed by us expatriates preferred to cook English food, as they were taught by their colonial masters, and it was difficult to persuade them to cook Nigerian food, since that was what their wives served at home."

Mrs. Fischer rejected Ejituru's offer to clear the table, explaining that Cecelia knew where the things were kept, and Ejituru should relax and talk with the guests. The party didn't finish until quite late. Before she left, Cecelia asked Ejituru if she'd like to accompany her for a walk along the canal the following day. Even though she wasn't a walker, Ejituru agreed, thinking it would be nice to talk to Cecelia, who lived in New York. She was an accountant for a famous law firm and had an apartment in the Tribeca area. She had gone to boarding school in Massachusetts when her parents were stationed in Nigeria and visited Nigeria only on school holidays.

On the walk the following day, Cecelia talked about the recreational clubs her parents had belonged to and how much she enjoyed going there to play tennis or to meet other young people from different countries. She talked about going to Bar Beach for picnics. She told Ejituru that her parents had night and day watchmen because of security problems. She never ventured beyond Victoria Island during her stay, but during a holiday she accompanied her mother to Oshogbo to see an artist. She'd never been that far east or north.

She wanted to know about Ejituru's childhood, and she explained that, like most middle-class Nigerians, she went to a single-sex boarding school when she was eleven. Before then, she attended the school where her mother was headmistress. She added that she spent two years at the university in Nigeria before coming to the US.

Cecelia had a few errands to run for her mother, so Ejituru didn't see her again before she left for New York.

On Sunday, Ejituru called her mother to inform her that the divorce was final. Nkechi said Nwakama was feeling poorly, so she was taking him to a specialist the following week.

"You're not to worry," Nkechi said. "It may be nothing."

Nkechi sat beside her husband's bed in Umuahia General Hospital, reflecting on her life. It saddened her to see Nwakama so helpless. His life was so full of unfulfilled promise. After getting his high school diploma, he had tried many things. He was never able to stick with one job and he lived beyond his means. His father once sent him to Calabar to learn a trade, but that didn't work either. Nkechi once arranged for him to be a trainee manager at the big palm oil estate, but instead he was a lightning rod for problems, because he didn't have the knack of managing people. *Would he have had a different life if he'd married into another family,* she wondered, *to an illiterate, meek, obedient woman willing to stay within the culturally prescribed role for women? In many ways, I've been a good wife. I never belittled him in public. Like my contemporaries, I haven't asked him to support me financially. Rather, I provided him with whatever he needed to maintain his position in society.*

I'm fond of him, but I can't say I love him. I've resented how I've had to bear the financial burden of his extended family. All the ventures he entered into, only to have me bail him out to save face. I don't want him to die though. I want him to live and see what Ejituru, my precious daughter, has accomplished without his help, even though I know he would claim the glory. Her mind turned to other events in her life. She thought of her business ventures. She needed to go home in a few days if Nwakama's condition stabilized. If he carried out the doctor's orders, he was expected to have a full recovery.

Nwakama had had a heart attack during an altercation at a meeting of the elders. Luckily, Nkechi had just acquired a van for her business, and she rushed him to the hospital in Umuahia for admission. The doctor said the hospital could do nothing for his arthritic knees, but Nwakama had to take medication to control his cholesterol.

Nkechi made frequent visits to Umuahia to see Nwakama in the hospital, but she couldn't afford to be away from home for more than a day with all her business interests. She asked Onyeka to help look after Nwakama at the hospital. Running back and forth to Aba during Nwakama's stay in the hospital also interrupted the rhythm of Nkechi's life, and she'd be glad when he could come home.

After she'd brought him into the hospital, she called Ejituru to apprise her of the situation, in case Nwakama's health became worse. She told her daughter not to worry, since the doctor had been trained in Russia and knew what he was doing. Once the danger was past, Nkechi's first thought was to convey the good news to Ejituru because she would be worried.

Nkechi was always close to her daughter, and talking with her always lifted her spirits. It was one of the many heartaches that she was away from her daughter during the years when Ejituru struggled to work and study. Nkechi's business was still in its infancy at the time, and she couldn't afford to send even small sums of money to contribute to Ejituru's education. She cursed the men in their lives for their treachery, especially Nwakama for sacrificing his daughter to his ambition.

Nkechi remembered how broken-hearted she felt during the negotiations leading up to Ejituru's marriage. She recalled all the times she had consulted with her dear friend Kanu and the advice he gave.

I have my wish, she thought. *My only daughter has become a doctor, but at what cost? On the other hand, I know that she is truly my daughter. Both of us can overcome any adversity placed in our way. Look at how determined she was to achieve her ambition. I pray I am able to see her walk down the aisle to receive her diploma.*

She cried silently, and her thoughts turned to Ignatius, the person she hated most. *They say the fruit doesn't fall far from the tree. Everyone said he was different from his father, more like his mother, but when one can't stand by his word, what does that say of a husband? Nwakama was deceived by both father and son. The promised joint business venture never materialized, and the son took my daughter to a foreign country and made her give up her training at Nsukka by promising he would pay for a better education overseas. Nwakama brought that into our lives and gave away my daughter. Am I supposed to forgive that?*

She decided not to tell Nwakama of the finality of the divorce and that Ejituru had a new boyfriend. He would learn of it later. She would wait until he was stronger, and she would start by talking about the child she heard that his son-in-law had with another woman, then progress to say it was sensible of Ejituru to deal with the situation by divorcing him. She vowed that when the time came for the graduation, she'd go alone. Nwakama had done nothing to contribute to Ejituru's education and was to blame for the length of time it took her to achieve that goal.

Her thoughts turned to Onyeka, who just entered the room. The bad times between them were in the past. Onyeka learned she couldn't bite the hand that fed her and came to her senses. She was again a loyal servant. She confessed she was led astray by the women in Nwakama's compound, who were jealous of her ties with Nkechi and wanted to sow discord between them. Apologizing, she promised to behave.

So far, she'd kept her promise and was very helpful with Nkechi, who was happy to have her back in the fold. Nkechi wondered how she would have managed during the time Nwakama was in the hospital and her business had so many funerals to cater.

I gave my problems to God, and he was good to me.

CHAPTER TWENTY-SEVEN

Ignatius left for Nigeria with his family on the same day Ejituru married Nduka. When everything was decided, Ignatius purchased tickets for his family to return. His children would grow up in Nigeria, and when the time came, they would go back to the US for their college education. Excited about the move, Ignatius reflected that his children were Americans by virtue of their being born in the country, but he wanted them rooted in Nigeria. He only regretted that his mother had died without seeing his beautiful children.

He had, over the years, prepared for the move, sending money to Nigeria to build apartment houses and a strip mall. His sacrifices paid off, and he owned several modern apartment buildings in Aba, in addition to the strip mall on the road between Aba and Umuahia. His uncle collected the rent for him, and Ignatius had a sizeable bank account. He owned the houses outright with no mortgages. His uncle was also negotiating for the purchase of another duplex whose owner had gone bankrupt and needed immediate cash. Ignatius also managed to ship several well-maintained used Mercedes Benz vehicles and Toyotas to Nigeria to start a car-hire service based at the Owerri airport. His uncle used his contacts to get the necessary clearance and registration for the cars, and his father-in-law helped register the business. Everything was set.

The last time Ndidi's parents had visited the US, they urged the couple to consider moving back to Nigeria. At first Ndidi was reluctant to commit to such a move. She had never lived in Nigeria, and during her rare visits, she found it confusing, even though her parents' social standing and income smoothed out many of the difficulties expatriates experienced in the country. Her father always provided her with a car and a good driver. Her parents had a nice home, and even minor irritants like power outages didn't impact her, because her parents had powerful generators.

To seal the deal, her parents promised to give her a house as a wedding present and to ensure she had good servants to take care of the children while she worked. Ben used his influence to secure her a job as the head of the physiotherapy department at the hospital in Owerri operated by several doctors trained in Russia. She hoped by the time the family arrived in Nigeria their furniture and cars would be available to them.

Ndidi reluctantly agreed to give it a try, on one condition—the house in Bethesda wouldn't be sold for at least a year, so she could return to the US if she hated living in Nigeria. Her parents reluctantly agreed and instructed a real estate friend on Westlake Drive to look for short-term renters.

It was a new life and a new beginning.

Ejituru was stressed. Adding to the difficulties of her medical program was her father's constant harping on her to start thinking of marriage now that she was free from Ignatius and had qualified as a doctor. Nwakama kept arranging for various unmarried men he considered good suitors to write and introduce themselves to her. Moreover, he wondered why she hadn't agreed to marry the young men from the US who came to the house to inquire about her and who he knew had written to her. All held important positions in America and would make good husbands.

When the news of her divorce became common knowledge at home, the villagers first blamed Ignatius for the failure of the marriage. Recently, after he married Ndidi, the only daughter of a wealthy couple from Owerri, the tide had turned in his favor. Miriam, his mother-in-law, was very well connected, and Ndidi's brothers and sisters held important positions in the public and private sectors. Ben, his father-in-law, served as the proprietor of one of the well-known secondary schools in the country that catered to children whose parents lived overseas, particularly in America. Many rich Nigerians also sent their children to that school, since most of its graduates had no difficulty gaining admission into American universities. Those who accompanied Okoro, Ignatius's uncle, to both the combined knocking-at-the-door and wine ceremonies at Owerri, returned with news regarding the family's wealth and began spreading that around. The village people soon began blaming Nkechi for the failure of Ejituru's marriage to Ignatius. It was Nkechi's ambition for her child that caused the divorce, they said.

Everyone agreed that Ignatius did very well. While Ejituru told her mother that Ignatius had found out about her boyfriend, a fellow doctor, and they planned to marry when they could, she hadn't told her father. Neither had her mother. Even though she told her mother some things, only Stella, who had moved to Atlanta, knew the full story.

Ejituru visited Stella few times over the holidays and marveled at how happy she was in her marriage. Stella and her husband were glad they were no longer subjected to the strains and stresses of extended family and were free to make their own decisions. However, Stella missed having more help with the kids. Finding domestic help in Atlanta was beyond their means, considering her husband's income, especially since she had recently enrolled in school. She barely managed to pay for a sitter for the children while she attended classes.

Stella took Ejituru's advice and enrolled in a graduate program in public health. In her final year, she was enjoying her stay in Atlanta and made many friends. She reminded Ejituru that she was the one who'd suggested she take the course, even though it wasn't easy with two children and their constant demand for attention.

Ejituru envied Stella her good fortune, with a husband who loved her and two beautiful, healthy children. Stella told her that she too hoped that in Nduka, Ejituru's wish for love would be fulfilled after years of a loveless marriage.

When she'd left for the US, Ejituru was cut off from all her friends at Nsukka except Stella. She always regretted leaving so abruptly without telling Nduka she was terminating her education and moving to the States to marry Ignatius. He knew her parents wanted her to marry Ignatius, but she gave the impression she was against marriage and wanted to continue at Nsukka. Many times during her first year in the US, she remembered Nduka and wondered what he thought of her behavior and whether he found another girl. Later, she learned he'd been selected for a residency in Kiev on a Soviet Union scholarship.

Then Stella wrote and told her of his marriage to a girl he befriended shortly after Ejituru left. Ejituru wondered what had happened to Nduka's marriage before his wife's tragic death. Was he too in a loveless marriage? Was he contemplating divorce before death released him from the obligation to his wife? Such thoughts consumed her for many nights. Despite his professed love for her, she couldn't helping wondering about it, especially when he was with her but seemed lost in thought.

On a beautiful spring day with temperatures above normal, Ejituru sat in her apartment looking at the offers for a position after her residency and had an unexpected visitor—Nduka. He suggested they go for a walk around the Tidal Basin to look at the cherry blossoms. He had just returned from his second interview in Dallas and wanted to discuss it with her.

Ejituru opted to drive them to Nineteenth Street and Pennsylvania Avenue NW, where she parked the car so they could walk down. At the Tidal Basin, they wandered among the trees, all in full bloom. The ground was strewn with petals. Nduka suggested they walk to the Smithsonian African Museum, where they could talk undisturbed.

Once they were there, he said, "I'd like us to be married before I move to Dallas. When I was done interviewing, I found out there are some practices in Dallas that might offer you a position if you wish. I'd prefer that we live in the same city. I'm tired of living apart from you."

Ejituru thought about that. "I wasn't quite sure what your thoughts on marriage were, so I was actually leaning toward Atlanta because of Stella, and because I didn't think you'd propose so soon. Furthermore, I'm under pressure from my mother to return home and set up a practice, but I don't feel I can do that with my large debt."

"Ejituru, my dear, you should know I've always loved you. After you left, I reconciled myself to life without you, but now I'm sure more than ever that you're meant to be with me. There's no point in wasting time now that you're free. It should be easy for of two us to repay your debt. Let's get married soon."

"I actually wrote a letter to my mother telling her how irrational it would be for me to return to Nigeria at this time. I know she's worried about my father. I've said that at some point in the future I'll invite her to visit, but she can't do that now because of his health. I also believe I need more experience. Perhaps we might consider going home to visit, perhaps next year."

"Would you like a fellowship in neonatology?" "Not immediately, but I would consider it."

"My brother will be here just before your graduation. Shall we plan on getting married immediately after? We can have a small celebration afterward, and you can invite Mrs. Fischer."

The wedding day was set.

"I'll call my mother and tell her we've decided to get married after graduation. She'll worry she won't be present, but I'll tell her we'll visit sometime in the future."

Ejituru looked worried for a moment.

"What's troubling you?" Nduka asked. "Is it your mother's reaction?" "Oh, no. It's just a small thing."

"What is it? Tell me. We shouldn't hide anything from each other." "I'm three months pregnant."

"Ejituru, my darling, why didn't you tell me?"

"I didn't want you to ask me to marry you because of the baby." He smiled. "Let's go out to dinner to celebrate."

As they relaxed over dinner, Ejituru said, "I feel as if I'm my grandfather, Achi, who went through so much before achieving happiness."

"Tell me about him."

"He was captured in one of the raids of the mighty Ibini Ukpabi people. As my mother told it, it was on a particularly beautiful evening. The sun was setting, the day's work was done, and people were returning to the village from their activities. Some farmers were setting out to the stream to wash away the day's dirt, while others were returning home from the stream.

"As the women cooked the evening meal, knots of children played and ran about in the village square. Grandmothers shooed the little ones away because they were distracting them from their work. A few groups of women gossiped, either about their husbands or about the latest misdeeds of their co-wives. A fresh breeze blew in from the surrounding hills, and people were busy with things they needed to finish before the sun set and they had to go to bed.

"Suddenly there were shouts. The raiders had come. The last time they attacked the village, the harvest was in and the yam barns were full. Now it was the beginning of planting season, so no one expected another attack.

"Women ran from them, dragging their children. Some carried meager possessions. Others had nothing more than a loincloth around their waists. Soon, the village was deserted except for the chief priestess, the keeper of the village altar. She refused to run, and invoked the protection of the Chi. Achi's mother took him to the altar, begging her sister to run away with them, but she refused, saying the Chi would protect her from the marauders. Grabbing Achi, his mother reluctantly ran toward the other women. It was the first time in the boy's young life he had to flee into the forest with his mother.

"The raids had become frequent in recent times. The raiders came from the south and were said to be people who lived on the Cross River and had the protection of a powerful god named Ibini Ukpabi. Although Achi's village in Udi was protected by hills on three sides, it was very fertile, and the Udi villages were always able to produce the food they needed.

"The last time he remembered running, they hadn't gone far and only hid until morning. When they returned, many men were missing from the village, the yam barns were empty, and there was nothing to eat. They ran deep into the forest, meeting up with other groups of women and men from other villages.

"The first night they slept near a river. The children cried, and mothers tried to quiet them by saying the raiders would hear. Sometimes during the night something happened. Achi never knew what. People began running again. The children cried, and the women couldn't stop them. In the dark, he felt the presence of other children, many too tired to stay awake. Mothers abandoned their children in the flight, and Achi was separated from his mother, so he huddled under a tree, praying for daylight.

"He must've fallen asleep, because when he awoke, the children left behind were in the river, splashing around, crying and not knowing where they were. Confused, he followed the older children, who decided to find their way back to the village in Udi.

"As they walked single file down a narrow track, they felt unseen eyes watching. Suddenly, the marauders caught some of them. They took Achi and the others to a camp somewhere in the forest. Later, they forced them to march from camp to camp until they reached the raiders' home at the Cross River town, where they still live.

"They sold Achi to Chief Igwe, who took him as a house slave and gave him his name. A hardworking young man, he soon gained the love and confidence of the chief. He rose to become the chief's confidant and trading arm. On behalf of his master, he traveled to many trading posts."

"I still can't see the parallel," Nduka said. "He was brought to the area against his will, while you came of your own free will."

"In a way you're right, but my grandfather persisted and redeemed himself. He married into the Amadi class. I too persisted and redeemed myself. I achieved my objective and am able to marry the love of my life." After dinner, back at the apartment in Foggy Bottom, they called Nkechi to tell her of the upcoming marriage and Ejituru's pregnancy. They would move to Dallas immediately after the wedding.

Review Requested:
If you loved this book, would you please provide a review at Amazon. com?